Meet ChocoMimi A WHO'S WHO!

WITH COOL PHOTO STICKERS OF THE CHOCOMIMI GANG!

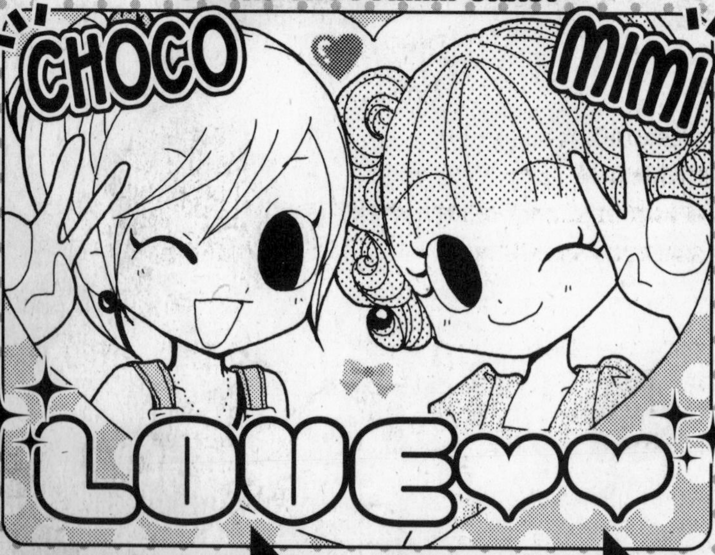
CHOCO
MIMI
LOVE♥♥

CHOCO SAKURAI, GRADE 8
SERIOUS AND MATURE

BIRTHDAY: MAY 5 ★
SIGN: TAURUS ★ BLOOD TYPE: A ★
HOBBIES: SEWING, READING, MOVIES
SKILLS: BAKING, SWIMMING

MIMI NEKOTA, GRADE 8
LIKES THINGS HER WAY

BIRTHDAY: MARCH 3 ★
SIGN: PISCES ★ BLOOD TYPE: AB ★
HOBBIES: COLLECTING BEARS, FASHION
SKILLS: MAKING EXCUSES, FAKING TEARS

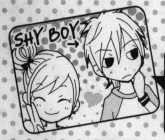

ANDO

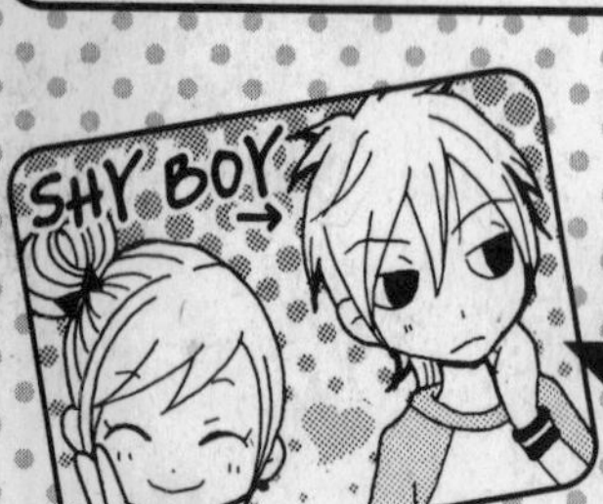
SHY BOY →

ANDO RYUNOSUKE, GRADE 8
QUIET AND SHY

BIRTHDAY: NOV. 3 ★
SIGN: SCORPIO ★ BLOOD TYPE: O ★
HOBBIES: GUITAR, FISHING
SKILLS: SPEAKS ENGLISH

MUMU

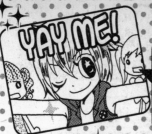

YAY ME!

MUMU MOMOYAMA, GRADE 8
TOTALLY *LOVES* HIMSELF!

BIRTHDAY: AUG. 20 ★
SIGN: LEO ★ BLOOD TYPE: B ★
HOBBIES: GAMES, TEASING MIMI ★
SKILLS: CUTE FACES, PLAYING PRANKS ★

MIKACHIN

KOUMEI MIKAMI, GRADE 8
SMART AND WEIRD

BIRTHDAY: OCT. 22 ★
SIGN: LIBRA ★ BLOOD TYPE: AB ★
HOBBIES: SAXOPHONE, READING ★
SKILLS: NOTHING SPECIAL ★

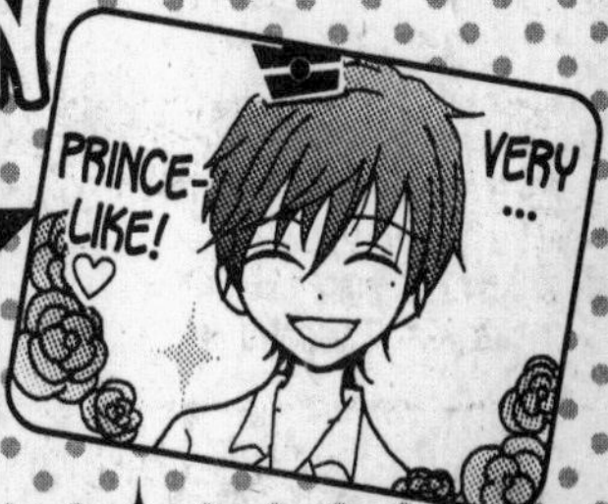

PRINCE-LIKE! ♥

VERY...

BAMBI

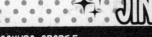

LET'S CHILL!

HEH.

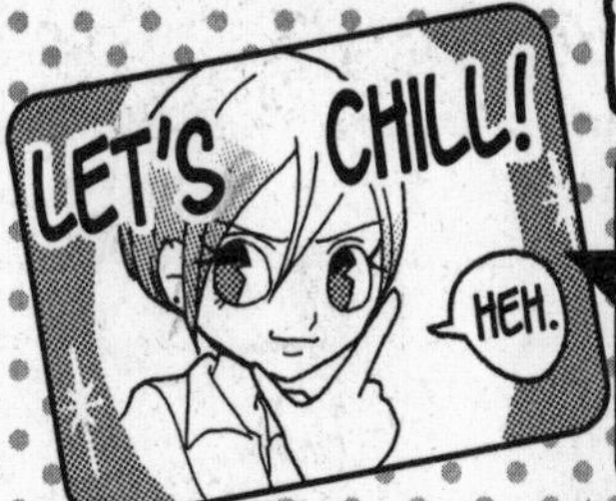

KOJIKA MORI, GRADE 8
A COOL CUTIE ♡

BIRTHDAY: APRIL 12 ★
SIGN: ARIES ★ BLOOD TYPE: A ★
HOBBIES: SINGING ★
SKILLS: SPORTS LIKE SOCCER ★

JIN

JIN SAKURA, GRADE 5
CHOCO'S LITTLE BROTHER

BIRTHDAY: NOV. 23 ★
SIGN: SAGITTARIUS ★ BLOOD TYPE: O ★
HOBBIES: GAMES, SPORTS ★
SKILLS: EATING FAST ★

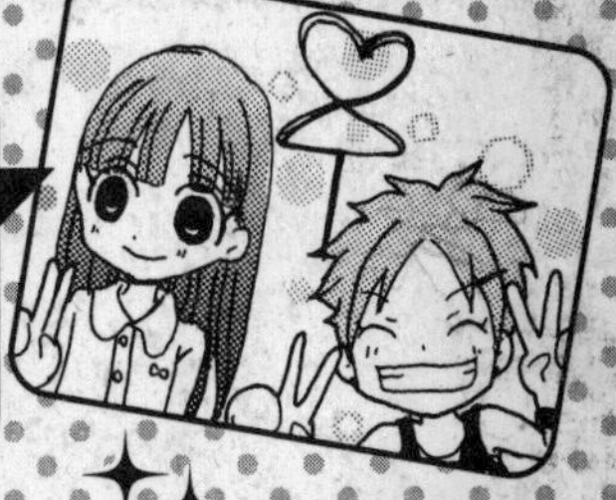

AOI

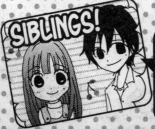

SIBLINGS!

AOI MIKAMI, GRADE 6
A SMILING BOOKWORM

BIRTHDAY: APRIL 29 ★
SIGN: TAURUS ★ BLOOD TYPE: A ★
HOBBIES: READING ★
SKILLS: PIANO ★

MR. TAKE

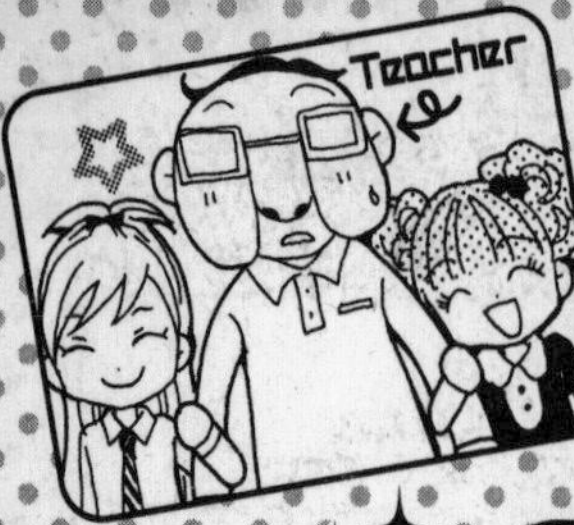
Teacher

MASATO TAKEDA
A STRICT TEACHER

BIRTHDAY: SEPT. 23 ★
SIGN: VIRGO ★ BLOOD TYPE: A ★
HOBBIES: JOGGING, GARDENING ★
SKILLS: D.I.Y. STUFF, CHINESE ★

PICHO

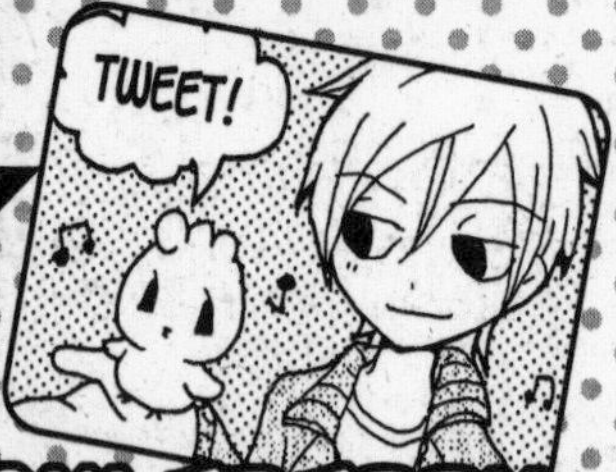
TWEET!

A LITTLE ANGEL

LIKES: "I DUNNO!" ★
HATES: "HUH?" ★
ANDO'S TREASURE! ♥

HUCKLEBERRY

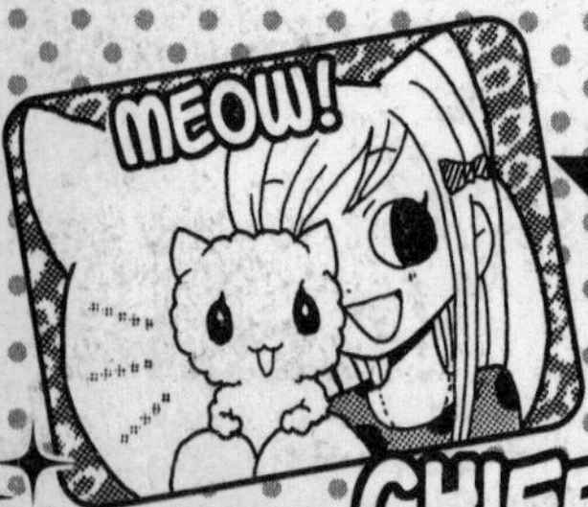
MEOW!

A VERY SMART KITTY

LIKES: PRETTY THINGS ★
HATES: UGLY THINGS ★
EX-STRAY. CHOCO RESCUED ME!

CHIFFON

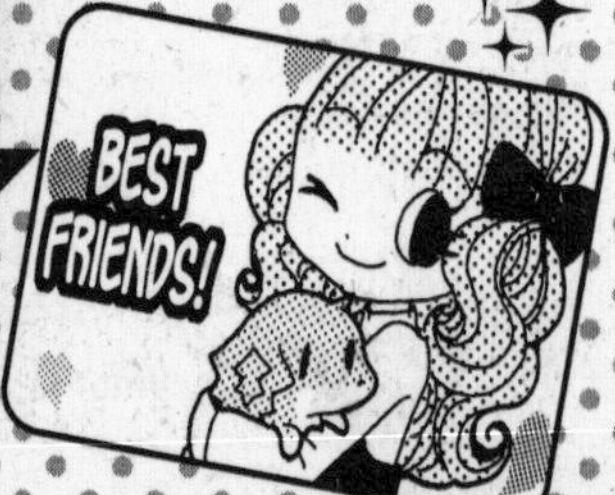
BEST FRIENDS!

A NICE SAMURAI DOG

LIKES: MASTER, SAMURAI STUFF ★
HATES: CLOTHES, GHOSTS ★
MY MASTER IS MIMI! ♥

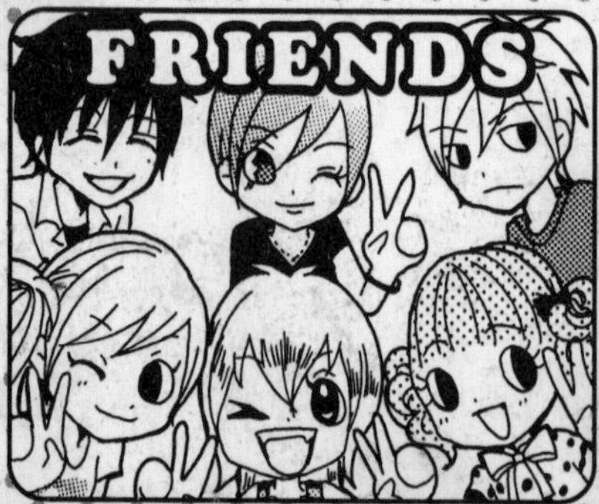
FRIENDS

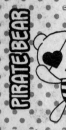

PIRATE BEAR

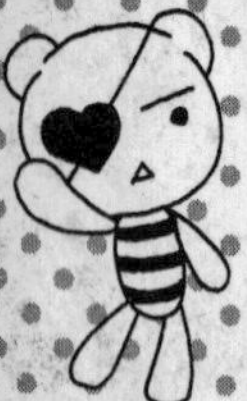

MIMI'S FAVE.
VERY POPULAR
(SHE SAYS).

DEATH BEAR

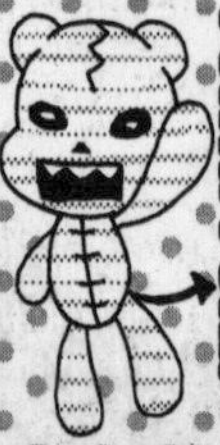

MUMU'S FAVE.
VERY RARE
(HE SAYS).

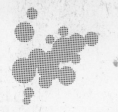

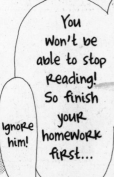

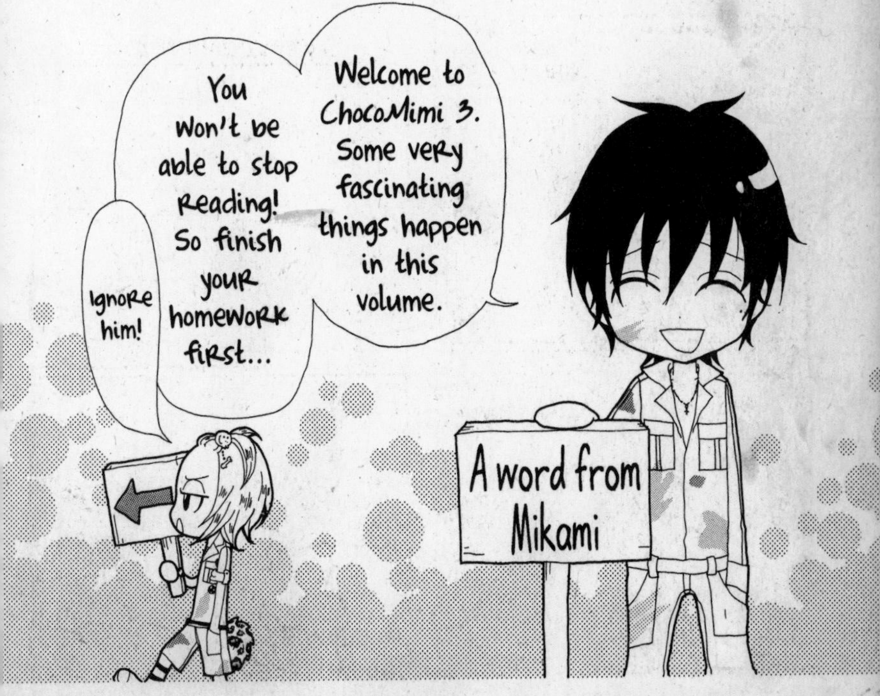

Welcome to ChocoMimi 3. Some very fascinating things happen in this volume.

You won't be able to stop reading! So finish your homework first...

Ignore him!

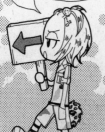

A word from Mikami

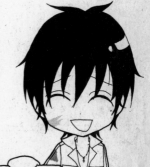

★Choco★Mimi★ 【3】

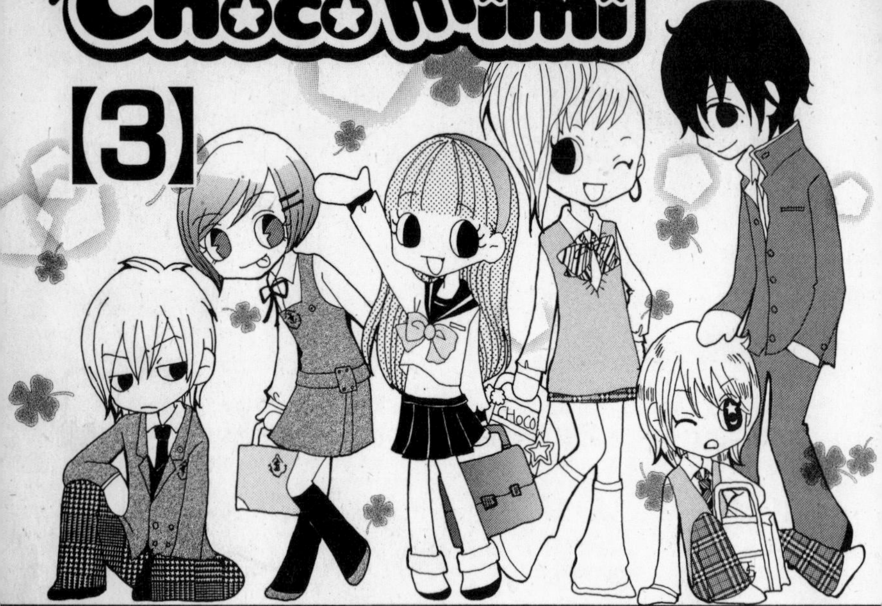

☆Homework☆

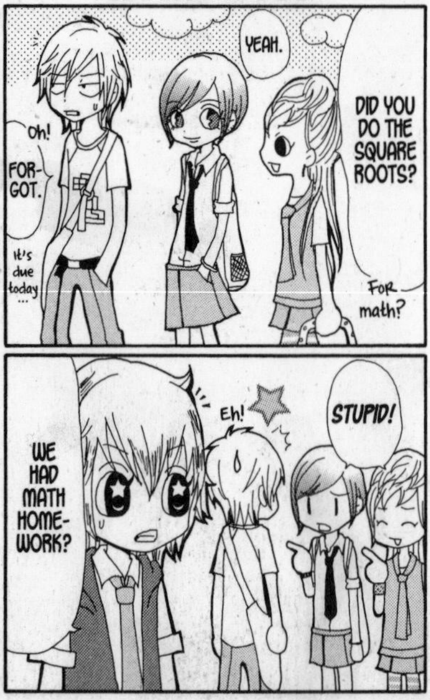
DID YOU DO THE SQUARE ROOTS?
For math?
YEAH.
Oh! FORGOT.
It's due today...
STUPID!
Eh!
WE HAD MATH HOMEWORK?

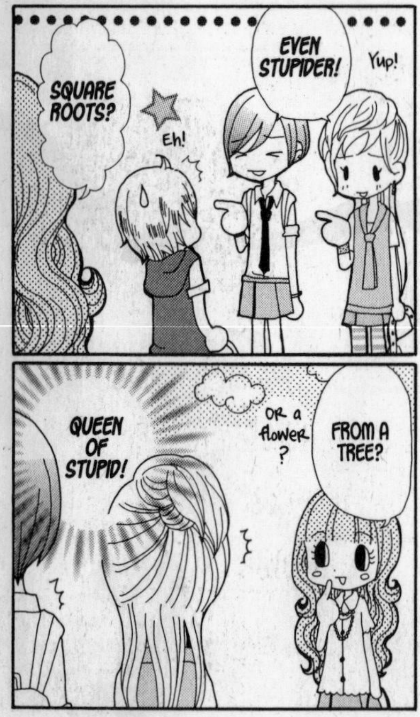
EVEN STUPIDER!
Yup!
Eh!
SQUARE ROOTS?
FROM A TREE?
OR a flower?
QUEEN OF STUPID!

☆ History ☆

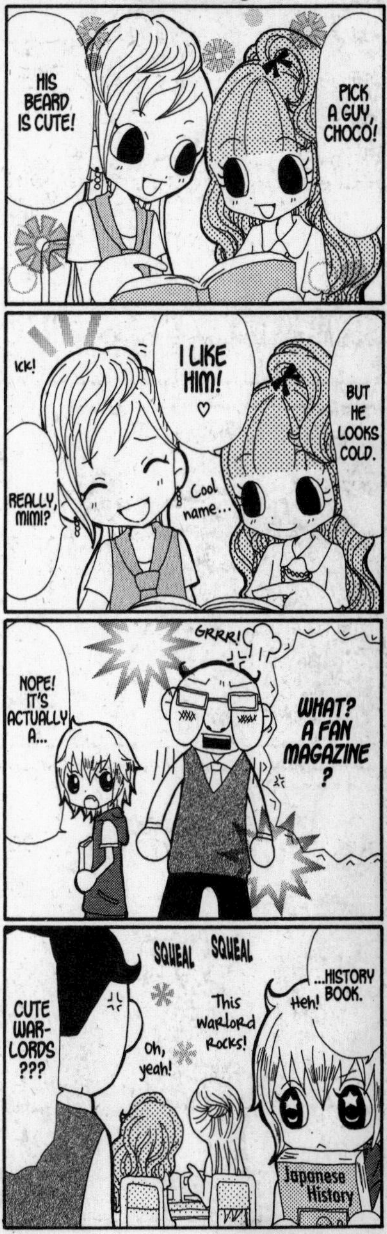
PICK A GUY, CHOCO!
HIS BEARD IS CUTE!
BUT HE LOOKS COLD.
I LIKE HIM! ♡
Ick!
Cool name...
REALLY, MIMI?
GRRR!
WHAT? A FAN MAGAZINE?
NOPE! IT'S ACTUALLY A...
...HISTORY BOOK.
Heh!
SQUEAL
SQUEAL
This warlord rocks!
Oh, yeah!
CUTE WARLORDS???
Japanese History

☆ P.E. ☆

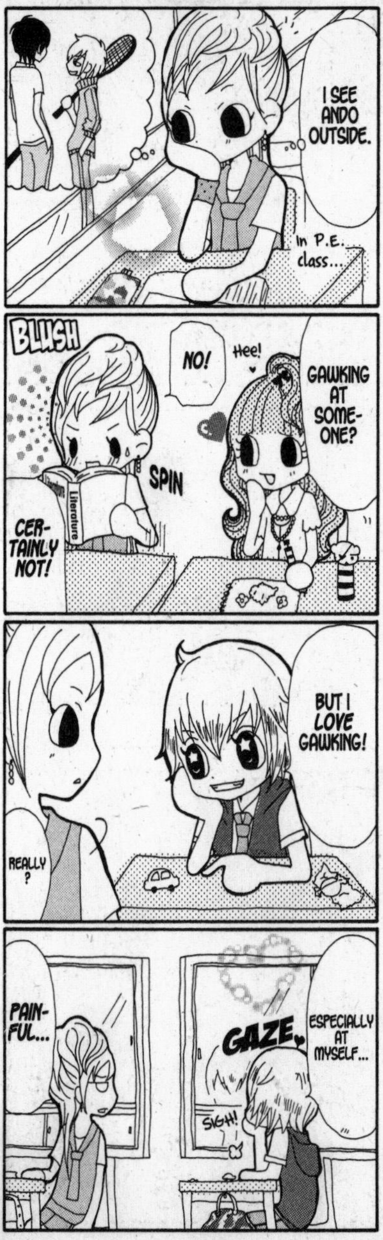
I SEE ANDO OUTSIDE.
In P.E. class...
GAWKING AT SOME-ONE?
Hee! ♥
NO!
BLUSH
SPIN
Literature
CERTAINLY NOT!
BUT I LOVE GAWKING!
REALLY?
ESPECIALLY AT MYSELF...
GAZE
SIGH!
PAIN-FUL...

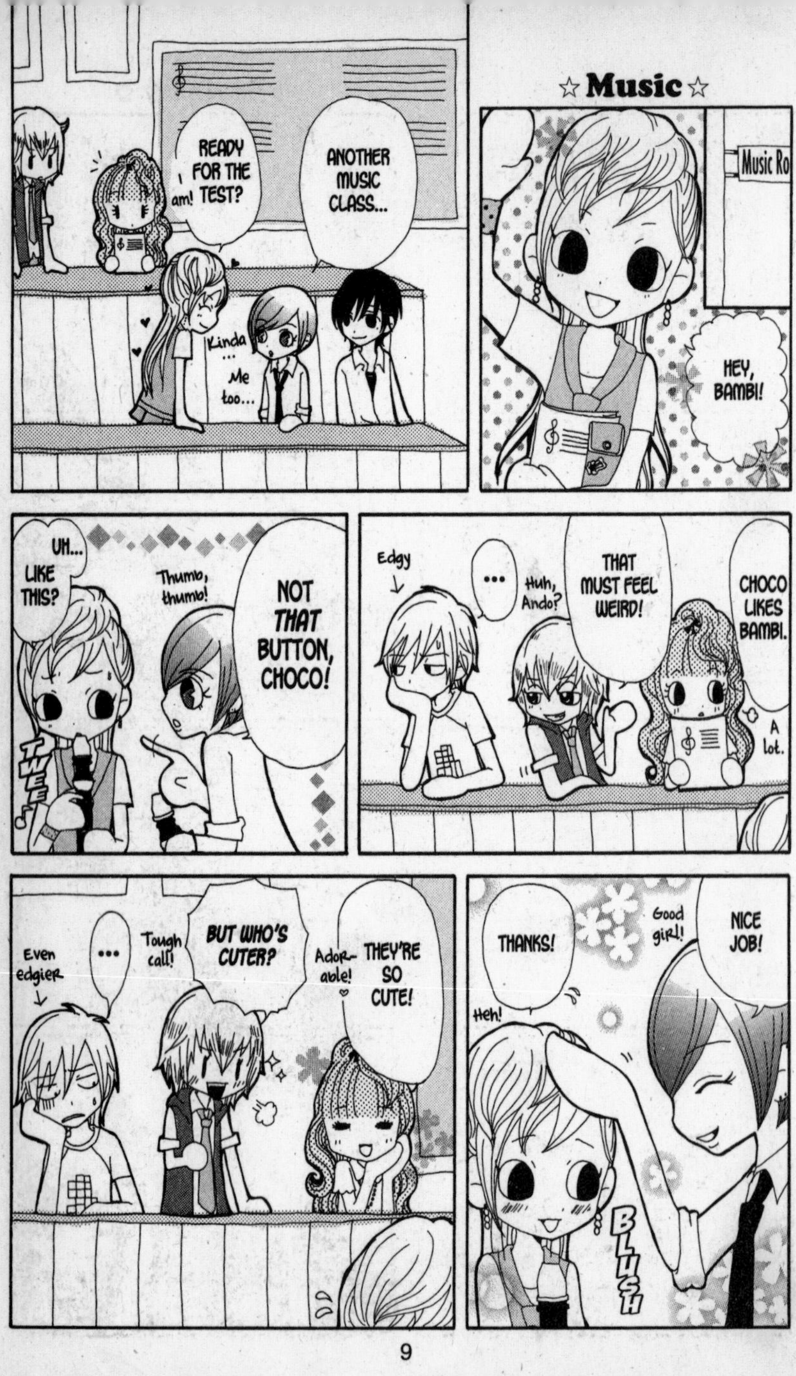
☆Music☆
Music Ro
HEY, BAMBI!
ANOTHER MUSIC CLASS...
READY FOR THE TEST?
I am!
Kinda...
Me too...
CHOCO LIKES BAMBI.
A lot.
THAT MUST FEEL WEIRD!
Huh, Ando?
...
Edgy
NOT THAT BUTTON, CHOCO!
Thumb, thumb!
UH... LIKE THIS?
TWEE
NICE JOB!
Good girl!
THANKS!
Heh!
BLUSH
THEY'RE SO CUTE!
Ador-able!
BUT WHO'S CUTER?
Tough call!
...
Even edgier

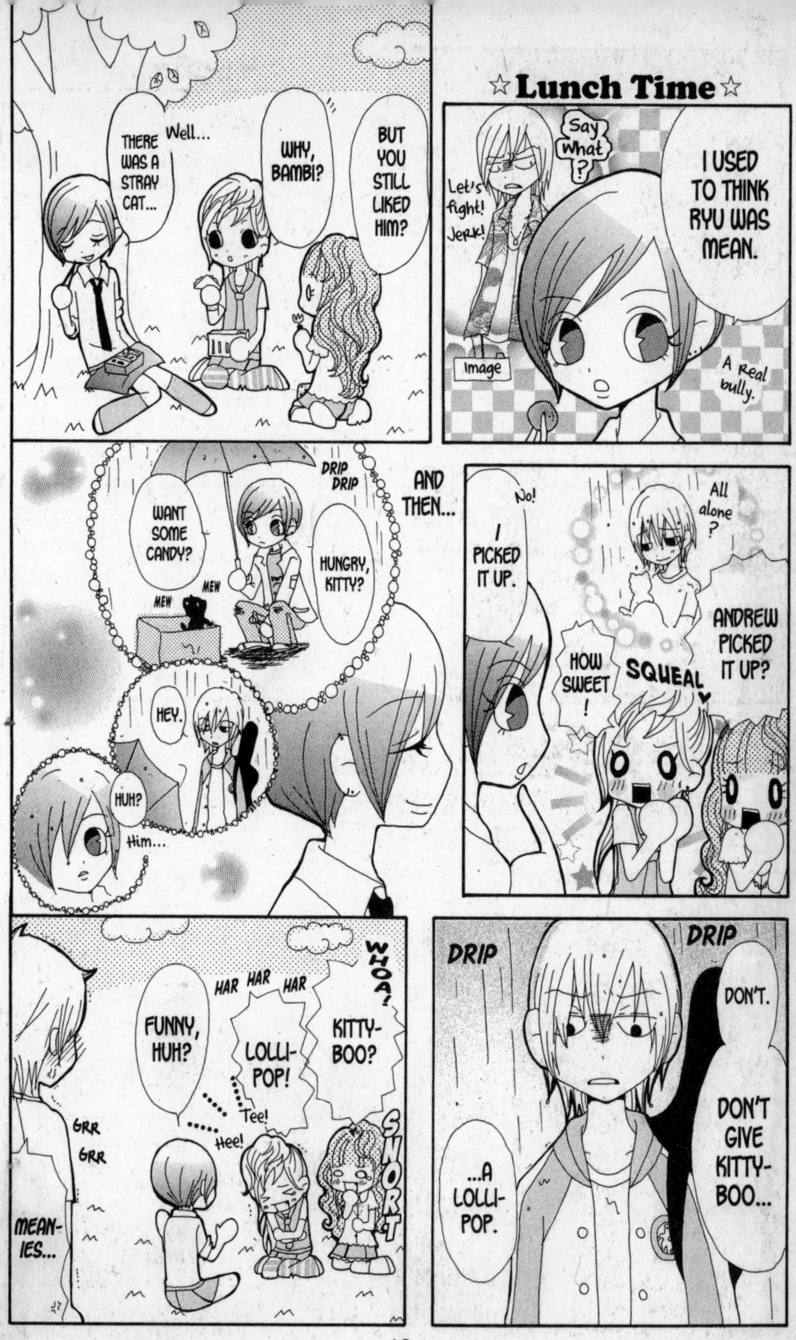
☆Lunch Time☆
I USED TO THINK RYU WAS MEAN.
A Real bully.
Say What?
Let's fight! Jerk!
Image
All alone?
ANDREW PICKED IT UP?
SQUEAL
HOW SWEET!
No!
I PICKED IT UP.
DRIP
DRIP
DON'T.
DON'T GIVE KITTY-BOO...
...A LOLLIPOP.
BUT YOU STILL LIKED HIM?
WHY, BAMBI?
Well...
THERE WAS A STRAY CAT...
AND THEN...
DRIP DRIP
HUNGRY, KITTY?
WANT SOME CANDY?
MEW
MEW
HEY.
HUH?
Him...
WHOA!
KITTY-BOO?
HAR HAR HAR
LOLLI-POP!
FUNNY, HUH?
Tee!
Hee!
SNORT
GRR
GRR
MEAN-IES...

☆English☆

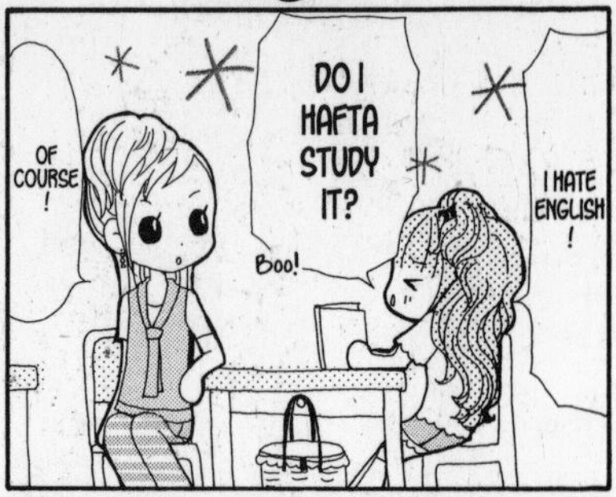
I HATE ENGLISH!
DO I HAFTA STUDY IT?
Boo!
OF COURSE!

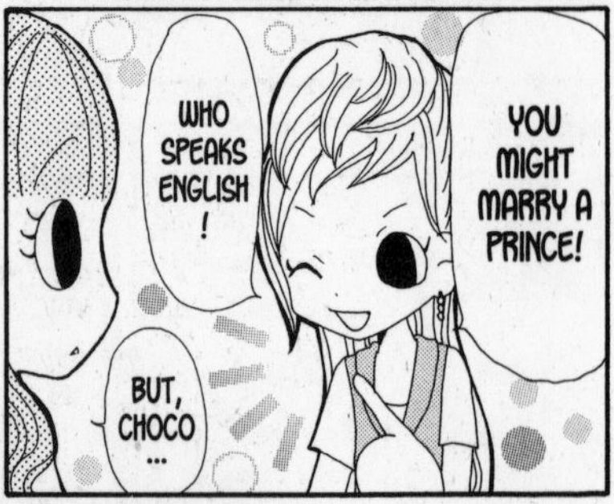
YOU MIGHT MARRY A PRINCE!
WHO SPEAKS ENGLISH!
BUT, CHOCO...

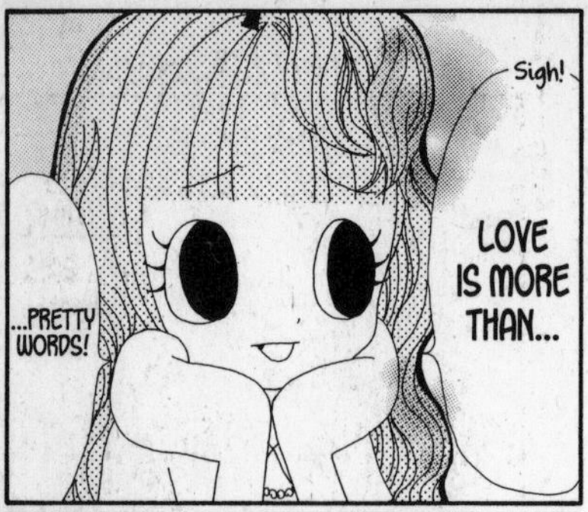
Sigh!
LOVE IS MORE THAN...
...PRETTY WORDS!

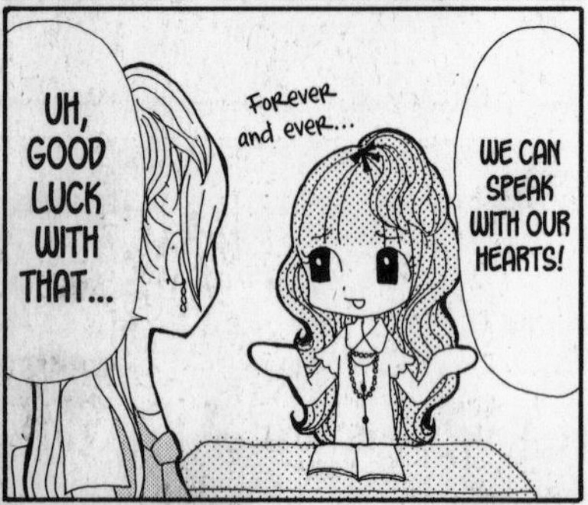
WE CAN SPEAK WITH OUR HEARTS!
Forever and ever...
UH, GOOD LUCK WITH THAT...

Choco Mimi Fashion Notes

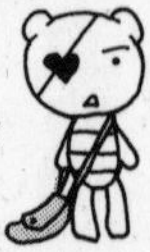

WHAT DO THE *CHOCOMIMI* GIRLS CARRY TO SCHOOL?
LET'S PEEK INSIDE THEIR BAGS!

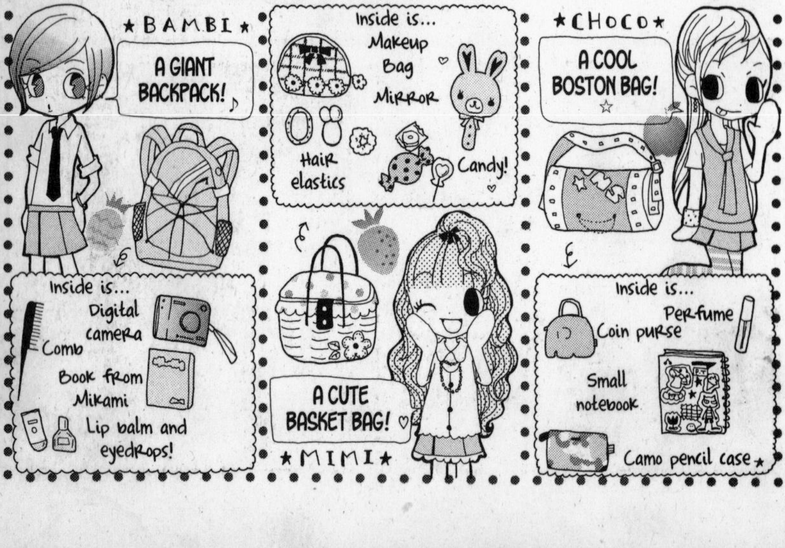
★BAMBI★
A GIANT BACKPACK!♪
Inside is...
Digital camera
Comb
Book from Mikami
Lip balm and eyedrops!
Inside is...
Makeup Bag
Mirror
Hair elastics
Candy!
A CUTE BASKET BAG!♡
★MIMI★
★CHOCO★
A COOL BOSTON BAG!
Inside is...
Perfume
Coin purse
Small notebook
Camo pencil case★

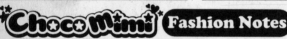

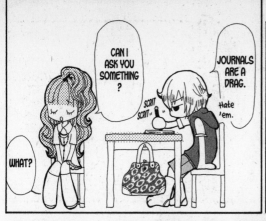

CAN I ASK YOU SOMETHING?

JOURNALS ARE A DRAG.

SCRIT SCRIT...

I Hate 'em.

WHAT?

| 4 | Music | Test |
| 5 | English | |

Absent
~~None~~

Journal

WHAT SHOULD I WRITE?

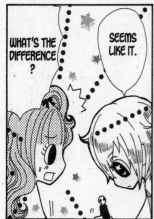

WHAT'S THE DIFFERENCE?

SEEMS LIKE IT.

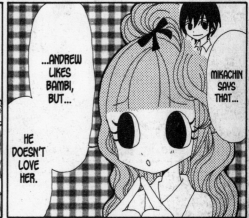

...ANDREW LIKES BAMBI, BUT...

HE DOESN'T LOVE HER.

MIKACHIN SAYS THAT...

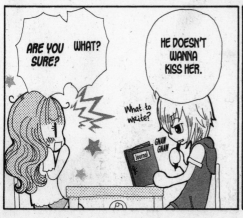

ARE YOU SURE?

WHAT?

HE DOESN'T WANNA KISS HER.

What to write?

GNAM GNAM

Journal

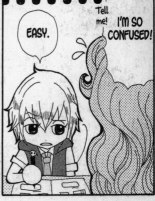

EASY.

Tell me!

I'M SO CONFUSED!

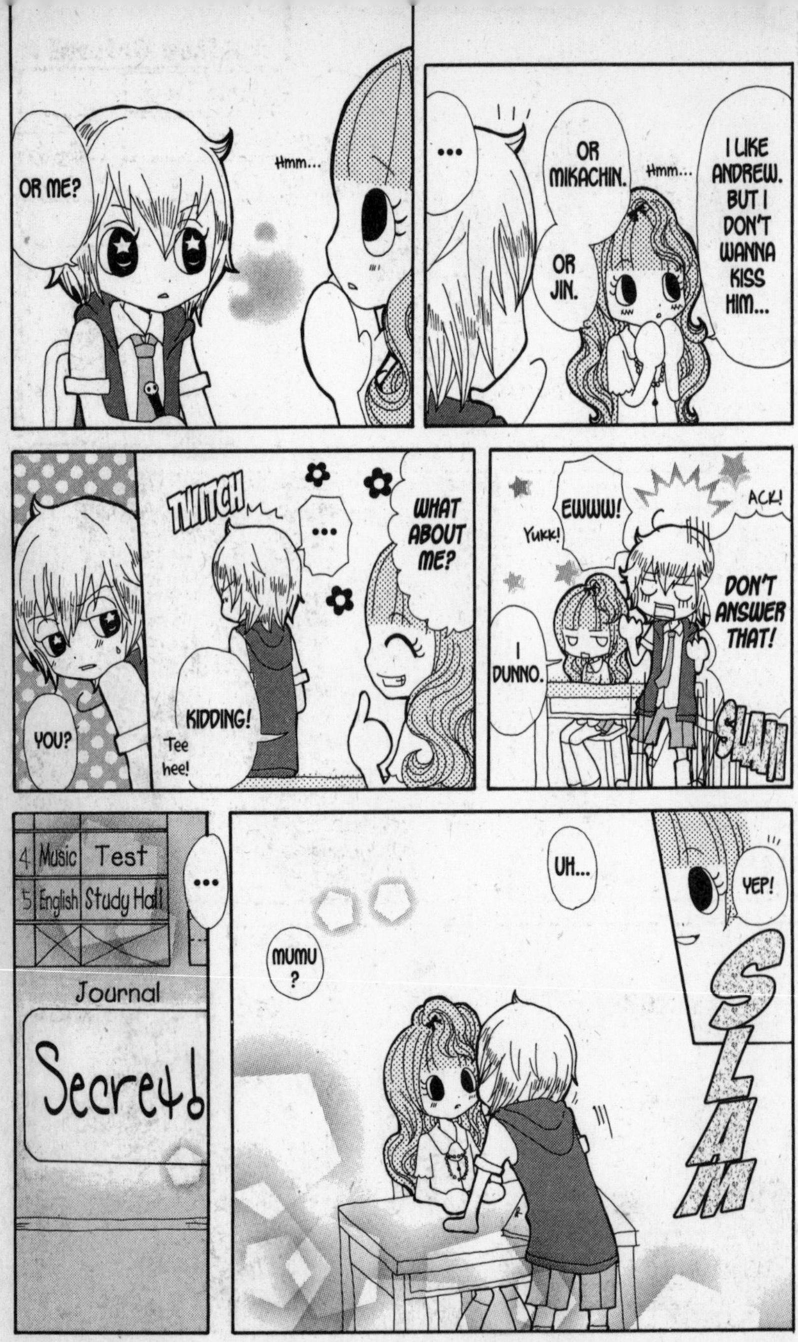
I LIKE ANDREW. BUT I DON'T WANNA KISS HIM...
Hmm...
OR MIKACHIN.
OR JIN.
...
Hmm...
OR ME?
ACK!
DON'T ANSWER THAT!
EWWW!
Yukk!
I DUNNO.
SLAM
WHAT ABOUT ME?
...
TWITCH
KIDDING!
Tee hee!
YOU?
YEP!
UH...
MUMU ?
SLAM
...
4 Music Test
5 English Study Hall
Journal
Secret!

All About Mr. Take

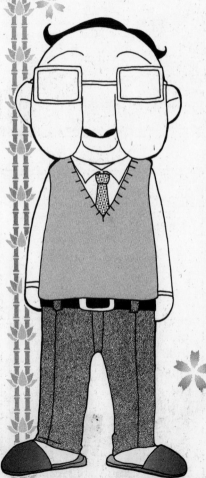

✿ By the Artist ✿

ChocoMimi's teacher

I based MR. Take on MR. Y, my middle school teacher. MR. Y was very strict, but in a good way. He scolded me all through eighth grade. When I got too crazy, he always said, "I'll be your teacher next year too!" Wonder how he's doing...

MR. Take and his wife have no children, but he dearly loves his students.

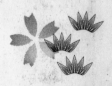

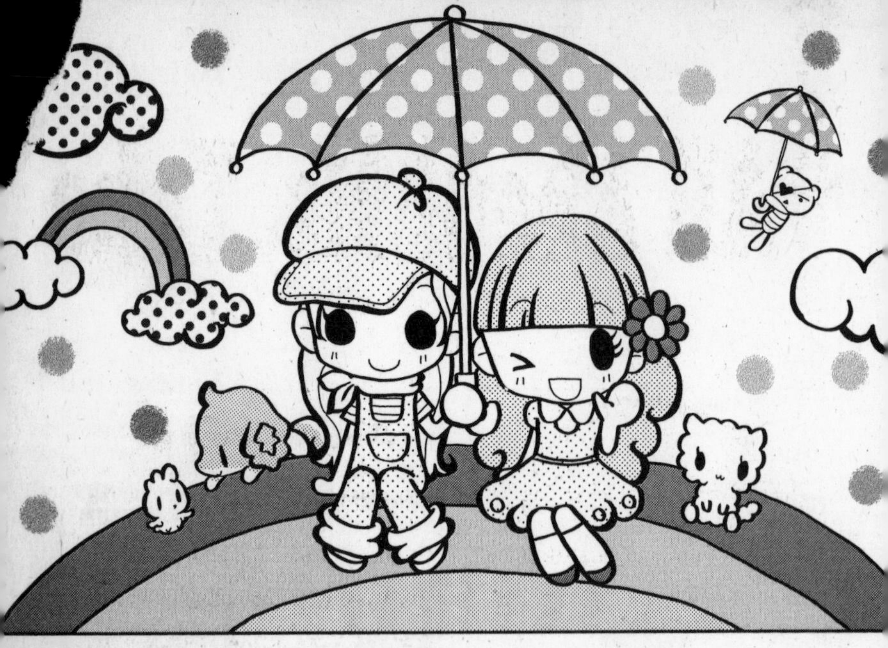

☆ **Rain** ☆

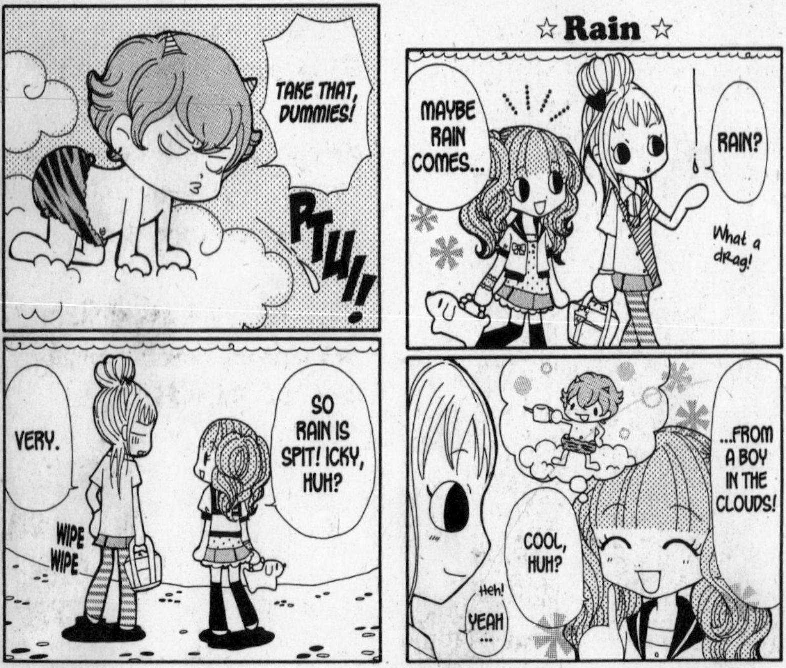
MAYBE RAIN COMES...
RAIN?
What a drag!
...FROM A BOY IN THE CLOUDS!
COOL, HUH?
Heh!
YEAH ...
TAKE THAT, DUMMIES!
PTUI!!
SO RAIN IS SPIT! ICKY, HUH?
VERY.
WIPE WIPE

☆Frizzy Hair☆

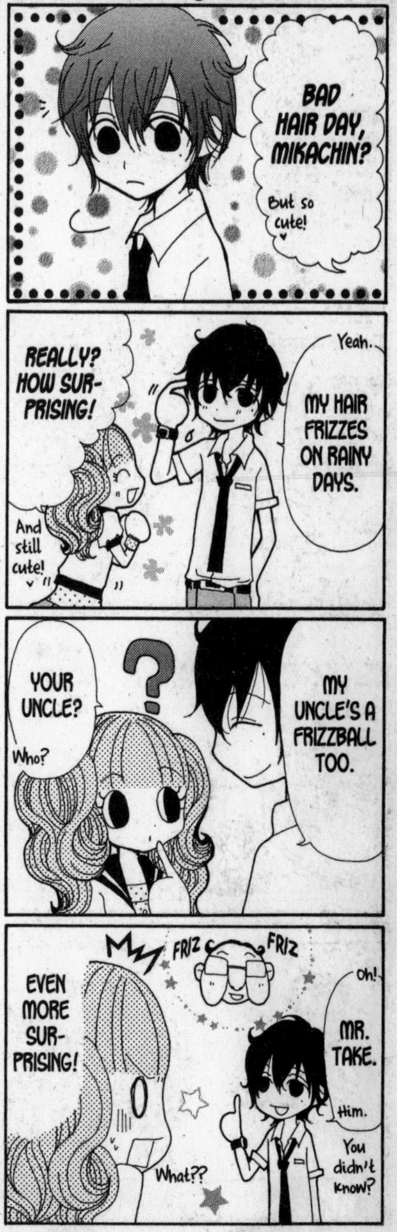
BAD HAIR DAY, MIKACHIN?
But so cute!
Yeah.
MY HAIR FRIZZES ON RAINY DAYS.
REALLY? HOW SUR-PRISING!
And still cute!
MY UNCLE'S A FRIZZBALL TOO.
YOUR UNCLE?
Who?
FRIZ
FRIZ
Oh!
MR. TAKE.
Him.
You didn't know?
EVEN MORE SUR-PRISING!
What??

☆Guitar☆

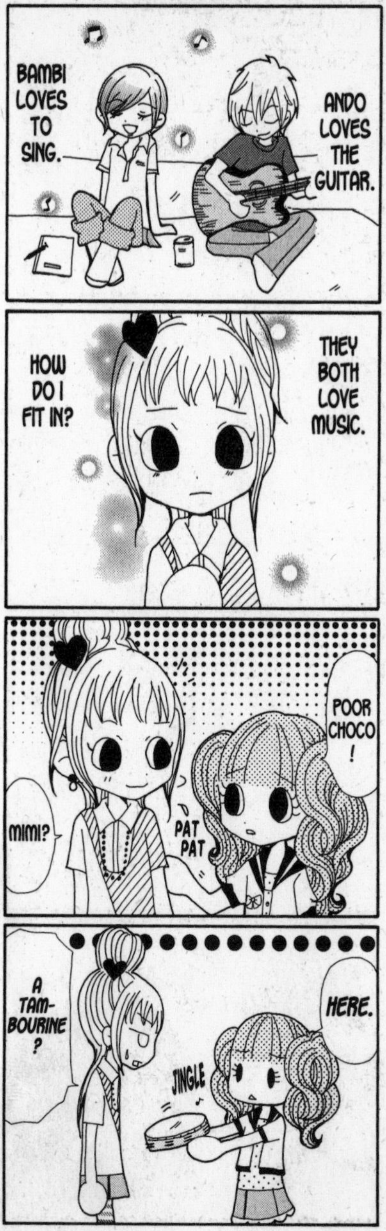
ANDO LOVES THE GUITAR.
BAMBI LOVES TO SING.
THEY BOTH LOVE MUSIC.
HOW DO I FIT IN?
POOR CHOCO!
PAT PAT
MIMI?
HERE.
JINGLE
A TAM-BOURINE?

☆ **Sunny Day Dolls** ☆

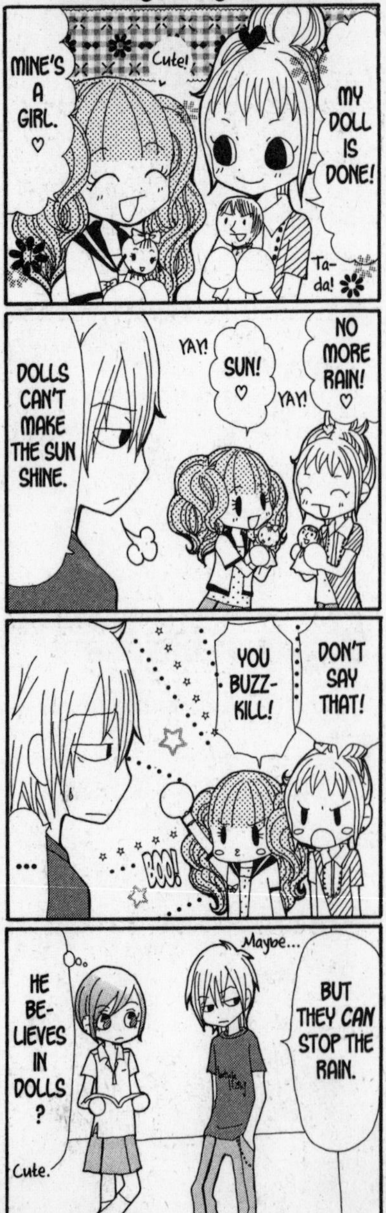
MY DOLL IS DONE!
Ta-da!
Cute!
MINE'S A GIRL. ♡
NO MORE RAIN! ♡
YAY!
SUN! ♡
YAY!
DOLLS CAN'T MAKE THE SUN SHINE.
DON'T SAY THAT!
YOU BUZZ-KILL!
BOO!
...
Maybe...
BUT THEY CAN STOP THE RAIN.
HE BE-LIEVES IN DOLLS?
Cute.

☆ **Side by Side** ☆

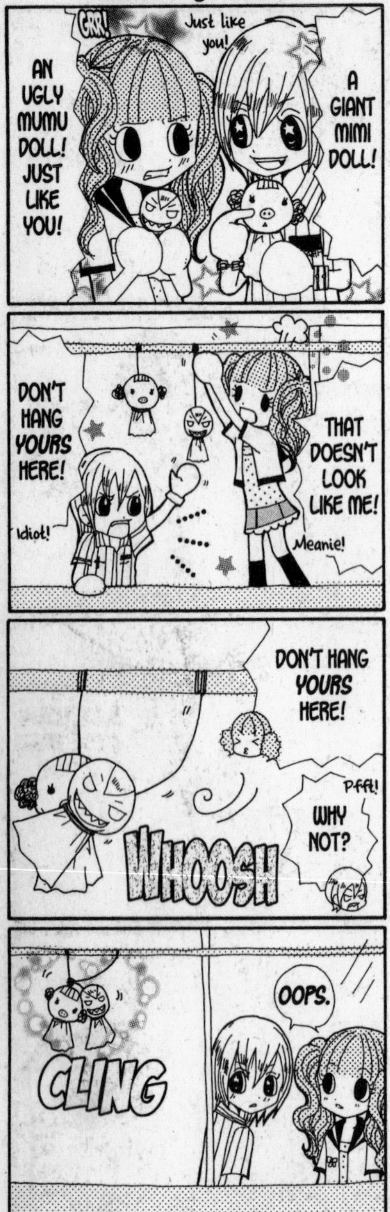
A GIANT MIMI DOLL!
Just like you!
GRR!
AN UGLY MUMU DOLL! JUST LIKE YOU!
THAT DOESN'T LOOK LIKE ME!
Meanie!
DON'T HANG YOURS HERE!
Idiot!
DON'T HANG YOURS HERE!
P-ffl!
WHY NOT?
WHOOSH
OOPS.
CLING

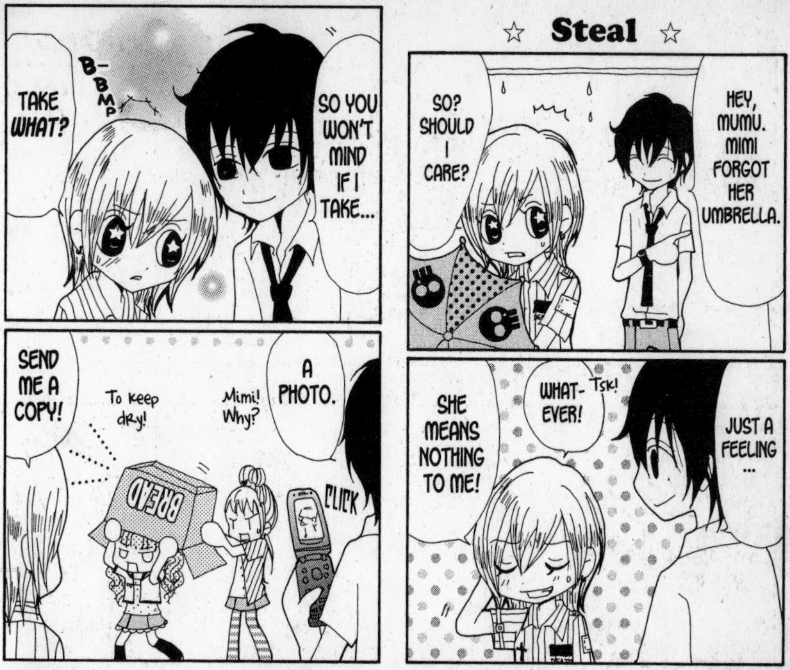
☆ Steal ☆
HEY, MUMU. MIMI FORGOT HER UMBRELLA.
SO? SHOULD I CARE?
JUST A FEELING ...
Tsk!
WHAT-EVER!
SHE MEANS NOTHING TO ME!
SO YOU WON'T MIND IF I TAKE...
B-BMP
TAKE WHAT?
A PHOTO.
CLICK
Mimi! Why?
To keep dry!
BREAD
SEND ME A COPY!

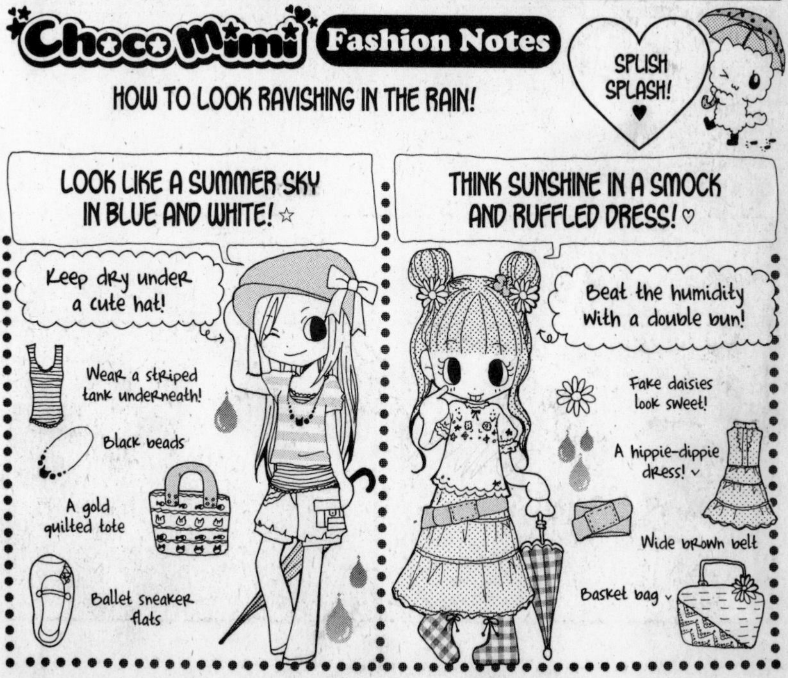
Choco Mimi Fashion Notes
HOW TO LOOK RAVISHING IN THE RAIN!
SPLISH SPLASH! ♥
THINK SUNSHINE IN A SMOCK AND RUFFLED DRESS! ♡
Beat the humidity with a double bun!
Fake daisies look sweet!
A hippie-dippie dress!
Wide brown belt
Basket bag
LOOK LIKE A SUMMER SKY IN BLUE AND WHITE! ☆
Keep dry under a cute hat!
Wear a striped tank underneath!
Black beads
A gold quilted tote
Ballet sneaker flats

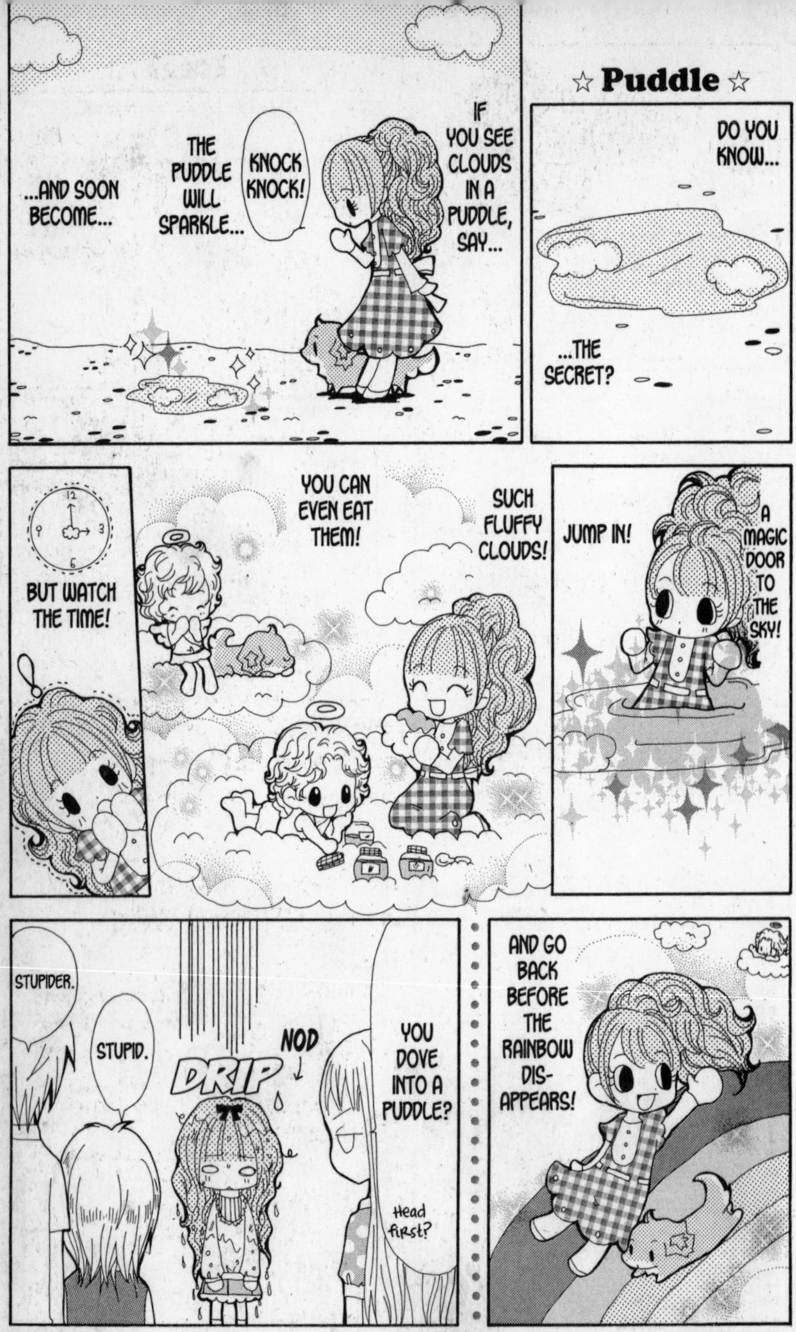
DO YOU KNOW...
...THE SECRET?
IF YOU SEE CLOUDS IN A PUDDLE, SAY...
KNOCK KNOCK!
THE PUDDLE WILL SPARKLE...
...AND SOON BECOME...
A MAGIC DOOR TO THE SKY!
JUMP IN!
SUCH FLUFFY CLOUDS!
YOU CAN EVEN EAT THEM!
BUT WATCH THE TIME!
AND GO BACK BEFORE THE RAINBOW DIS-APPEARS!
YOU DOVE INTO A PUDDLE?
Head first?
NOD
DRIP
STUPID.
STUPIDER.

☆Raincoat☆

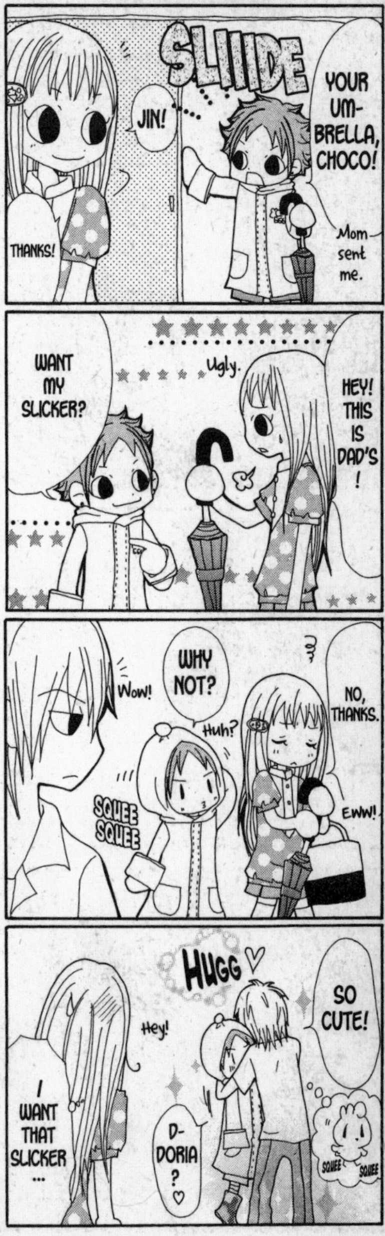
YOUR UM-BRELLA, CHOCO!
Mom sent me.
SLIIDE
JIN!
THANKS!
HEY! THIS IS DAD'S!
Ugly.
WANT MY SLICKER?
NO, THANKS.
EWW!
WHY NOT?
Huh?
Wow!
SQUEE SQUEE
SO CUTE!
SQUEE SQUEE
HUGG ♡
Hey!
D-DORIA?♡
I WANT THAT SLICKER...

☆Song☆

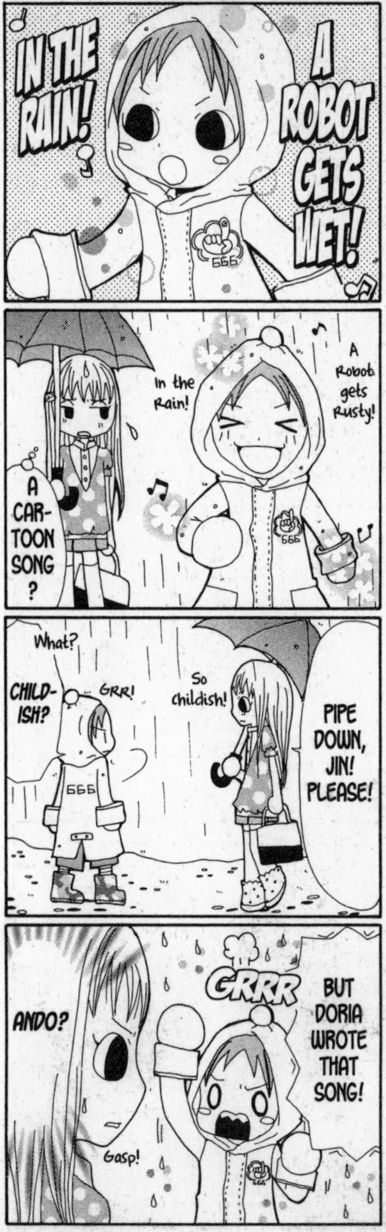
A ROBOT GETS WET!
IN THE RAIN!
A Robot gets Rusty!
In the Rain!
A CAR-TOON SONG?
PIPE DOWN, JIN! PLEASE!
So childish!
...GRR!
What?
CHILD-ISH?
BUT DORIA WROTE THAT SONG!
GRRR
ANDO?
Gasp!

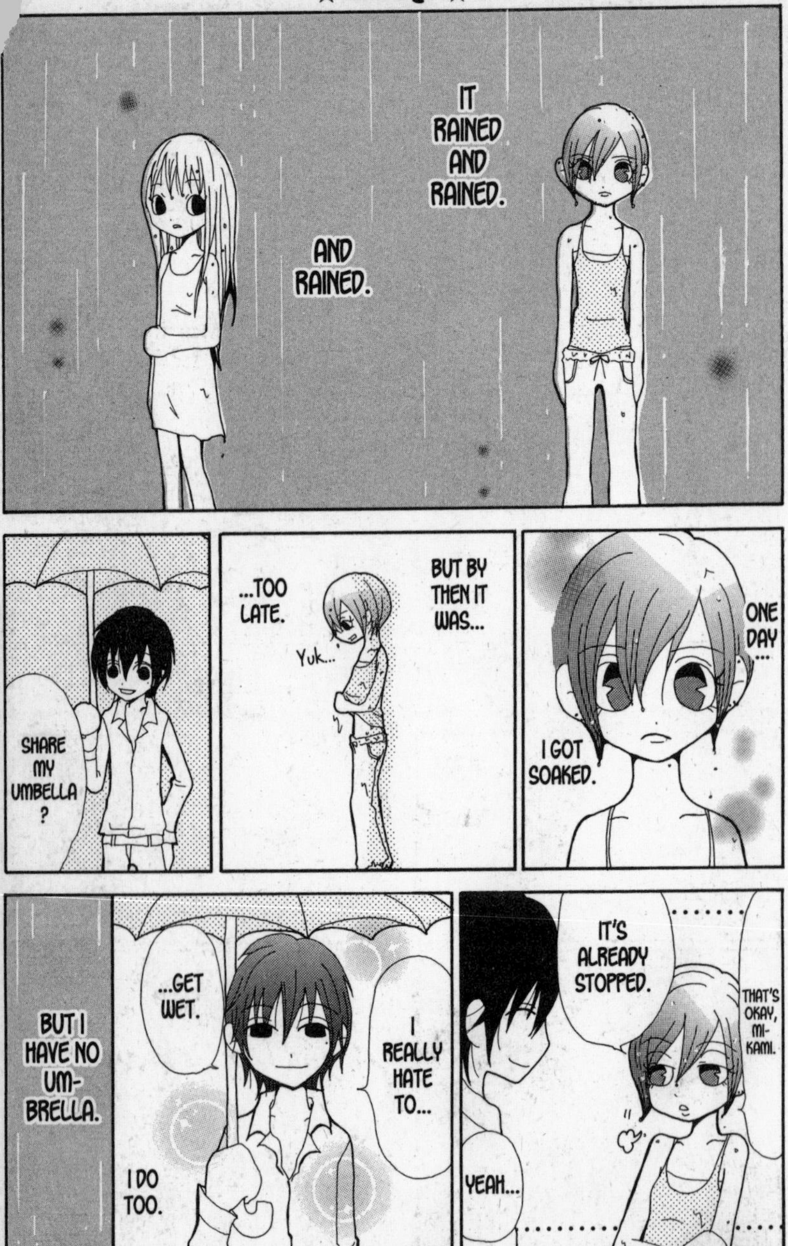
IT RAINED AND RAINED.
AND RAINED.
ONE DAY...
I GOT SOAKED.
BUT BY THEN IT WAS...
...TOO LATE.
Yuk...
SHARE MY UMBRELLA?
......
IT'S ALREADY STOPPED.
THAT'S OKAY, MI-KAMI.
YEAH...
......
I REALLY HATE TO...
...GET WET.
I DO TOO.
BUT I HAVE NO UM-BRELLA.

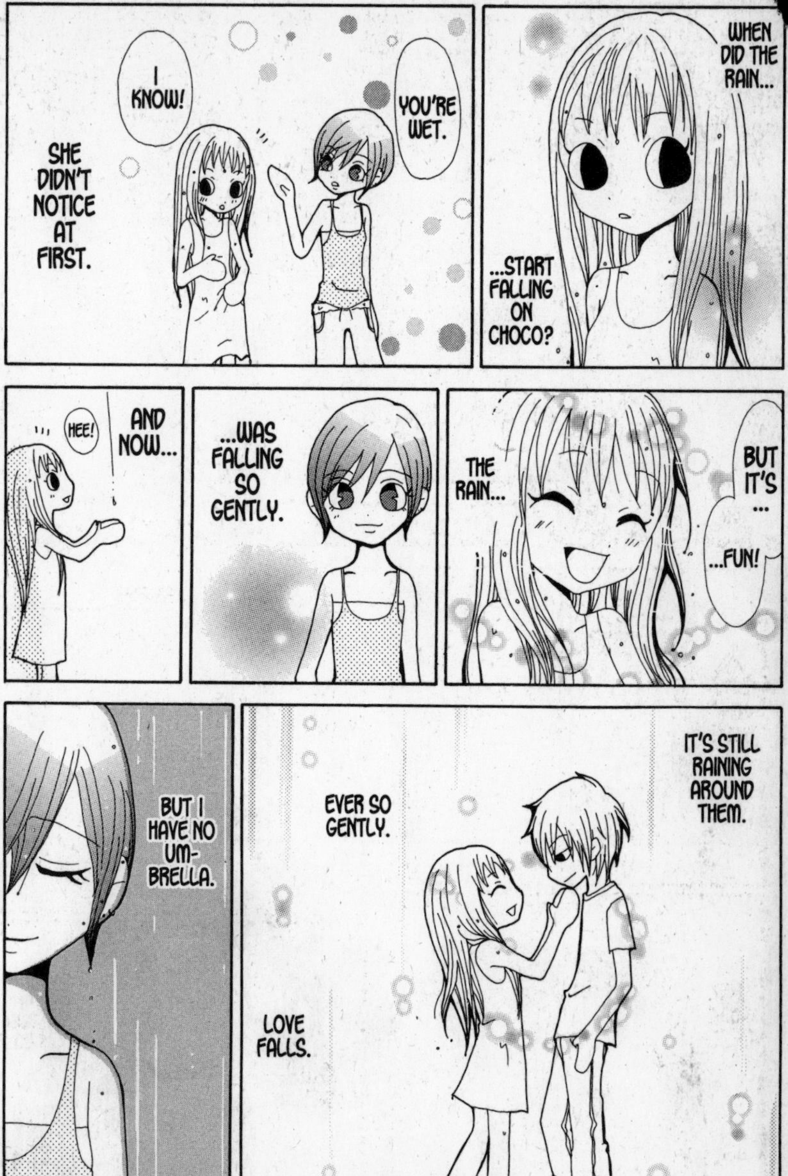
WHEN DID THE RAIN...
...START FALLING ON CHOCO?
YOU'RE WET.
I KNOW!
SHE DIDN'T NOTICE AT FIRST.
BUT IT'S...
...FUN!
THE RAIN...
...WAS FALLING SO GENTLY.
AND NOW...
HEE!
IT'S STILL RAINING AROUND THEM.
EVER SO GENTLY.
LOVE FALLS.
BUT I HAVE NO UM-BRELLA.

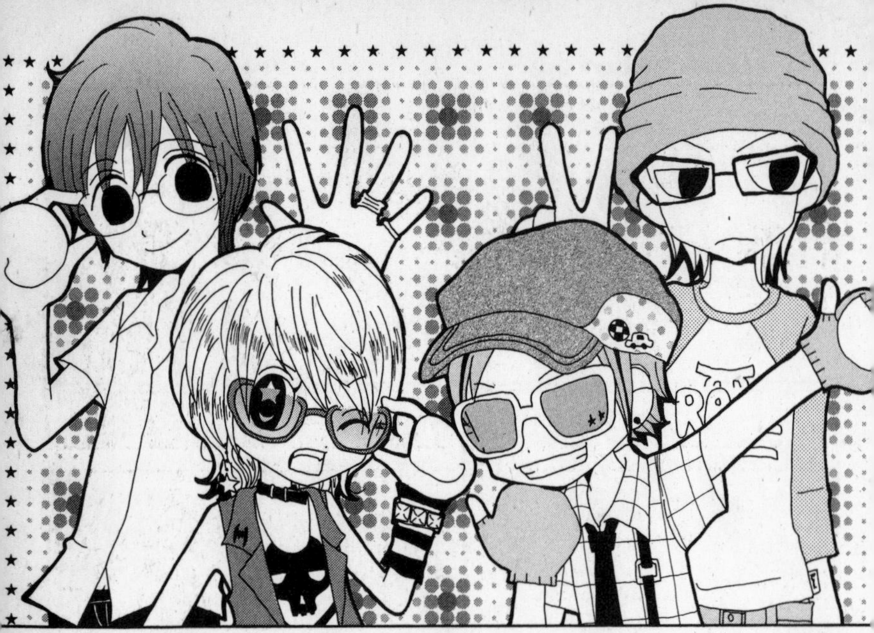

☆ **Glasses** ☆

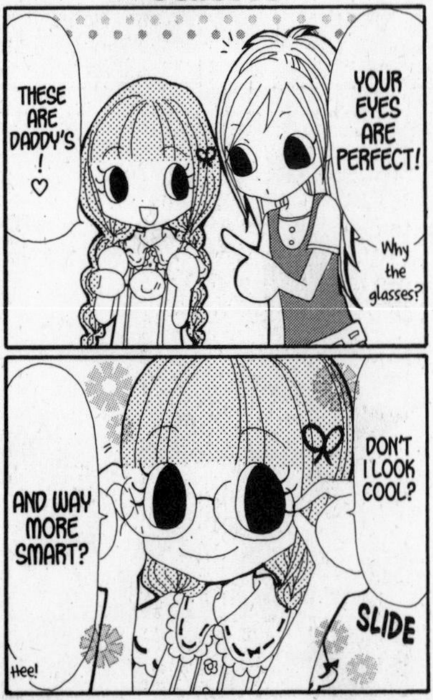
YOUR EYES ARE PERFECT!
Why the glasses?
THESE ARE DADDY'S! ♡
DON'T I LOOK COOL?
AND WAY MORE SMART?
SLIDE
Hee!

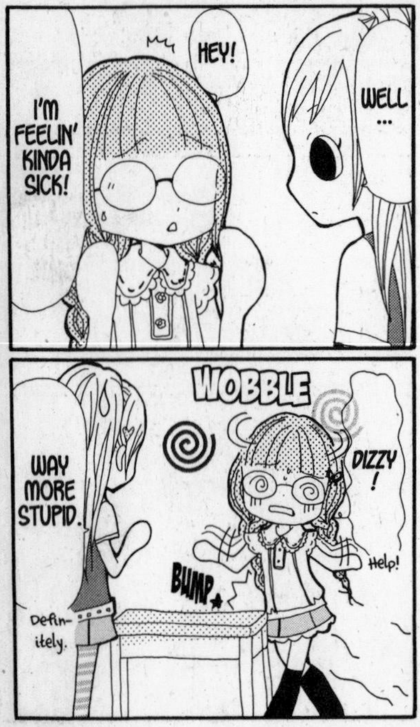
HEY!
WELL...
I'M FEELIN' KINDA SICK!
DIZZY!
WOBBLE
Help!
WAY MORE STUPID.
BUMP
Defin-itely.

☆ Need ☆

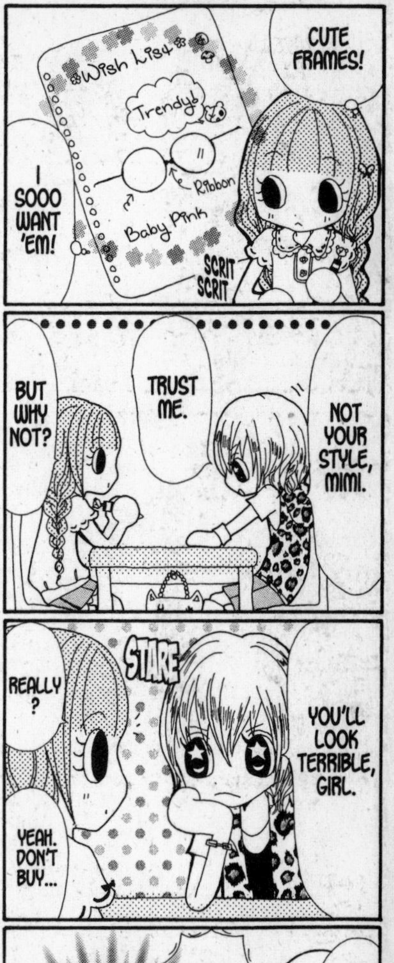
CUTE FRAMES!
Wish List
Trendy!
Ribbon
Baby Pink
I SOOO WANT 'EM!
SCRIT SCRIT
NOT YOUR STYLE, MIMI.
TRUST ME.
BUT WHY NOT?
YOU'LL LOOK TERRIBLE, GIRL.
STARE
REALLY?
YEAH. DON'T BUY...
...THAT BIKINI!
YOU DOOFUS!
THEY'RE GLAS-SES!

☆ Girl in Love ☆

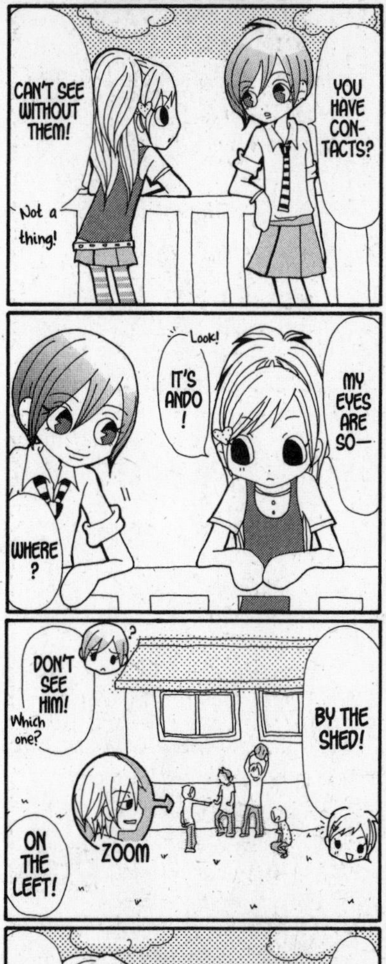
YOU HAVE CON-TACTS?
CAN'T SEE WITHOUT THEM!
Not a thing!
MY EYES ARE SO—
Look!
IT'S ANDO!
WHERE?
BY THE SHED!
DON'T SEE HIM!
Which one?
ZOOM
ON THE LEFT!
LOOK, LOOK!
Giggle!
THE EYES OF LOVE.
Sigh!

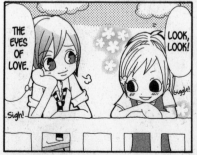

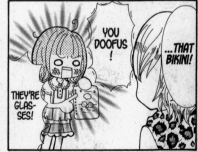

☆ My Glasses ☆

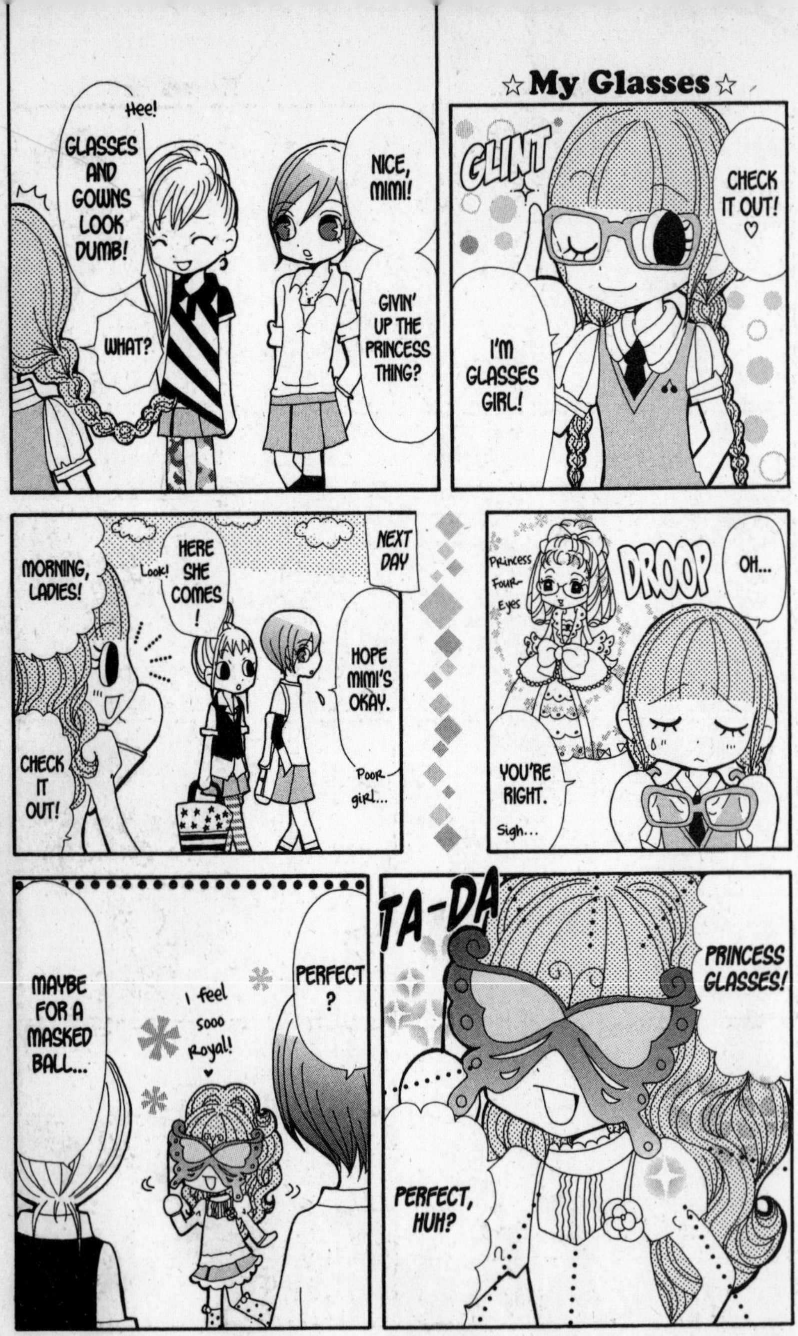
GLINT
CHECK IT OUT! ♡
I'M GLASSES GIRL!
NICE, MIMI!
GIVIN' UP THE PRINCESS THING?
Hee!
GLASSES AND GOWNS LOOK DUMB!
WHAT?
OH...
DROOP
Princess Four-Eyes
YOU'RE RIGHT.
Sigh...
NEXT DAY
HOPE MIMI'S OKAY.
Poor girl...
HERE SHE COMES!
Look!
MORNING, LADIES!
CHECK IT OUT!
PRINCESS GLASSES!
TA-DA
PERFECT, HUH?
PERFECT?
I feel sooo Royal! ♥
MAYBE FOR A MASKED BALL...

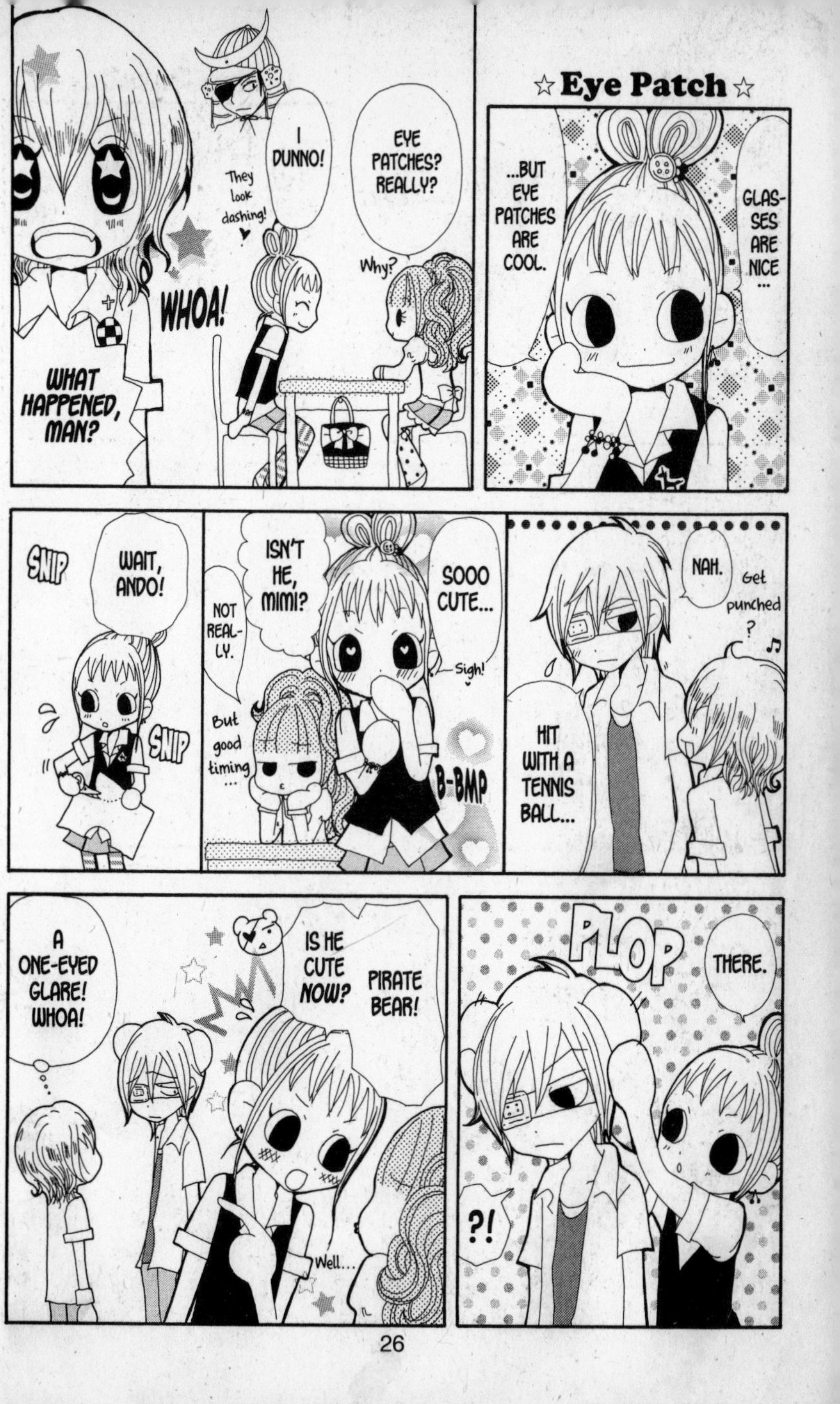
☆Eye Patch☆
GLASSES ARE NICE...
...BUT EYE PATCHES ARE COOL.
EYE PATCHES? REALLY?
Why?
I DUNNO!
They look dashing!
WHOA!
WHAT HAPPENED, MAN?
NAH.
Get punched?
HIT WITH A TENNIS BALL...
SOOO CUTE...
Sigh!
ISN'T HE, MIMI?
NOT REALLY.
But good timing...
B-BMP
WAIT, ANDO!
SNIP
SNIP
PLOP
THERE.
?!
PIRATE BEAR!
IS HE CUTE NOW?
A ONE-EYED GLARE! WHOA!
Well...

☆ Eye Patch 2 ☆

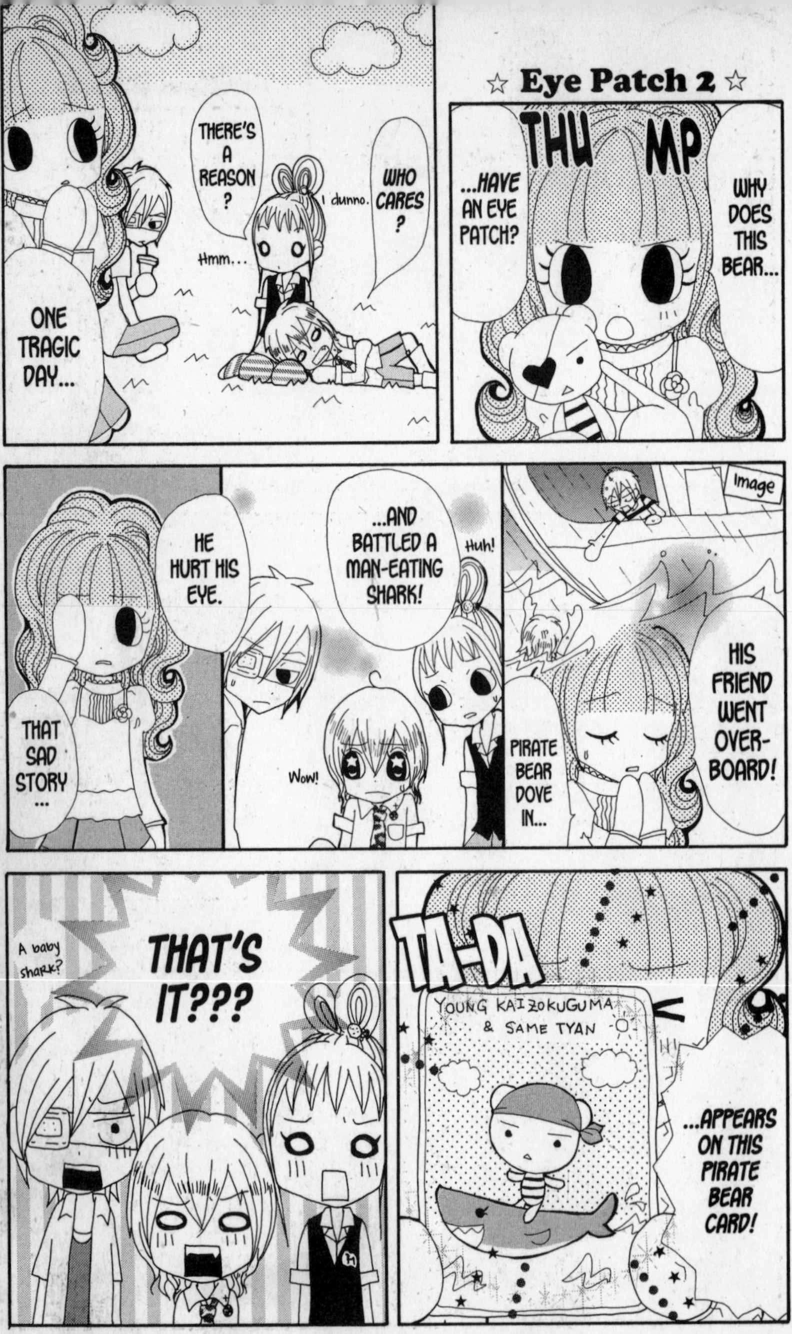
THUMP
WHY DOES THIS BEAR...
...HAVE AN EYE PATCH?
THERE'S A REASON?
WHO CARES?
I dunno.
Hmm...
ONE TRAGIC DAY...
Image
HIS FRIEND WENT OVERBOARD!
PIRATE BEAR DOVE IN...
...AND BATTLED A MAN-EATING SHARK!
Huh!
HE HURT HIS EYE.
Wow!
THAT SAD STORY...
TA-DA
YOUNG KAIZOKUGUMA & SAME TYAN
...APPEARS ON THIS PIRATE BEAR CARD!
THAT'S IT???
A baby shark?

☆ Caviar with Jin ☆

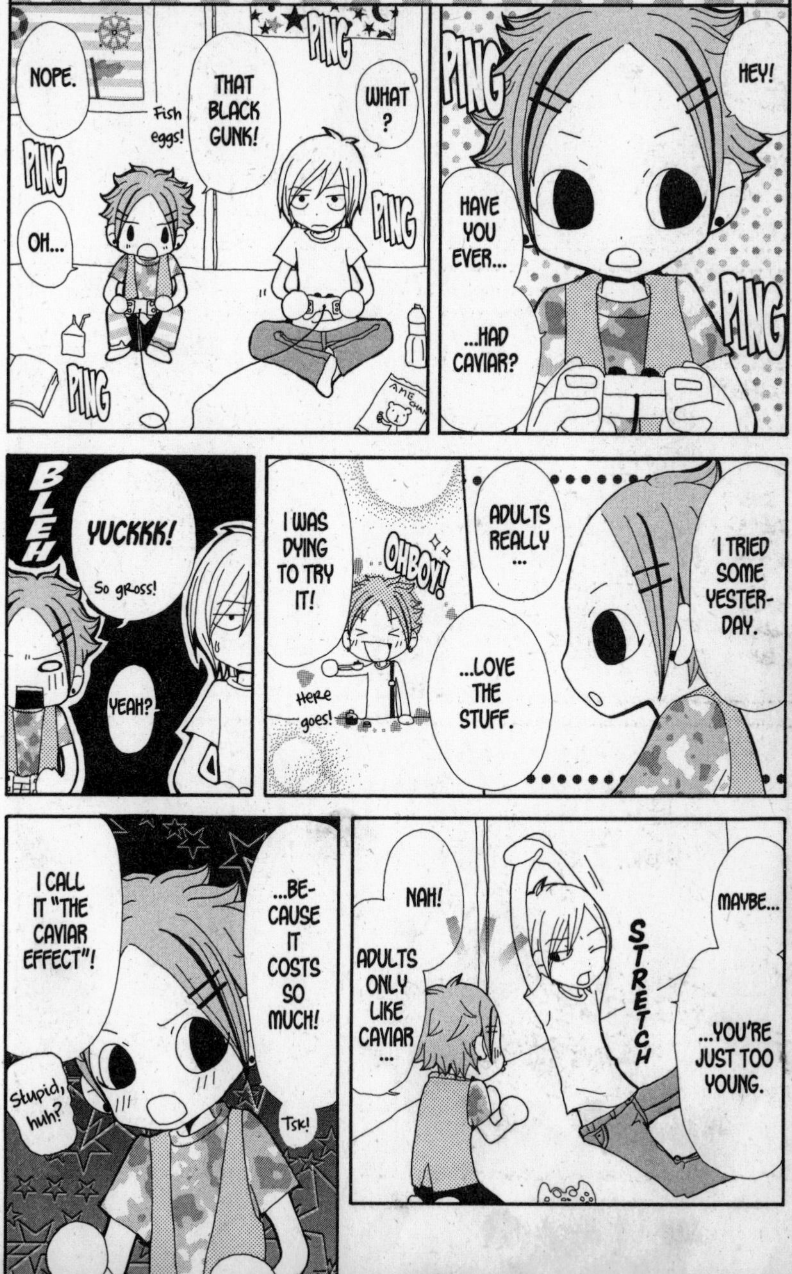
HEY!
PING
HAVE YOU EVER...
...HAD CAVIAR?
PING
PING
WHAT?
THAT BLACK GUNK!
Fish eggs!
NOPE.
PING
OH...
PING
PING
I TRIED SOME YESTER-DAY.
ADULTS REALLY...
...LOVE THE STUFF.
I WAS DYING TO TRY IT!
OHBOY!
Here goes!
YUCKKK!
So gross!
BLEH
YEAH?
MAYBE...
...YOU'RE JUST TOO YOUNG.
STRETCH
NAH!
ADULTS ONLY LIKE CAVIAR...
...BE-CAUSE IT COSTS SO MUCH!
I CALL IT "THE CAVIAR EFFECT"!
Tsk!
Stupid, huh?

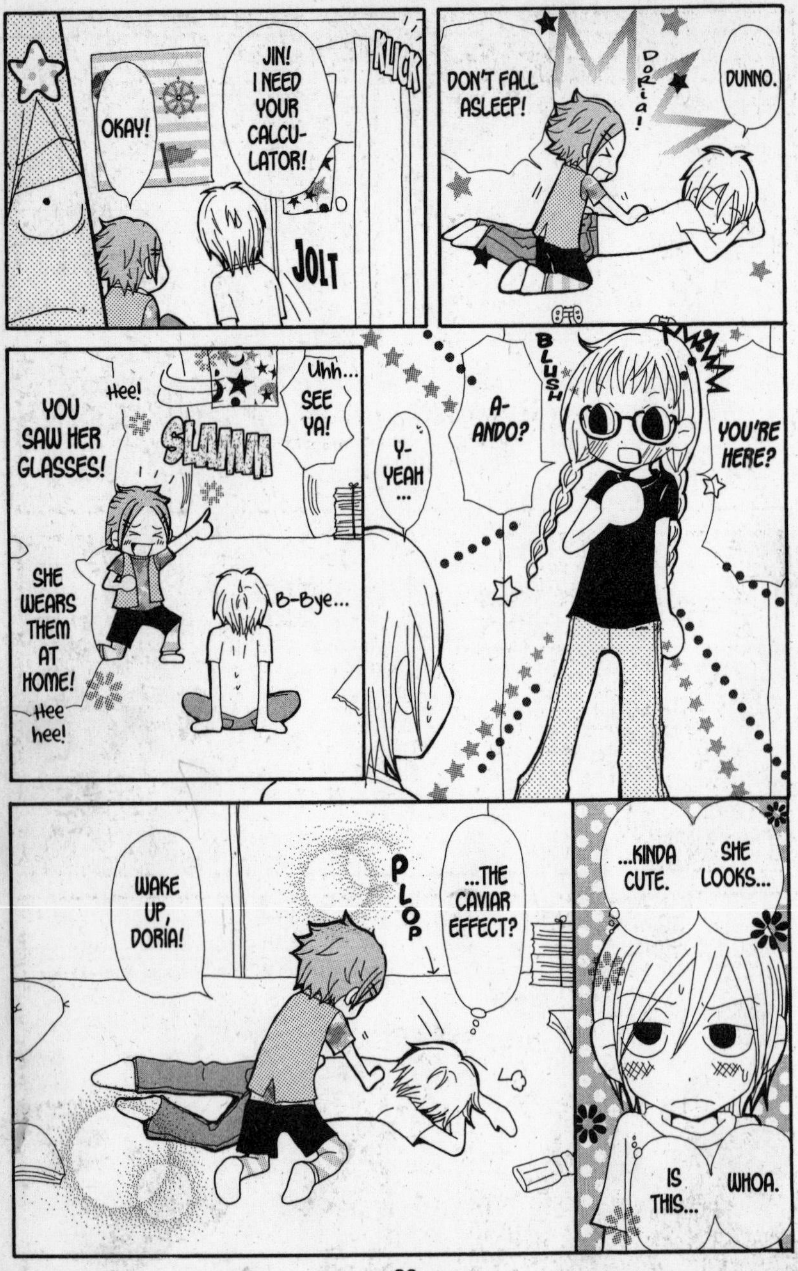
DUNNO.
DORIA!
DON'T FALL ASLEEP!
KLICK
JIN! I NEED YOUR CALCULATOR!
OKAY!
JOLT
YOU'RE HERE?
BLUSH
A-ANDO?
Y-YEAH...
Uhh... SEE YA!
SLAMM
Hee!
YOU SAW HER GLASSES!
B-Bye...
SHE WEARS THEM AT HOME!
Hee hee!
SHE LOOKS...
...KINDA CUTE.
WHOA.
IS THIS...
...THE CAVIAR EFFECT?
PLOP
WAKE UP, DORIA!

☆Collection☆

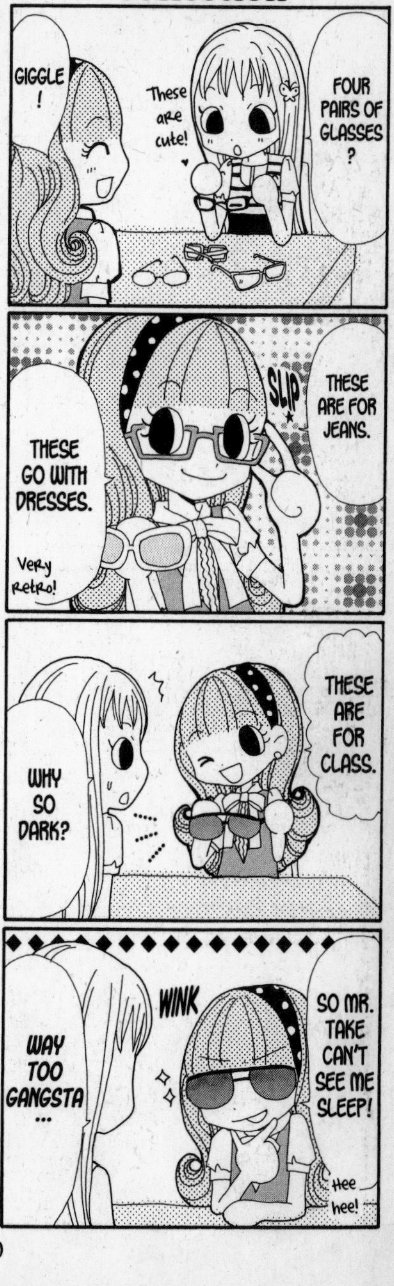
FOUR PAIRS OF GLASSES?
These are cute! ♥
GIGGLE!
THESE ARE FOR JEANS.
SLIP
THESE GO WITH DRESSES.
Very retro!
THESE ARE FOR CLASS.
WHY SO DARK?
SO MR. TAKE CAN'T SEE ME SLEEP!
WINK
WAY TOO GANGSTA...
Hee hee!

☆Contacts☆

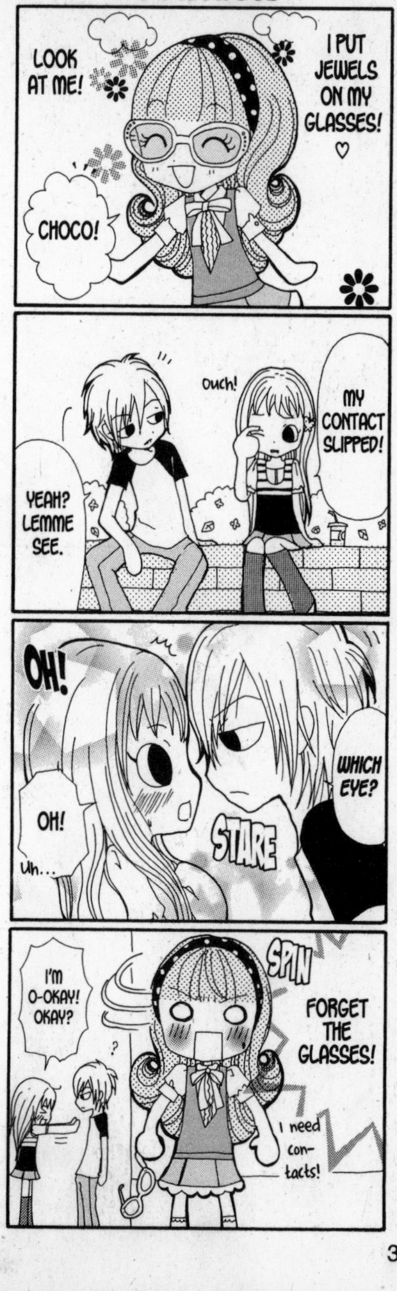
I PUT JEWELS ON MY GLASSES! ♡
LOOK AT ME!
CHOCO!
MY CONTACT SLIPPED!
Ouch!
YEAH? LEMME SEE.
WHICH EYE?
STARE
OH!
OH!
Uh...
SPIN
FORGET THE GLASSES!
I need con-tacts!
I'm O-OKAY! OKAY?

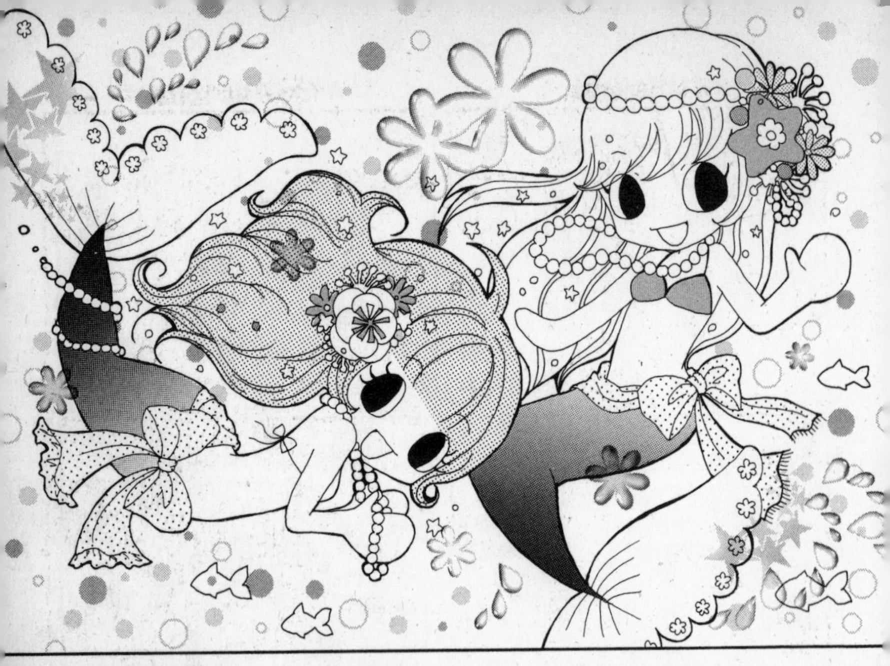

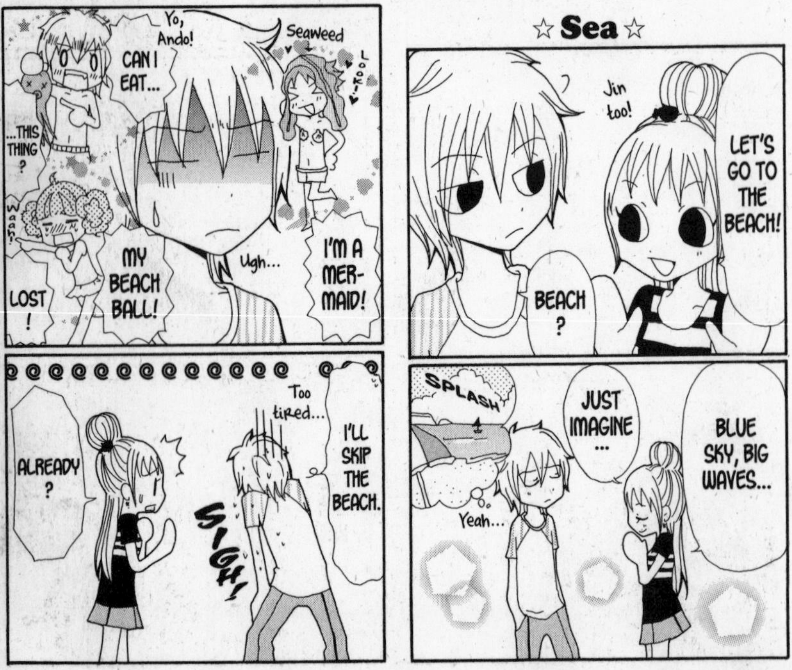
☆ Sea ☆
LET'S GO TO THE BEACH!
Jin too!
BEACH?
BLUE SKY, BIG WAVES...
JUST IMAGINE...
SPLASH
Yeah...
Seaweed
LOOK
Yo, Ando!
CAN I EAT...
...THIS THING?
I'M A MER-MAID!
Ugh...
MY BEACH BALL!
Waah!
LOST!
I'LL SKIP THE BEACH.
Too tired...
SIGH!
ALREADY?

☆Guessing Game☆

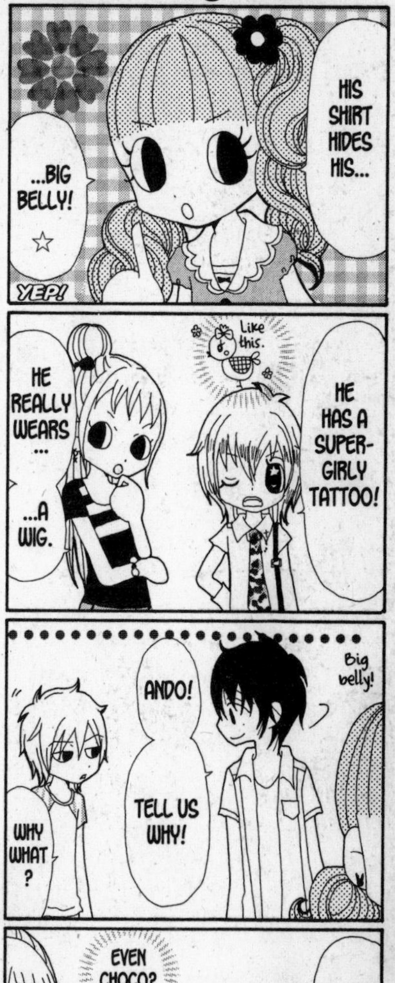
HIS SHIRT HIDES HIS...
...BIG BELLY! ☆
YEP!
HE HAS A SUPER-GIRLY TATTOO!
Like this.
HE REALLY WEARS ...
...A WIG.
Big belly!
ANDO!
TELL US WHY!
WHY WHAT ?
YOU WON'T GO TO THE BEACH.
EVEN CHOCO?
SO CRUEL!
A hairy chest?

☆Sunburn☆

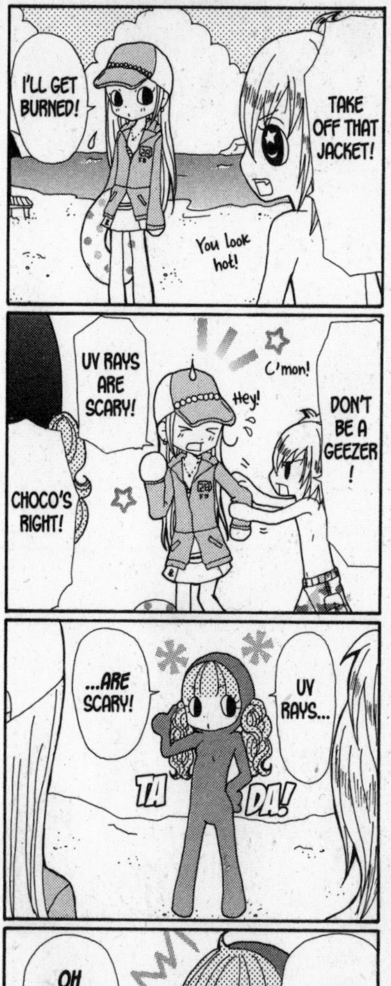
TAKE OFF THAT JACKET!
I'LL GET BURNED!
You look hot!
DON'T BE A GEEZER!
C'mon!
Hey!
UV RAYS ARE SCARY!
CHOCO'S RIGHT!
UV RAYS...
...ARE SCARY!
TA DA!
BUT WHAT ABOUT MY FACE?
OH BROTHER!
Oh no!

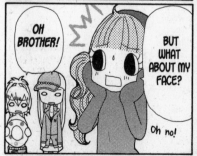

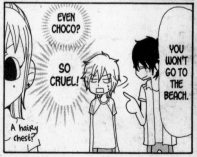

☆ Sunscreen ☆

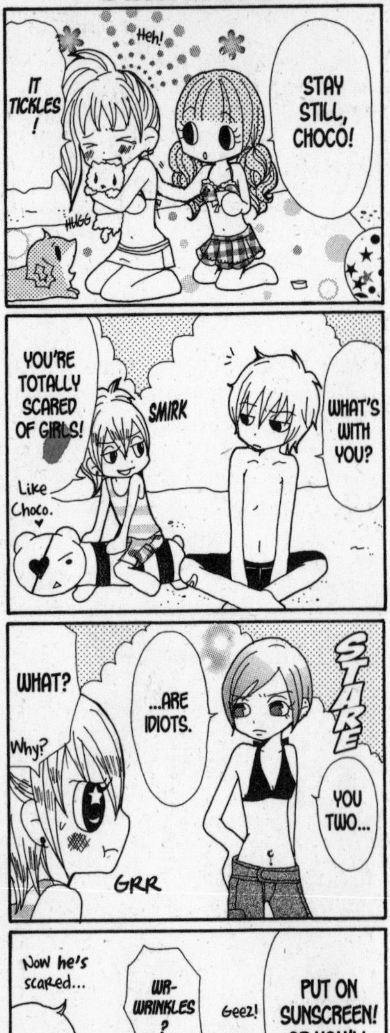
STAY STILL, CHOCO!
Heh!
IT TICKLES!
HUGG
WHAT'S WITH YOU?
SMIRK
YOU'RE TOTALLY SCARED OF GIRLS!
Like Choco.
STARE
YOU TWO...
...ARE IDIOTS.
WHAT?
Why?
GRR
PUT ON SUNSCREEN! OR YOU'LL GET WRINKLES!
Geez!
WR-WRINKLES?
Now he's scared...
JOLT

☆ Choice ☆

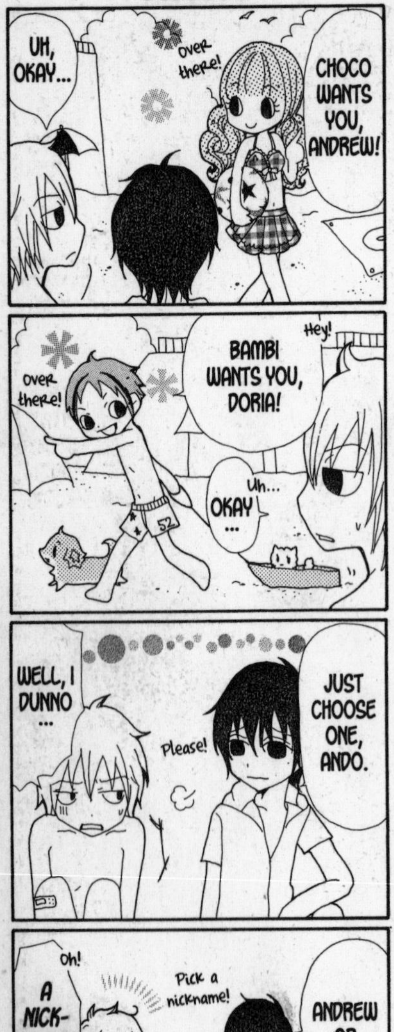
CHOCO WANTS YOU, ANDREW!
over there!
UH, OKAY...
Hey!
BAMBI WANTS YOU, DORIA!
Uh... OKAY...
over there!
JUST CHOOSE ONE, ANDO.
Please!
WELL, I DUNNO...
ANDREW OR DORIA?
Pick a nickname!
Oh!
A NICK-NAME!
Yeah!

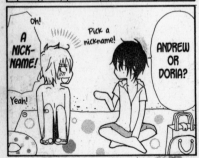

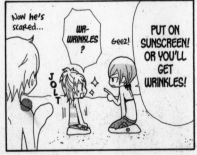

☆Foreign Country☆

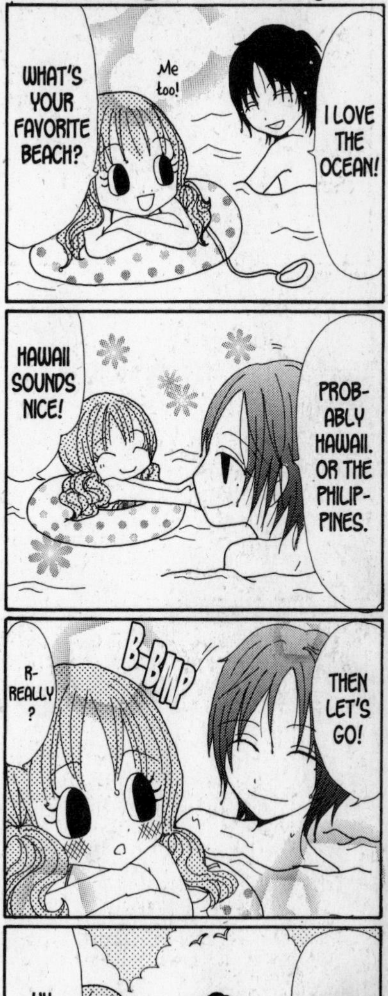
I LOVE THE OCEAN!
Me too!
WHAT'S YOUR FAVORITE BEACH?
PROBABLY HAWAII. OR THE PHILIPPINES.
HAWAII SOUNDS NICE!
THEN LET'S GO!
B-BMP
R-REALLY?
SURE! WE START SWIMMING THATAWAY!
For two months...
UH, YOU GO AHEAD...
I'll catch up...

☆Tunnel☆

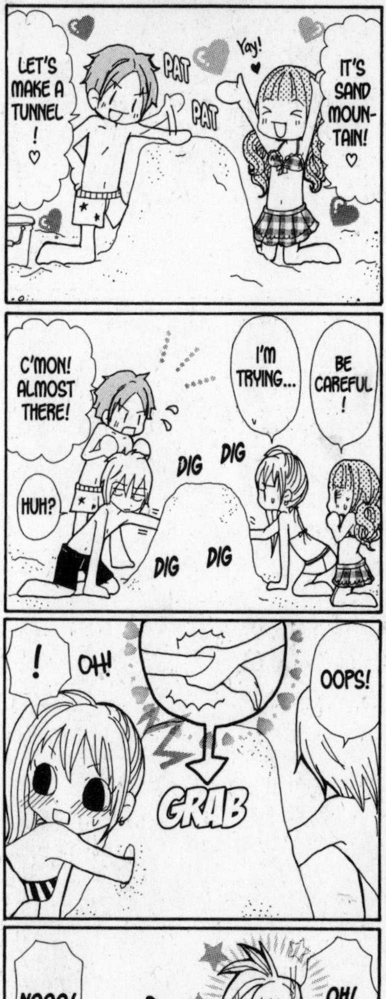
IT'S SAND MOUNTAIN! ♡
Yay! ♥
PAT
PAT
LET'S MAKE A TUNNEL! ♡
BE CAREFUL!
I'M TRYING...
C'MON! ALMOST THERE!
DIG DIG
DIG DIG
HUH?
OOPS!
GRAB
OH!
!
OH!
POP
BLUSH
NOOO!

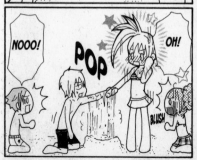

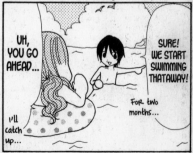

☆ Seashell ☆

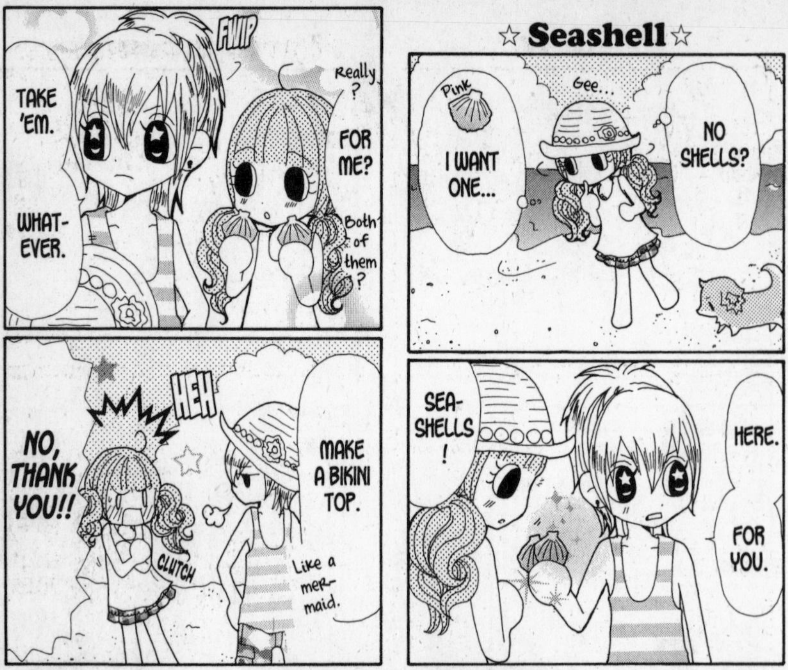
Pink
I WANT ONE...
Gee...
NO SHELLS?
SEA-SHELLS!
HERE.
FOR YOU.
FWIP
Really? FOR ME?
Both of them?
TAKE 'EM.
WHAT-EVER.
MAKE A BIKINI TOP.
Like a mer-maid.
HEH
NO, THANK YOU!!
CLUTCH

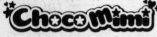

Choco Mimi Fashion Notes

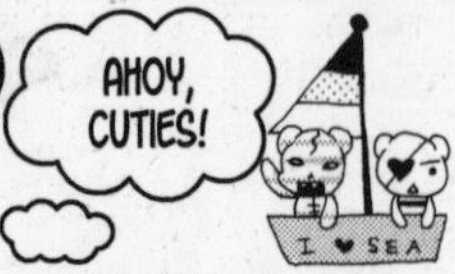
AHOY, CUTIES!
I ♥ SEA

HIT THE SAND IN YOUR FAVORITE BEACHWEAR! ♪

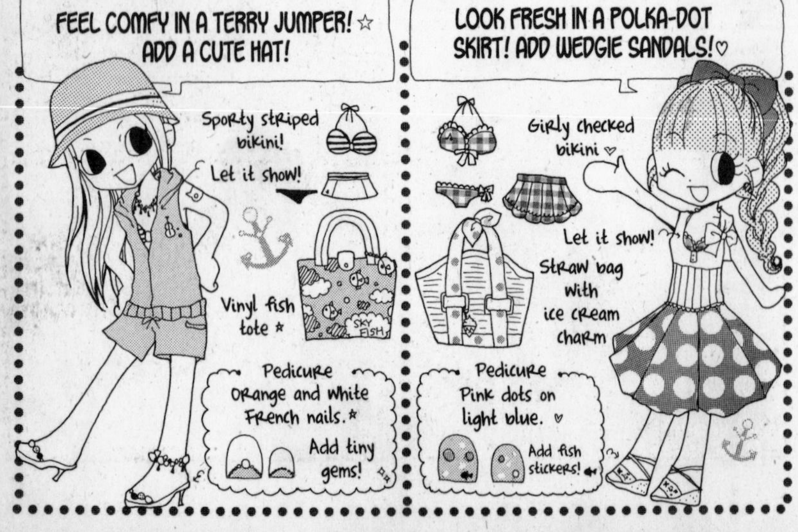
LOOK FRESH IN A POLKA-DOT SKIRT! ADD WEDGIE SANDALS! ♡
Girly checked bikini ♡
Let it show!
Straw bag with ice cream charm
Pedicure
Pink dots on light blue. ♡
Add fish stickers!
FEEL COMFY IN A TERRY JUMPER! ☆ ADD A CUTE HAT!
Sporty striped bikini!
Let it show!
Vinyl fish tote ☆
SKY FISH
Pedicure
Orange and white French nails. ☆
Add tiny gems!

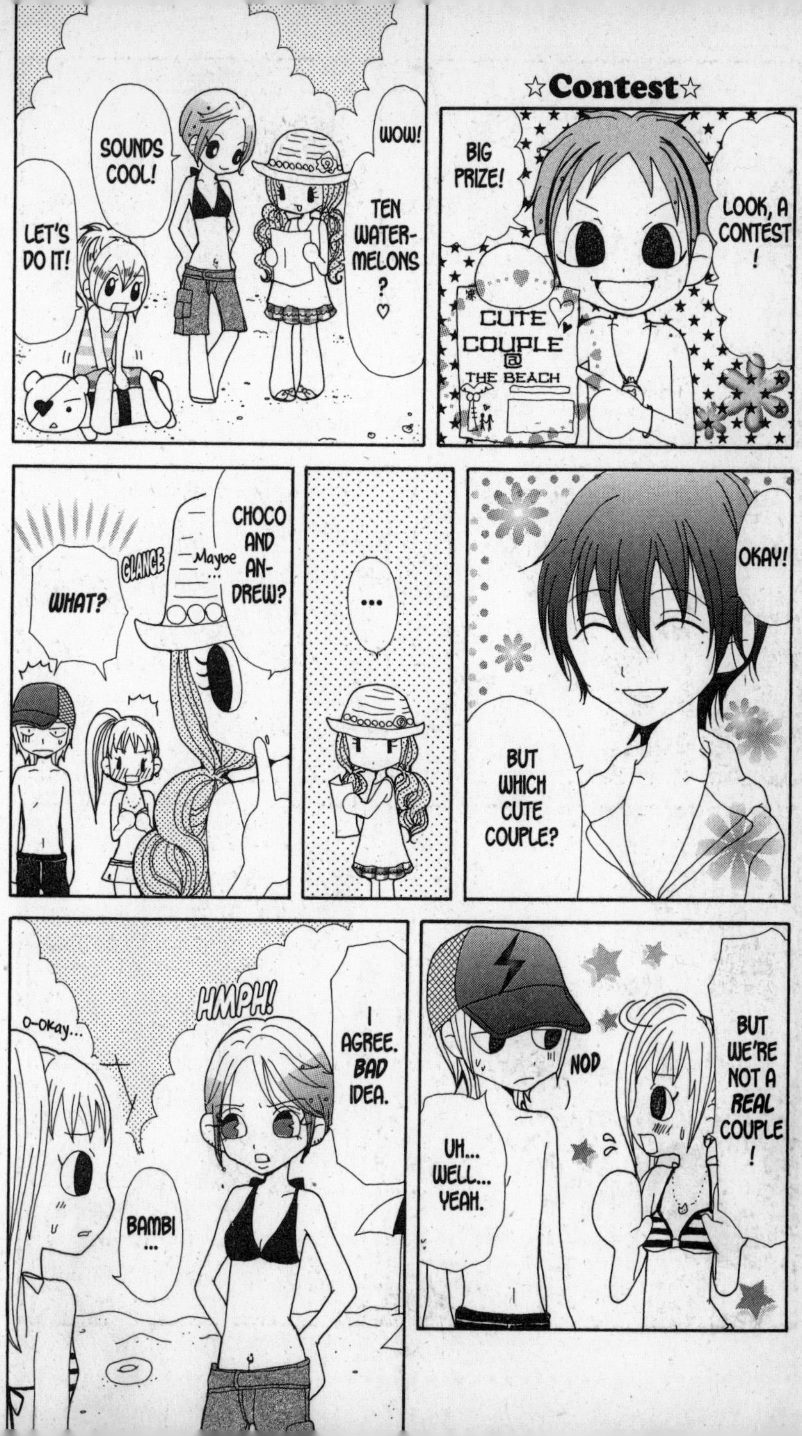
☆Contest☆
LOOK, A CONTEST!
BIG PRIZE!
CUTE COUPLE @ THE BEACH
WOW!
TEN WATER-MELONS? ♡
SOUNDS COOL!
LET'S DO IT!
OKAY!
BUT WHICH CUTE COUPLE?
...
CHOCO AND AN-DREW?
Maybe...
GLANCE
WHAT?
BUT WE'RE NOT A REAL COUPLE!
NOD
UH... WELL... YEAH.
I AGREE. BAD IDEA.
HMPH!
O-OKAY...
BAMBI...

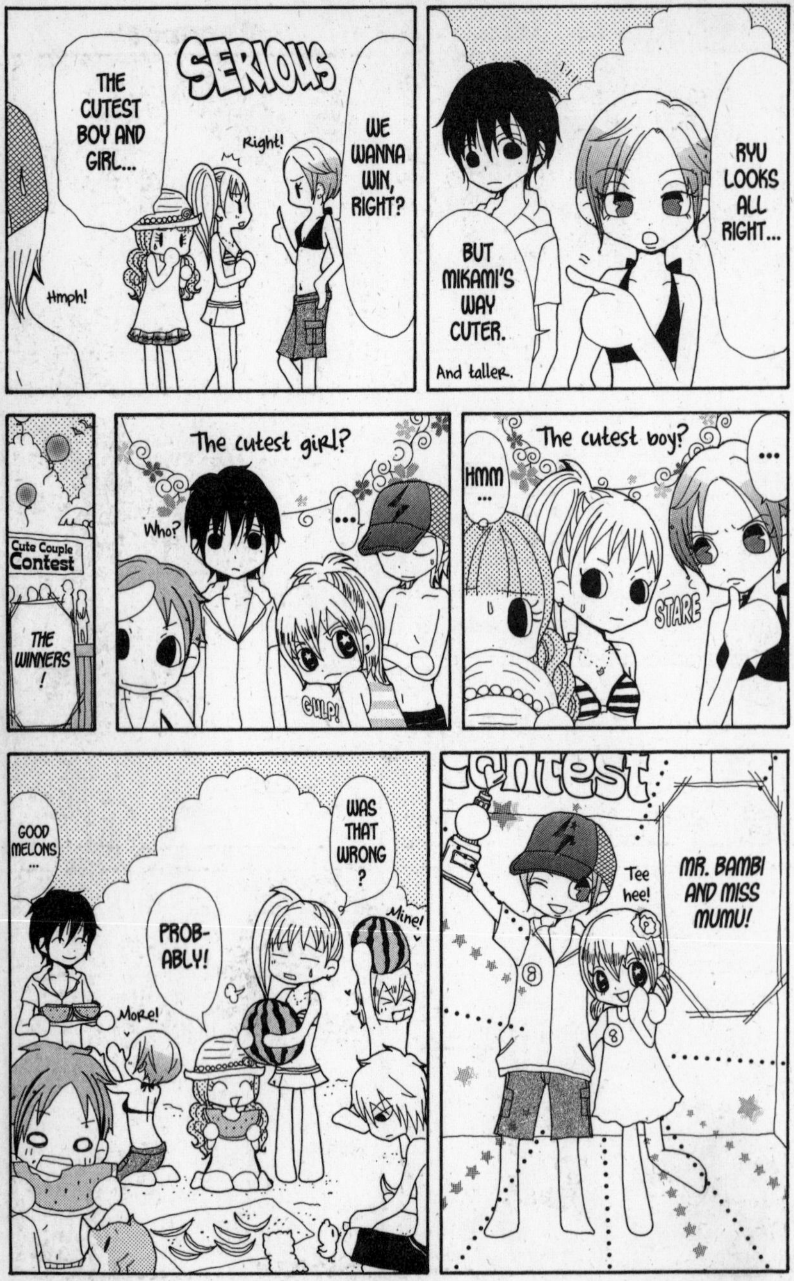
RYU LOOKS ALL RIGHT...
BUT MIKAMI'S WAY CUTER.
And taller.
WE WANNA WIN, RIGHT?
Right!
THE CUTEST BOY AND GIRL...
SERIOUS
Hmph!
The cutest boy?
...
HMM...
STARE
The cutest girl?
...
Who?
GULP!
Cute Couple Contest
THE WINNERS!
Contest
MR. BAMBI AND MISS MUMU!
Tee hee!
WAS THAT WRONG?
Mine!
PROB-ABLY!
GOOD MELONS...
More!

☆ Mermaid ☆

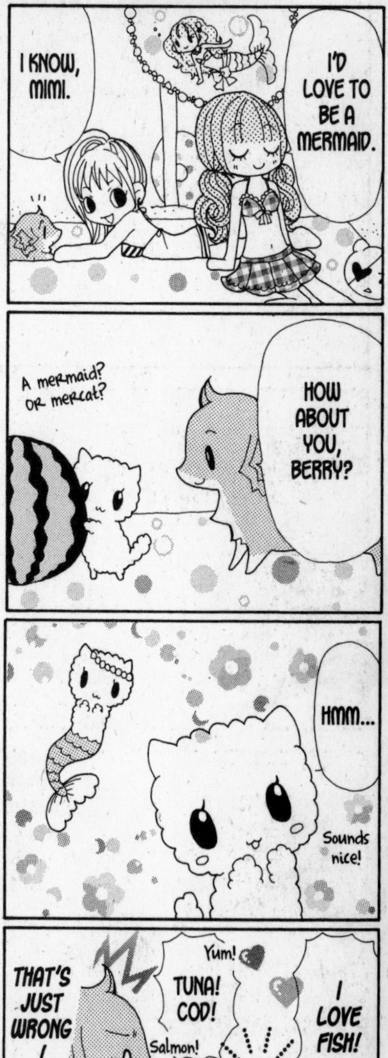
I'D LOVE TO BE A MERMAID.
I KNOW, MIMI.
HOW ABOUT YOU, BERRY?
A mermaid? Or mercat?
HMM...
Sounds nice!
I LOVE FISH!
Yum!
TUNA! COD!
Salmon!
THAT'S JUST WRONG!
B-BMP
B-BMP
Get a grip!

☆ Shaved Ice ☆

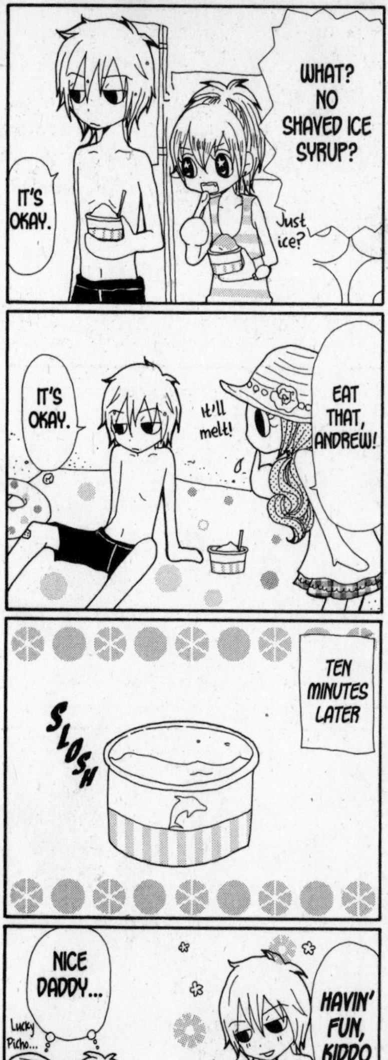
WHAT? NO SHAVED ICE SYRUP?
Just ice?
IT'S OKAY.
EAT THAT, ANDREW!
It'll melt!
IT'S OKAY.
TEN MINUTES LATER
SLOSH
HAVIN' FUN, KIDDO?
SPLSH
SPLSH
NICE DADDY...
Lucky Picho...

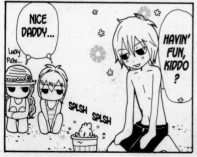

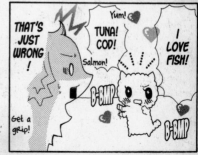

☆Help☆

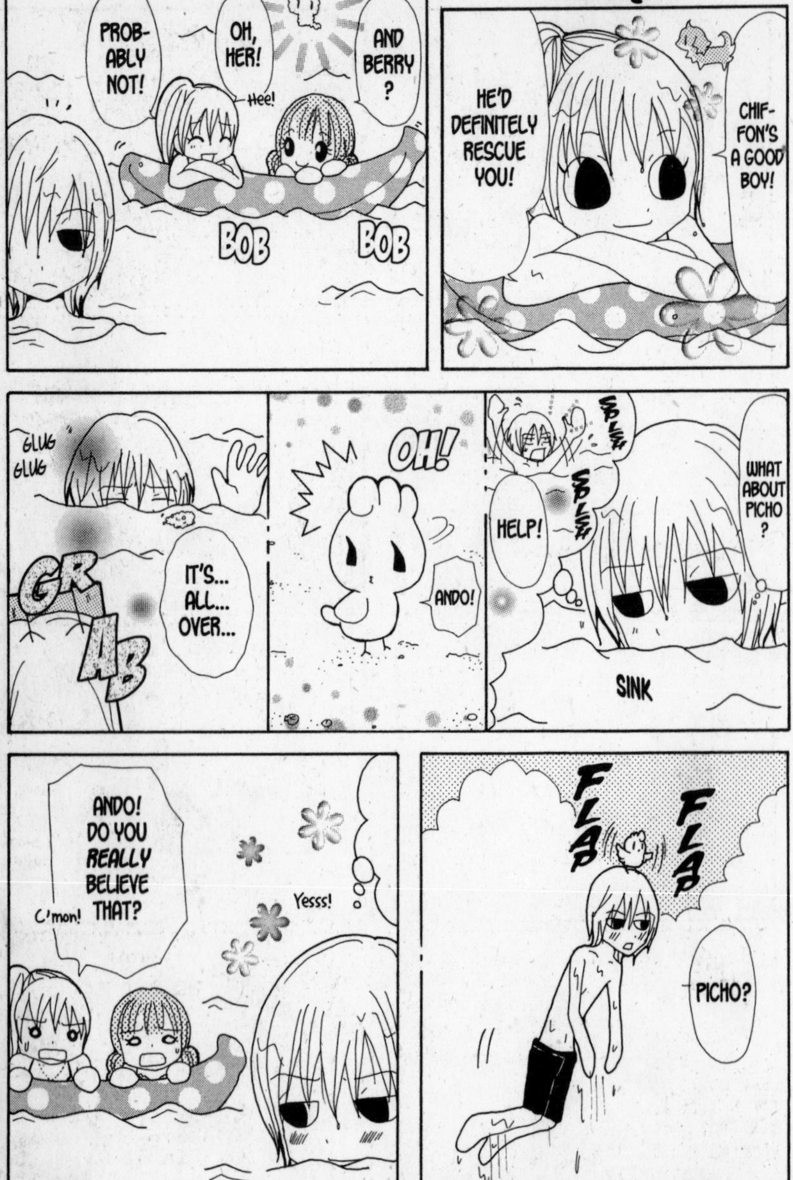

CHIF-FON'S A GOOD BOY!
HE'D DEFINITELY RESCUE YOU!
AND BERRY?
OH, HER!
Hee!
PROB-ABLY NOT!
BOB
BOB
WHAT ABOUT PICHO?
SPLISH
SPLISH
HELP!
SINK
OH!
ANDO!
GLUG GLUG
IT'S... ALL... OVER...
GRAB
FLAP
FLAP
PICHO?
Yesss!
ANDO! DO YOU REALLY BELIEVE THAT?
C'mon!

☆ Sunset ☆

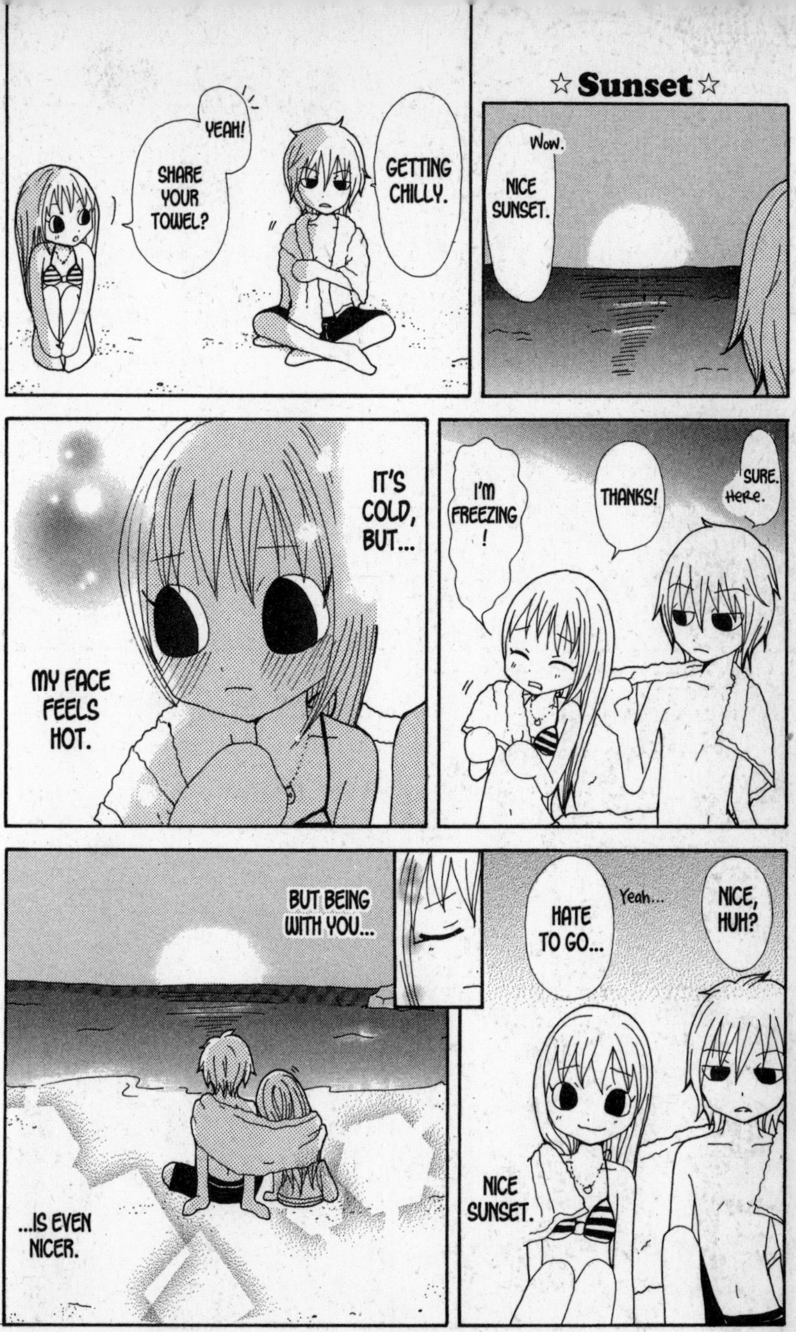
Wow.
NICE SUNSET.
GETTING CHILLY.
YEAH!
SHARE YOUR TOWEL?
SURE. Here.
THANKS!
I'M FREEZING!
IT'S COLD, BUT...
MY FACE FEELS HOT.
NICE, HUH?
Yeah...
HATE TO GO...
NICE SUNSET.
BUT BEING WITH YOU...
...IS EVEN NICER.

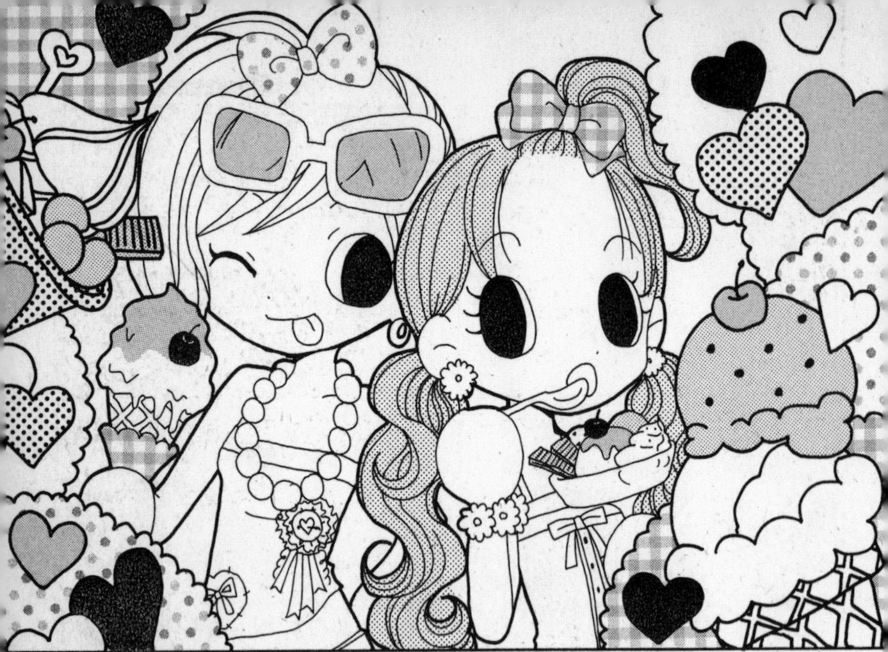

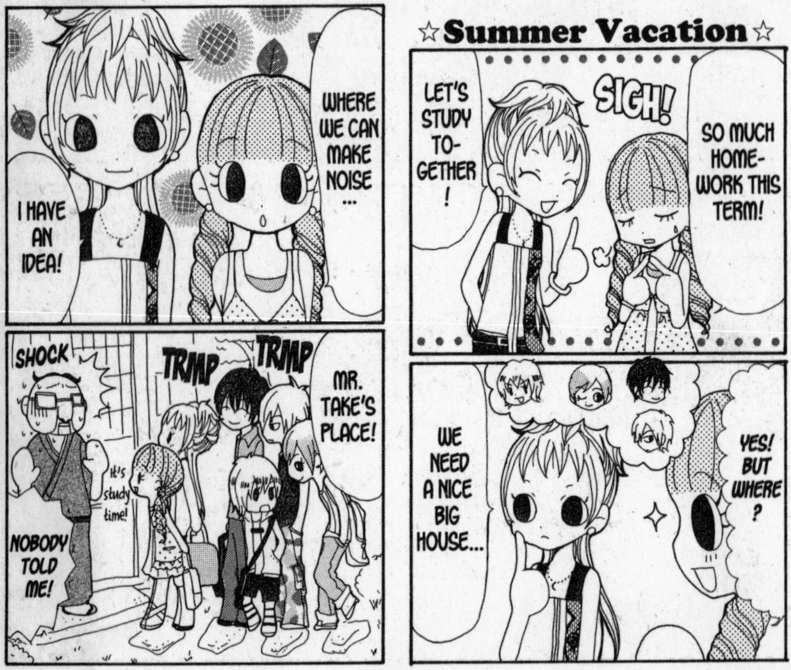
☆Summer Vacation☆
SO MUCH HOMEWORK THIS TERM!
SIGH!
LET'S STUDY TOGETHER!
YES! BUT WHERE?
WE NEED A NICE BIG HOUSE...
WHERE WE CAN MAKE NOISE...
I HAVE AN IDEA!
MR. TAKE'S PLACE!
TRMP
TRMP
It's study time!
SHOCK
NOBODY TOLD ME!

☆In Charge☆

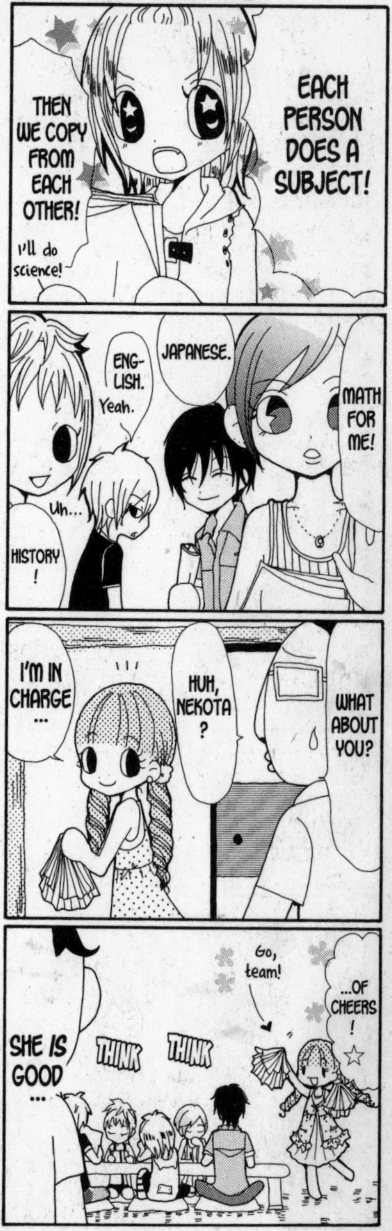
EACH PERSON DOES A SUBJECT!
THEN WE COPY FROM EACH OTHER!
I'll do science!
MATH FOR ME!
JAPANESE.
ENG-LISH.
Yeah.
Uh...
HISTORY!
WHAT ABOUT YOU?
HUH, NEKOTA?
I'M IN CHARGE...
...OF CHEERS!
Go, team!
THINK
THINK
SHE IS GOOD...

☆Sunflower☆

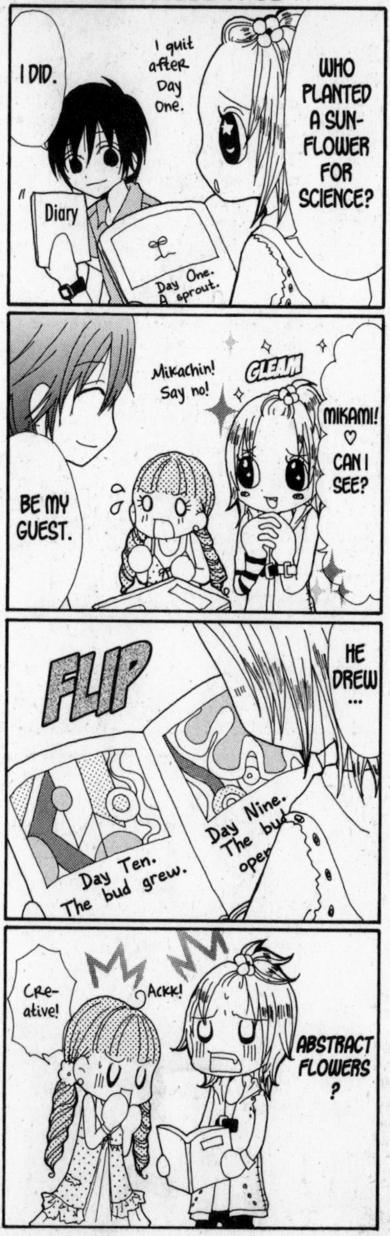
WHO PLANTED A SUN-FLOWER FOR SCIENCE?
I quit after Day One.
I DID.
Diary
Day One. A sprout.
MIKAMI! ♡ CAN I SEE?
GLEAM
Mikachin! Say no!
BE MY GUEST.
HE DREW...
FLIP
Day Nine. The bud oper
Day Ten. The bud grew.
ABSTRACT FLOWERS?
Ackk!
Cre-ative!

☆Book Report☆

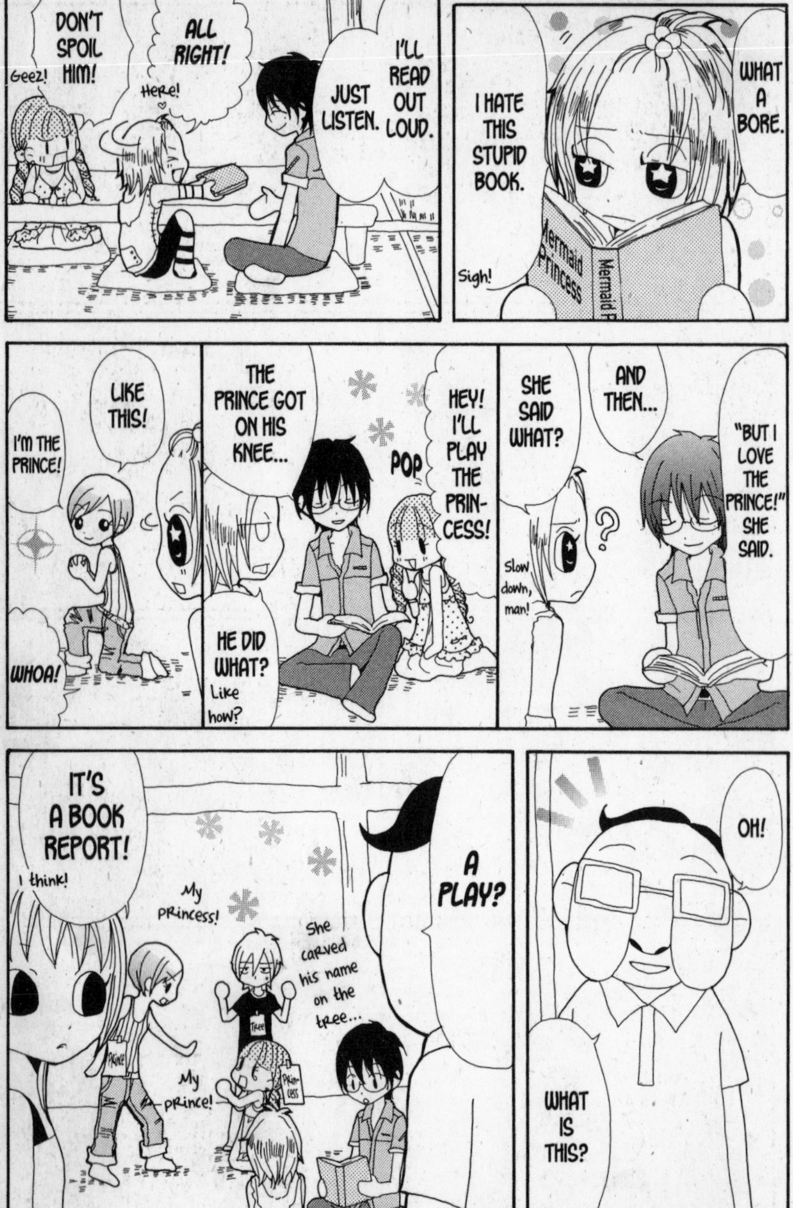
WHAT A BORE.
I HATE THIS STUPID BOOK.
Mermaid Princess
Sigh!
I'LL READ OUT LOUD.
JUST LISTEN.
ALL RIGHT!
Here!
DON'T SPOIL HIM!
Geez!
"BUT I LOVE THE PRINCE!" SHE SAID.
AND THEN...
SHE SAID WHAT?
Slow down, man!
HEY! I'LL PLAY THE PRIN-CESS!
POP
THE PRINCE GOT ON HIS KNEE...
HE DID WHAT?
Like how?
LIKE THIS!
I'M THE PRINCE!
WHOA!
OH!
WHAT IS THIS?
A PLAY?
IT'S A BOOK REPORT!
I think!
My princess!
She carved his name on the tree...
My prince!
Prince
Tree
Prin-cess

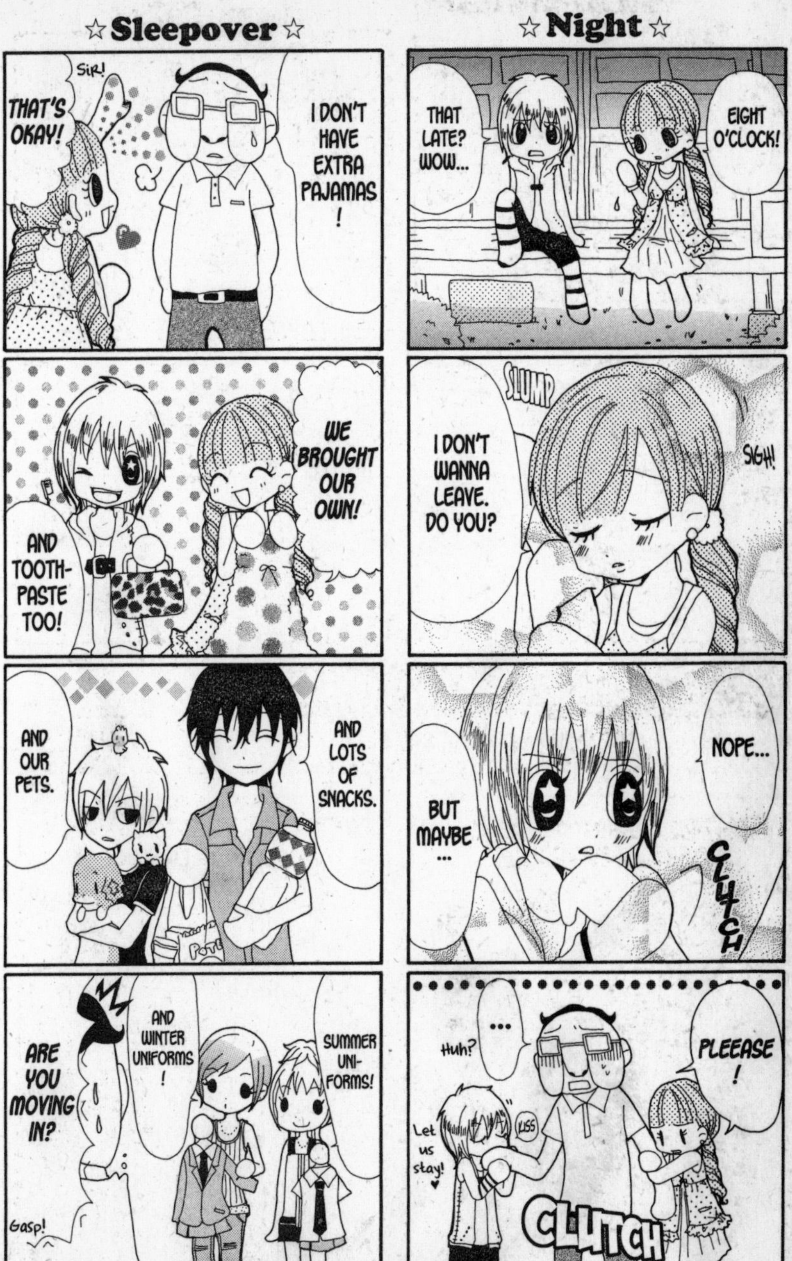
☆Night☆
EIGHT O'CLOCK!
THAT LATE? WOW...
SIGH!
SLUMP
I DON'T WANNA LEAVE. DO YOU?
NOPE...
CLUTCH
BUT MAYBE...
PLEEASE!
...
Huh?
KISS
Let us stay! ♥
CLUTCH
☆Sleepover☆
I DON'T HAVE EXTRA PAJAMAS!
SIR!
THAT'S OKAY!
WE BROUGHT OUR OWN!
AND TOOTH-PASTE TOO!
AND LOTS OF SNACKS.
AND OUR PETS.
SUMMER UNI-FORMS!
AND WINTER UNIFORMS!
ARE YOU MOVING IN?
Gasp!

☆Love Talk☆

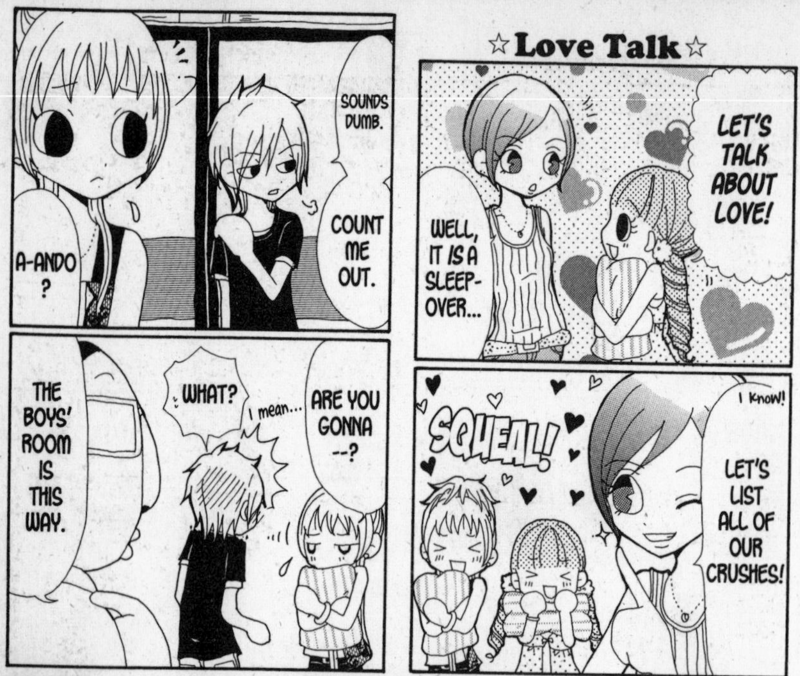
LET'S TALK ABOUT LOVE!
WELL, IT IS A SLEEP-OVER...
I know!
LET'S LIST ALL OF OUR CRUSHES!
SQUEAL!
SOUNDS DUMB.
COUNT ME OUT.
A-ANDO?
ARE YOU GONNA--?
I mean...
WHAT?
THE BOYS' ROOM IS THIS WAY.

Choco Mimi Fashion Notes

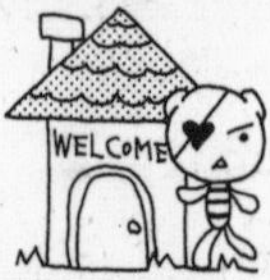
WELCOME

TIME FOR SUMMER VACATION!
LET'S PEEK INTO THEIR SUITCASES!

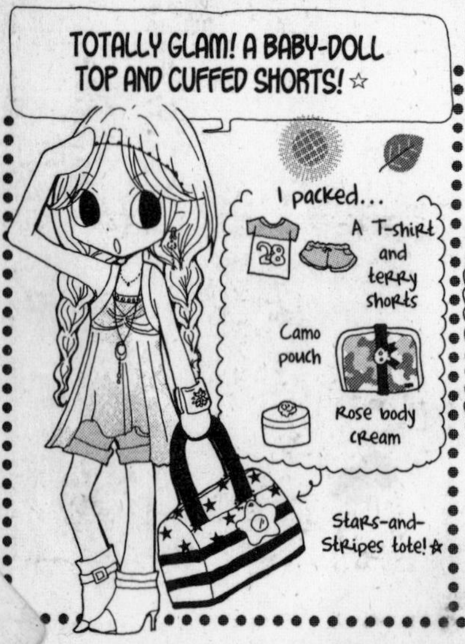
TOTALLY GLAM! A BABY-DOLL TOP AND CUFFED SHORTS! ☆
I packed...
A T-shirt and terry shorts
Camo pouch
Rose body cream
Stars-and-Stripes tote! ☆

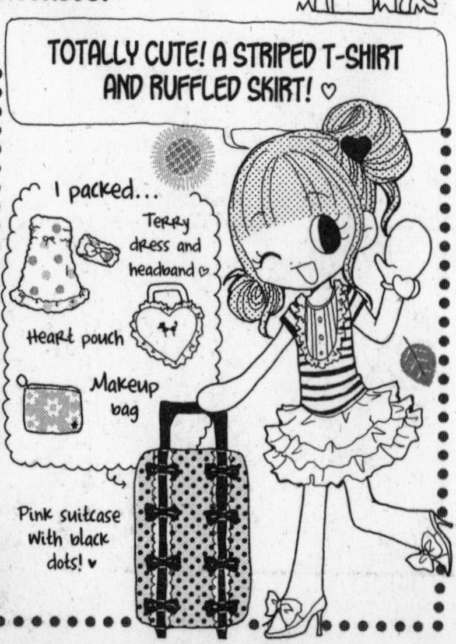
TOTALLY CUTE! A STRIPED T-SHIRT AND RUFFLED SKIRT! ♡
I packed...
Terry dress and headband ♡
Heart pouch
Makeup bag
Pink suitcase with black dots! ♥

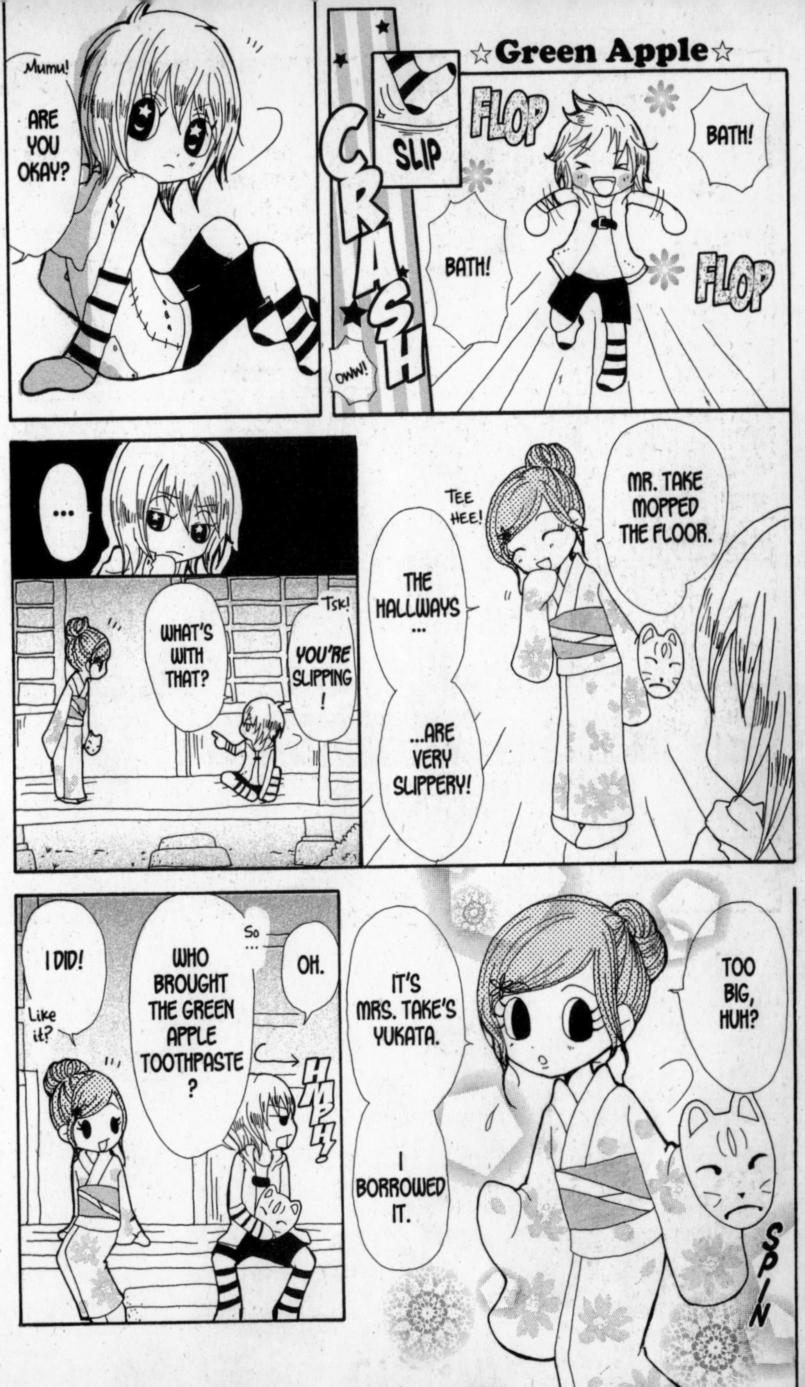
BATH!
FLOP
BATH!
FLOP
SLIP
CRASH
OWW!
Mumu!
ARE YOU OKAY?
MR. TAKE MOPPED THE FLOOR.
TEE HEE!
THE HALLWAYS ...
...ARE VERY SLIPPERY!
...
TSK!
YOU'RE SLIPPING!
WHAT'S WITH THAT?
TOO BIG, HUH?
SPIN
IT'S MRS. TAKE'S YUKATA.
I BORROWED IT.
So ...
OH.
WHO BROUGHT THE GREEN APPLE TOOTHPASTE?
HMPH!
I DID!
Like it?

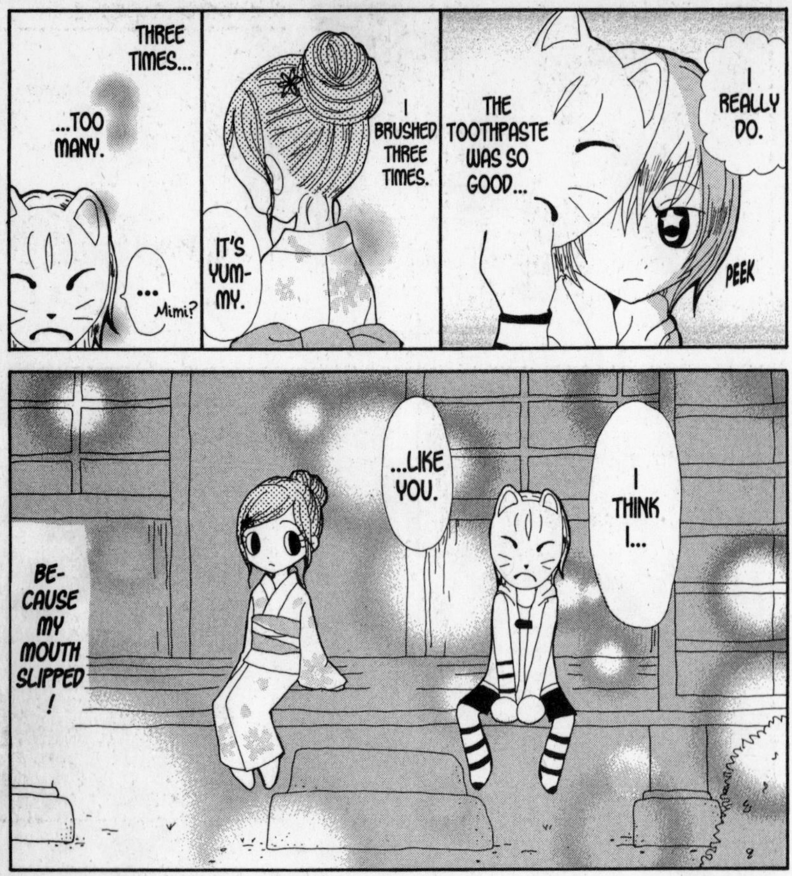
I REALLY DO.
THE TOOTHPASTE WAS SO GOOD...
PEEK
I BRUSHED THREE TIMES.
IT'S YUM-MY.
THREE TIMES...
...TOO MANY.
...
Mimi?
I THINK I...
...LIKE YOU.
BE-CAUSE MY MOUTH SLIPPED!

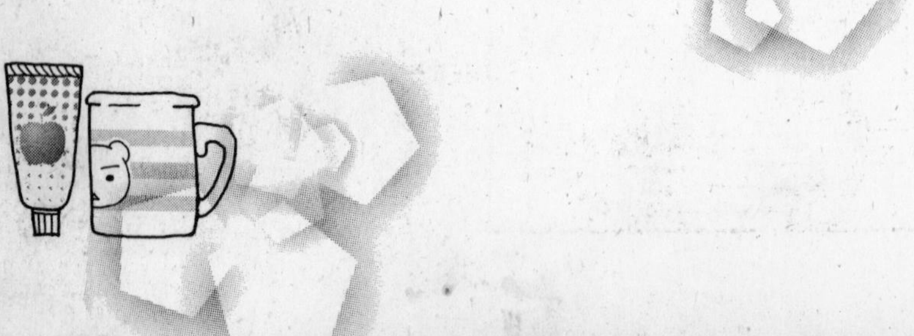

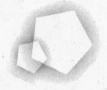

Extra 1

My new PJs!
Super girly! ♡

SO DOLL-LIKE!
Cute! ♥
DID MUMU SEE YOU?
TEE HEE!
BAMBI!
WHO CARES ABOUT HIM?
GEEZ!
NOW, NOW...
HA HA!
SLAM
SHUT UP, WOMEN!
GO TO SLEEP!
TA-DAA!
CUUUUUTE! ♡
EWW!
How old is he?

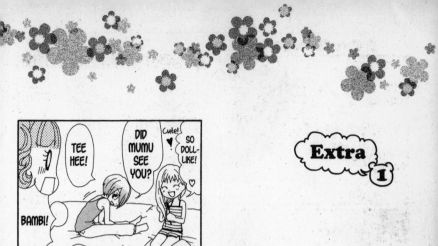

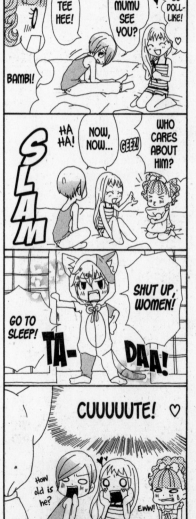

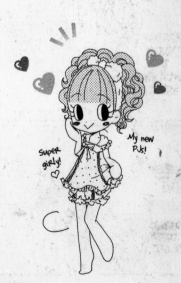

♡ Love ♡

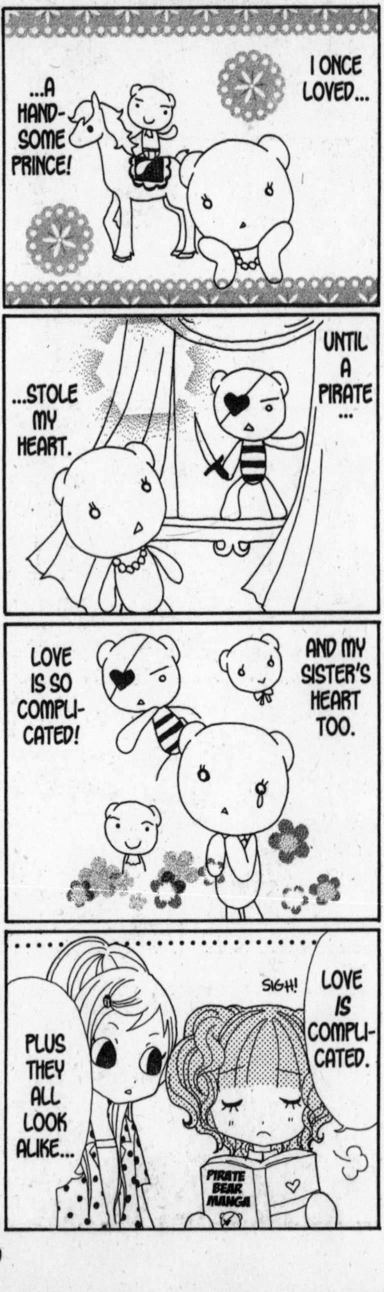
I ONCE LOVED...
...A HANDSOME PRINCE!
UNTIL A PIRATE...
...STOLE MY HEART.
AND MY SISTER'S HEART TOO.
LOVE IS SO COMPLICATED!
LOVE IS COMPLICATED.
SIGH!
PLUS THEY ALL LOOK ALIKE...
PIRATE BEAR MANGA

♡ Confession ♡

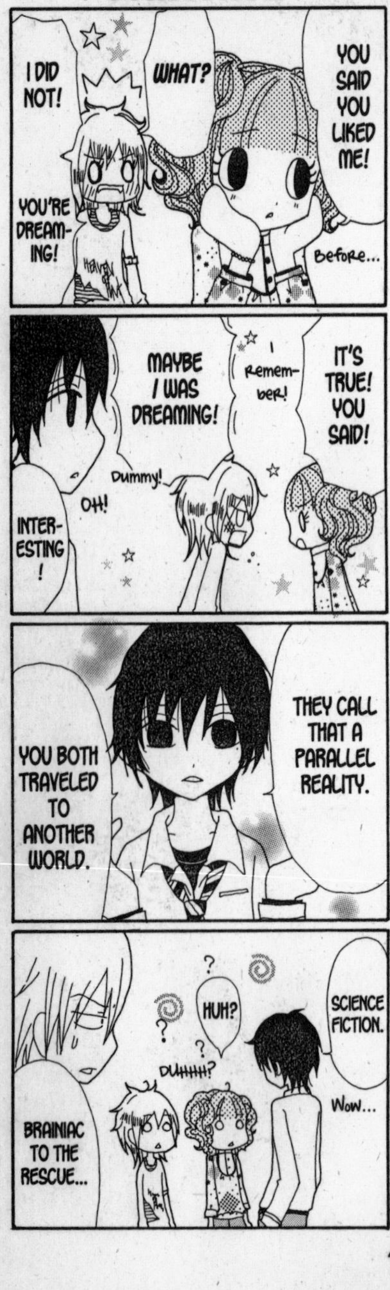
YOU SAID YOU LIKED ME!
Before...
WHAT?
I DID NOT!
YOU'RE DREAMING!
IT'S TRUE! YOU SAID!
I Remember!
MAYBE I WAS DREAMING!
Dummy!
OH!
INTERESTING!
THEY CALL THAT A PARALLEL REALITY.
YOU BOTH TRAVELED TO ANOTHER WORLD.
SCIENCE FICTION.
Wow...
HUH?
DUHHH?
BRAINIAC TO THE RESCUE...

♡Going Out♡

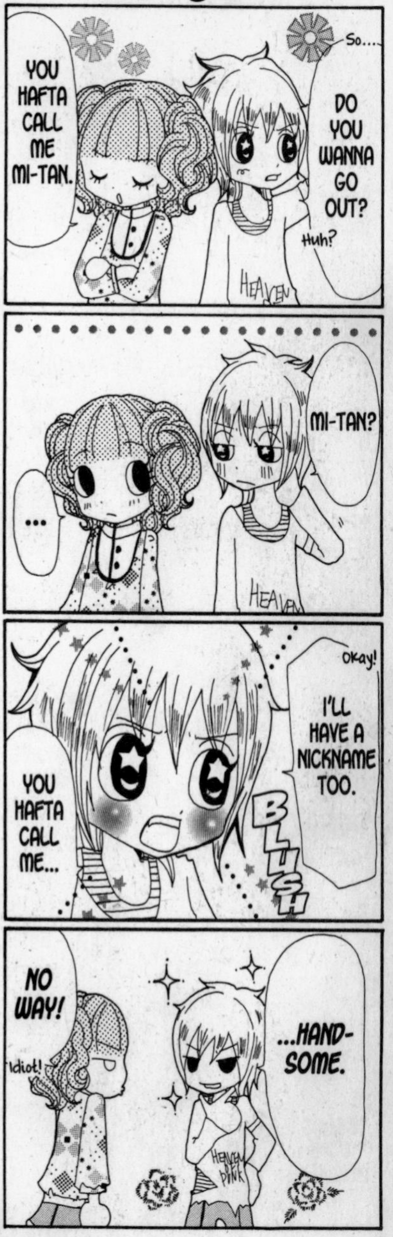
So....
DO YOU WANNA GO OUT?
Huh?
YOU HAFTA CALL ME MI-TAN.
HEAVEN
MI-TAN?
...
HEAVEN
Okay!
I'LL HAVE A NICKNAME TOO.
BLUSH
YOU HAFTA CALL ME...
...HAND-SOME.
NO WAY!
Idiot!
HEAVEN PINK

♡Lonely♡

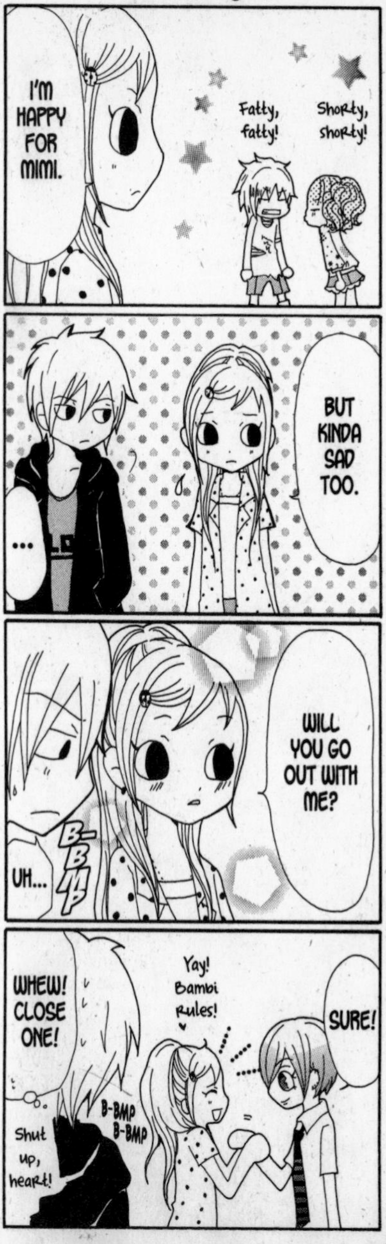
Shorty, shorty!
Fatty, fatty!
I'M HAPPY FOR MIMI.
BUT KINDA SAD TOO.
...
WILL YOU GO OUT WITH ME?
B-BMP
UH...
SURE!
Yay! Bambi rules!
B-BMP B-BMP
WHEW! CLOSE ONE!
Shut up, heart!

♡Dating♡

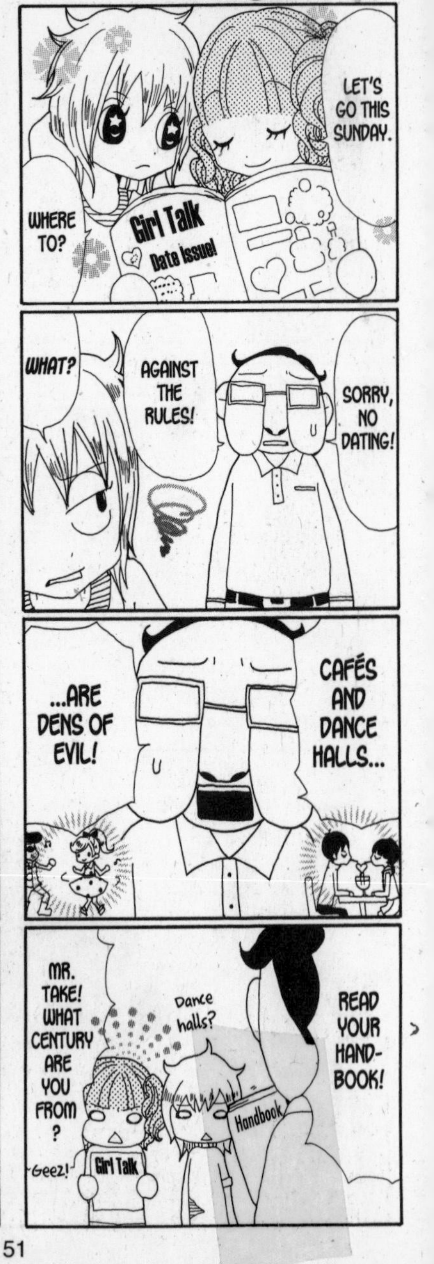
LET'S GO THIS SUNDAY.
WHERE TO?
Girl Talk
Date Issue!
SORRY, NO DATING!
AGAINST THE RULES!
WHAT?
CAFÉS AND DANCE HALLS...
...ARE DENS OF EVIL!
READ YOUR HANDBOOK!
Handbook
Dance halls?
MR. TAKE! WHAT CENTURY ARE YOU FROM?
Geez!
Girl Talk

♡Crowds♡

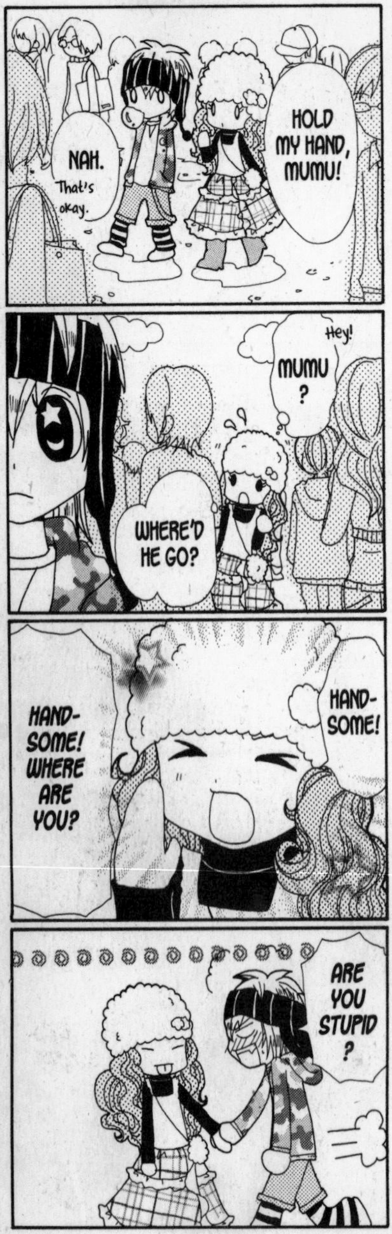
HOLD MY HAND, MUMU!
NAH.
That's okay.
Hey!
MUMU?
WHERE'D HE GO?
HANDSOME!
HANDSOME! WHERE ARE YOU?
ARE YOU STUPID?

♡Heart Sticker♡

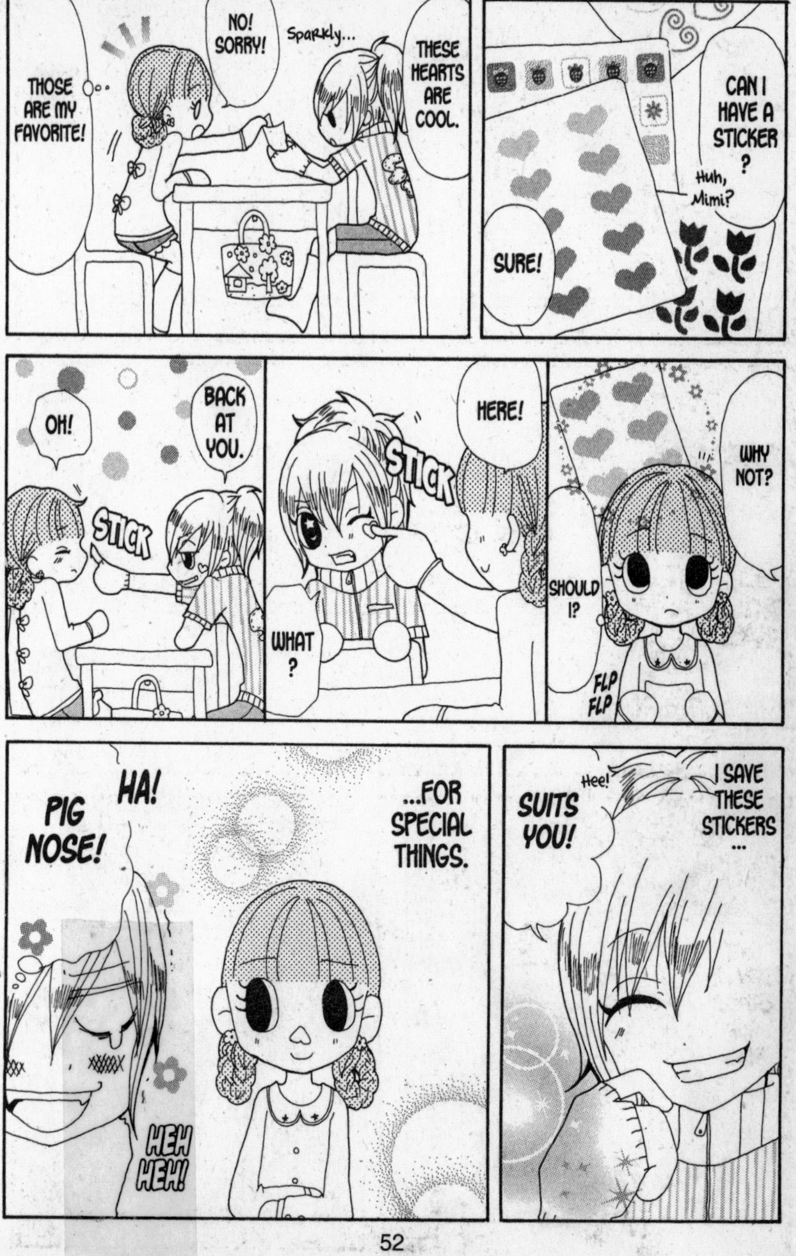
CAN I HAVE A STICKER ?
Huh, Mimi?
SURE!
THESE HEARTS ARE COOL.
Sparkly...
NO! SORRY!
THOSE ARE MY FAVORITE!
WHY NOT?
SHOULD I?
FLP FLP
HERE!
STICK
WHAT ?
BACK AT YOU.
STICK
OH!
I SAVE THESE STICKERS ...
Hee!
SUITS YOU!
...FOR SPECIAL THINGS.
HA!
PIG NOSE!
HEH HEH!

♡ Cupcake ♡

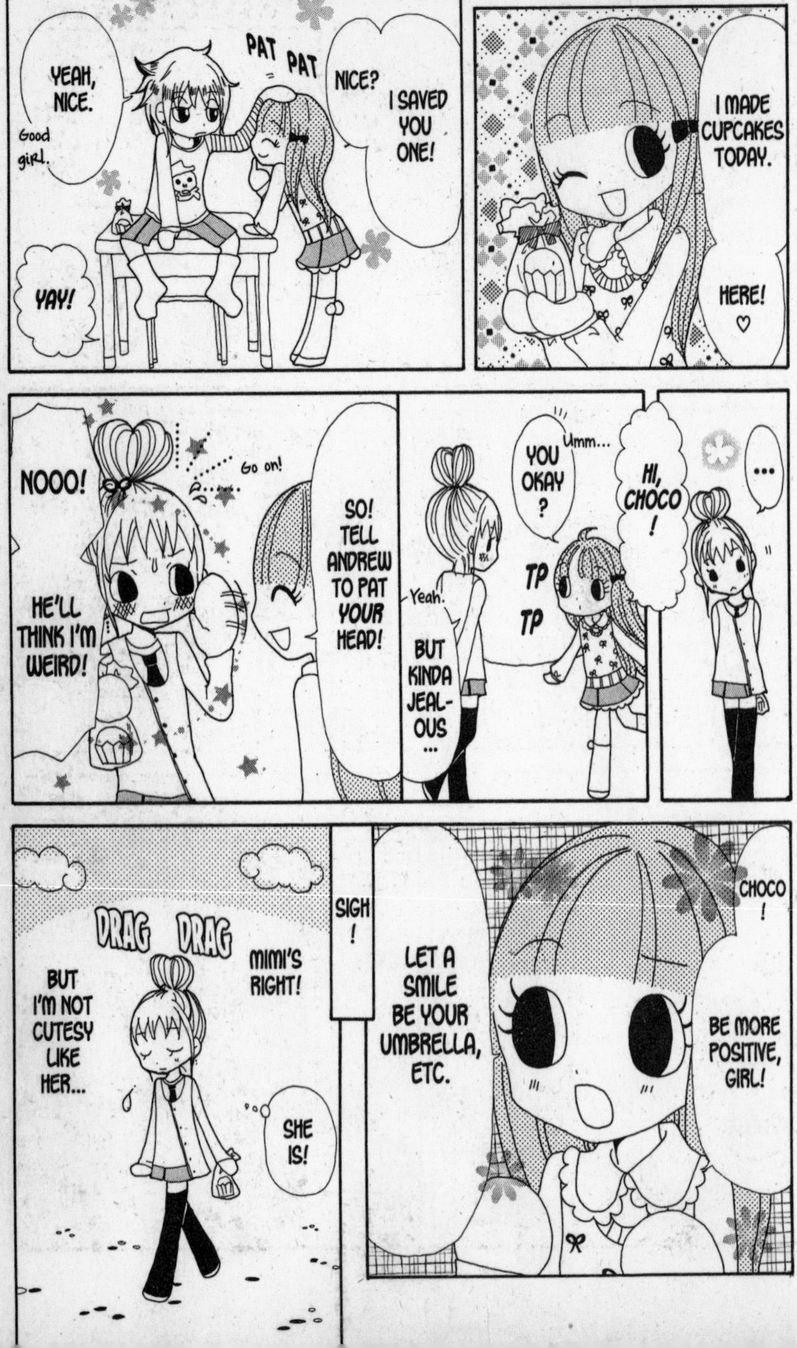

I MADE CUPCAKES TODAY.
HERE! ♡
NICE?
I SAVED YOU ONE!
PAT PAT
YEAH, NICE.
Good girl.
YAY!
...
HI, CHOCO!
YOU OKAY?
Umm...
TP TP
Yeah.
BUT KINDA JEAL-OUS...
SO! TELL ANDREW TO PAT YOUR HEAD!
Go on!
NOOO!
HE'LL THINK I'M WEIRD!
CHOCO!
BE MORE POSITIVE, GIRL!
LET A SMILE BE YOUR UMBRELLA, ETC.
SIGH!
MIMI'S RIGHT!
DRAG DRAG
BUT I'M NOT CUTESY LIKE HER...
SHE IS!

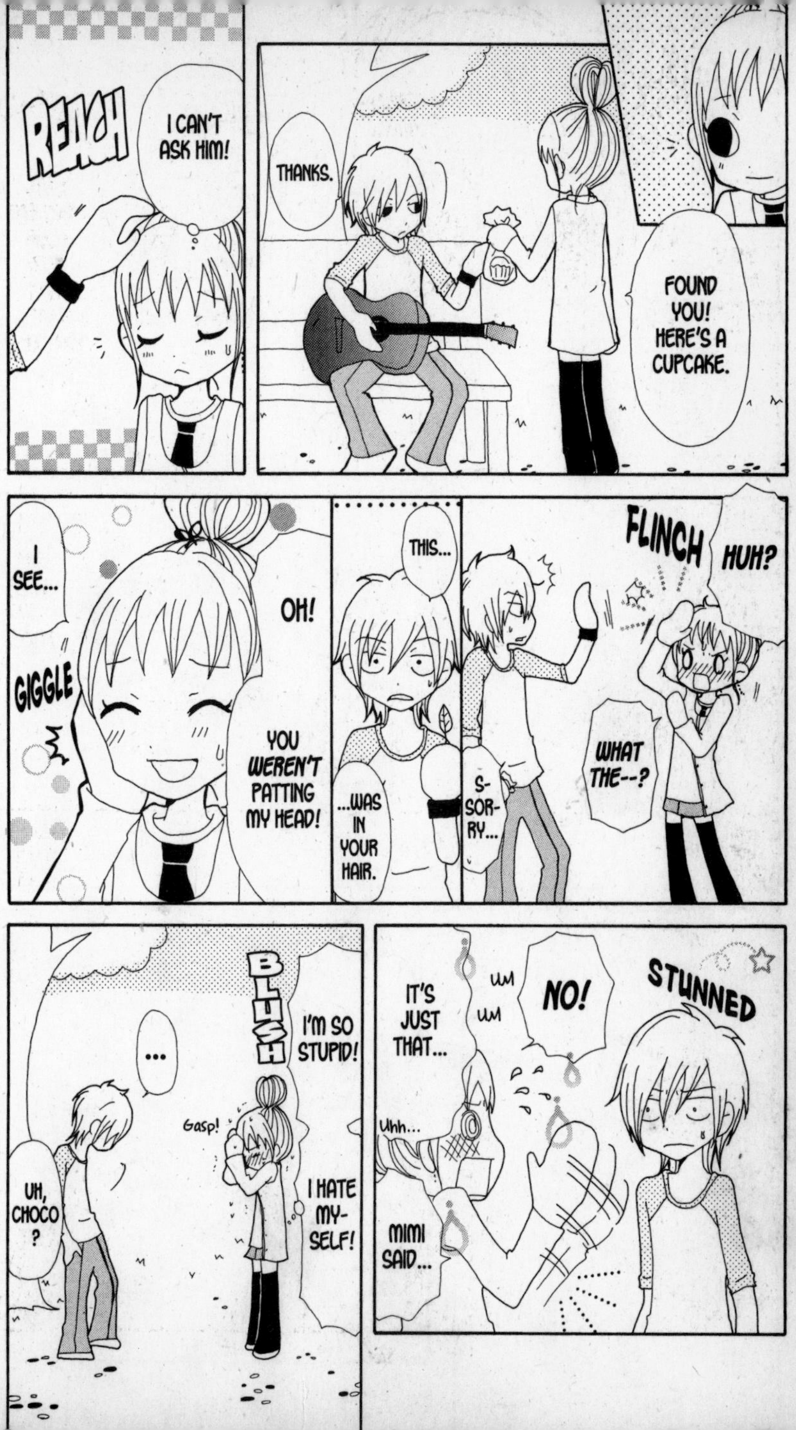
FOUND YOU! HERE'S A CUPCAKE.
THANKS.
REACH
I CAN'T ASK HIM!
FLINCH
HUH?
WHAT THE--?
S-SORRY...
THIS...
...WAS IN YOUR HAIR.
OH!
YOU WEREN'T PATTING MY HEAD!
GIGGLE
I SEE...
STUNNED
NO!
UM
UM
IT'S JUST THAT...
Uhh...
MIMI SAID...
BLUSH
I'M SO STUPID!
I HATE MYSELF!
Gasp!
...
UH, CHOCO?

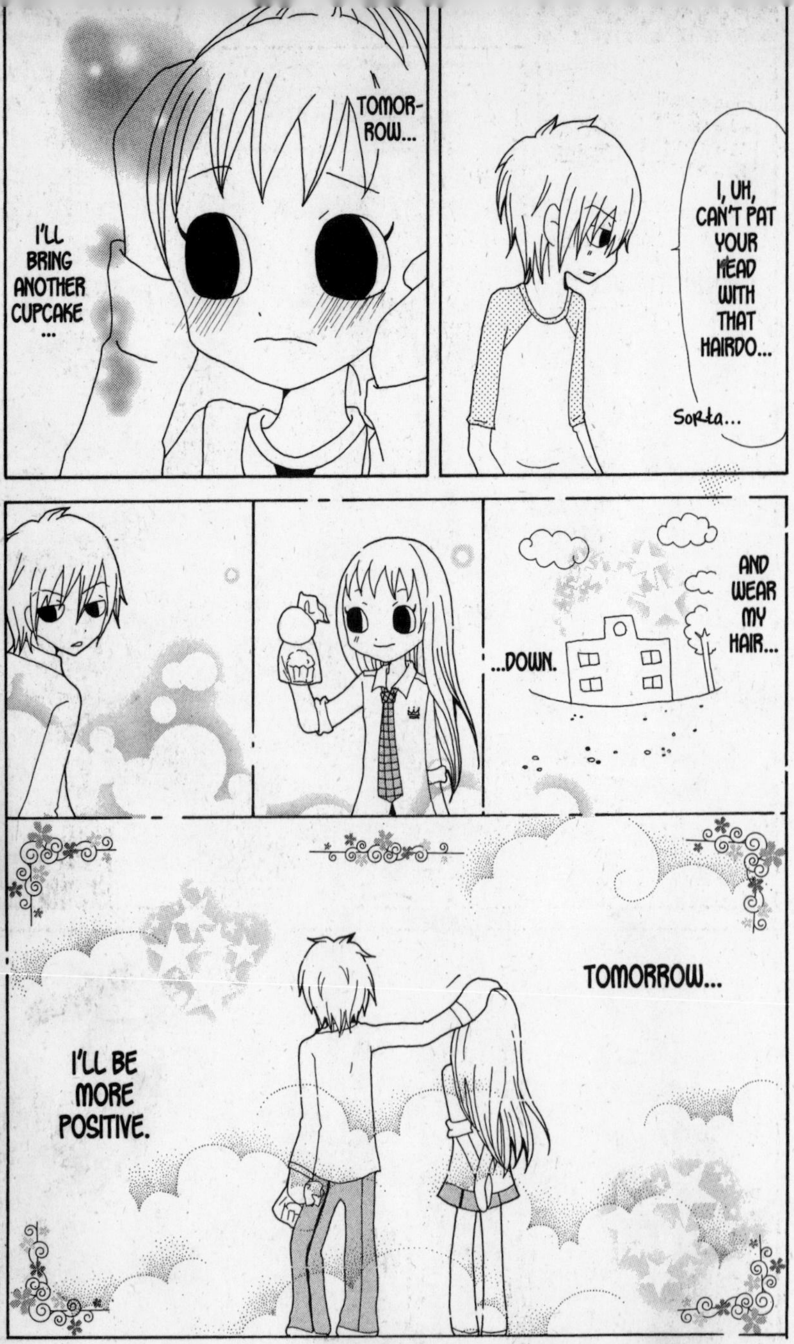
I, UH, CAN'T PAT YOUR HEAD WITH THAT HAIRDO...
Sorta...
TOMOR-ROW...
I'LL BRING ANOTHER CUPCAKE...
AND WEAR MY HAIR...
...DOWN.
TOMORROW...
I'LL BE MORE POSITIVE.

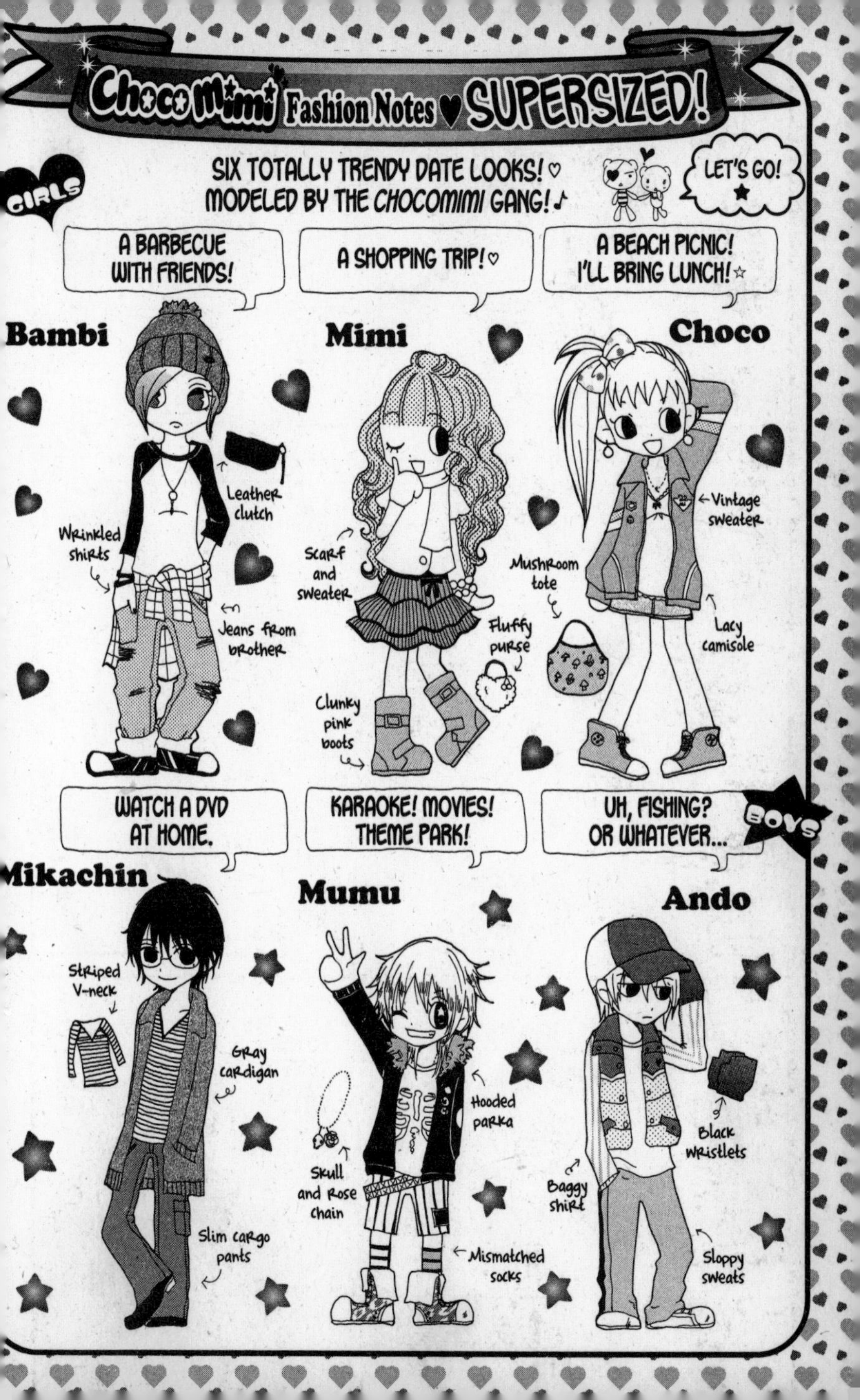
Chocomimi Fashion Notes ♥ SUPERSIZED!
GIRLS
SIX TOTALLY TRENDY DATE LOOKS! ♡
MODELED BY THE CHOCOMIMI GANG! ♪
LET'S GO! ★
A BARBECUE WITH FRIENDS!
A SHOPPING TRIP! ♡
A BEACH PICNIC! I'LL BRING LUNCH! ☆
Bambi
Leather clutch
Wrinkled shirts
Jeans from brother
Mimi
Scarf and sweater
Fluffy purse
Clunky pink boots
Choco
Vintage sweater
Mushroom tote
Lacy camisole
WATCH A DVD AT HOME.
KARAOKE! MOVIES! THEME PARK!
UH, FISHING? OR WHATEVER...
BOYS
Mikachin
Striped V-neck
Gray cardigan
Slim cargo pants
Mumu
Hooded parka
Skull and Rose chain
Mismatched socks
Ando
Black wristlets
Baggy shirt
Sloppy sweats

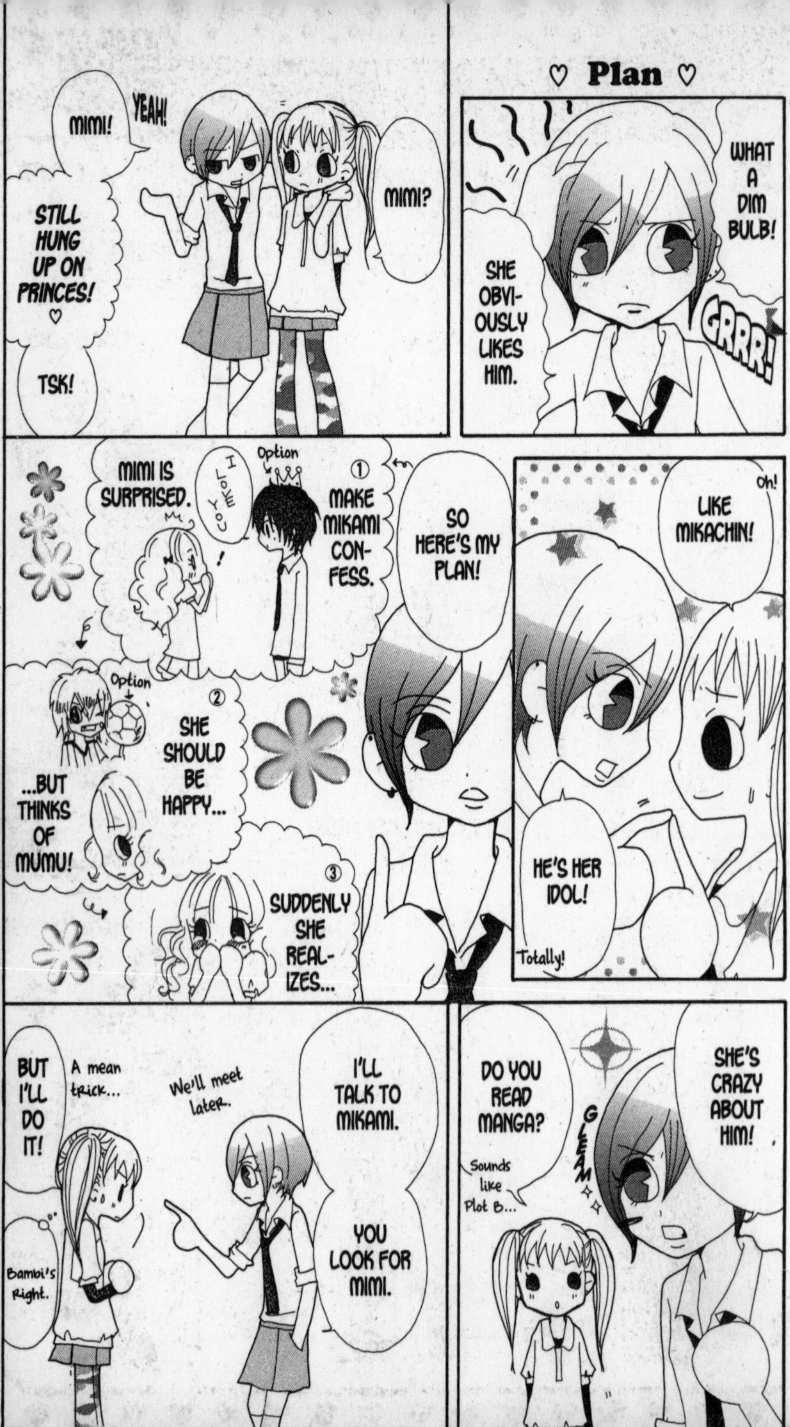
♡ Plan ♡
WHAT A DIM BULB!
SHE OBVIOUSLY LIKES HIM.
GRRR!
Oh!
LIKE MIKACHIN!
HE'S HER IDOL!
Totally!
SHE'S CRAZY ABOUT HIM!
GLEAM
DO YOU READ MANGA?
Sounds like Plot B...
YEAH!
MIMI!
MIMI?
STILL HUNG UP ON PRINCES! ♡
TSK!
SO HERE'S MY PLAN!
① MAKE MIKAMI CONFESS.
Option
I LOVE YOU
MIMI IS SURPRISED.
② SHE SHOULD BE HAPPY...
Option
...BUT THINKS OF MUMU!
③ SUDDENLY SHE REALIZES...
I'LL TALK TO MIKAMI.
YOU LOOK FOR MIMI.
We'll meet later.
BUT I'LL DO IT!
A mean trick...
Bambi's right.

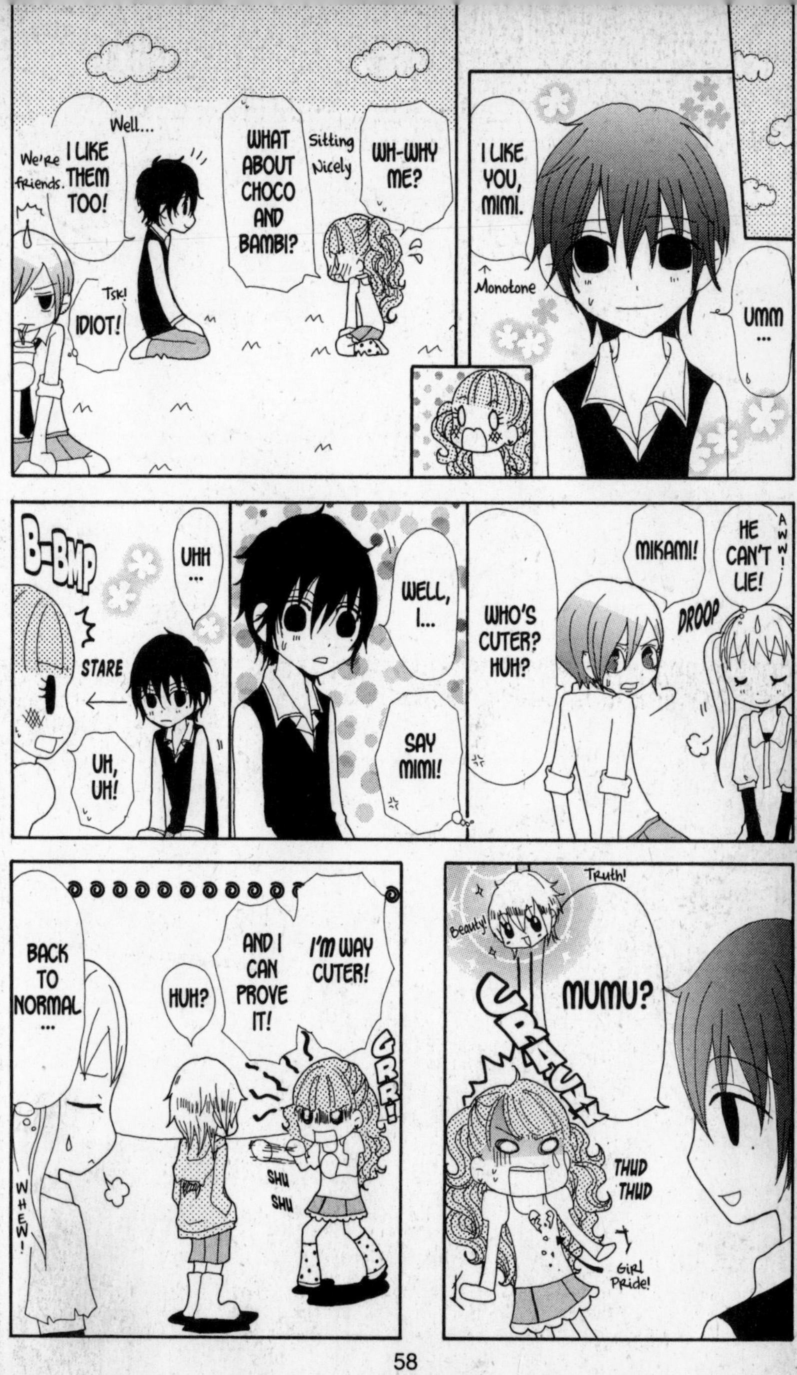
I LIKE YOU, MIMI.
Monotone
UMM ...
WH-WHY ME?
Sitting Nicely
WHAT ABOUT CHOCO AND BAMBI?
Well...
I LIKE THEM TOO!
We're friends.
Tsk!
IDIOT!
HE CAN'T LIE!
AWW!
MIKAMI!
DROOP
WHO'S CUTER? HUH?
WELL, I...
SAY MIMI!
UHH ...
B-BMP
STARE
UH, UH!
Truth!
Beauty!
MUMU?
URAUKK
THUD THUD
Girl Pride!
I'M WAY CUTER!
AND I CAN PROVE IT!
GRR!
HUH?
SHU SHU
BACK TO NORMAL ...
WHEW!

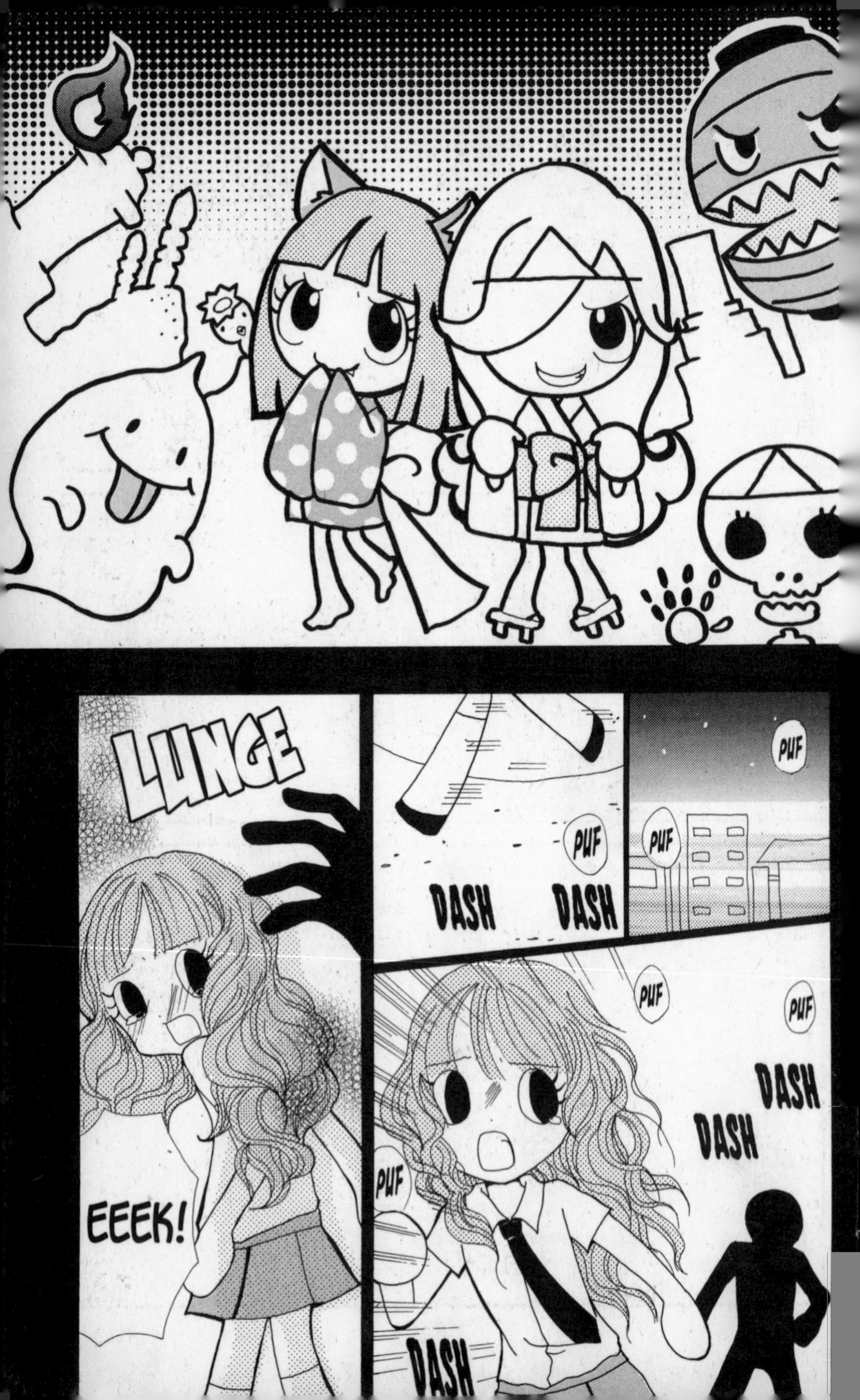
PUF
PUF
PUF
DASH
DASH
PUF
PUF
DASH
DASH
PUF
DASH
LUNGE
EEEK!

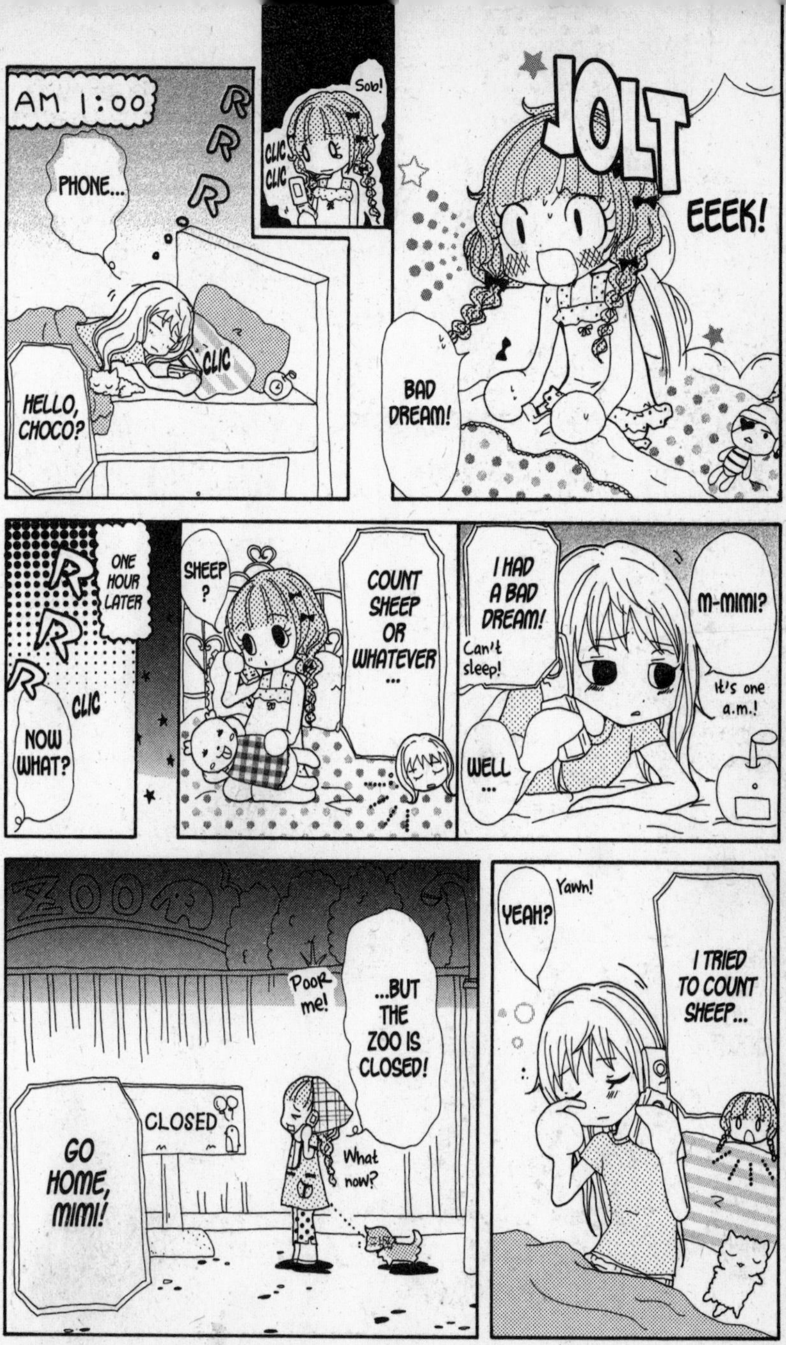
JOLT
EEEK!
BAD DREAM!
Sob!
CLIC CLIC
AM 1:00
R R R
PHONE...
CLIC
HELLO, CHOCO?
M-MIMI?
It's one a.m.!
I HAD A BAD DREAM!
Can't sleep!
WELL ...
COUNT SHEEP OR WHATEVER ...
SHEEP ?
ONE HOUR LATER
R R R
CLIC
NOW WHAT?
Yawn!
YEAH?
I TRIED TO COUNT SHEEP...
...BUT THE ZOO IS CLOSED!
Poor me!
ZOO
CLOSED
What now?
GO HOME, MIMI!

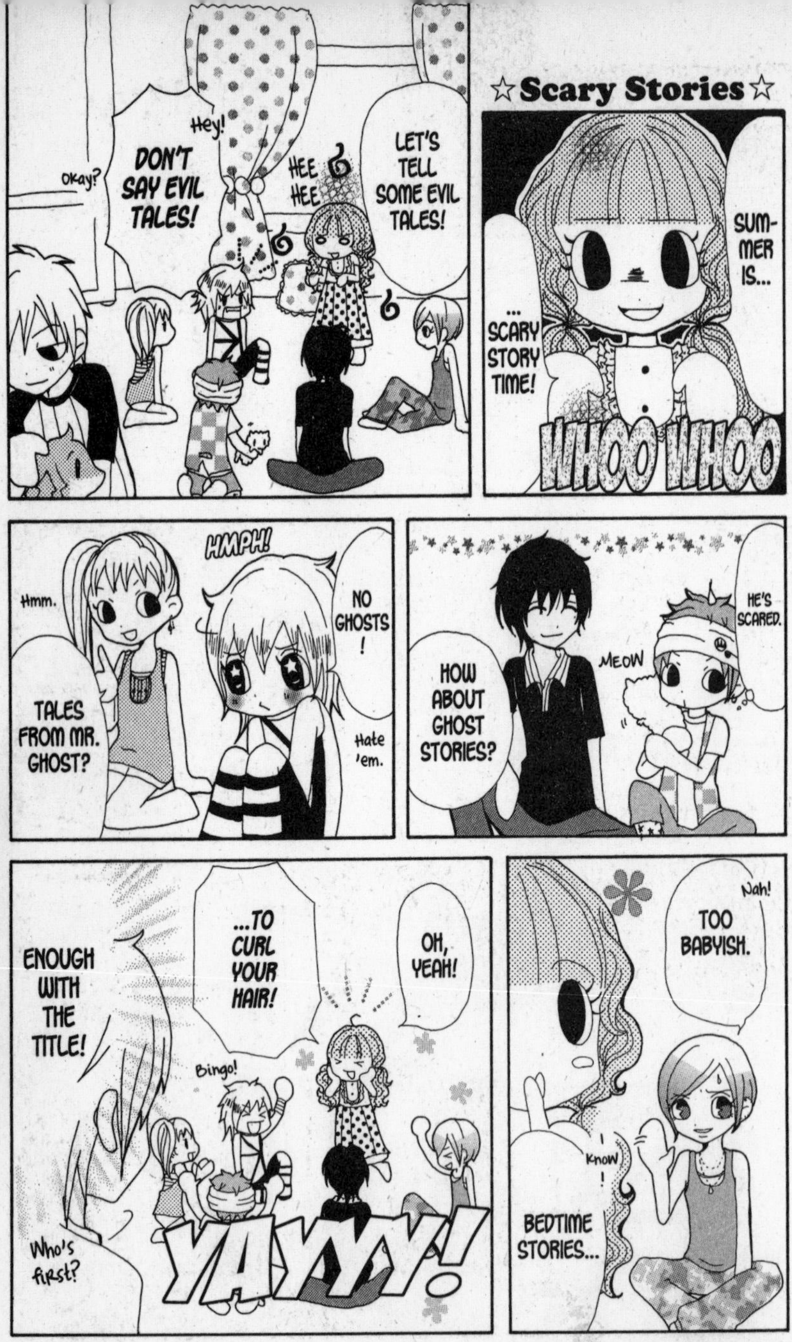
☆Scary Stories☆
SUMMER IS...
...SCARY STORY TIME!
WHOO WHOO
LET'S TELL SOME EVIL TALES!
HEE HEE
Hey!
DON'T SAY EVIL TALES!
Okay?
HE'S SCARED.
MEOW
HOW ABOUT GHOST STORIES?
NO GHOSTS!
HMPH!
Hate 'em.
Hmm.
TALES FROM MR. GHOST?
Nah!
TOO BABYISH.
I know!
BEDTIME STORIES...
OH, YEAH!
...TO CURL YOUR HAIR!
ENOUGH WITH THE TITLE!
Bingo!
YAYYY!
Who's first?

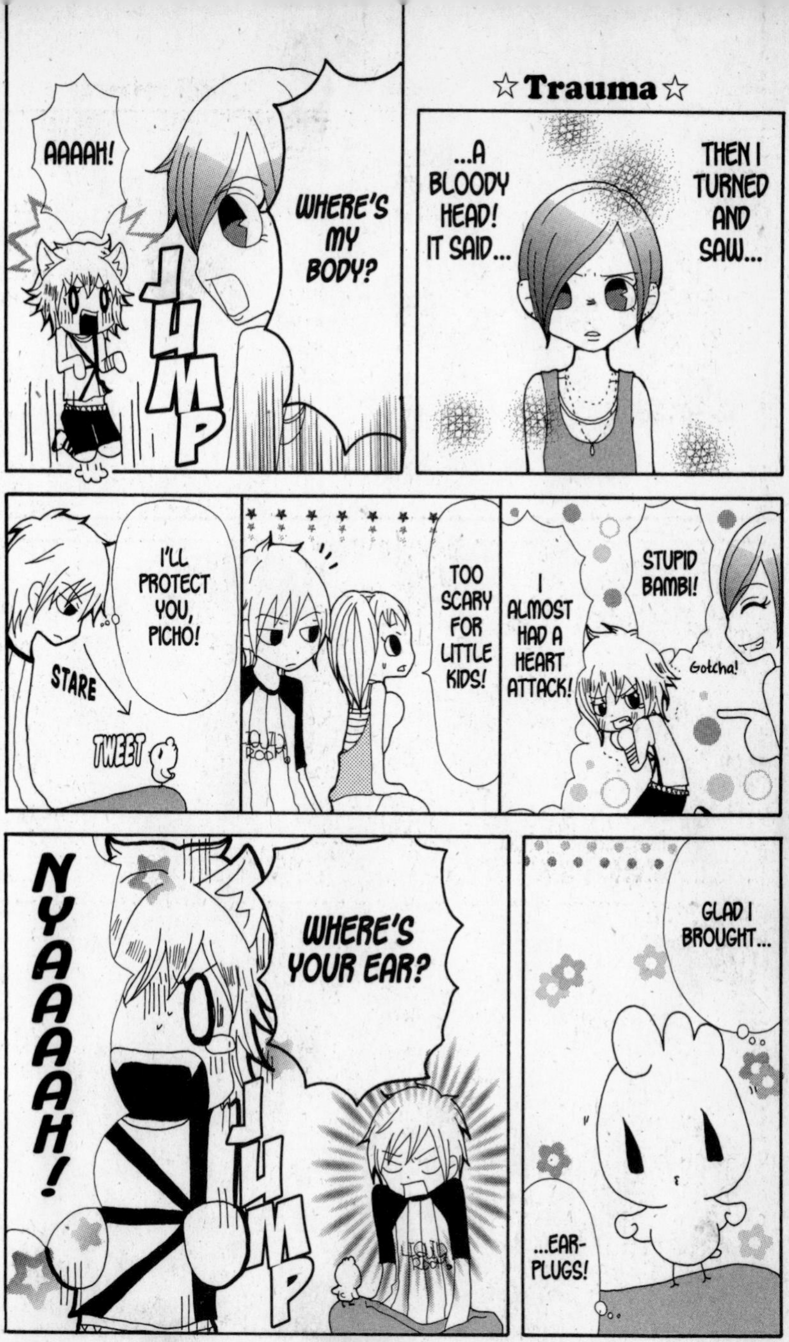
☆Trauma☆
THEN I TURNED AND SAW...
...A BLOODY HEAD! IT SAID...
WHERE'S MY BODY?
JUMP
AAAAH!
STUPID BAMBI!
Gotcha!
I ALMOST HAD A HEART ATTACK!
TOO SCARY FOR LITTLE KIDS!
I'LL PROTECT YOU, PICHO!
STARE
TWEET
GLAD I BROUGHT...
...EAR-PLUGS!
WHERE'S YOUR EAR?
JUMP
NYAAAAAH!

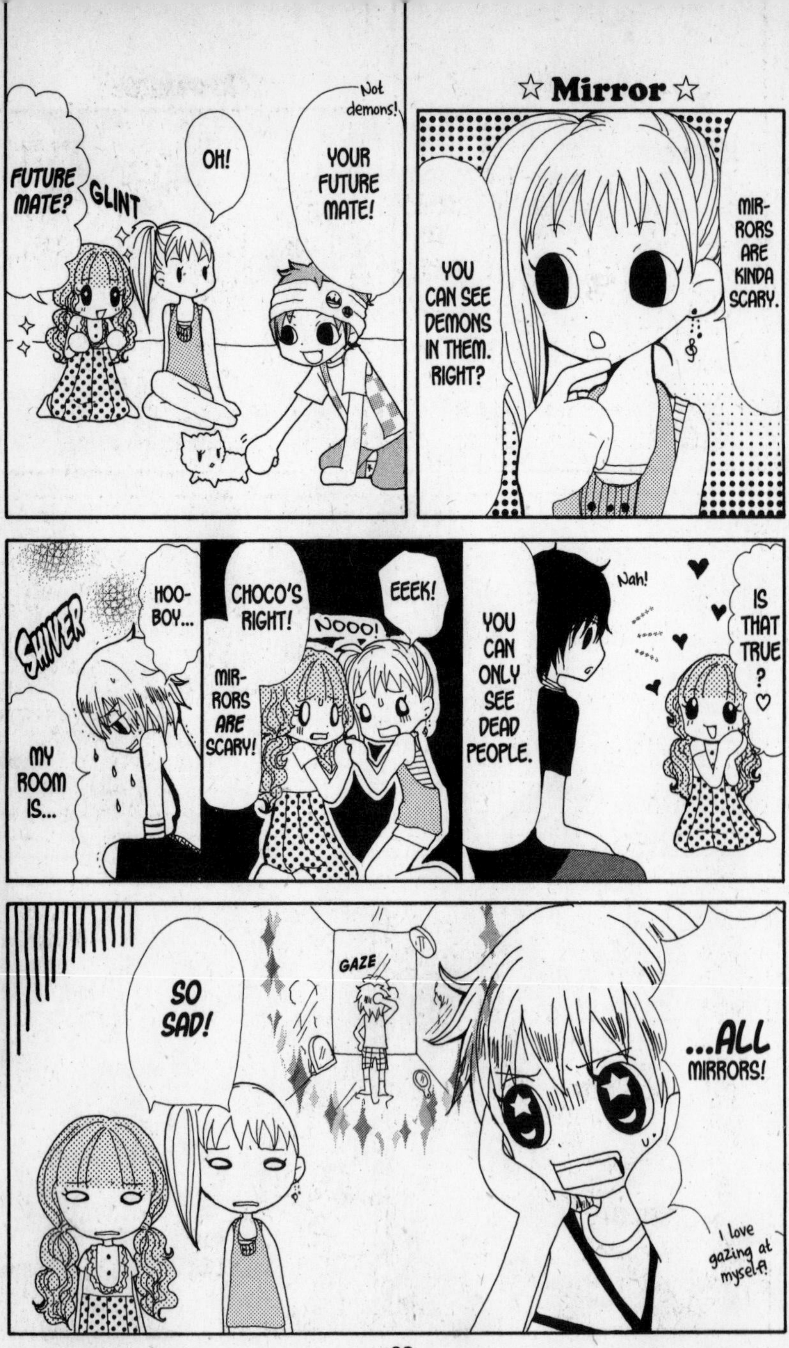
☆ Mirror ☆
MIRRORS ARE KINDA SCARY.
YOU CAN SEE DEMONS IN THEM. RIGHT?
Not demons!
YOUR FUTURE MATE!
OH!
FUTURE MATE?
GLINT
IS THAT TRUE? ♡
Nah!
YOU CAN ONLY SEE DEAD PEOPLE.
EEEK!
NOOO!
CHOCO'S RIGHT!
MIRRORS ARE SCARY!
HOO-BOY...
SHIVER
MY ROOM IS...
...ALL MIRRORS!
I love gazing at myself♪
GAZE
SO SAD!

☆ Doll ☆

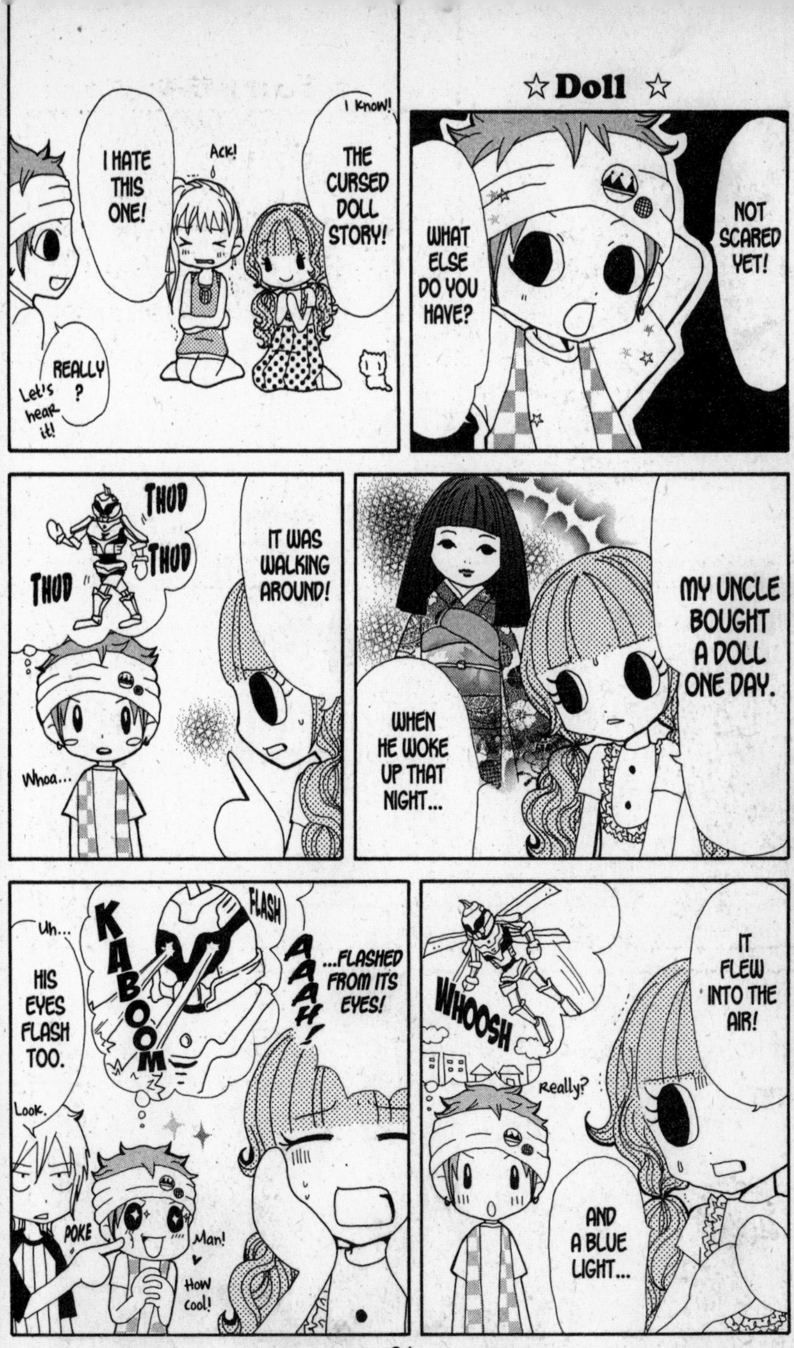
NOT SCARED YET!
WHAT ELSE DO YOU HAVE?
I know!
THE CURSED DOLL STORY!
Ack!
I HATE THIS ONE!
REALLY?
Let's hear it!
MY UNCLE BOUGHT A DOLL ONE DAY.
WHEN HE WOKE UP THAT NIGHT...
IT WAS WALKING AROUND!
THUD
THUD
THUD
Whoa...
IT FLEW INTO THE AIR!
WHOOSH
Really?
AND A BLUE LIGHT...
...FLASHED FROM ITS EYES!
AAAH!
FLASH
KABOOM
Uh...
HIS EYES FLASH TOO.
Look.
POKE
Man!
How cool!

☆ Scary Story ☆

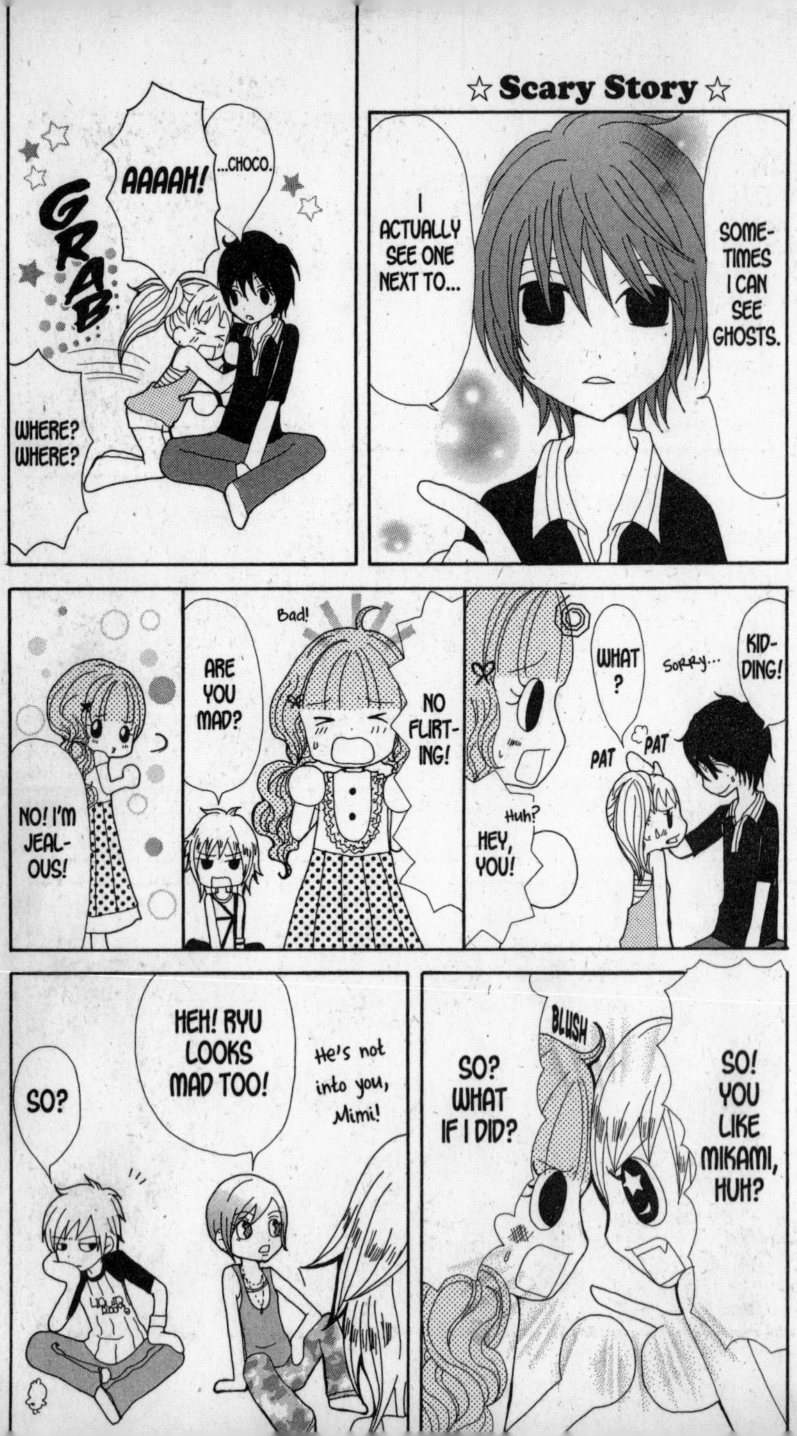
SOMETIMES I CAN SEE GHOSTS.
I ACTUALLY SEE ONE NEXT TO...
...CHOCO.
AAAAH!
GRAB
WHERE? WHERE?
KIDDING!
Sorry...
WHAT?
PAT PAT
Huh?
HEY, YOU!
NO FLIRTING!
Bad!
ARE YOU MAD?
NO! I'M JEALOUS!
SO! YOU LIKE MIKAMI, HUH?
BLUSH
SO? WHAT IF I DID?
He's not into you, Mimi!
HEH! RYU LOOKS MAD TOO!
SO?

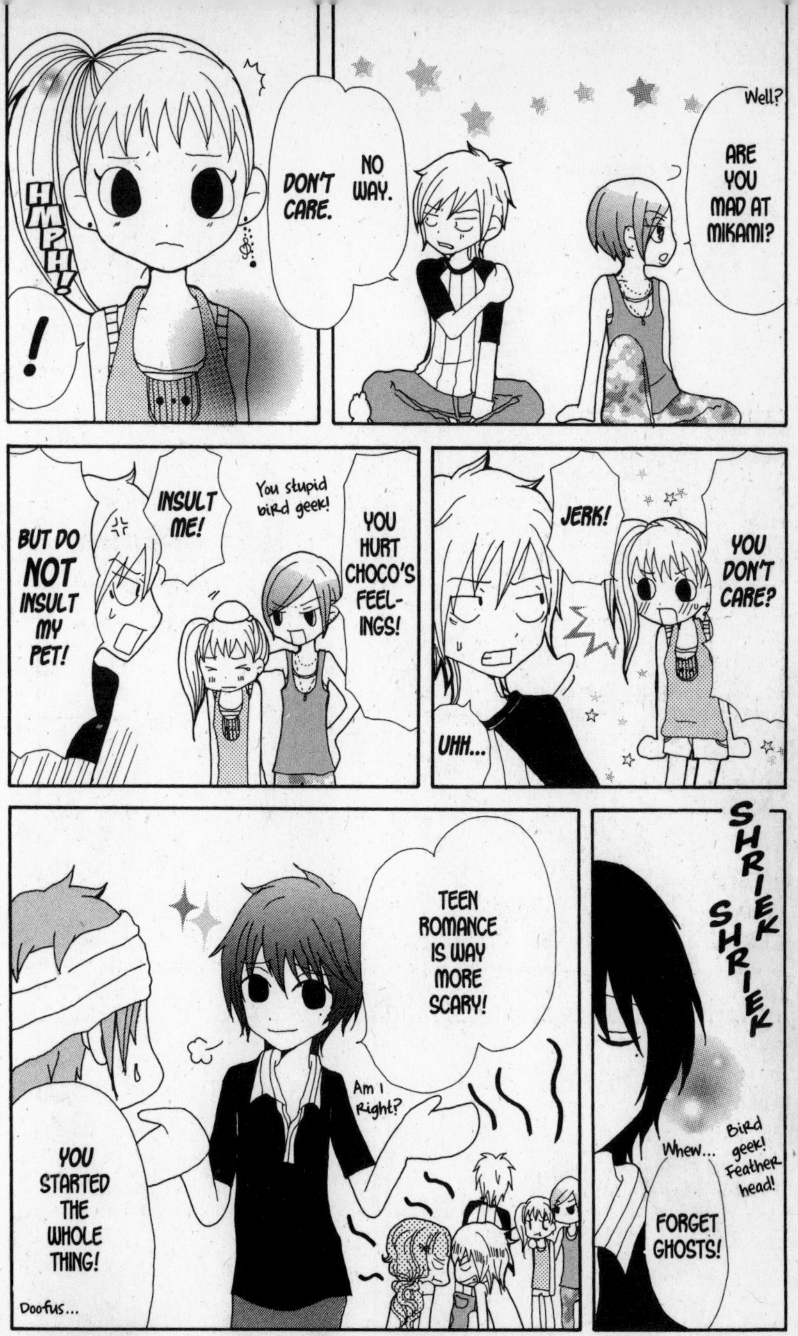
Well?
ARE YOU MAD AT MIKAMI?
NO WAY.
DON'T CARE.
HMPH!
!
YOU DON'T CARE?
JERK!
UHH...
YOU HURT CHOCO'S FEEL-INGS!
You stupid bird geek!
INSULT ME!
BUT DO NOT INSULT MY PET!
SHRIEK SHRIEK
Bird geek! Feather head!
Whew...
FORGET GHOSTS!
TEEN ROMANCE IS WAY MORE SCARY!
Am I right?
YOU STARTED THE WHOLE THING!
Doofus...

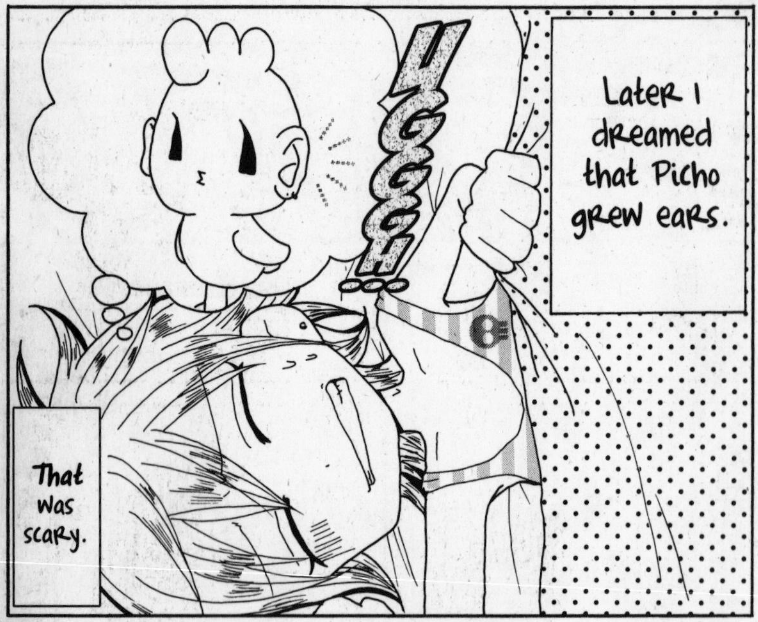
Later I dreamed that Picho grew ears.
UGGGH!...
That was scary.

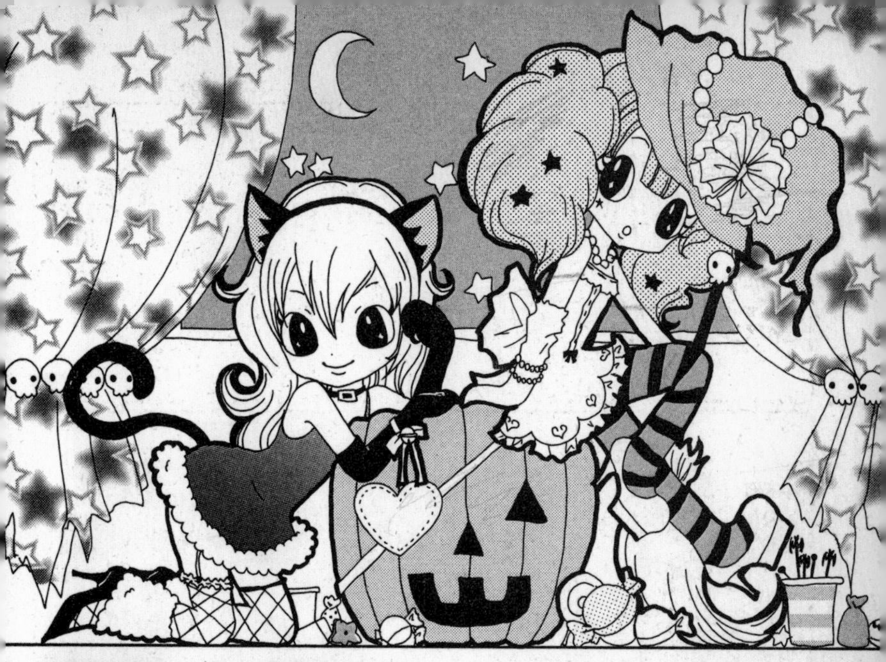

☆**Halloween**☆

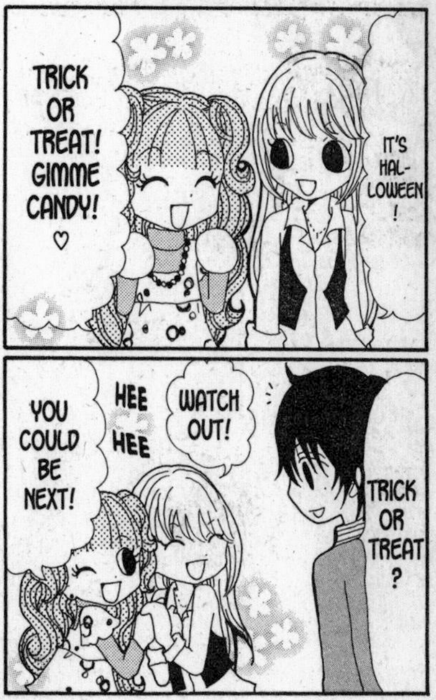
IT'S HALLOWEEN!
TRICK OR TREAT! GIMME CANDY! ♡
TRICK OR TREAT?
WATCH OUT!
HEE HEE
YOU COULD BE NEXT!

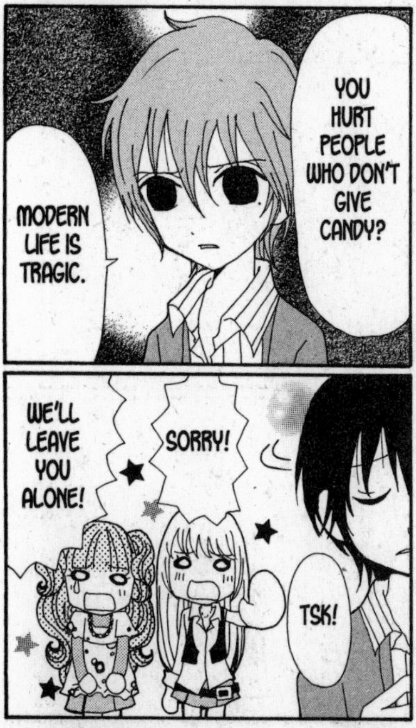
YOU HURT PEOPLE WHO DON'T GIVE CANDY?
MODERN LIFE IS TRAGIC.
SORRY!
WE'LL LEAVE YOU ALONE!
TSK!

☆Café☆

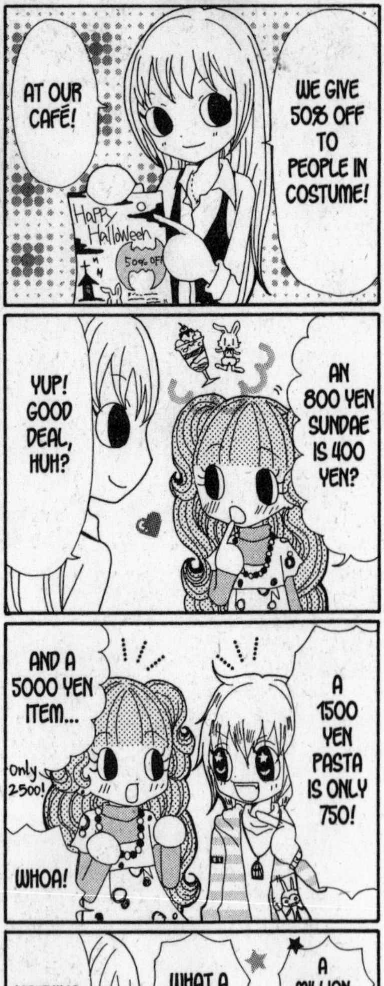
WE GIVE 50% OFF TO PEOPLE IN COSTUME!
AT OUR CAFÉ!
Happy Halloween 50% OFF
AN 800 YEN SUNDAE IS 400 YEN?
YUP! GOOD DEAL, HUH?
A 1500 YEN PASTA IS ONLY 750!
AND A 5000 YEN ITEM...
Only 2500!
WHOA!
A MILLION YEN IS 500,000!
WHAT A BUY!
Gasp!
NOTHING COSTS A MILLION YEN!
Sorry!

☆Pumpkin☆

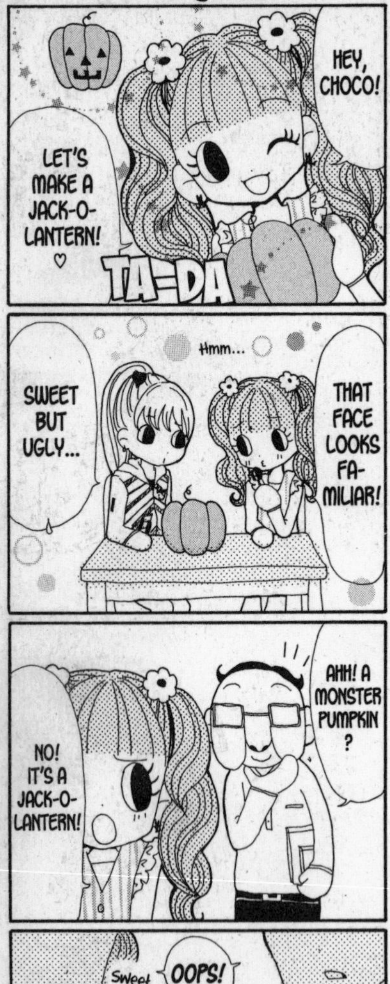
HEY, CHOCO!
LET'S MAKE A JACK-O-LANTERN! ♡
TA-DA
THAT FACE LOOKS FA-MILIAR!
Hmm...
SWEET BUT UGLY...
AHH! A MONSTER PUMPKIN?
NO! IT'S A JACK-O-LANTERN!
OOPS!
Sweet but ugly.

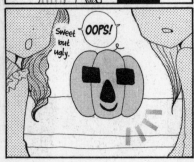

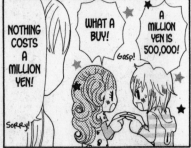

☆ Monster ☆

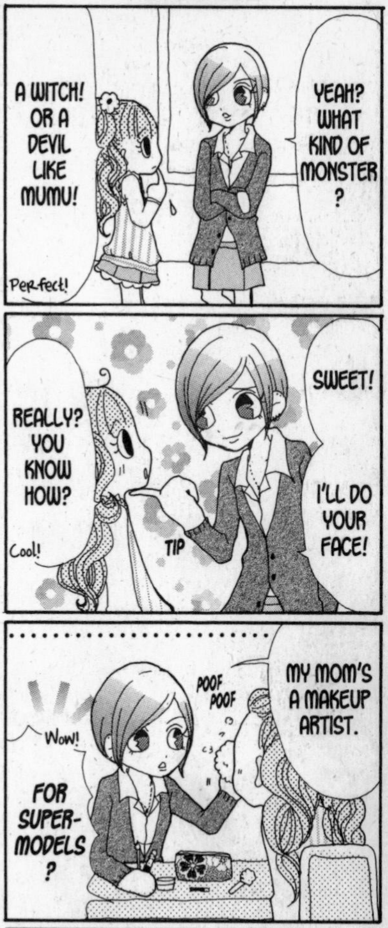
YEAH? WHAT KIND OF MONSTER?
A WITCH! OR A DEVIL LIKE MUMU!
Perfect!
SWEET!
I'LL DO YOUR FACE!
REALLY? YOU KNOW HOW?
TIP
Cool!
......
MY MOM'S A MAKEUP ARTIST.
POOF POOF
Wow!
FOR SUPER-MODELS?
FOR HORROR MOVIES.
Special effects.
ENOUGH!

☆Costume☆

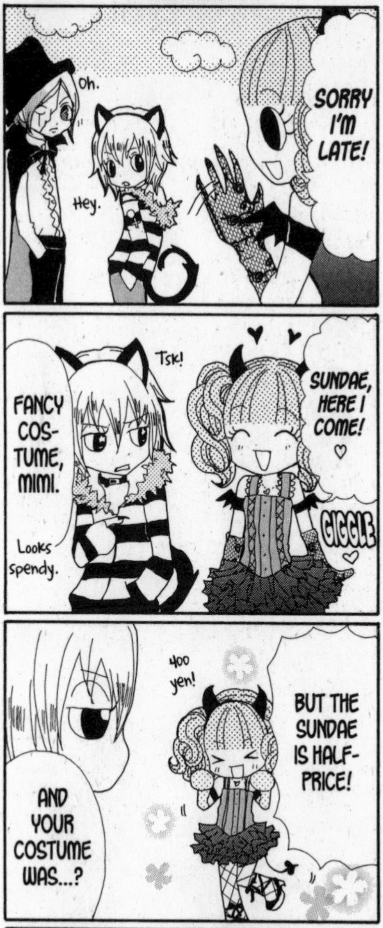
SORRY I'M LATE!
Oh.
Hey.
SUNDAE, HERE I COME!
GIGGLE
Tsk!
FANCY COSTUME, MIMI.
Looks spendy.
BUT THE SUNDAE IS HALF-PRICE!
400 yen!
AND YOUR COSTUME WAS...?
4000 YEN.
MATH ISN'T HER THING...

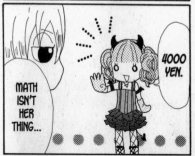

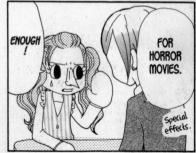

☆ Item ☆

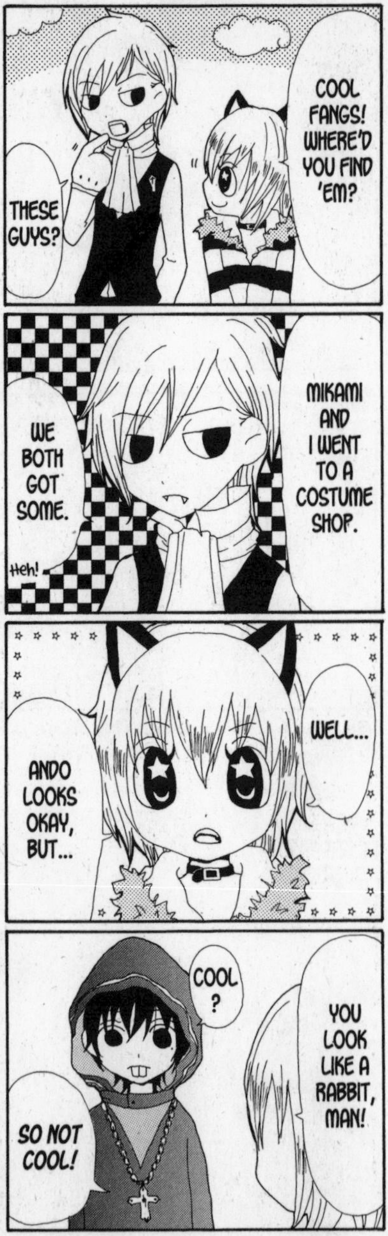
COOL FANGS! WHERE'D YOU FIND 'EM?
THESE GUYS?
MIKAMI AND I WENT TO A COSTUME SHOP.
WE BOTH GOT SOME.
Heh!
WELL...
ANDO LOOKS OKAY, BUT...
YOU LOOK LIKE A RABBIT, MAN!
COOL?
SO NOT COOL!

☆At the Café☆

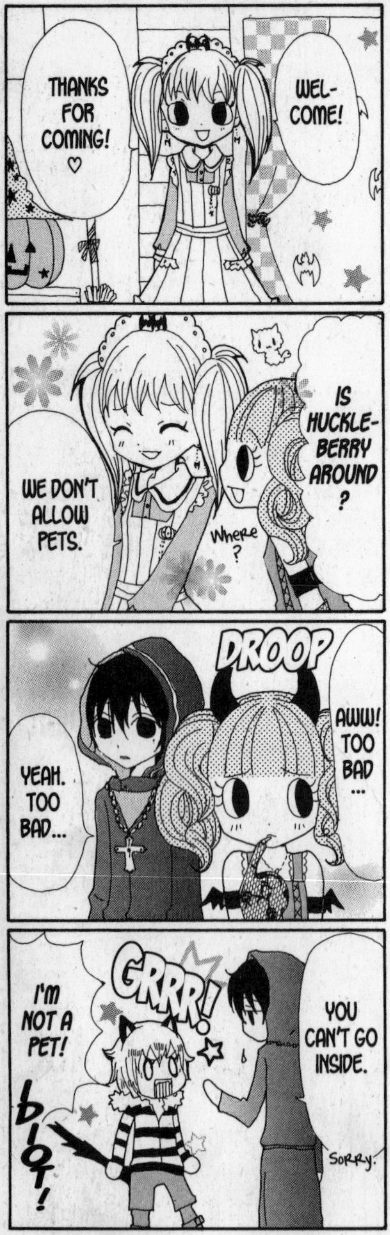
WEL-COME!
THANKS FOR COMING! ♡
IS HUCKLE-BERRY AROUND?
Where?
WE DON'T ALLOW PETS.
AWW! TOO BAD...
DROOP
YEAH. TOO BAD...
YOU CAN'T GO INSIDE.
Sorry.
GRRR!
I'M NOT A PET!
BLOT!

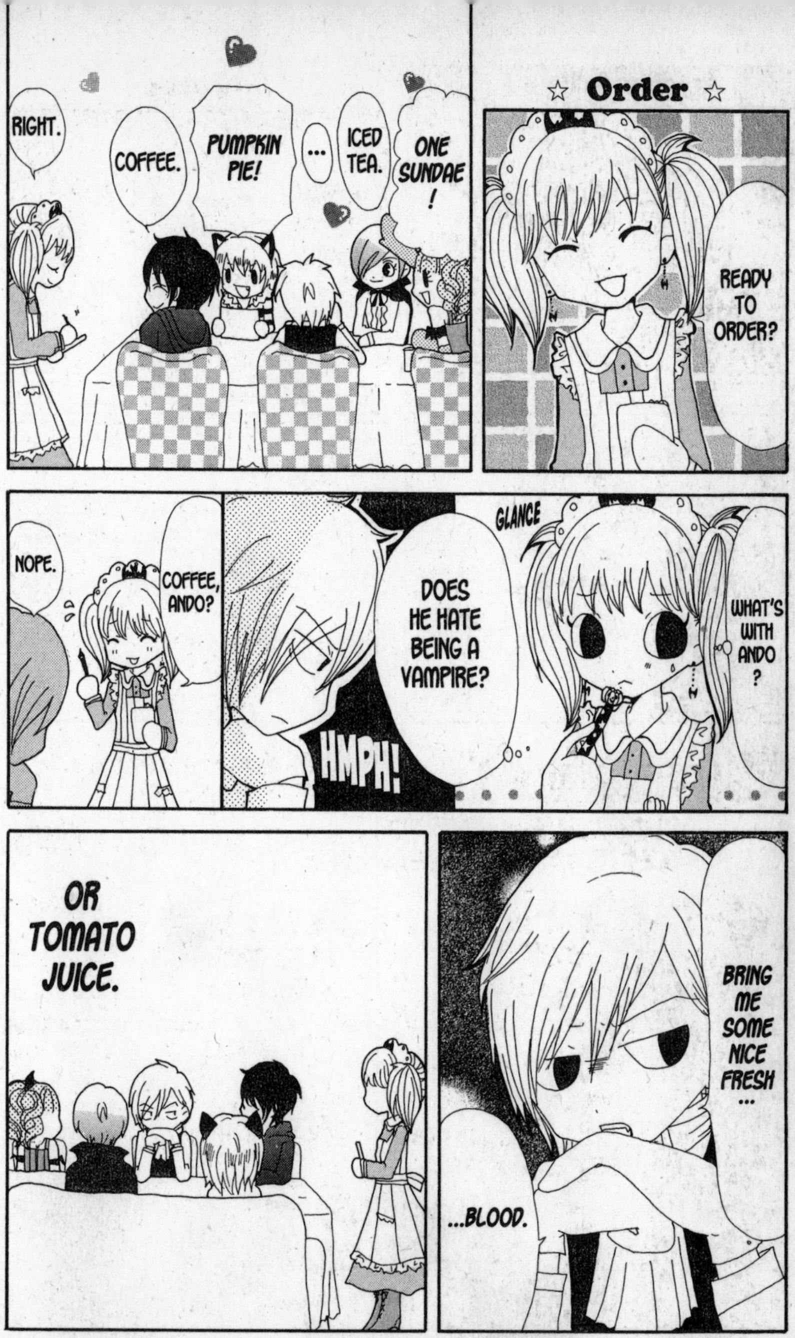
☆ Order ☆
READY TO ORDER?
ONE SUNDAE!
ICED TEA.
...
PUMPKIN PIE!
COFFEE.
RIGHT.
WHAT'S WITH ANDO?
GLANCE
DOES HE HATE BEING A VAMPIRE?
HMPH!
COFFEE, ANDO?
NOPE.
BRING ME SOME NICE FRESH...
...BLOOD.
OR TOMATO JUICE.

☆Fruits☆

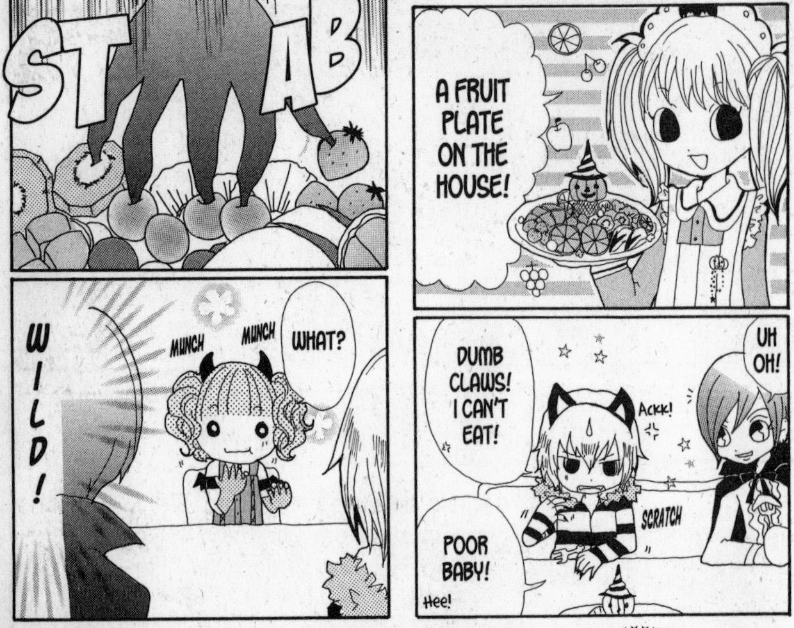
A FRUIT PLATE ON THE HOUSE!
DUMB CLAWS! I CAN'T EAT!
UH OH!
Ackk!
SCRATCH
POOR BABY!
Hee!
STAB
WHAT?
MUNCH
MUNCH
WILD!

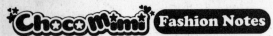

Choco Mimi Fashion Notes

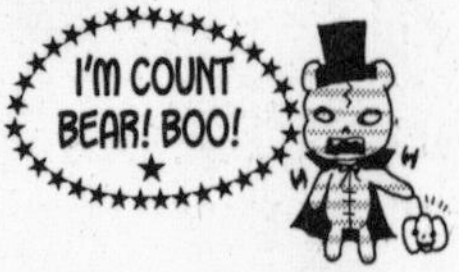
I'M COUNT BEAR! BOO!

GOING TO A HALLOWEEN PARTY? DON'T BE SCARED TO LOOK CUTE!

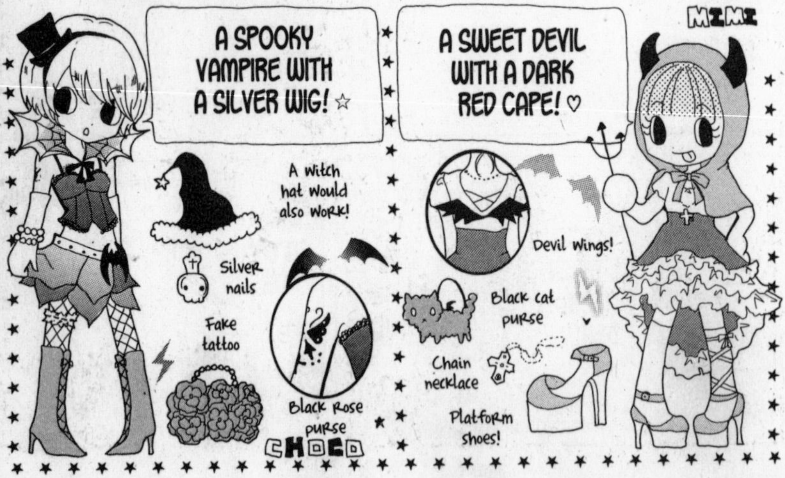
A SPOOKY VAMPIRE WITH A SILVER WIG! ☆
A witch hat would also work!
Silver nails
Fake tattoo
Black Rose purse
CHOCO
MIMI
A SWEET DEVIL WITH A DARK RED CAPE! ♡
Devil wings!
Black cat purse
Chain necklace
Platform shoes!

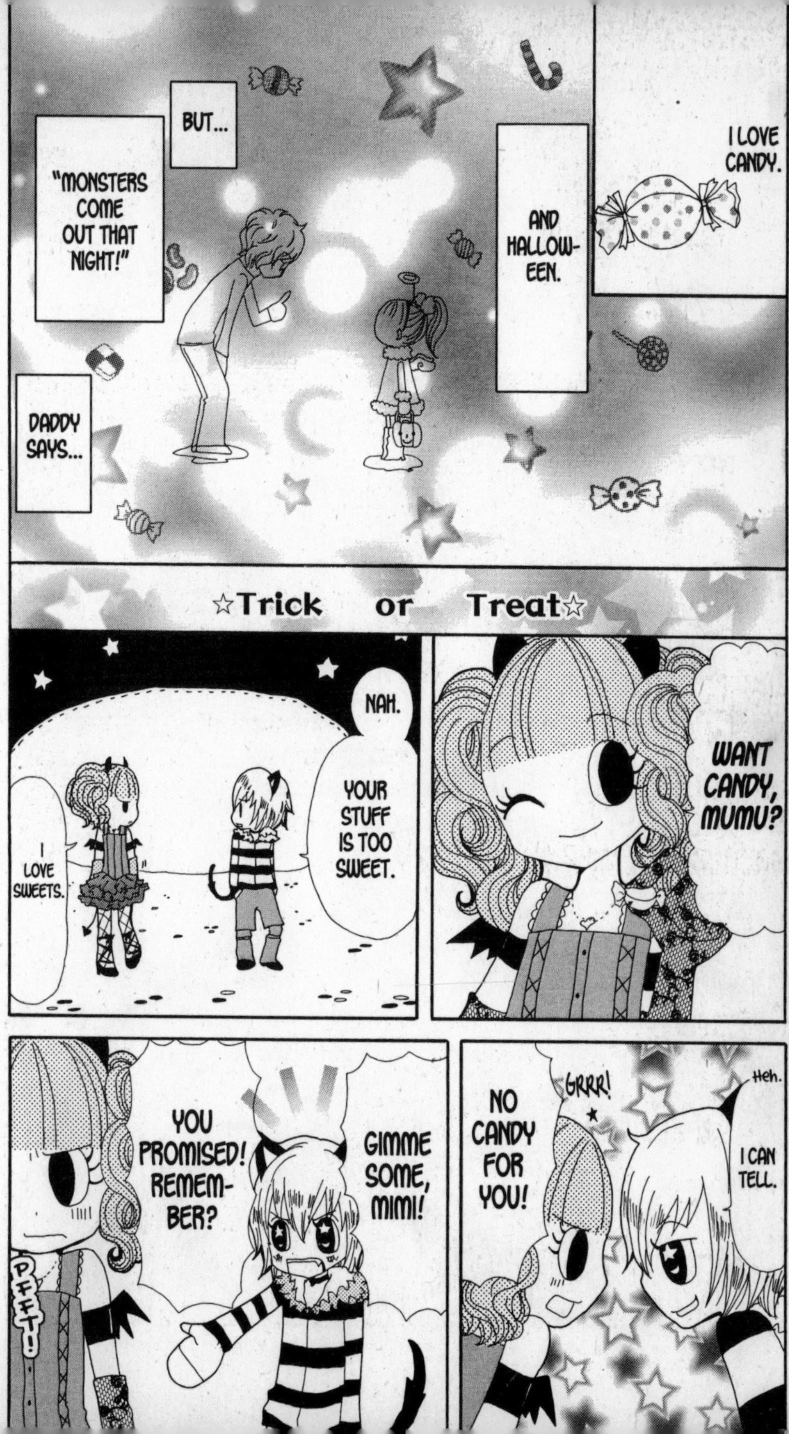
I LOVE CANDY.
AND HALLOW-EEN.
BUT...
"MONSTERS COME OUT THAT NIGHT!"
DADDY SAYS...
☆Trick or Treat☆
WANT CANDY, MUMU?
NAH.
YOUR STUFF IS TOO SWEET.
I LOVE SWEETS.
Heh.
I CAN TELL.
GRRR!
NO CANDY FOR YOU!
GIMME SOME, MIMI!
YOU PROMISED! REMEM-BER?
PFFT!

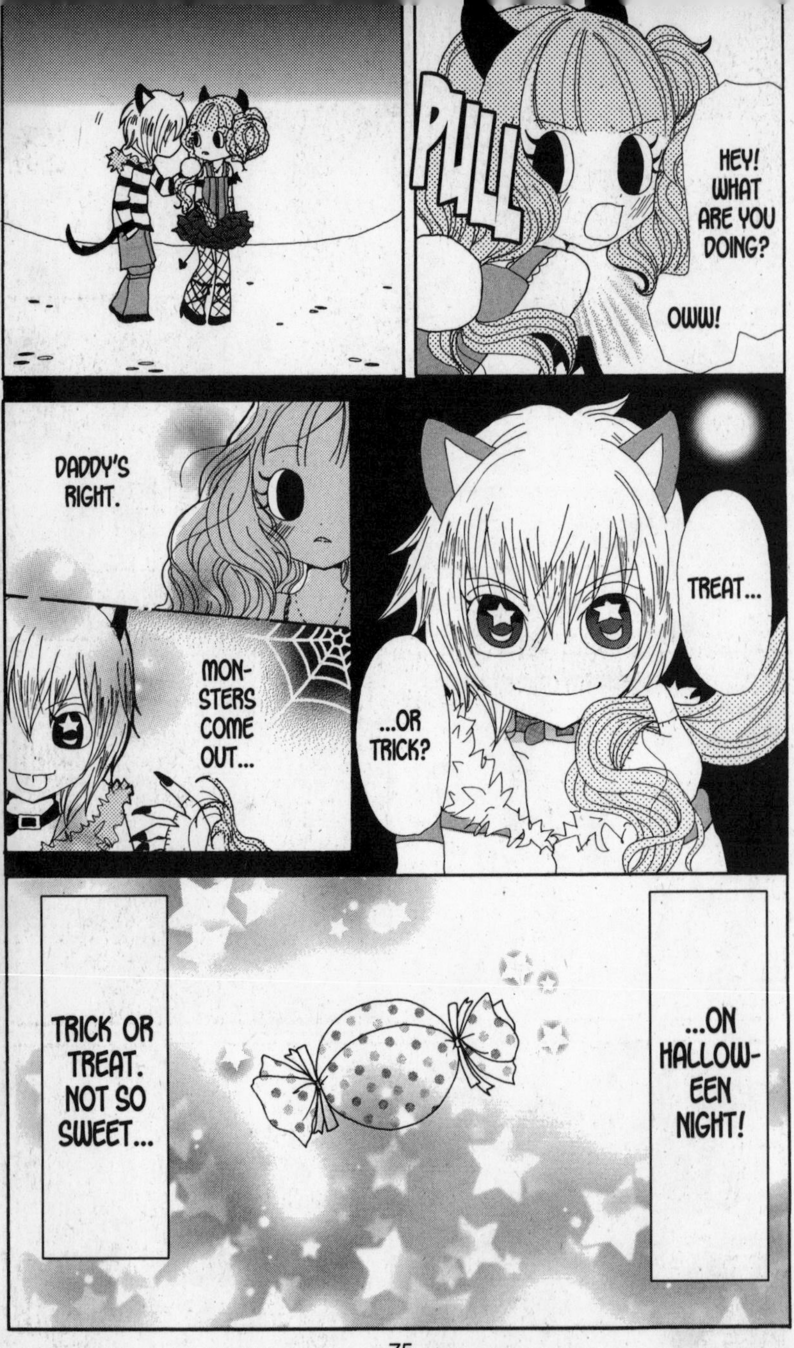
PULL
HEY! WHAT ARE YOU DOING?
OWW!
TREAT...
...OR TRICK?
DADDY'S RIGHT.
MON-STERS COME OUT...
...ON HALLOW-EEN NIGHT!
TRICK OR TREAT. NOT SO SWEET...

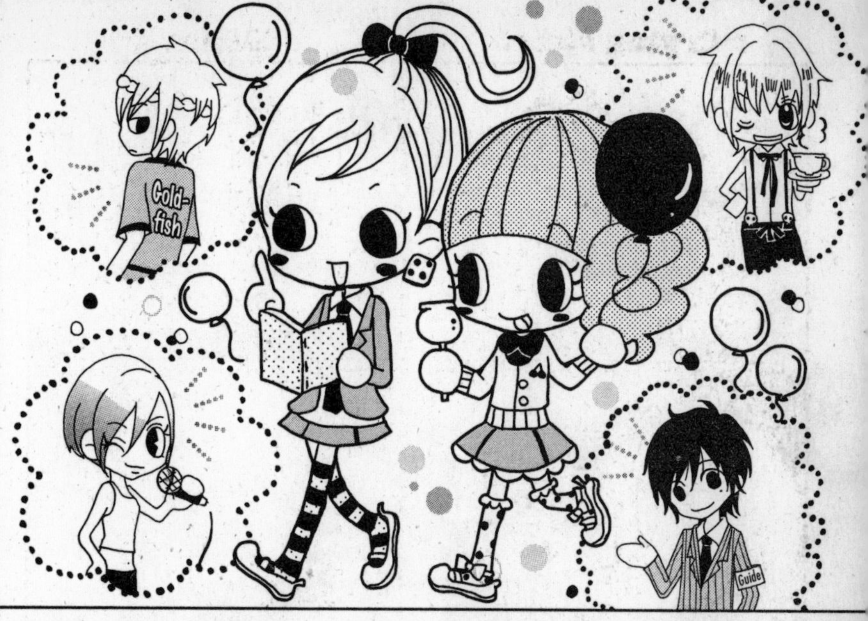
Gold-
fish
Guide

☆**School Festival**☆

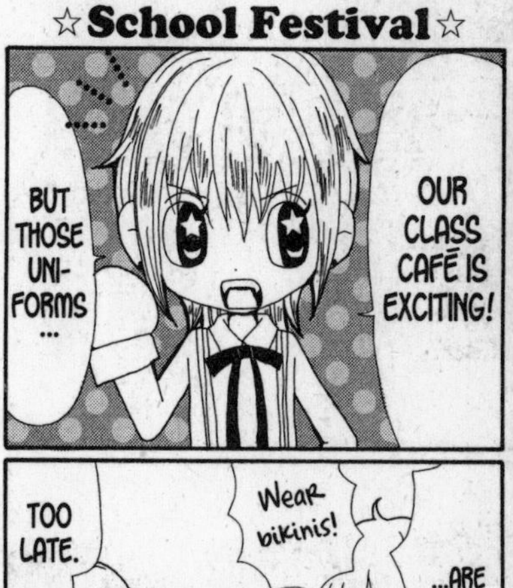
OUR CLASS CAFÉ IS EXCITING!
BUT THOSE UNI-FORMS...
...ARE SO YESTER-DAY!
Wear bikinis!
TOO LATE.

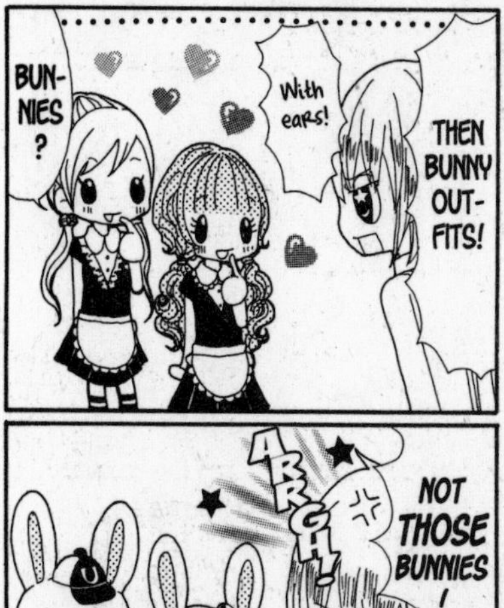
THEN BUNNY OUT-FITS!
With ears!
BUN-NIES?
NOT THOSE BUNNIES!
ARRGH!
PLUS CHOCO'S A GUY!

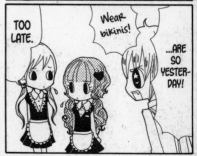

☆ Bunny ☆

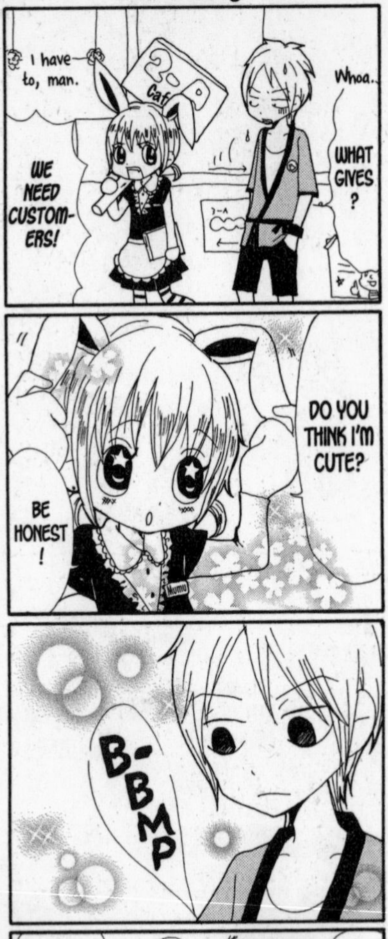
Whoa..
WHAT GIVES?
I have to, man.
Café
WE NEED CUSTOMERS!
DO YOU THINK I'M CUTE?
BE HONEST!
B-BMP
I'M ALLERGIC TO RABBITS.
..CHOO!
HE CALLED ME AN ANIMAL!
Hit him!
AH...
SNIFF

☆ Crying Mole ☆

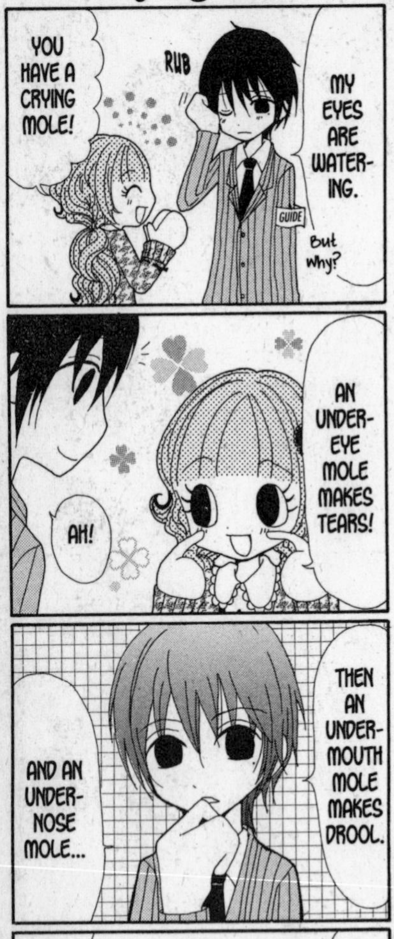
MY EYES ARE WATERING.
RUB
YOU HAVE A CRYING MOLE!
GUIDE
But why?
AN UNDER-EYE MOLE MAKES TEARS!
AH!
THEN AN UNDER-MOUTH MOLE MAKES DROOL.
AND AN UNDER-NOSE MOLE...
...MAKES SNOT!
NO!
PRINCES DON'T SAY "SNOT"!

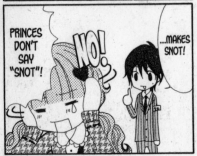

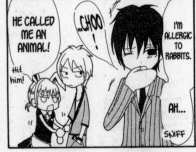

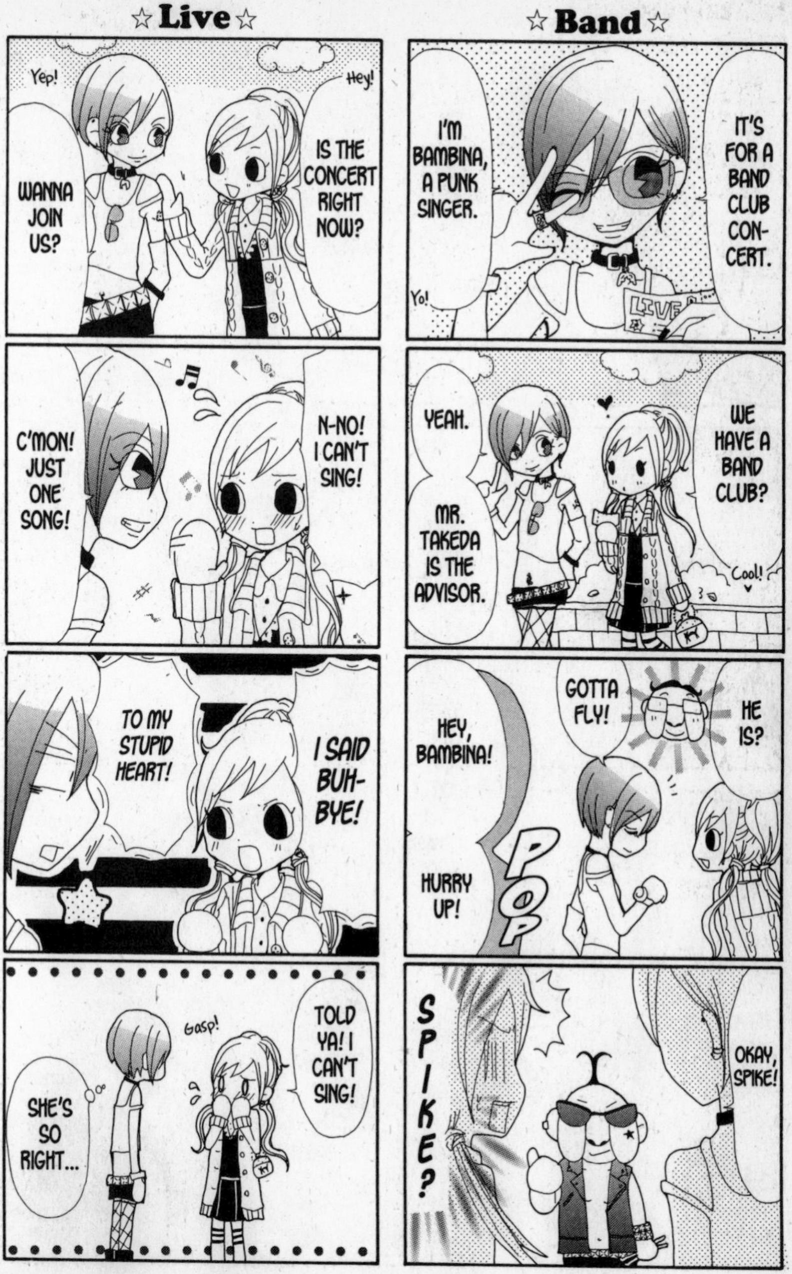
☆Band☆
IT'S FOR A BAND CLUB CONCERT.
I'M BAMBINA, A PUNK SINGER.
Yo!
LIVE
WE HAVE A BAND CLUB?
Cool!
YEAH.
MR. TAKEDA IS THE ADVISOR.
HE IS?
GOTTA FLY!
HEY, BAMBINA!
HURRY UP!
POP
OKAY, SPIKE!
SPIKE?
☆Live☆
Hey!
IS THE CONCERT RIGHT NOW?
Yep!
WANNA JOIN US?
N-NO! I CAN'T SING!
C'MON! JUST ONE SONG!
I SAID BUH-BYE!
TO MY STUPID HEART!
TOLD YA! I CAN'T SING!
Gasp!
SHE'S SO RIGHT...

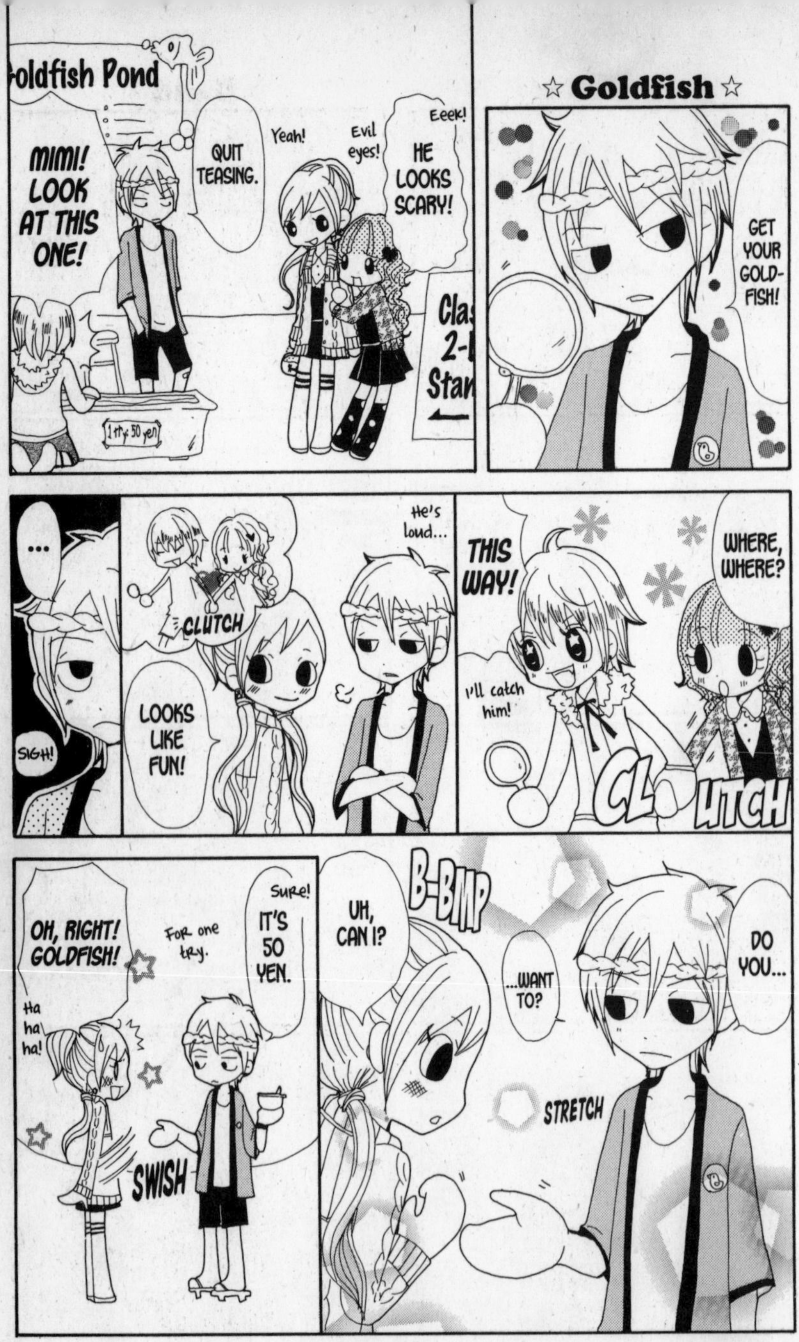
☆ Goldfish ☆
GET YOUR GOLD-FISH!
Eeek!
HE LOOKS SCARY!
Evil eyes!
Yeah!
QUIT TEASING.
Goldfish Pond
MIMI! LOOK AT THIS ONE!
1 try: 50 yen
WHERE, WHERE?
THIS WAY!
I'll catch him!
CLUTCH
He's loud...
CLUTCH
LOOKS LIKE FUN!
...
SIGH!
DO YOU...
B-BMP
...WANT TO?
UH, CAN I?
STRETCH
Sure!
IT'S 50 YEN.
For one try.
OH, RIGHT! GOLDFISH!
Ha ha ha!
SWISH

☆Smile☆

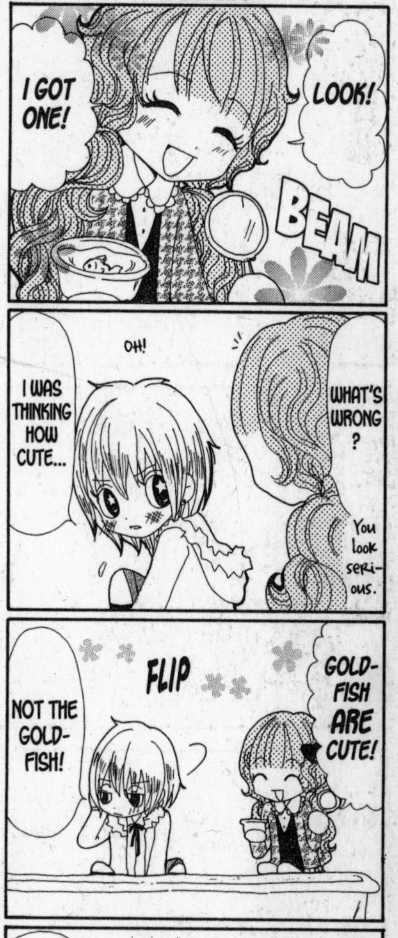
LOOK!
I GOT ONE!
BEAM
WHAT'S WRONG?
You look seri-ous.
OH!
I WAS THINKING HOW CUTE...
GOLD-FISH ARE CUTE!
FLIP
NOT THE GOLD-FISH!
WHAT?
B-BMP B-BMP
MY REFLEC-TION...
Adorable!

☆ Pet ☆

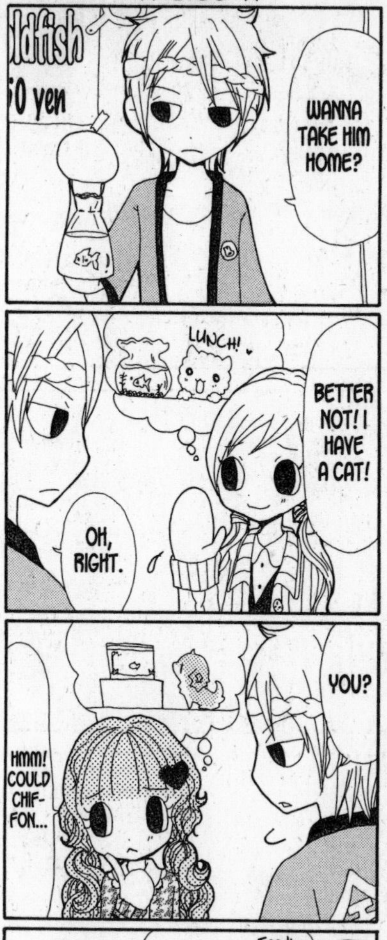
WANNA TAKE HIM HOME?
ldfish
50 yen
BETTER NOT! I HAVE A CAT!
LUNCH!
OH, RIGHT.
YOU?
HMM! COULD CHIF-FON...
...TAKE CARE OF A GOLD-FISH?
Feeding time!
YOU'RE THAT LAZY?
Geez!

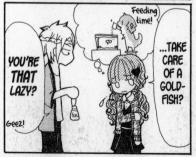

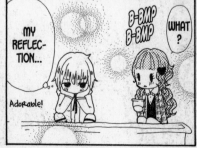

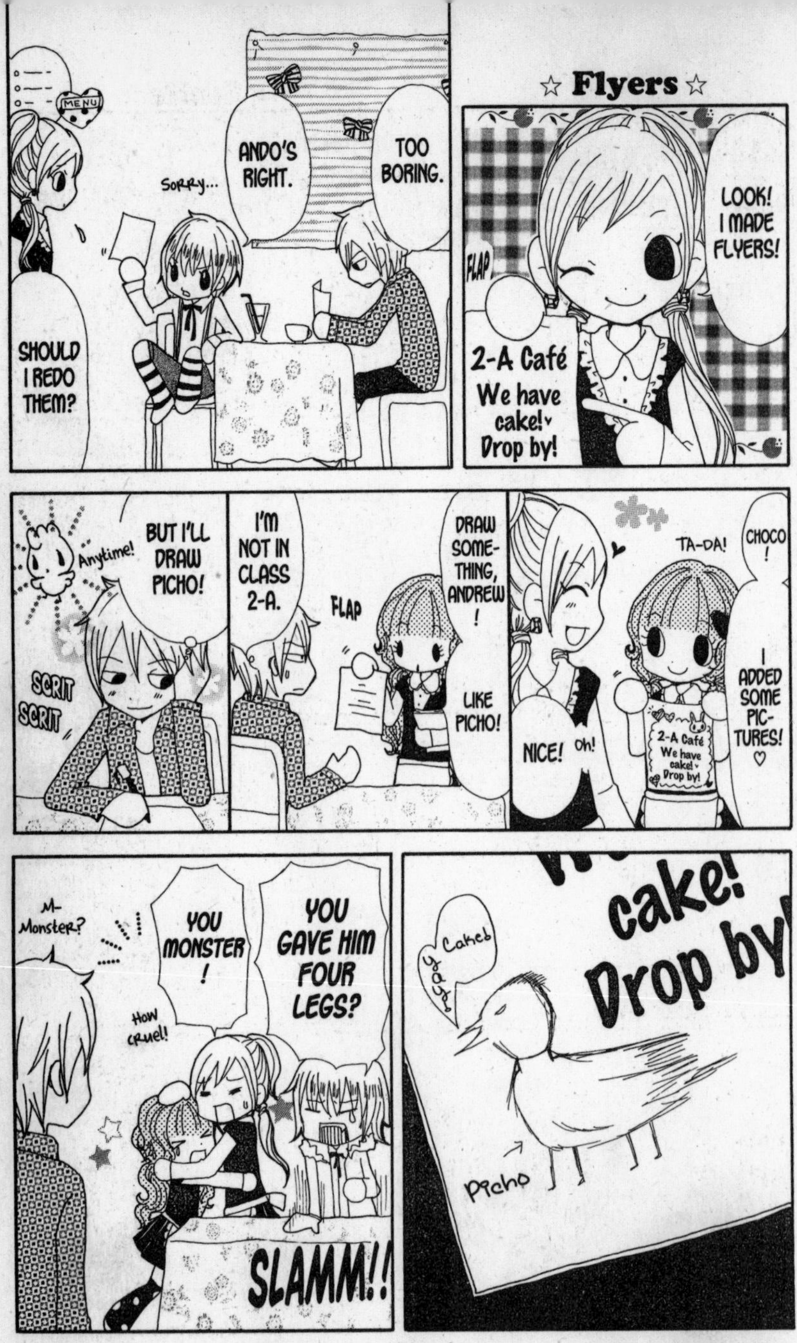
☆ Flyers ☆
LOOK! I MADE FLYERS!
FLAP
2-A Café We have cake! Drop by!
TOO BORING.
ANDO'S RIGHT.
MENU
Sorry...
SHOULD I REDO THEM?
CHOCO!
TA-DA!
I ADDED SOME PICTURES!
Oh!
NICE!
2-A Café We have cake! Drop by!
DRAW SOMETHING, ANDREW!
LIKE PICHO!
FLAP
I'M NOT IN CLASS 2-A.
BUT I'LL DRAW PICHO!
Anytime!
SCRIT SCRIT
cake! Drop by!
Cake!
yay
Picho
YOU GAVE HIM FOUR LEGS?
YOU MONSTER!
M-Monster?
How cruel!
SLAMM!!

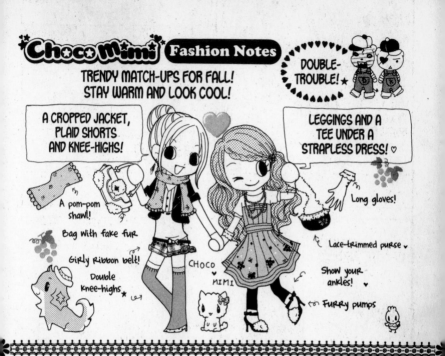

Choco Mimi Fashion Notes
TRENDY MATCH-UPS FOR FALL! STAY WARM AND LOOK COOL!
DOUBLE-TROUBLE! ★
A CROPPED JACKET, PLAID SHORTS AND KNEE-HIGHS!
LEGGINGS AND A TEE UNDER A STRAPLESS DRESS! ♡
A pom-pom shawl!
Bag with fake fur
Girly Ribbon belt!
Double knee-highs ★
CHOCO ♥ MIMI
Long gloves!
Lace-trimmed purse ♥
Show your ankles! ♥
Furry pumps

Mommy!
I saw an alien!
...

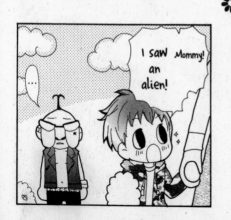

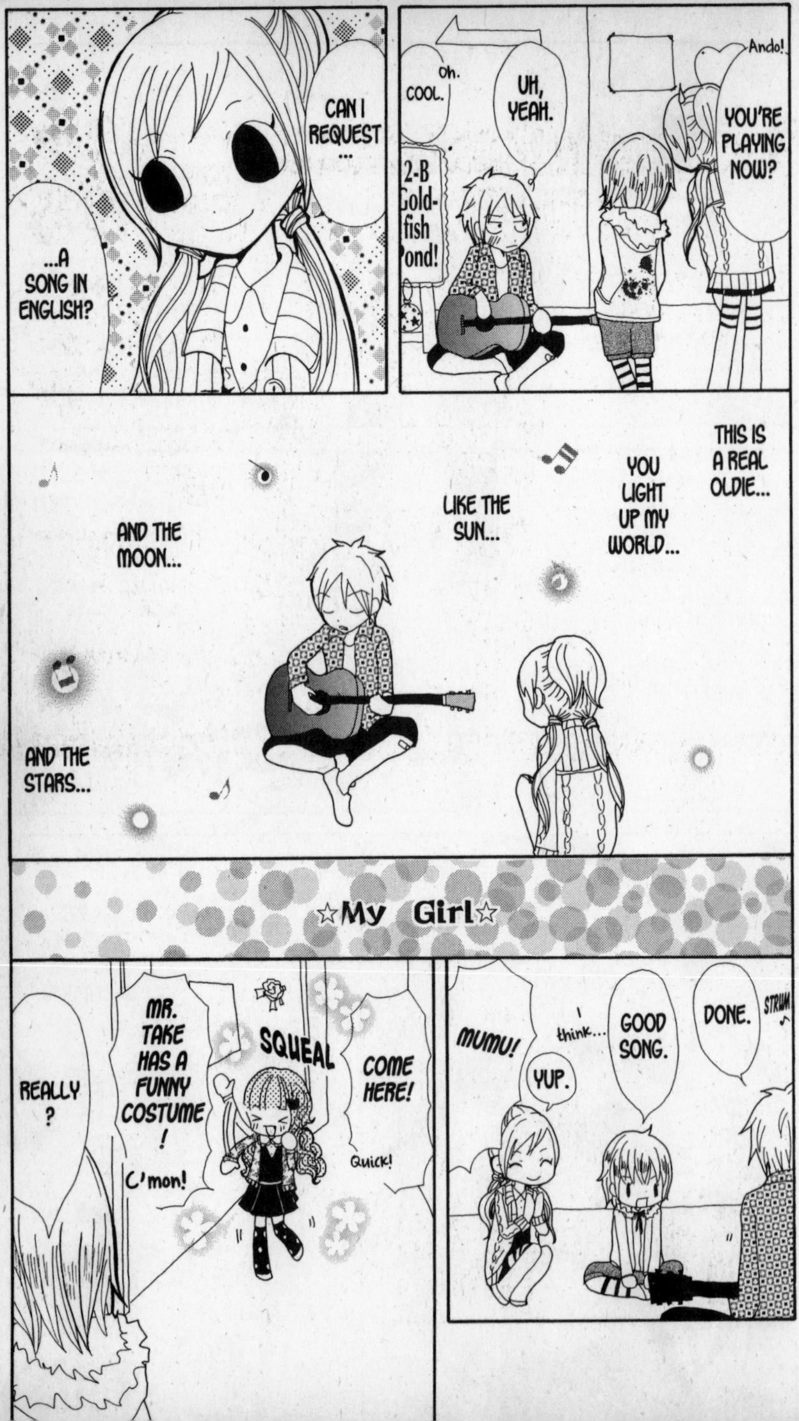
Ando!
YOU'RE PLAYING NOW?
UH, YEAH.
Oh. COOL.
2-B Goldfish Pond!
CAN I REQUEST ...
...A SONG IN ENGLISH?
THIS IS A REAL OLDIE...
YOU LIGHT UP MY WORLD...
LIKE THE SUN...
AND THE MOON...
AND THE STARS...
☆My Girl☆
STRUM
DONE.
GOOD SONG.
I think...
MUMU!
YUP.
COME HERE!
Quick!
SQUEAL
MR. TAKE HAS A FUNNY COSTUME!
C'mon!
REALLY?

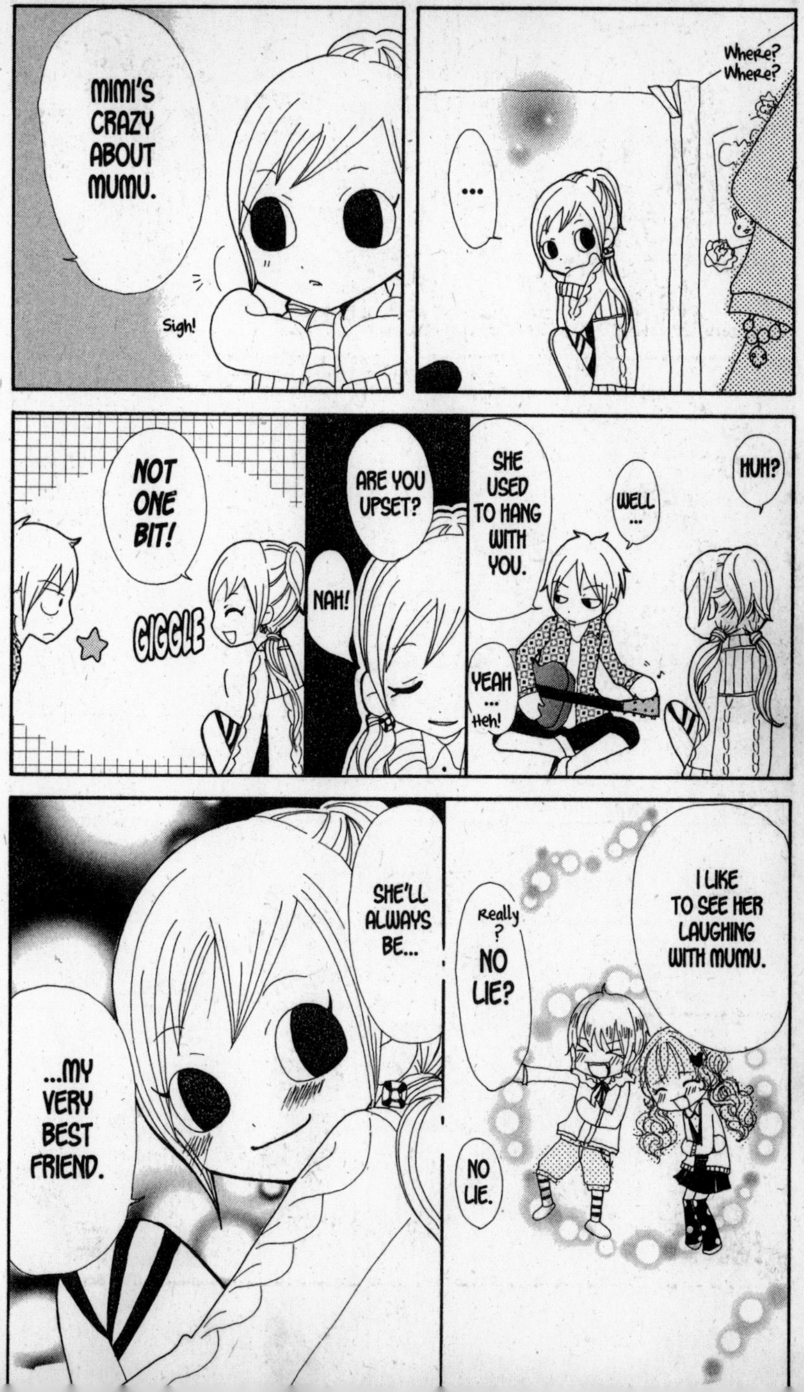
Where? Where?
...
MIMI'S CRAZY ABOUT MUMU.
Sigh!
HUH?
WELL ...
SHE USED TO HANG WITH YOU.
YEAH ... Heh!
ARE YOU UPSET?
NAH!
NOT ONE BIT!
GIGGLE
I LIKE TO SEE HER LAUGHING WITH MUMU.
Really? NO LIE?
NO LIE.
SHE'LL ALWAYS BE...
...MY VERY BEST FRIEND.

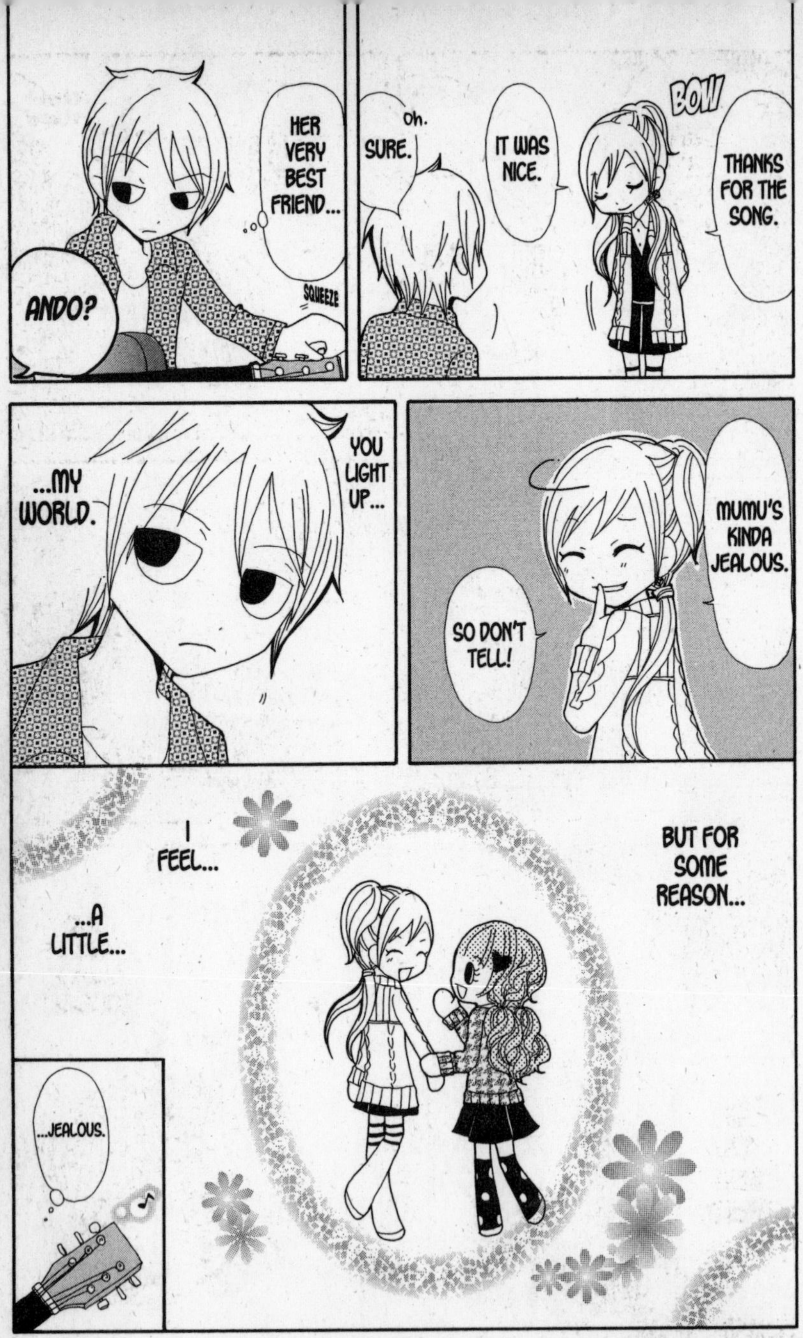
BOW
THANKS FOR THE SONG.
IT WAS NICE.
Oh. SURE.
HER VERY BEST FRIEND...
SQUEEZE
ANDO?
MUMU'S KINDA JEALOUS.
SO DON'T TELL!
YOU LIGHT UP...
...MY WORLD.
BUT FOR SOME REASON...
I FEEL...
...A LITTLE...
...JEALOUS.

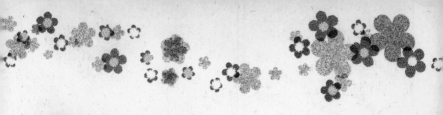

Extra 2

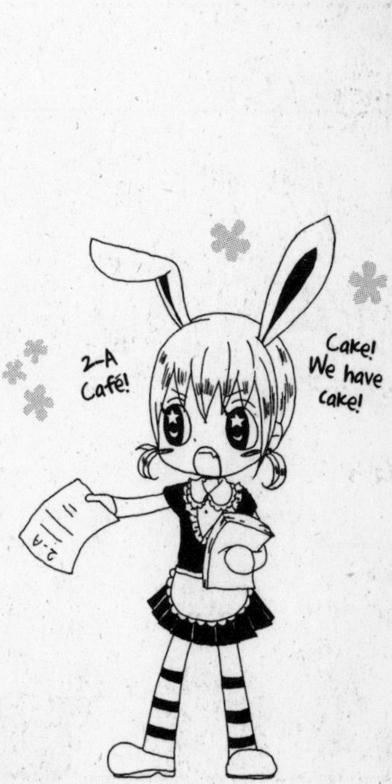
Cake! We have cake!
2-A Café!

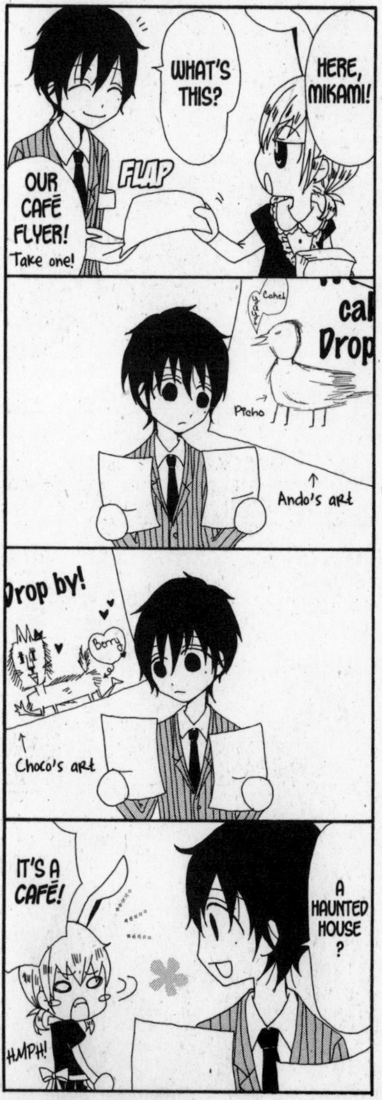
HERE, MIKAMI!
WHAT'S THIS?
FLAP
OUR CAFÉ FLYER!
Take one!
Drop
Picho
Ando's art
Drop by!
Berry
Choco's art
A HAUNTED HOUSE?
IT'S A CAFÉ!
HMPH!

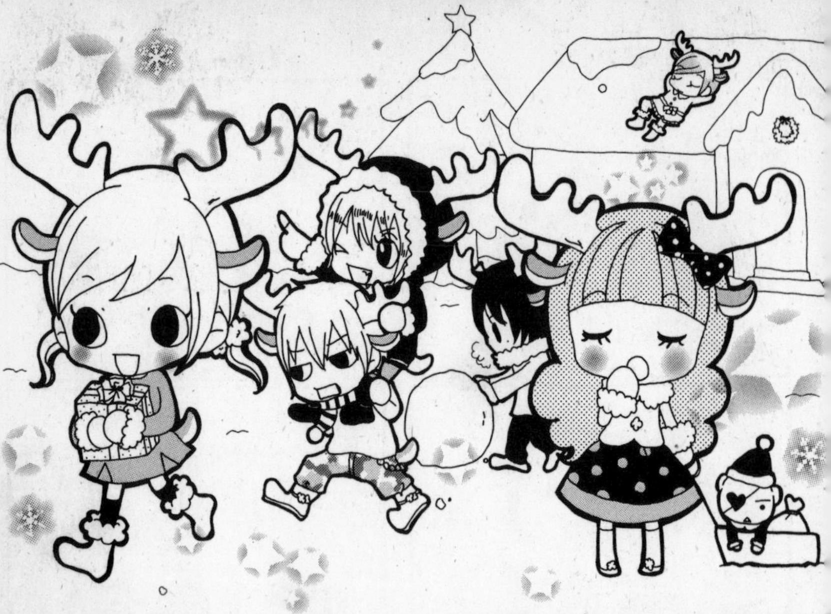

☆ **December 20** ☆

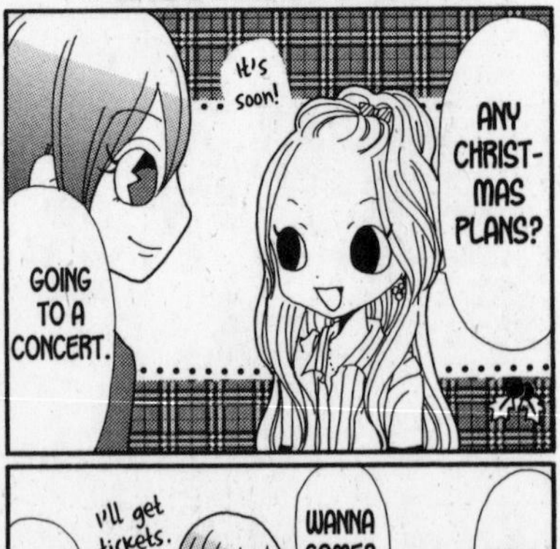
ANY CHRISTMAS PLANS?
It's soon!
GOING TO A CONCERT.
WOW, LUCKY!
WANNA COME?
I'll get tickets.
DANG!

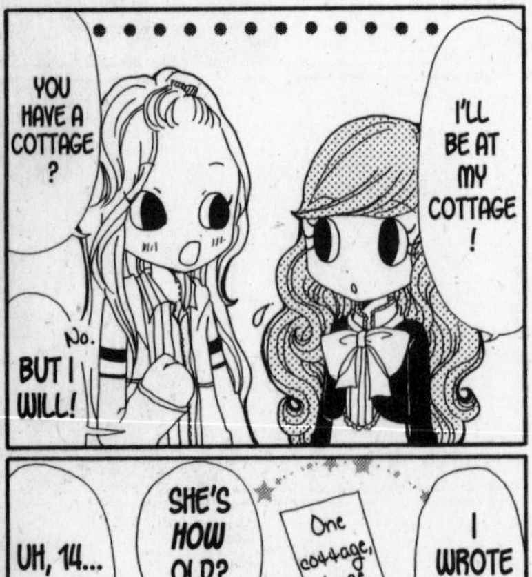
I'LL BE AT MY COTTAGE!
YOU HAVE A COTTAGE?
No.
BUT I WILL!
I WROTE TO SANTA!
One cottage, please. -Mimi
SHE'S *HOW* OLD?
Santa?
UH, 14...

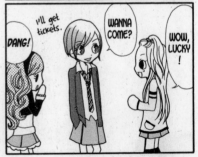

☆Christmas☆

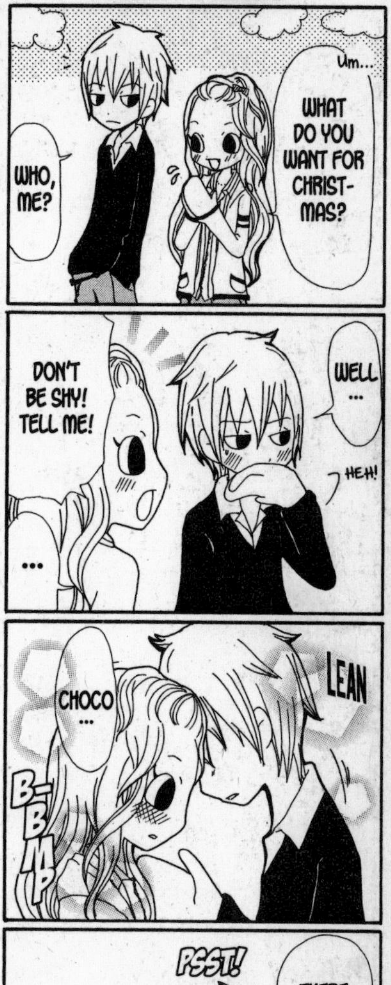
Um...
WHAT DO YOU WANT FOR CHRIST-MAS?
WHO, ME?
WELL...
HEH!
DON'T BE SHY! TELL ME!
...
LEAN
CHOCO...
B-BMP
PSST!
THERE IS NO SANTA.
Don't expect presents.
OH, REALLY?

☆Santa☆

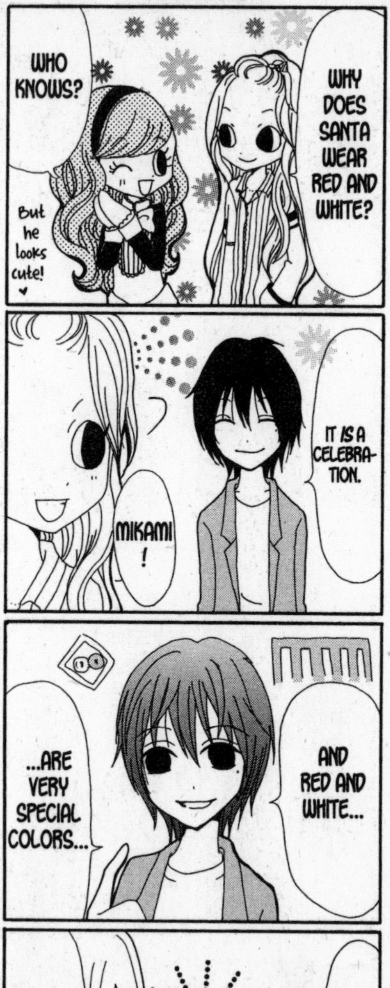
WHY DOES SANTA WEAR RED AND WHITE?
WHO KNOWS?
But he looks cute! ♥
IT IS A CELEBRA-TION.
MIKAMI!
AND RED AND WHITE...
...ARE VERY SPECIAL COLORS...
...IN JAPAN.
WOW!
Brilliant!
SANTA ISN'T JAPAN-ESE!

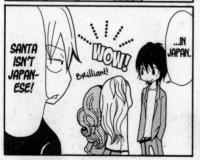

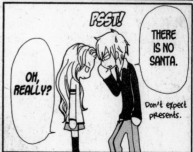

☆ Idea ☆

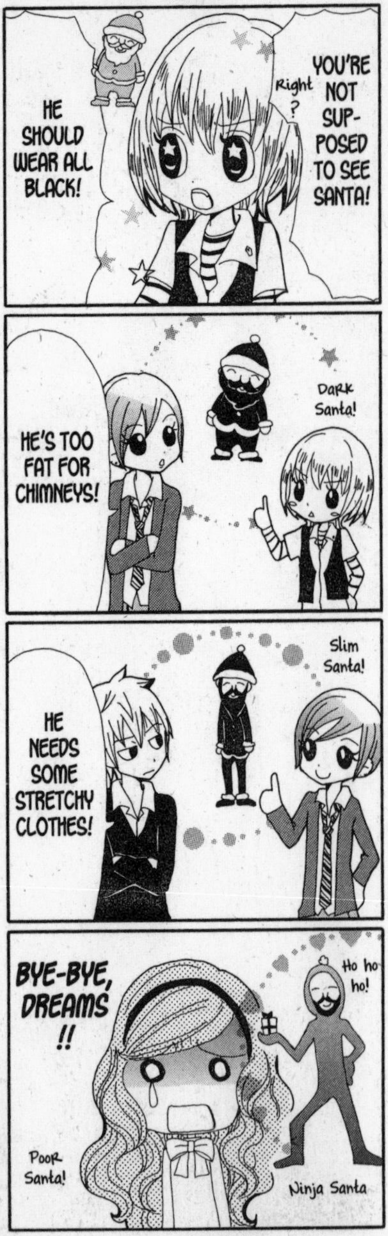
YOU'RE NOT SUP-POSED TO SEE SANTA!
Right?
HE SHOULD WEAR ALL BLACK!
Dark Santa!
HE'S TOO FAT FOR CHIMNEYS!
Slim Santa!
HE NEEDS SOME STRETCHY CLOTHES!
Ho ho ho!
BYE-BYE, DREAMS!!
Ninja Santa
Poor Santa!

☆ December 21 ☆

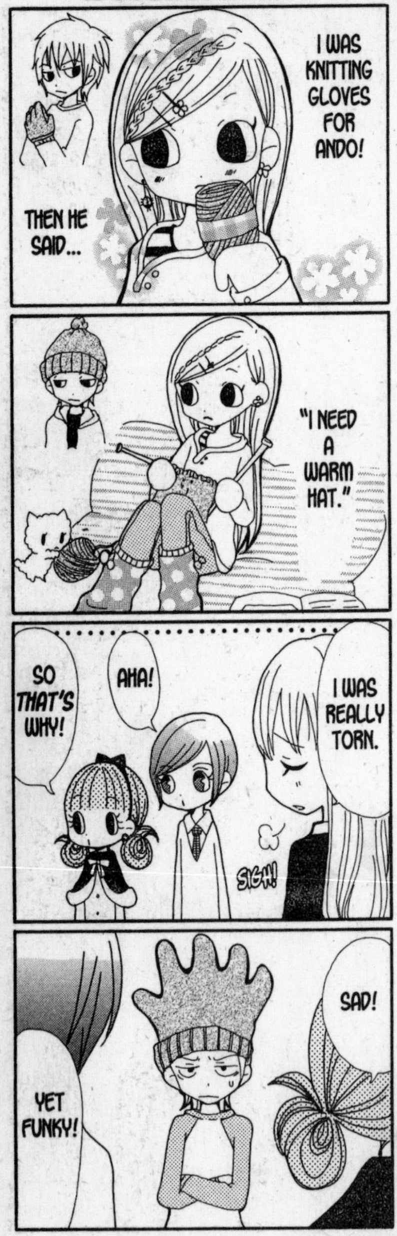
I WAS KNITTING GLOVES FOR ANDO!
THEN HE SAID...
"I NEED A WARM HAT."
I WAS REALLY TORN.
SIGH!
AHA!
SO THAT'S WHY!
SAD!
YET FUNKY!

☆ December 22 ☆

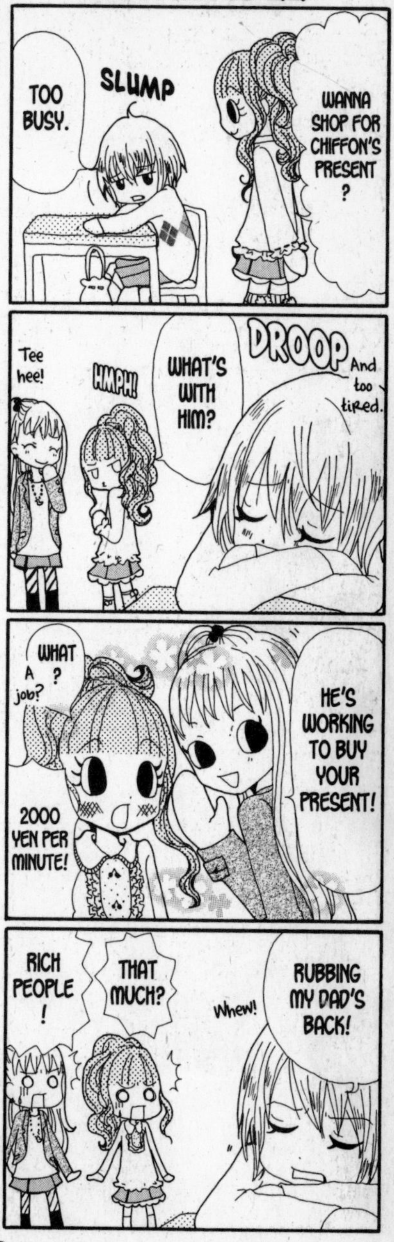
WANNA SHOP FOR CHIFFON'S PRESENT?
SLUMP
TOO BUSY.
DROOP
And too tired.
WHAT'S WITH HIM?
HMPH!
Tee hee!
HE'S WORKING TO BUY YOUR PRESENT!
WHAT ?
A job?
2000 YEN PER MINUTE!
RUBBING MY DAD'S BACK!
Whew!
THAT MUCH?
RICH PEOPLE!

☆ Serious ☆

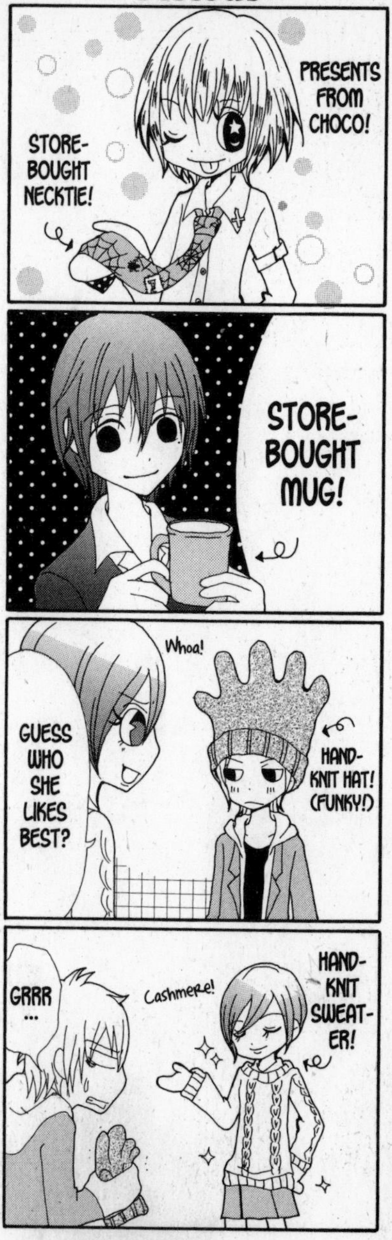
PRESENTS FROM CHOCO!
STORE-BOUGHT NECKTIE!
STORE-BOUGHT MUG!
HAND-KNIT HAT! (FUNKY!)
Whoa!
GUESS WHO SHE LIKES BEST?
HAND-KNIT SWEATER!
Cashmere!
GRRR...

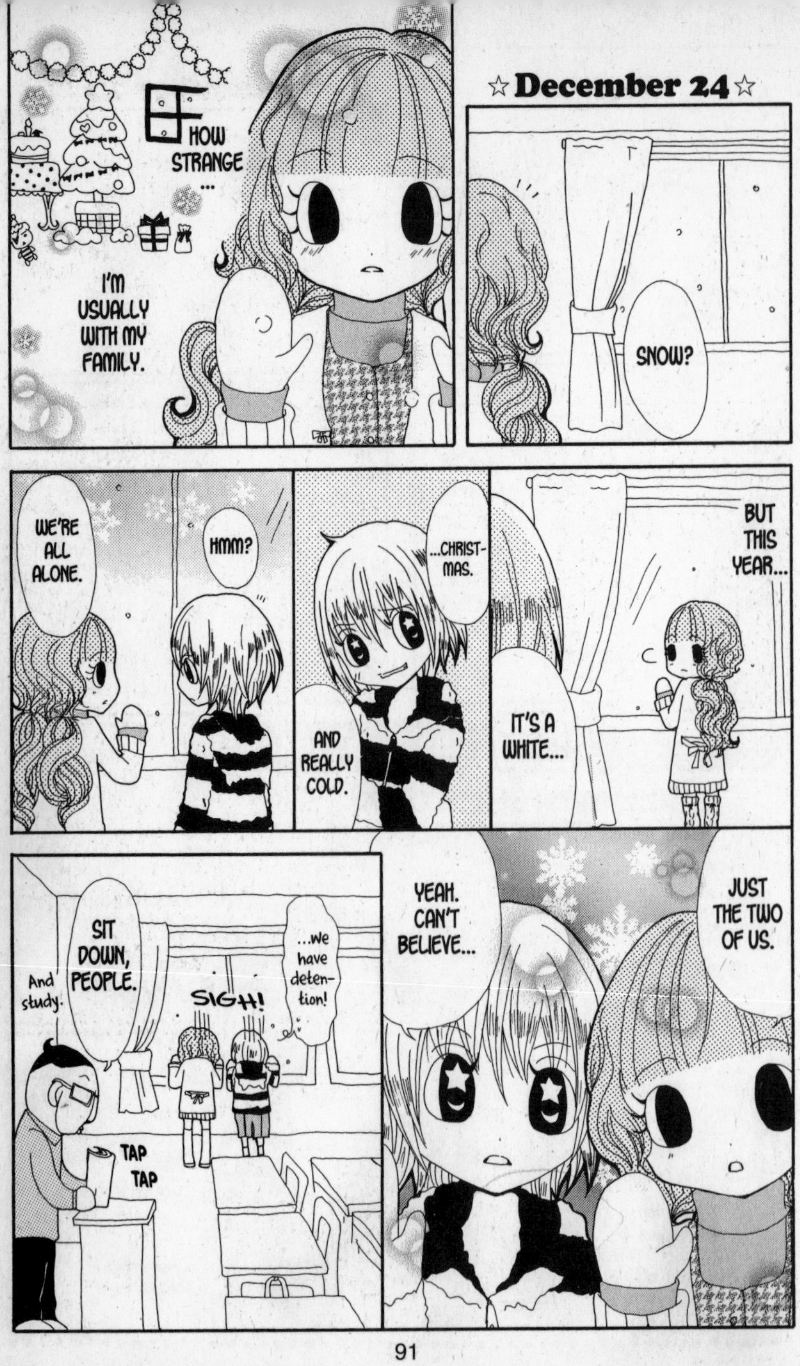
☆December 24☆
SNOW?
HOW STRANGE...
I'M USUALLY WITH MY FAMILY.
BUT THIS YEAR...
IT'S A WHITE...
...CHRISTMAS.
AND REALLY COLD.
HMM?
WE'RE ALL ALONE.
JUST THE TWO OF US.
YEAH. CAN'T BELIEVE...
...we have detention!
SIGH!
SIT DOWN, PEOPLE.
And study.
TAP TAP

☆Good Kid☆

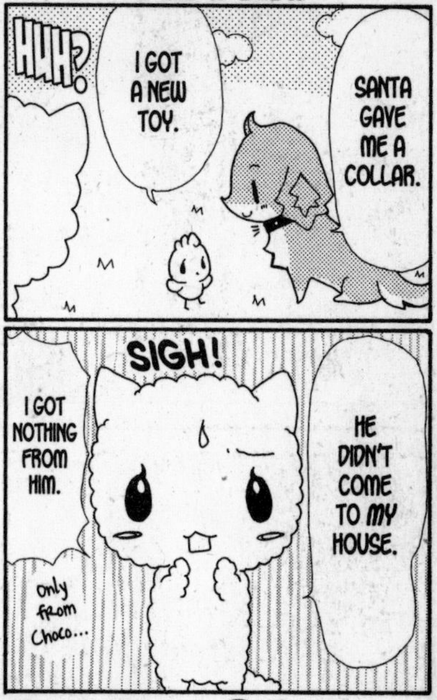
SANTA GAVE ME A COLLAR.
I GOT A NEW TOY.
HUH?
HE DIDN'T COME TO MY HOUSE.
I GOT NOTHING FROM HIM.
SIGH!
Only from Choco...

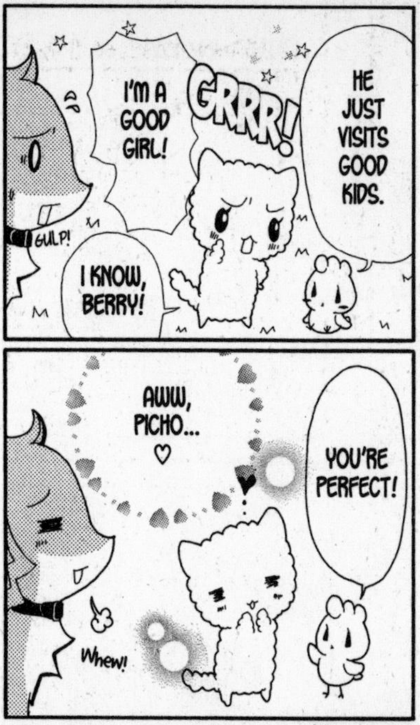
HE JUST VISITS GOOD KIDS.
GRRR!
I'M A GOOD GIRL!
GULP!
I KNOW, BERRY!
YOU'RE PERFECT!
AWW, PICHO... ♡
Whew!

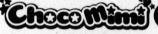

ChocoMimi Fashion Notes

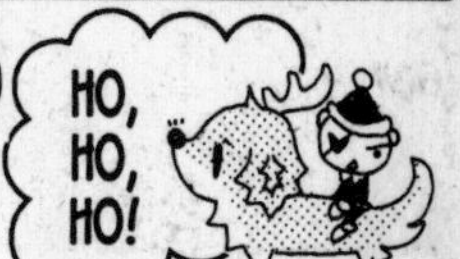
HO, HO, HO!

DRESS HAPPY FOR THE HOLIDAYS!
CHOCOMIMI ♥ STYLE!

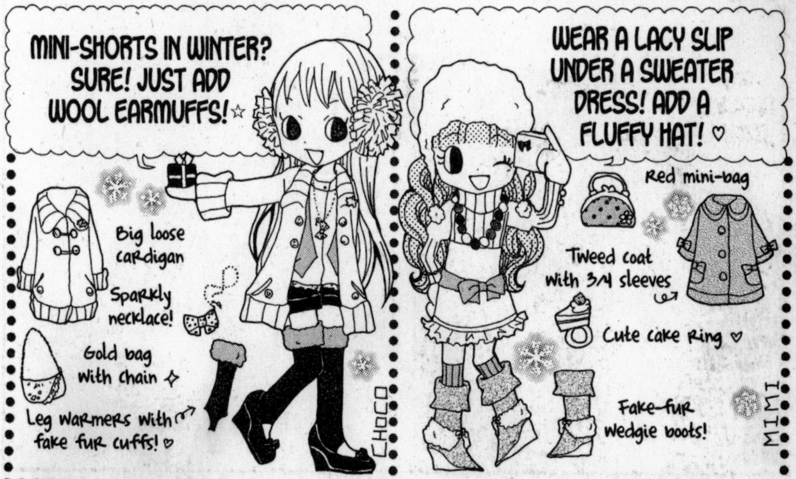
WEAR A LACY SLIP UNDER A SWEATER DRESS! ADD A FLUFFY HAT! ♡
Red mini-bag
Tweed coat with 3/4 sleeves
Cute cake Ring ♡
Fake-fur wedgie boots!
MIMI
MINI-SHORTS IN WINTER? SURE! JUST ADD WOOL EARMUFFS! ☆
Big loose cardigan
Sparkly necklace!
Gold bag with chain ✧
Leg warmers with fake fur cuffs! ♡
CHOCO

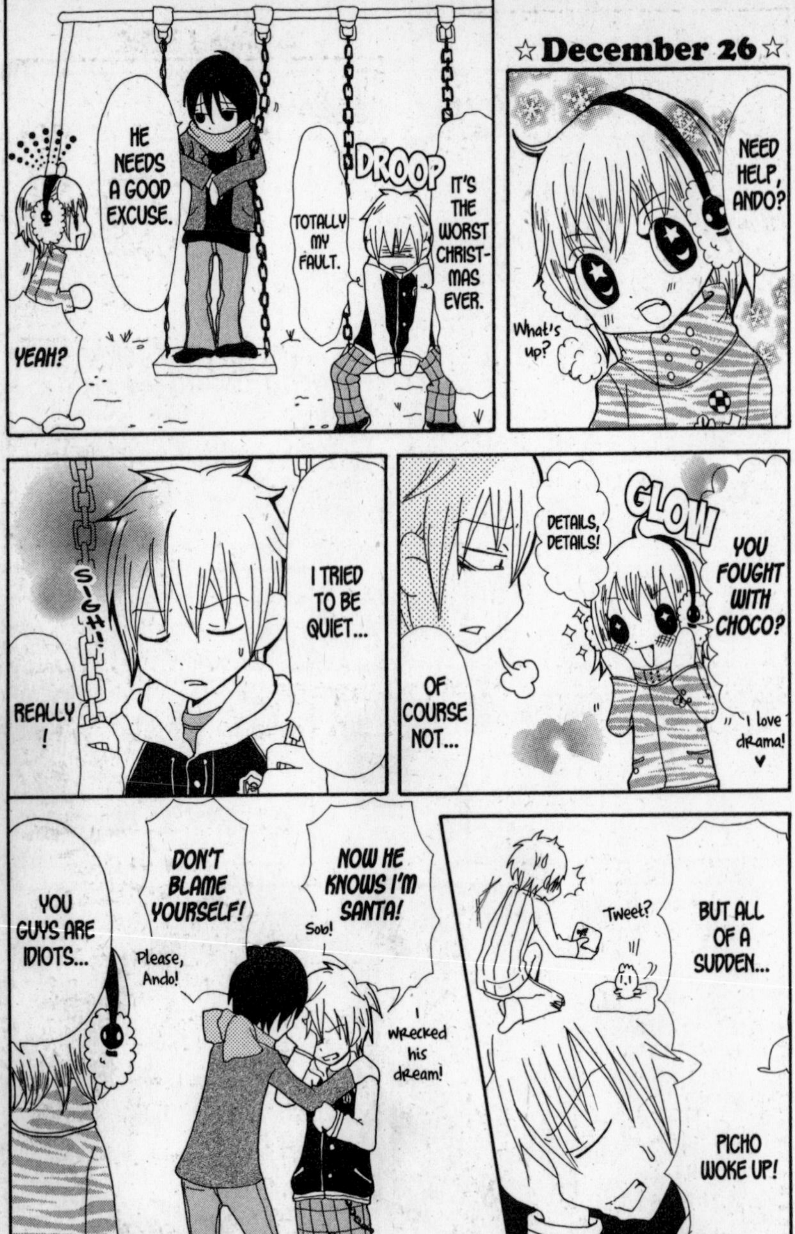
☆December 26☆
NEED HELP, ANDO?
What's up?
IT'S THE WORST CHRISTMAS EVER.
DROOP
TOTALLY MY FAULT.
HE NEEDS A GOOD EXCUSE.
YEAH?
YOU FOUGHT WITH CHOCO?
GLOW
I love drama!
DETAILS, DETAILS!
OF COURSE NOT...
I TRIED TO BE QUIET...
SIGH!
REALLY!
BUT ALL OF A SUDDEN...
Tweet?
PICHO WOKE UP!
NOW HE KNOWS I'M SANTA!
Sob!
I wrecked his dream!
DON'T BLAME YOURSELF!
Please, Ando!
YOU GUYS ARE IDIOTS...

☆Christmas Present☆

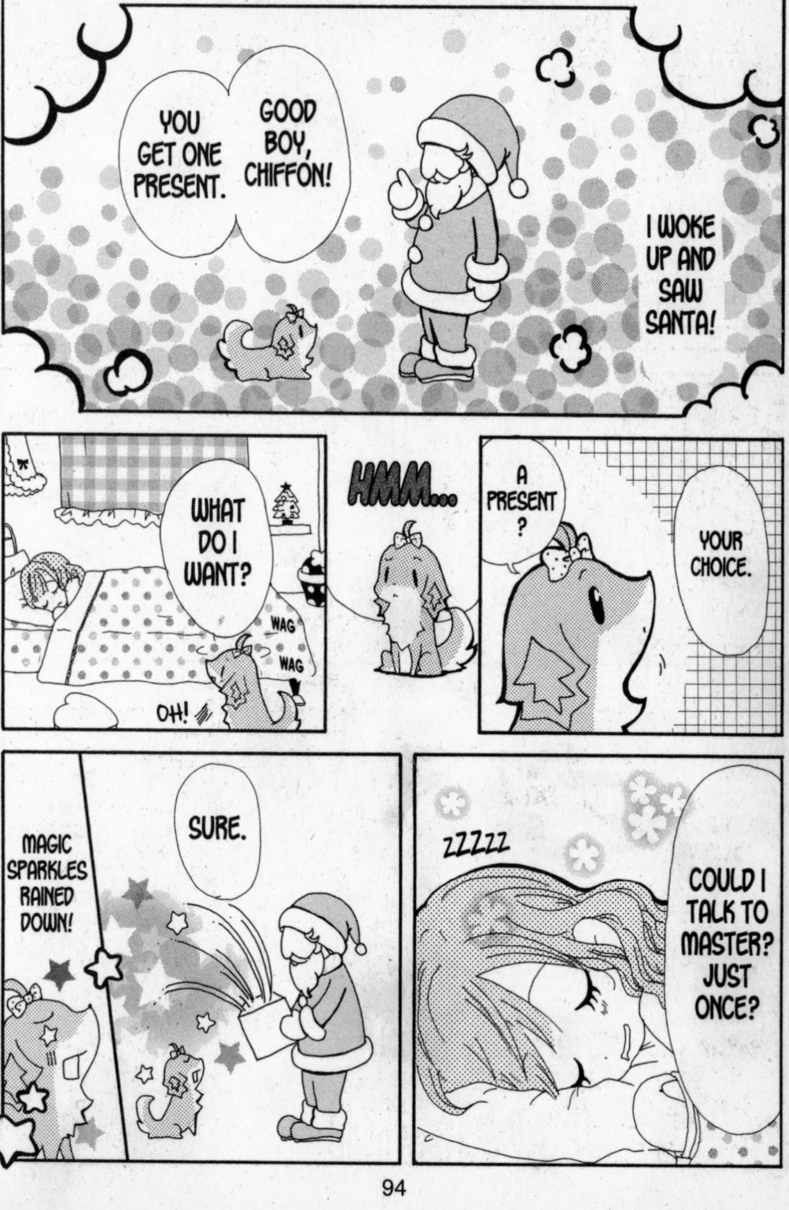
I WOKE UP AND SAW SANTA!
GOOD BOY, CHIFFON!
YOU GET ONE PRESENT.
YOUR CHOICE.
A PRESENT?
HMM...
WHAT DO I WANT?
WAG
WAG
OH!
COULD I TALK TO MASTER? JUST ONCE?
ZZZZZ
SURE.
MAGIC SPARKLES RAINED DOWN!

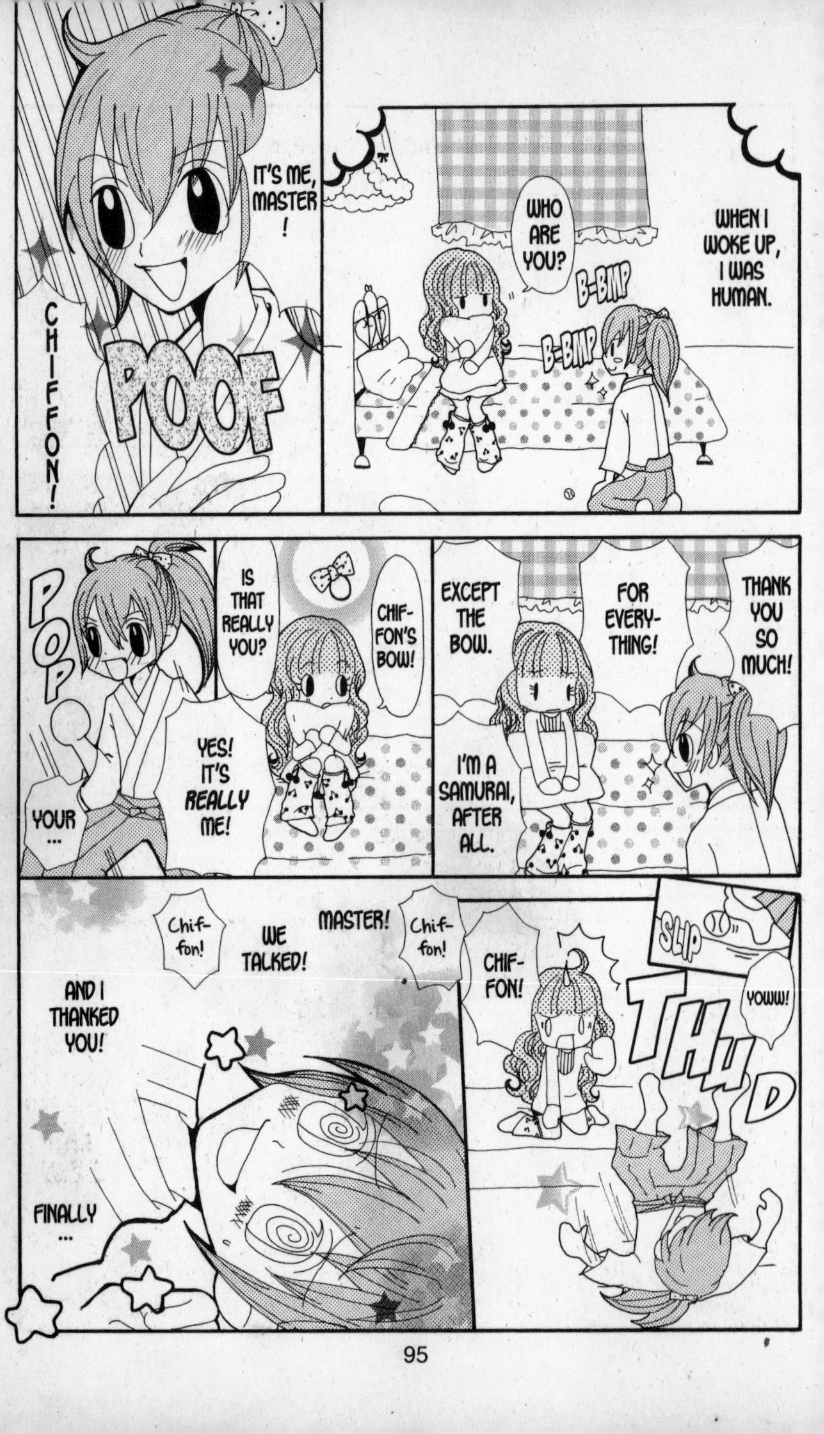
WHEN I WOKE UP, I WAS HUMAN.
WHO ARE YOU?
B-BMP
B-BMP
IT'S ME, MASTER!
CHIFFON!
POOF
THANK YOU SO MUCH!
FOR EVERY-THING!
EXCEPT THE BOW.
I'M A SAMURAI, AFTER ALL.
CHIF-FON'S BOW!
IS THAT REALLY YOU?
YES! IT'S REALLY ME!
POP
YOUR...
SLIP
YOWW!
THUD
CHIF-FON!
Chif-fon!
MASTER!
WE TALKED!
Chif-fon!
AND I THANKED YOU!
FINALLY...

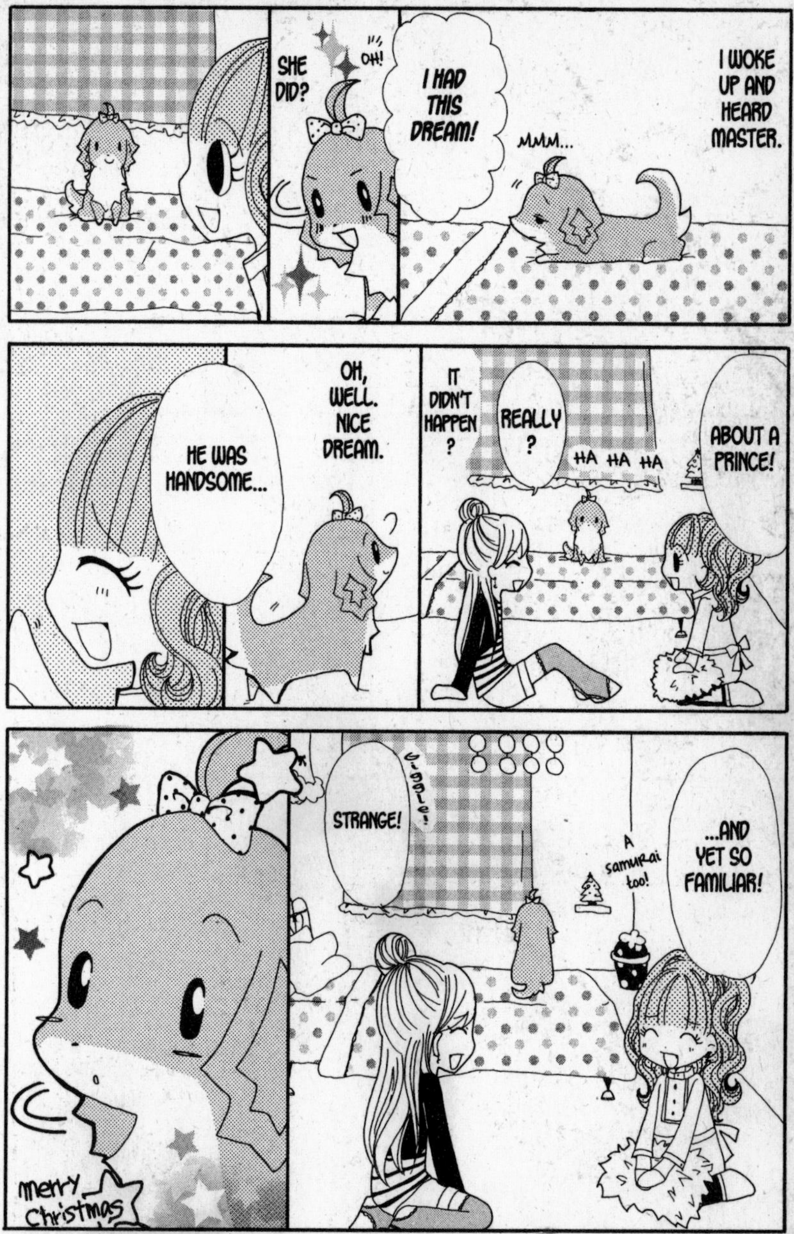
I WOKE UP AND HEARD MASTER.
MMM...
I HAD THIS DREAM!
OH!
SHE DID?
ABOUT A PRINCE!
HA HA HA
REALLY?
IT DIDN'T HAPPEN?
OH, WELL. NICE DREAM.
HE WAS HANDSOME...
...AND YET SO FAMILIAR!
A samurai too!
Giggle!
STRANGE!
merry Christmas

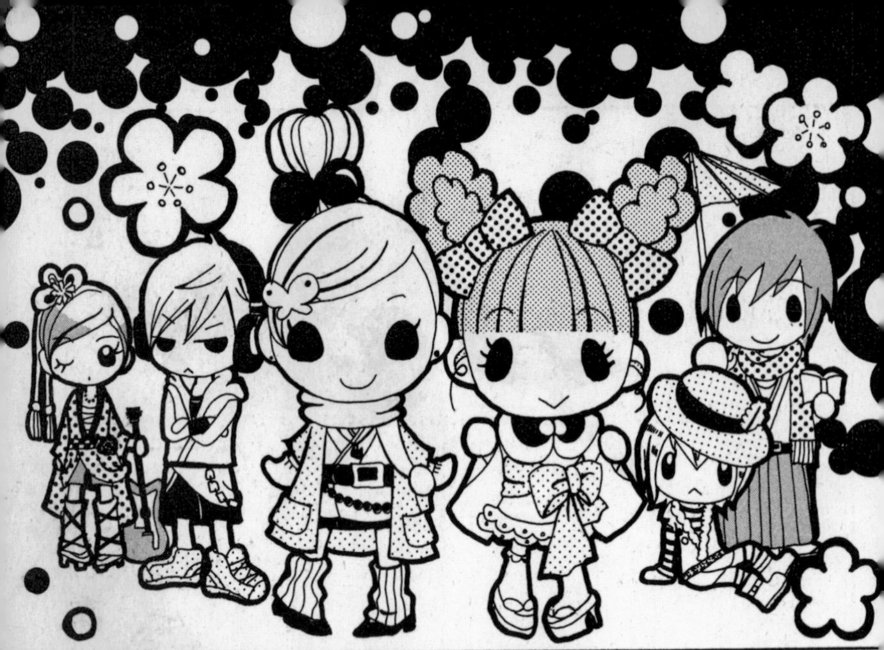

☆ New Year's Cards ☆

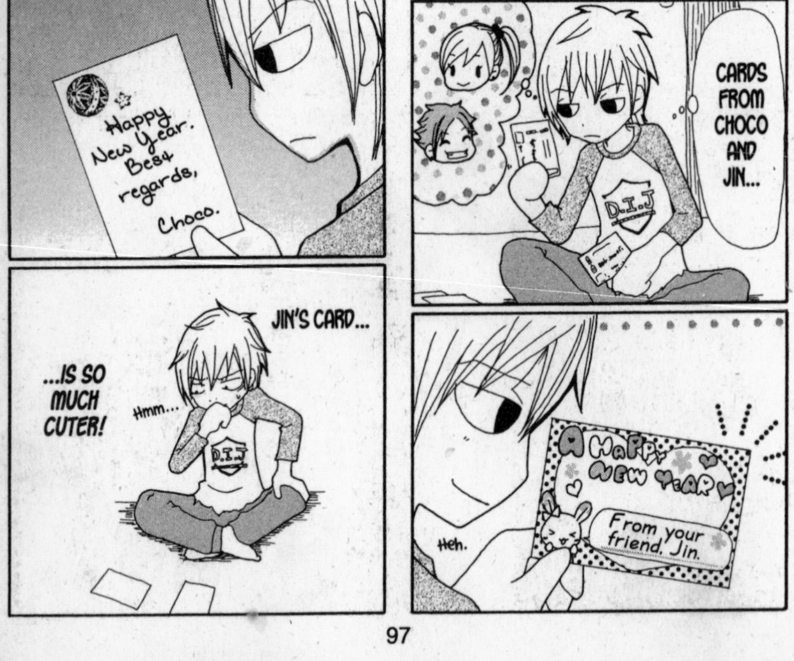

CARDS FROM CHOCO AND JIN...
A HAPPY NEW YEAR
From your friend, Jin.
Heh.
Happy New Year. Best regards, Choco.
JIN'S CARD...
...IS SO MUCH CUTER!
Hmm...

☆ Charms ☆

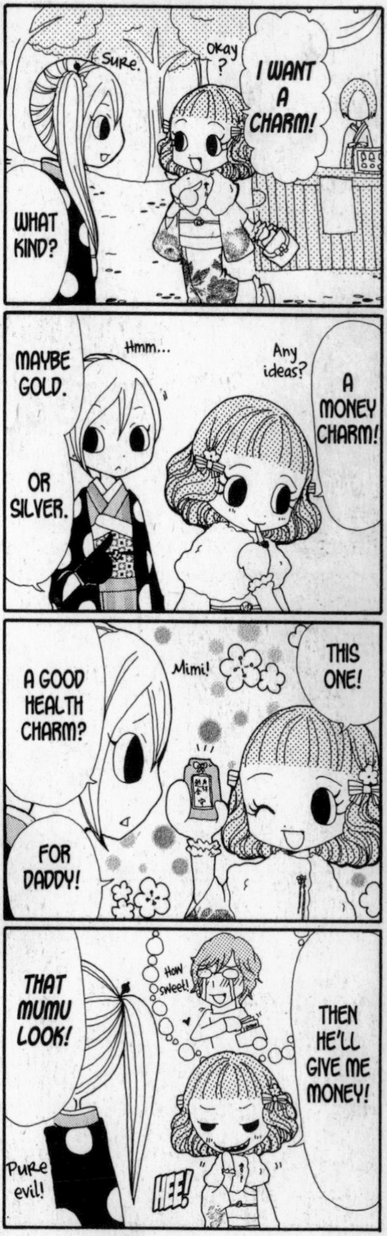
I WANT A CHARM!
Okay ?
Sure.
WHAT KIND?
A MONEY CHARM!
Any ideas?
Hmm...
MAYBE GOLD.
OR SILVER.
THIS ONE!
Mimi!
A GOOD HEALTH CHARM?
FOR DADDY!
THEN HE'LL GIVE ME MONEY!
How sweet!
THAT MUMU LOOK!
HEE!
Pure evil!

☆ Wishes ☆

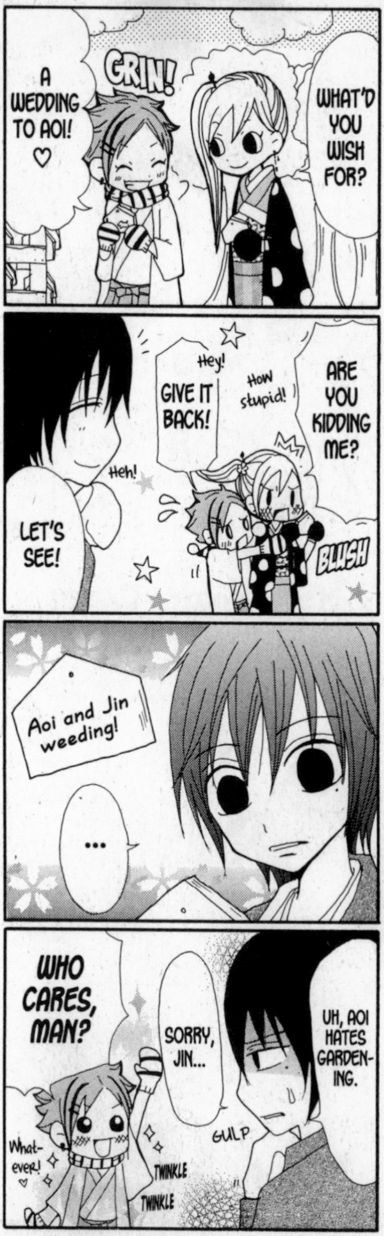
WHAT'D YOU WISH FOR?
GRIN!
A WEDDING TO AOI! ♡
ARE YOU KIDDING ME?
How stupid!
Hey!
GIVE IT BACK!
BLUSH
Heh!
LET'S SEE!
Aoi and Jin weeding!
...
UH, AOI HATES GARDEN-ING.
SORRY, JIN...
GULP
WHO CARES, MAN?
TWINKLE
TWINKLE
What-ever!

☆ Interest ☆

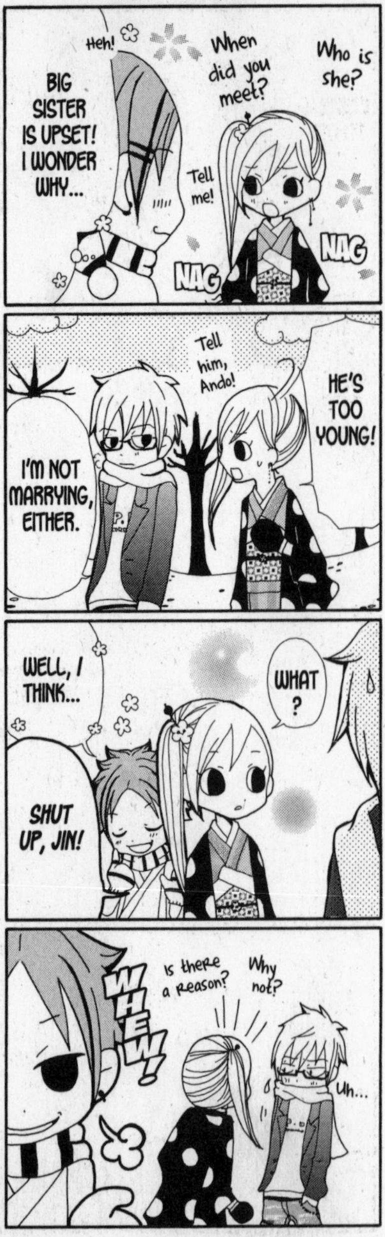

Who is she?
When did you meet?
Heh!
BIG SISTER IS UPSET! I WONDER WHY...
Tell me!
NAG
NAG
HE'S TOO YOUNG!
Tell him, Ando!
I'M NOT MARRYING, EITHER.
WHAT?
WELL, I THINK...
SHUT UP, JIN!
Uh...
Why not?
Is there a reason?
WHEW!

☆ Man ☆

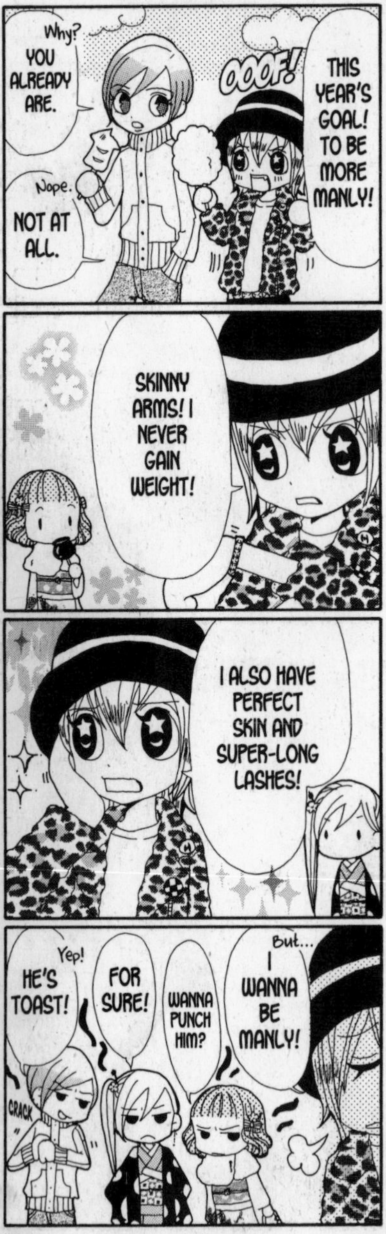

THIS YEAR'S GOAL! TO BE MORE MANLY!
OOOF!
Why?
YOU ALREADY ARE.
Nope.
NOT AT ALL.
SKINNY ARMS! I NEVER GAIN WEIGHT!
I ALSO HAVE PERFECT SKIN AND SUPER-LONG LASHES!
But...
I WANNA BE MANLY!
WANNA PUNCH HIM?
FOR SURE!
Yep!
HE'S TOAST!
CRACK

☆More Wishes☆

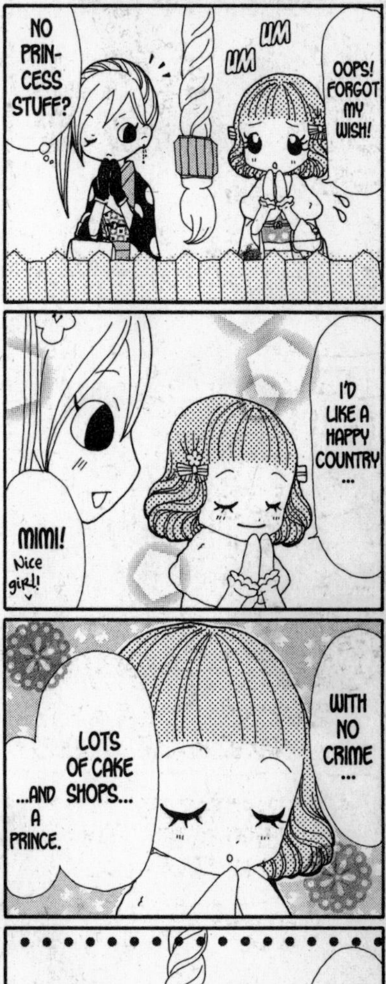
OOPS! FORGOT MY WISH!
UM UM
NO PRINCESS STUFF?
I'D LIKE A HAPPY COUNTRY...
MIMI!
Nice girl!
WITH NO CRIME...
LOTS OF CAKE SHOPS...
...AND A PRINCE.
I'M THE PRINCESS.
SAME OLD, SAME OLD.

☆Adult☆

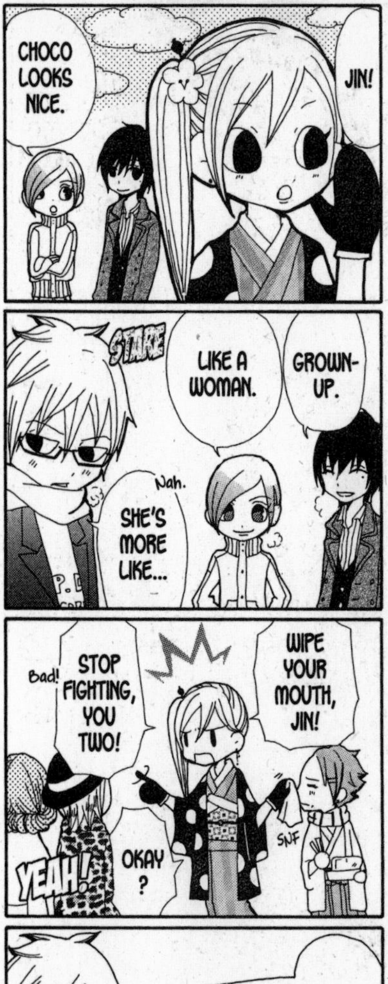
JIN!
CHOCO LOOKS NICE.
GROWN-UP.
LIKE A WOMAN.
STARE
Nah.
SHE'S MORE LIKE...
WIPE YOUR MOUTH, JIN!
STOP FIGHTING, YOU TWO!
Bad!
SNF
OKAY?
YEAH!
...A MOTHER.
Oh!
Bingo!

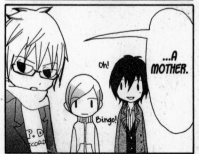

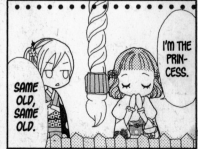

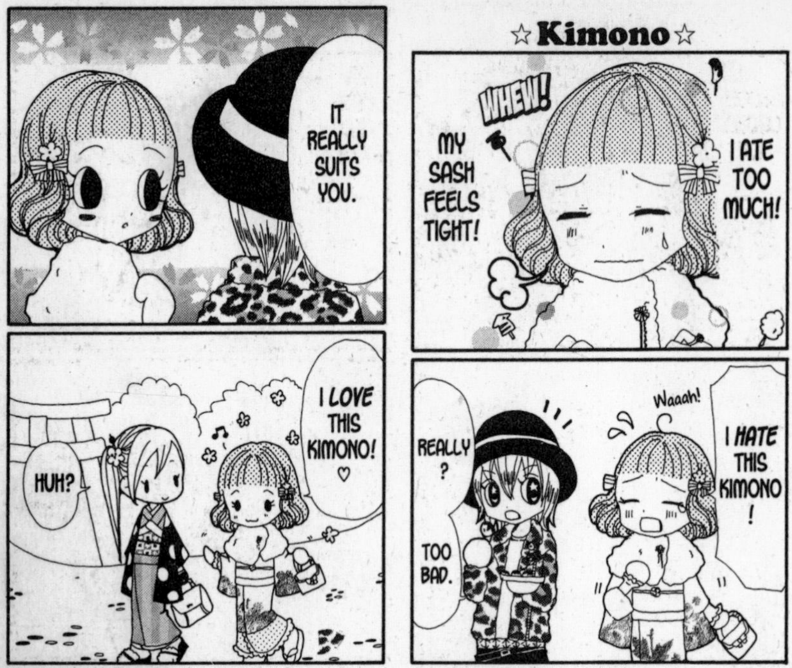
☆Kimono☆
WHEW!
I ATE TOO MUCH!
MY SASH FEELS TIGHT!
IT REALLY SUITS YOU.
Waaah!
I HATE THIS KIMONO!
REALLY?
TOO BAD.
I LOVE THIS KIMONO! ♡
HUH?

Choco Mimi Fashion Notes

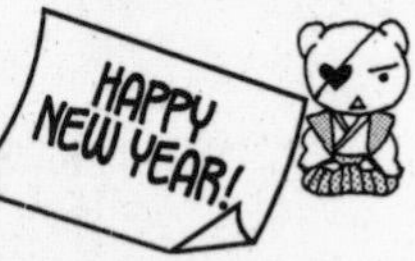
HAPPY NEW YEAR!

RING IN THE NEW YEAR IN A LOVELY KIMONO! ♡
ADD YOUR OWN SPECIAL TOUCHES!

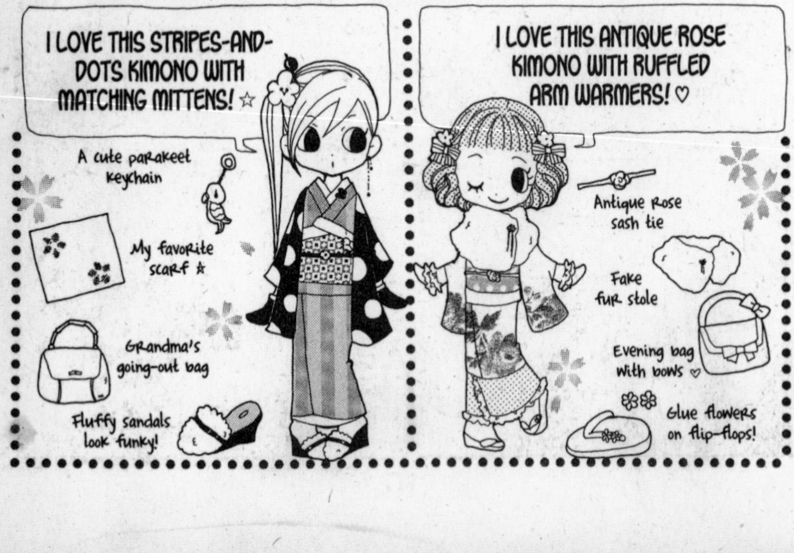
I LOVE THIS STRIPES-AND-DOTS KIMONO WITH MATCHING MITTENS! ☆
A cute parakeet keychain
My favorite scarf ☆
Grandma's going-out bag
Fluffy sandals look funky!
I LOVE THIS ANTIQUE ROSE KIMONO WITH RUFFLED ARM WARMERS! ♡
Antique rose sash tie
Fake fur stole
Evening bag with bows ♡
Glue flowers on flip-flops!

☆**Dress-up**☆

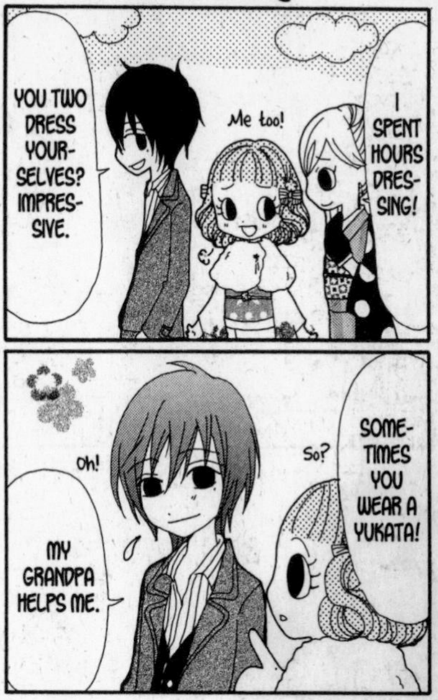
I SPENT HOURS DRESSING!
Me too!
YOU TWO DRESS YOURSELVES? IMPRESSIVE.
SOMETIMES YOU WEAR A YUKATA!
So?
Oh!
MY GRANDPA HELPS ME.

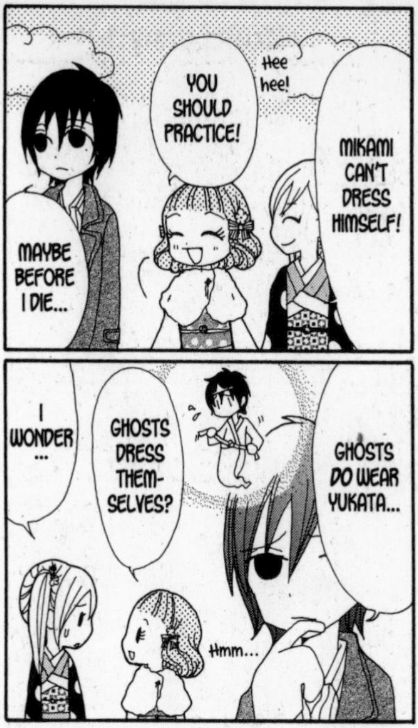
MIKAMI CAN'T DRESS HIMSELF!
Hee hee!
YOU SHOULD PRACTICE!
MAYBE BEFORE I DIE...
GHOSTS DO WEAR YUKATA...
GHOSTS DRESS THEMSELVES?
I WONDER...
Hmm...

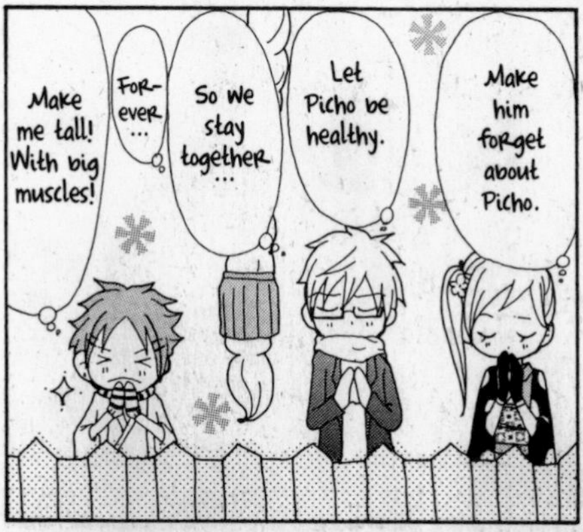
Make him forget about Picho.
Let Picho be healthy.
So we stay together...
Forever...
Make me tall! With big muscles!

☆ Calligraphy ☆

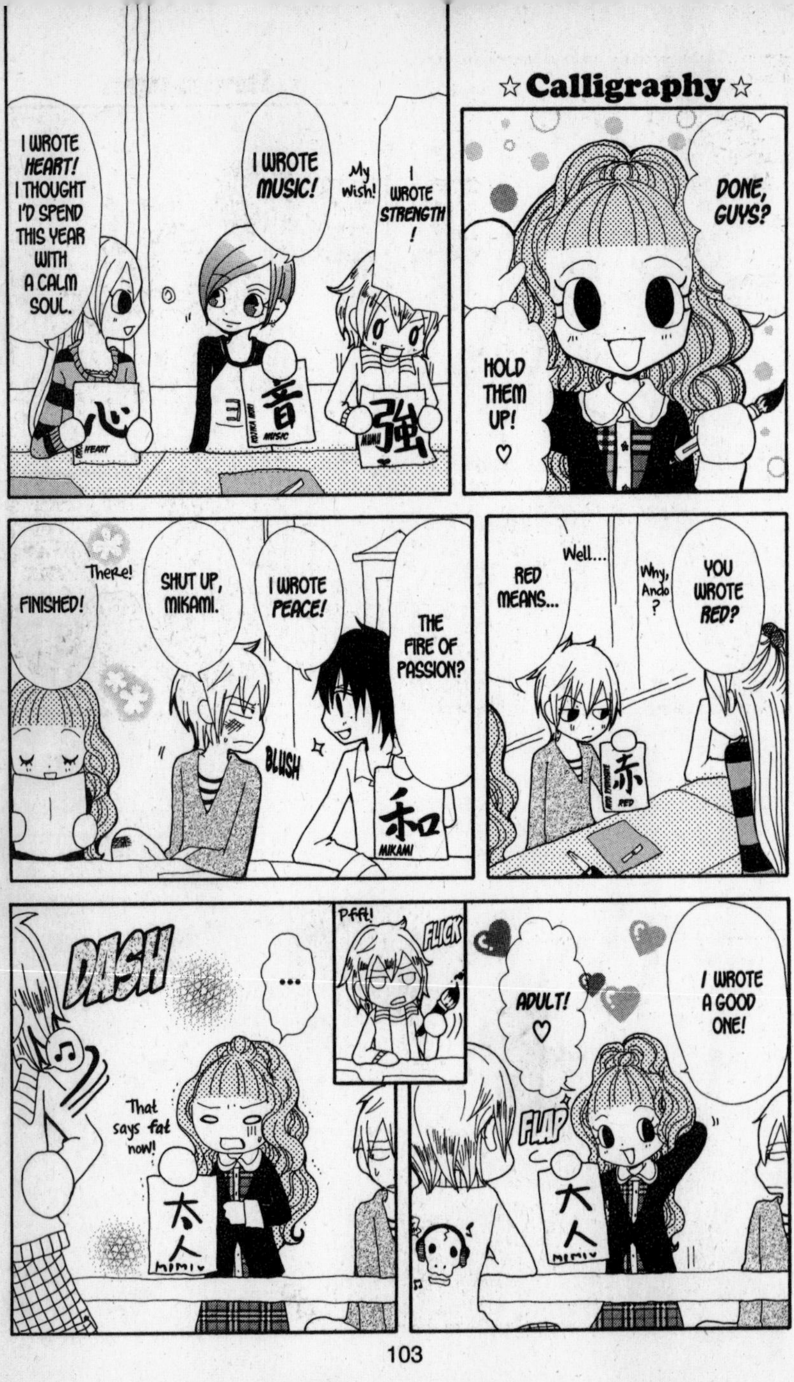

DONE, GUYS?
HOLD THEM UP! ♡
I WROTE STRENGTH!
My Wish!
I WROTE MUSIC!
I WROTE HEART! I THOUGHT I'D SPEND THIS YEAR WITH A CALM SOUL.
YOU WROTE RED?
Why, Ando?
Well...
RED MEANS...
THE FIRE OF PASSION?
I WROTE PEACE!
SHUT UP, MIKAMI.
BLUSH
There!
FINISHED!
I WROTE A GOOD ONE!
ADULT! ♡
FLAP
FLICK
Pfft!
...
DASH
That says fat now!

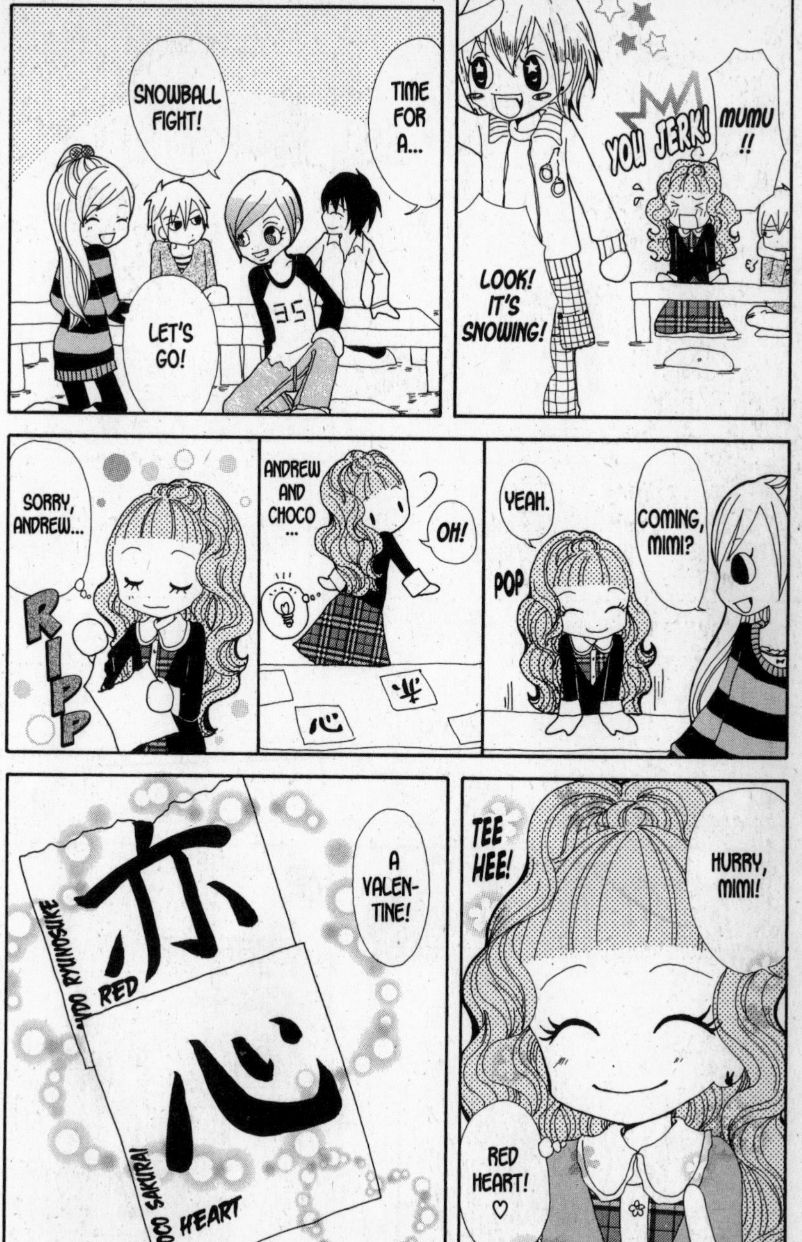
YOU JERK!
MUMU !!
LOOK! IT'S SNOWING!
TIME FOR A...
SNOWBALL FIGHT!
LET'S GO!
COMING, MIMI?
YEAH.
POP
ANDREW AND CHOCO ...
OH!
SORRY, ANDREW...
RIPP
HURRY, MIMI!
TEE HEE!
RED HEART! ♡
A VALEN-TINE!
RYUNOSUKE
RED
心
CHOCO SAKURAI
HEART

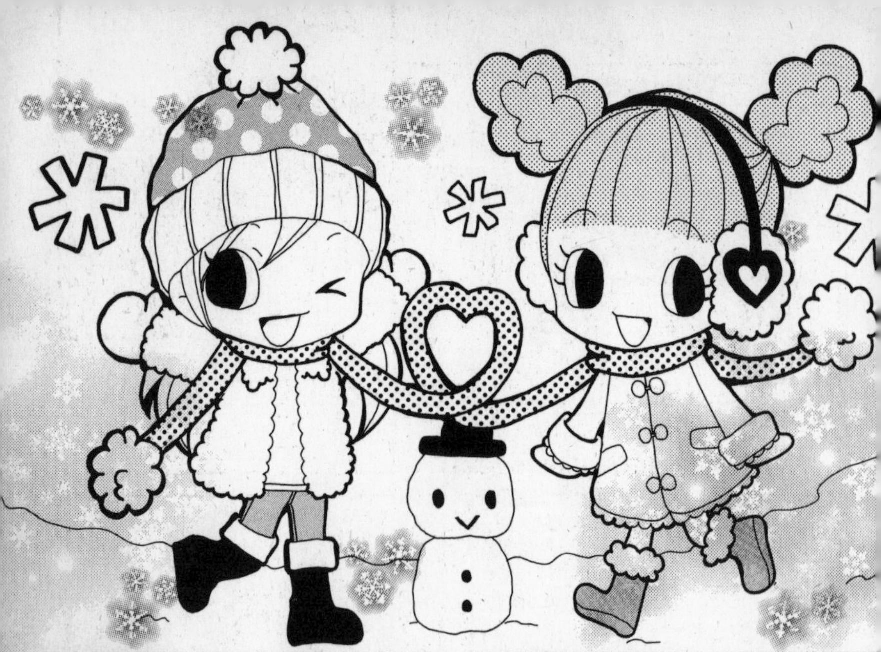

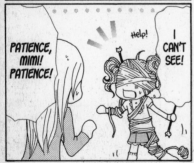

☆**Knitting**☆

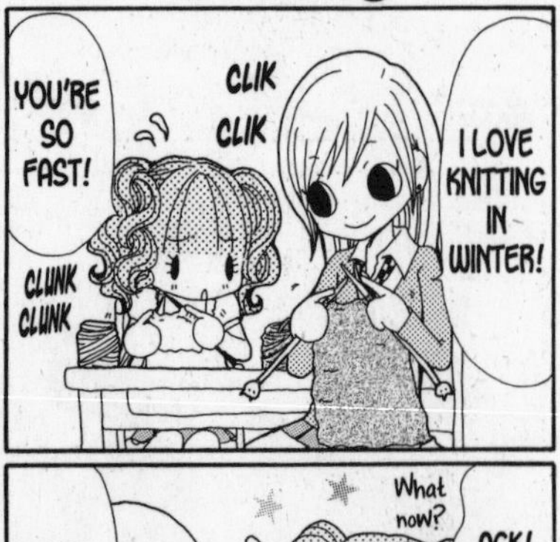
I LOVE KNITTING IN WINTER!
CLIK CLIK
YOU'RE SO FAST!
CLUNK CLUNK
ACK! WHAT A MESS!
What now?
JUST UN-TANGLE IT.

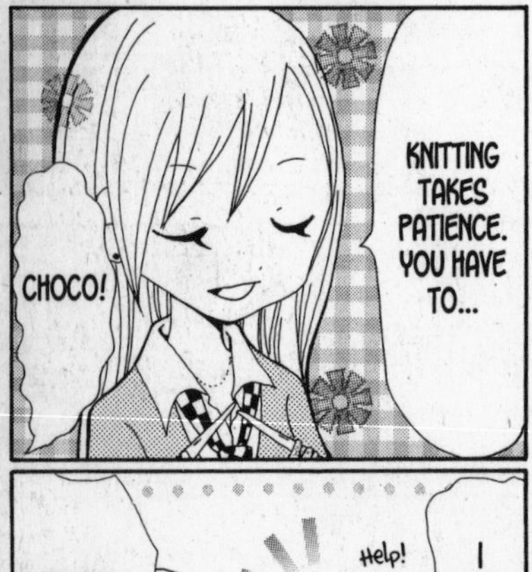
KNITTING TAKES PATIENCE. YOU HAVE TO...
CHOCO!
I CAN'T SEE!
Help!
PATIENCE, MIMI! PATIENCE!

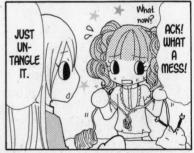

☆ Wish ☆

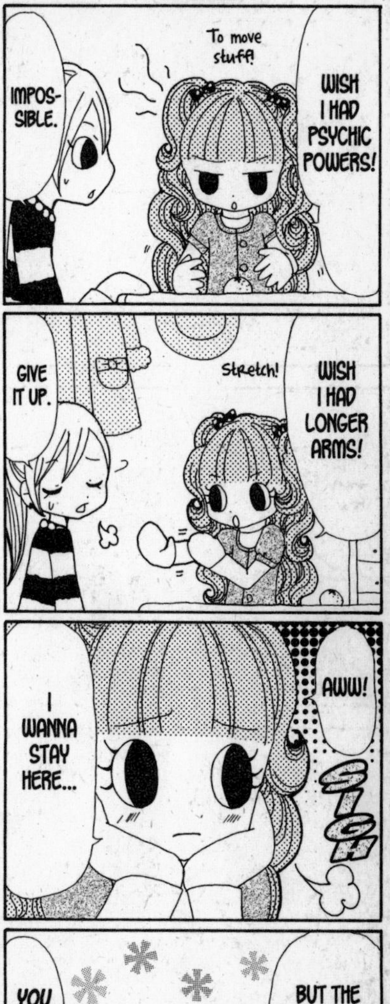
WISH I HAD PSYCHIC POWERS!
To move stuff!
IMPOSSIBLE.
WISH I HAD LONGER ARMS!
Stretch!
GIVE IT UP.
AWW!
SIGH
I WANNA STAY HERE...
BUT THE SNACKS ARE OVER THERE!
YOU LAZY BUM.
Move, Mimi! Move!

☆ Winter ☆

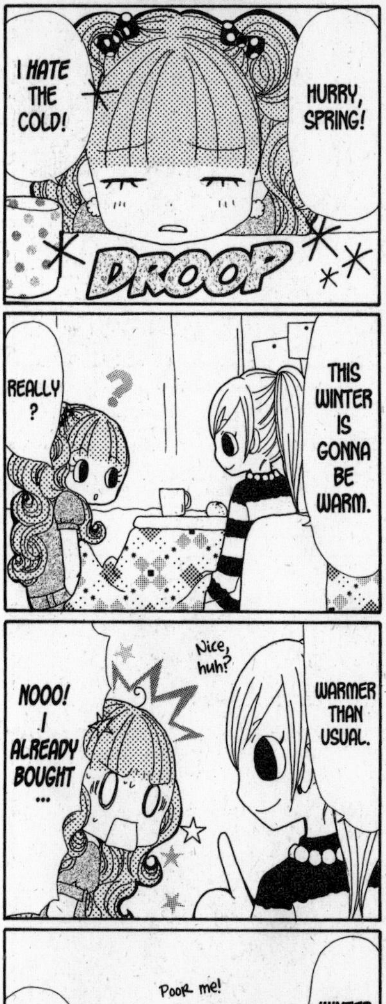
HURRY, SPRING!
I HATE THE COLD!
DROOP
THIS WINTER IS GONNA BE WARM.
REALLY?
WARMER THAN USUAL.
Nice, huh?
NOOO! I ALREADY BOUGHT...
WINTER CLOTHES!
Poor me!
WARMER, MIMI! NOT HOT!

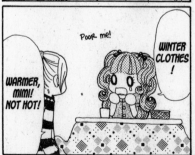

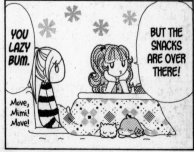

☆Sorry to Bother You☆

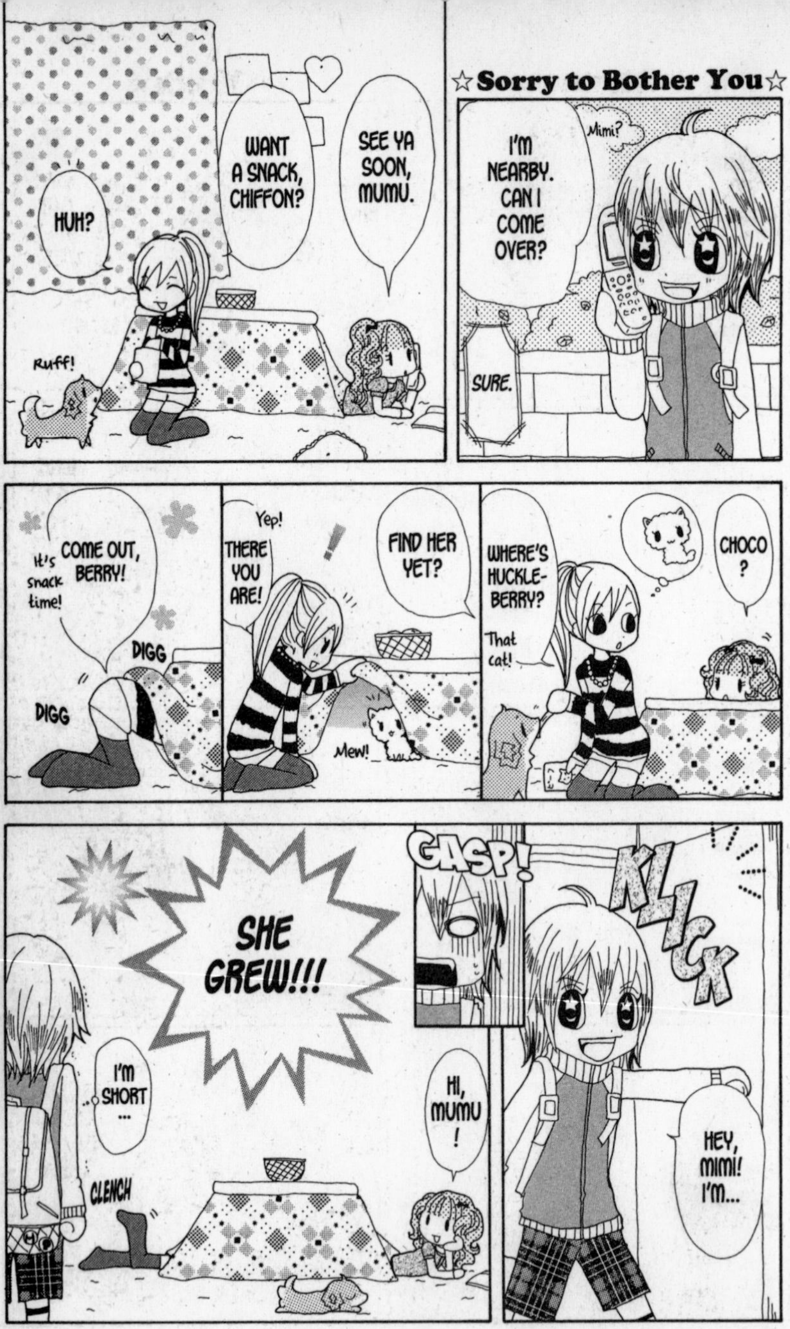
Mimi?
I'M NEARBY. CAN I COME OVER?
SURE.
SEE YA SOON, MUMU.
WANT A SNACK, CHIFFON?
HUH?
Ruff!
CHOCO?
WHERE'S HUCKLE-BERRY?
That cat!
FIND HER YET?
Yep!
THERE YOU ARE!
Mew!
COME OUT, BERRY!
It's snack time!
DIGG
DIGG
KLICK
HEY, MIMI! I'M...
GASP!
HI, MUMU!
SHE GREW!!!
I'M SHORT...
CLENCH

☆ Outside ☆

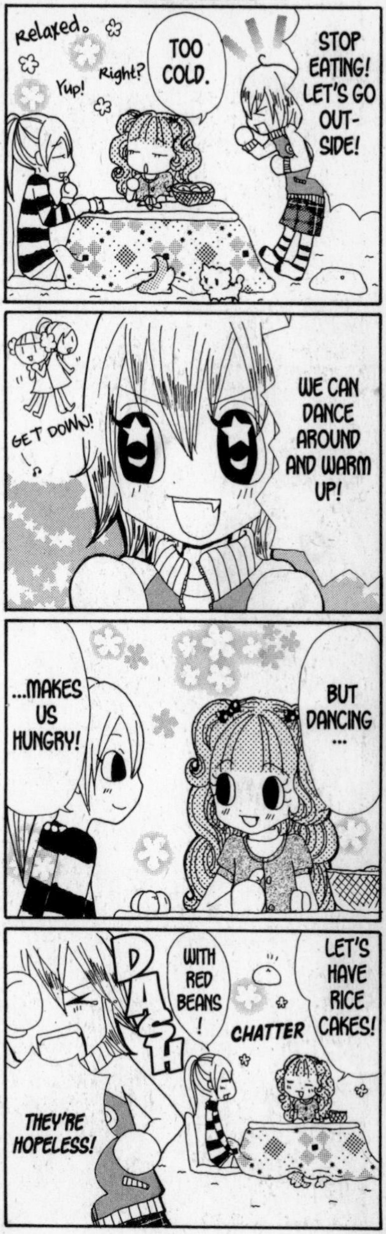
STOP EATING! LET'S GO OUT-SIDE!
TOO COLD.
Right?
Yup!
Relaxed.
WE CAN DANCE AROUND AND WARM UP!
GET DOWN!
BUT DANCING ...
...MAKES US HUNGRY!
LET'S HAVE RICE CAKES!
CHATTER
WITH RED BEANS!
DASH
THEY'RE HOPELESS!

☆ Snacks ☆

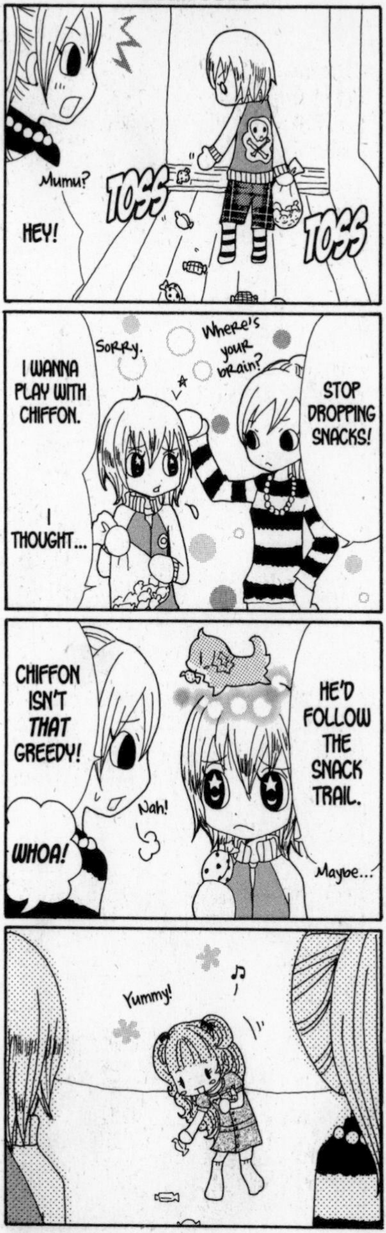
TOSS
TOSS
Mumu?
HEY!
STOP DROPPING SNACKS!
Where's your brain?
Sorry.
I WANNA PLAY WITH CHIFFON.
I THOUGHT...
HE'D FOLLOW THE SNACK TRAIL.
Maybe...
Nah!
CHIFFON ISN'T THAT GREEDY!
WHOA!
Yummy!

☆Going Out☆

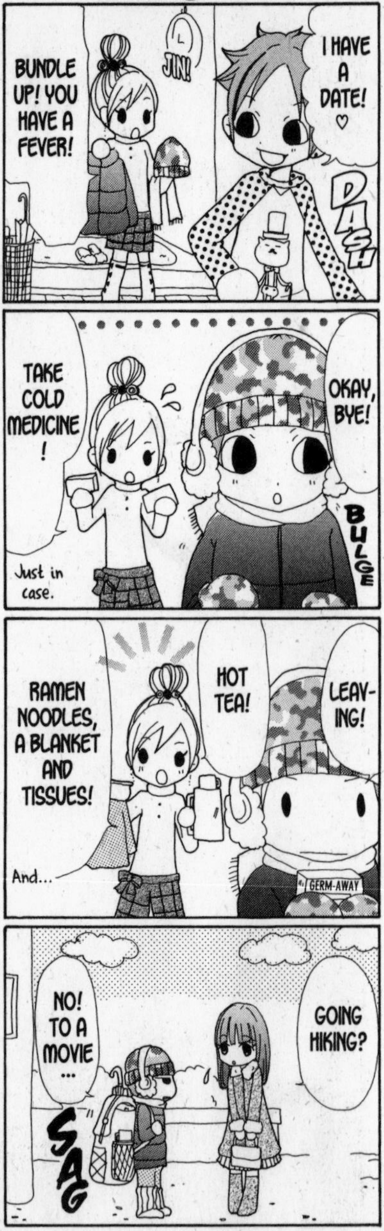
I HAVE A DATE! ♡
JIN!
BUNDLE UP! YOU HAVE A FEVER!
DASH
OKAY, BYE!
TAKE COLD MEDICINE!
BULGE
Just in case.
LEAV-ING!
HOT TEA!
RAMEN NOODLES, A BLANKET AND TISSUES!
GERM-AWAY
And...
GOING HIKING?
NO! TO A MOVIE...
SAG

☆Scarf☆

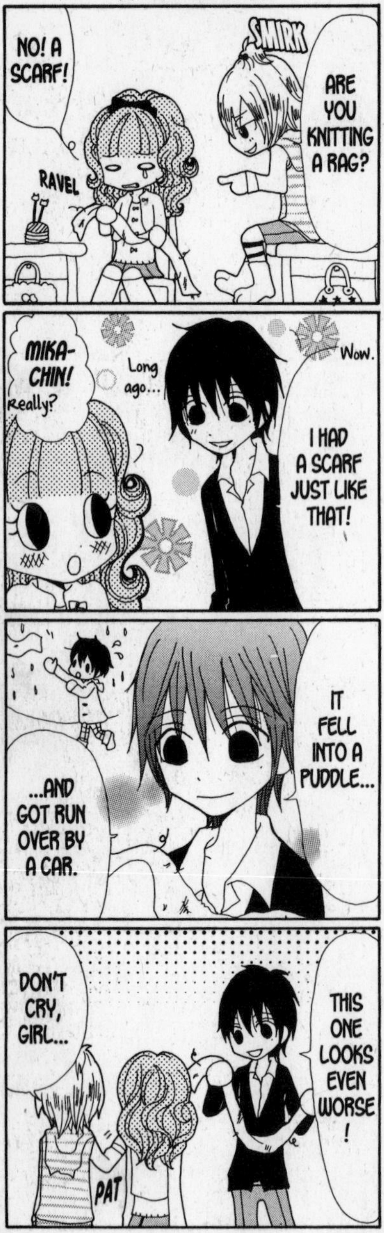
SMIRK
ARE YOU KNITTING A RAG?
NO! A SCARF!
RAVEL
Wow.
I HAD A SCARF JUST LIKE THAT!
Long ago...
MIKA-CHIN!
Really?
IT FELL INTO A PUDDLE...
...AND GOT RUN OVER BY A CAR.
THIS ONE LOOKS EVEN WORSE!
DON'T CRY, GIRL...
PAT

☆ Fur ☆

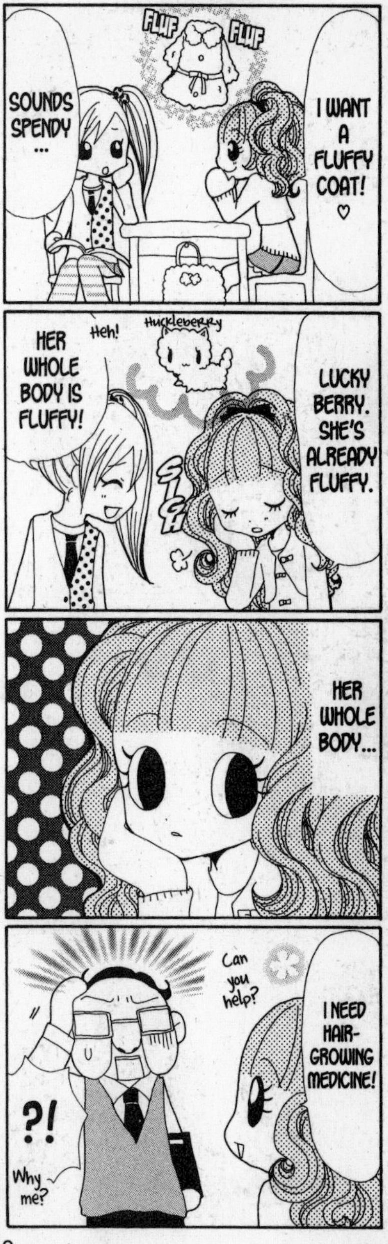
I WANT A FLUFFY COAT! ♡
FLUF
FLUF
SOUNDS SPENDY ...
LUCKY BERRY. SHE'S ALREADY FLUFFY.
Huckleberry
SIGH
Heh!
HER WHOLE BODY IS FLUFFY!
HER WHOLE BODY...
I NEED HAIR-GROWING MEDICINE!
Can you help?
?!
Why me?

☆ The Layered Look ☆

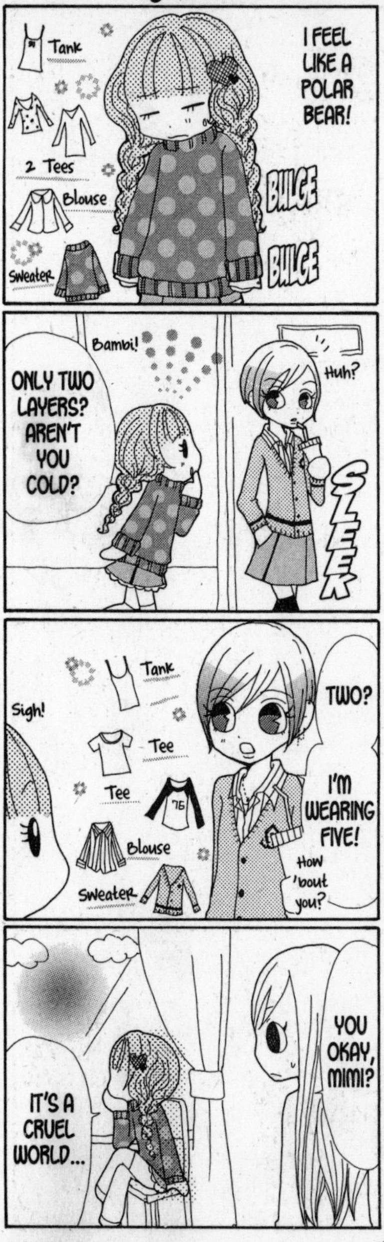
I FEEL LIKE A POLAR BEAR!
BULGE
BULGE
Tank
2 Tees
Blouse
Sweater
Huh?
SLEEK
Bambi!
ONLY TWO LAYERS? AREN'T YOU COLD?
TWO?
I'M WEARING FIVE!
How 'bout you?
Tank
Tee
Tee
Blouse
Sweater
Sigh!
YOU OKAY, MIMI?
IT'S A CRUEL WORLD...

☆ Love ☆ ☆ Squeeze ☆

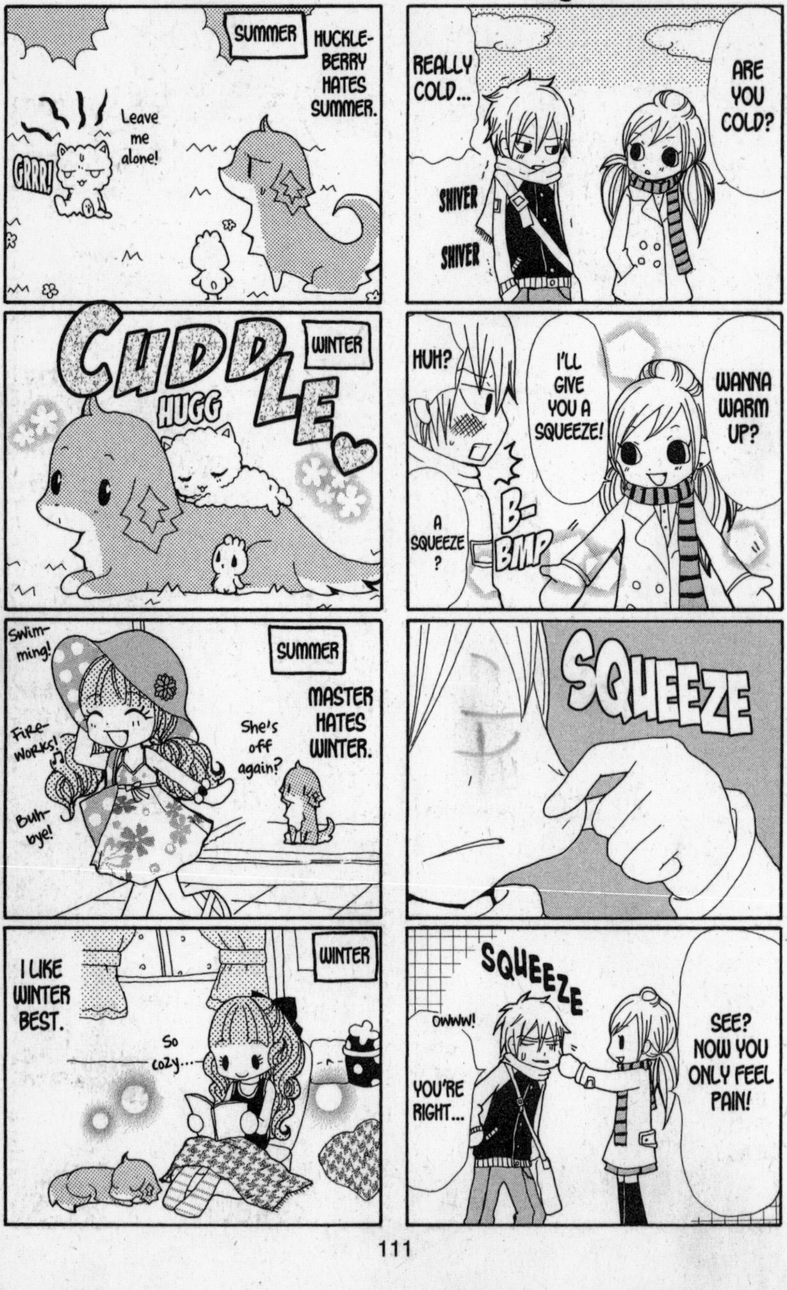
ARE YOU COLD?
REALLY COLD...
SHIVER
SHIVER
WANNA WARM UP?
I'LL GIVE YOU A SQUEEZE!
HUH?
B-BMP
A SQUEEZE?
SQUEEZE
SEE? NOW YOU ONLY FEEL PAIN!
SQUEEZE
OWWW!
YOU'RE RIGHT...
SUMMER
HUCKLE-BERRY HATES SUMMER.
Leave me alone!
GRRR!
WINTER
CUDDLE
HUGG
SUMMER
MASTER HATES WINTER.
She's off again?
Swim-ming!
Fire-works!
Buh-bye!
WINTER
I LIKE WINTER BEST.
So cozy....

☆ A Snow Globe Story ☆

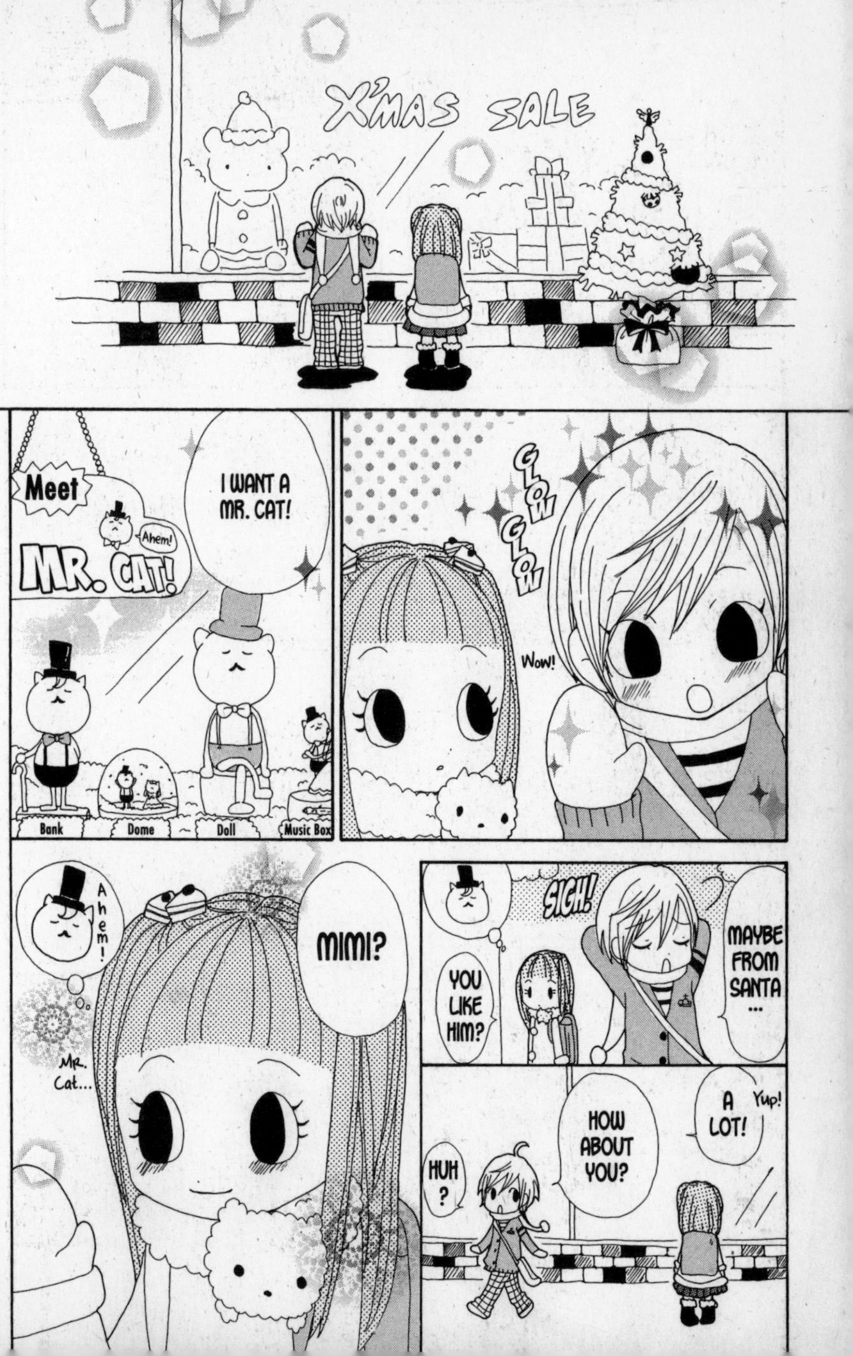
X'MAS SALE
GLOW GLOW
Wow!
I WANT A MR. CAT!
Meet MR. CAT!
Ahem!
Bank
Dome
Doll
Music Box
MAYBE FROM SANTA...
SIGH!
YOU LIKE HIM?
A LOT!
Yup!
HOW ABOUT YOU?
HUH?
MIMI?
Ahem!
Mr. Cat...

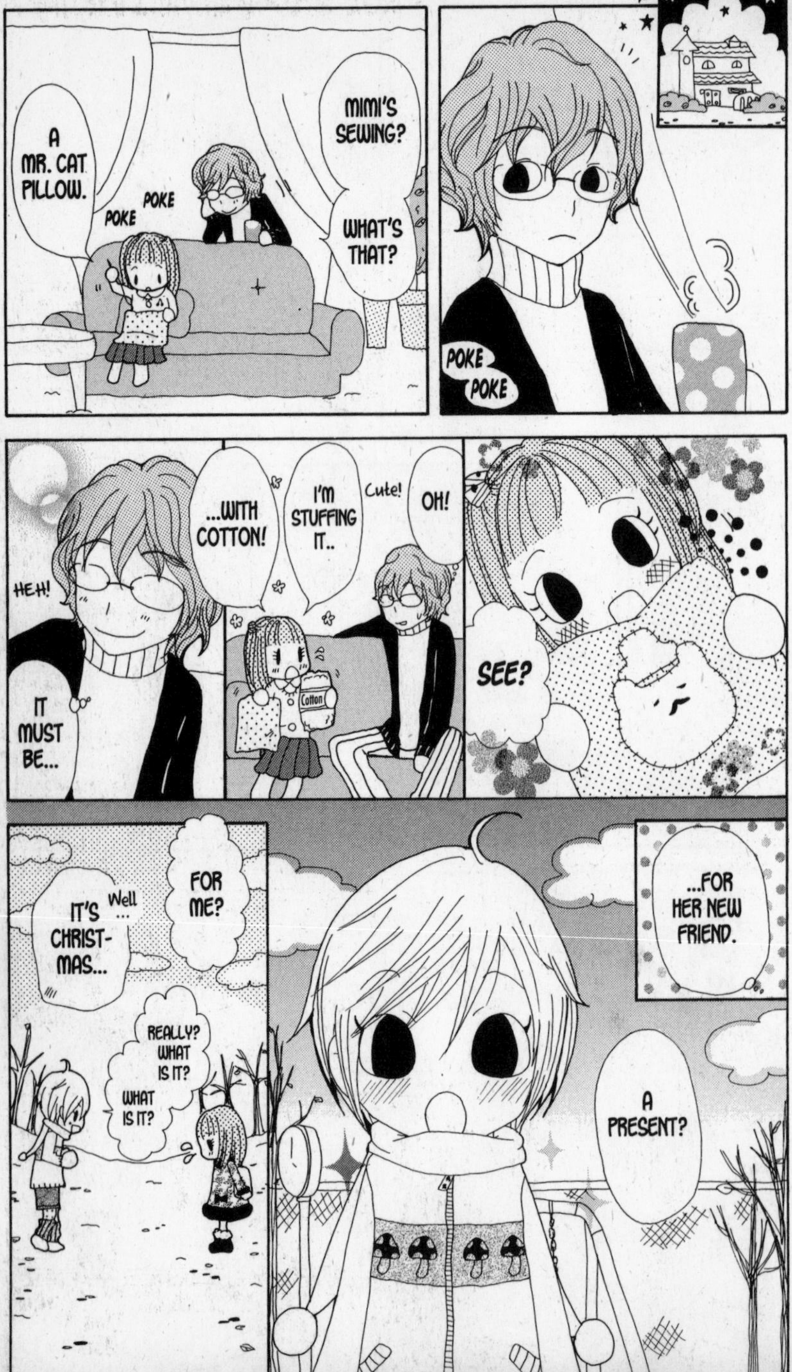
POKE
POKE
MIMI'S SEWING?
WHAT'S THAT?
A MR. CAT PILLOW.
POKE
POKE
OH!
SEE?
Cute!
I'M STUFFING IT..
...WITH COTTON!
Cotton
HEH!
IT MUST BE...
...FOR HER NEW FRIEND.
A PRESENT?
FOR ME?
Well ...
IT'S CHRIST-MAS...
REALLY? WHAT IS IT?
WHAT IS IT?

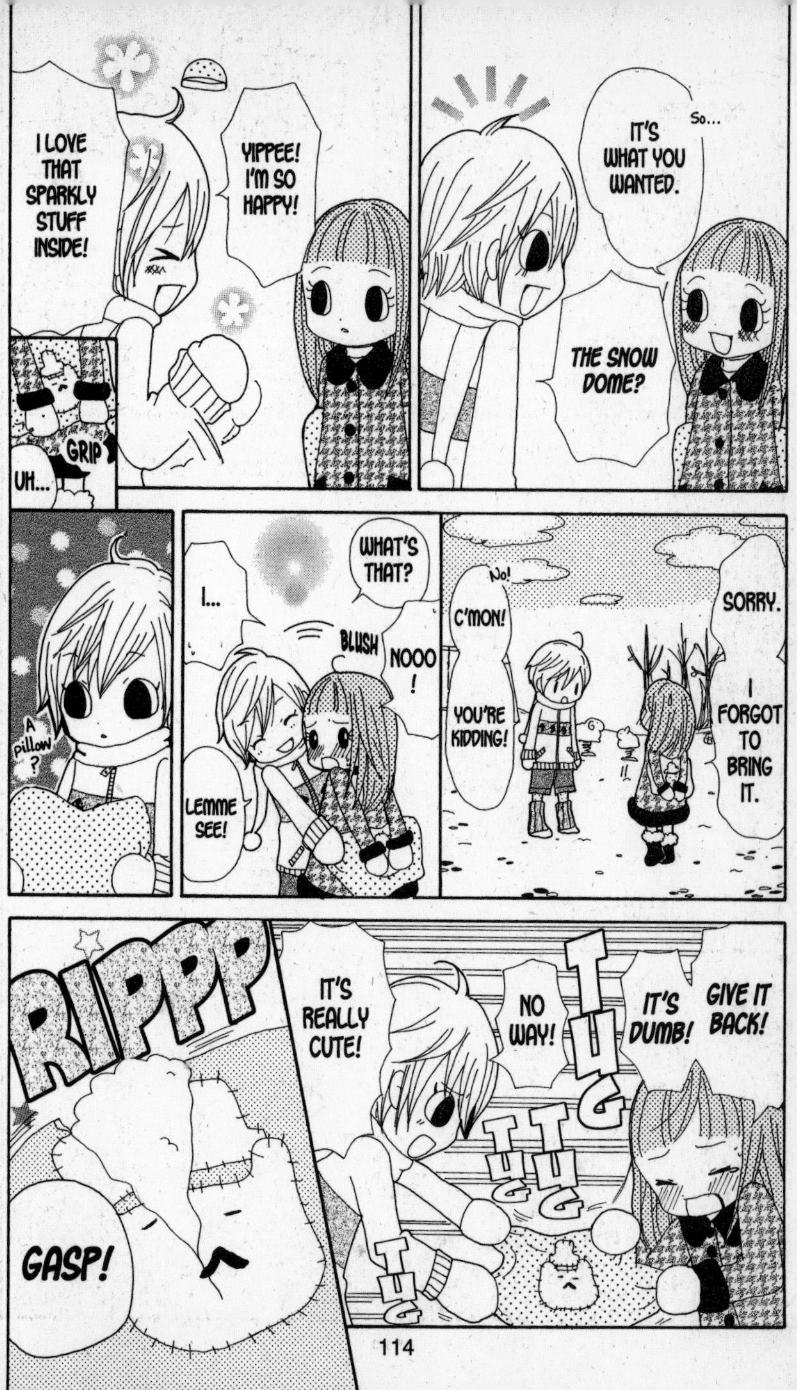
So...
IT'S WHAT YOU WANTED.
THE SNOW DOME?
YIPPEE! I'M SO HAPPY!
I LOVE THAT SPARKLY STUFF INSIDE!
GRIP
UH...
SORRY.
I FORGOT TO BRING IT.
No!
C'MON!
YOU'RE KIDDING!
WHAT'S THAT?
NOOO!
BLUSH
I...
LEMME SEE!
A pillow?
GIVE IT BACK!
IT'S DUMB!
TUG
NO WAY!
IT'S REALLY CUTE!
TUG
TUG
TUG
RIPPP
GASP!

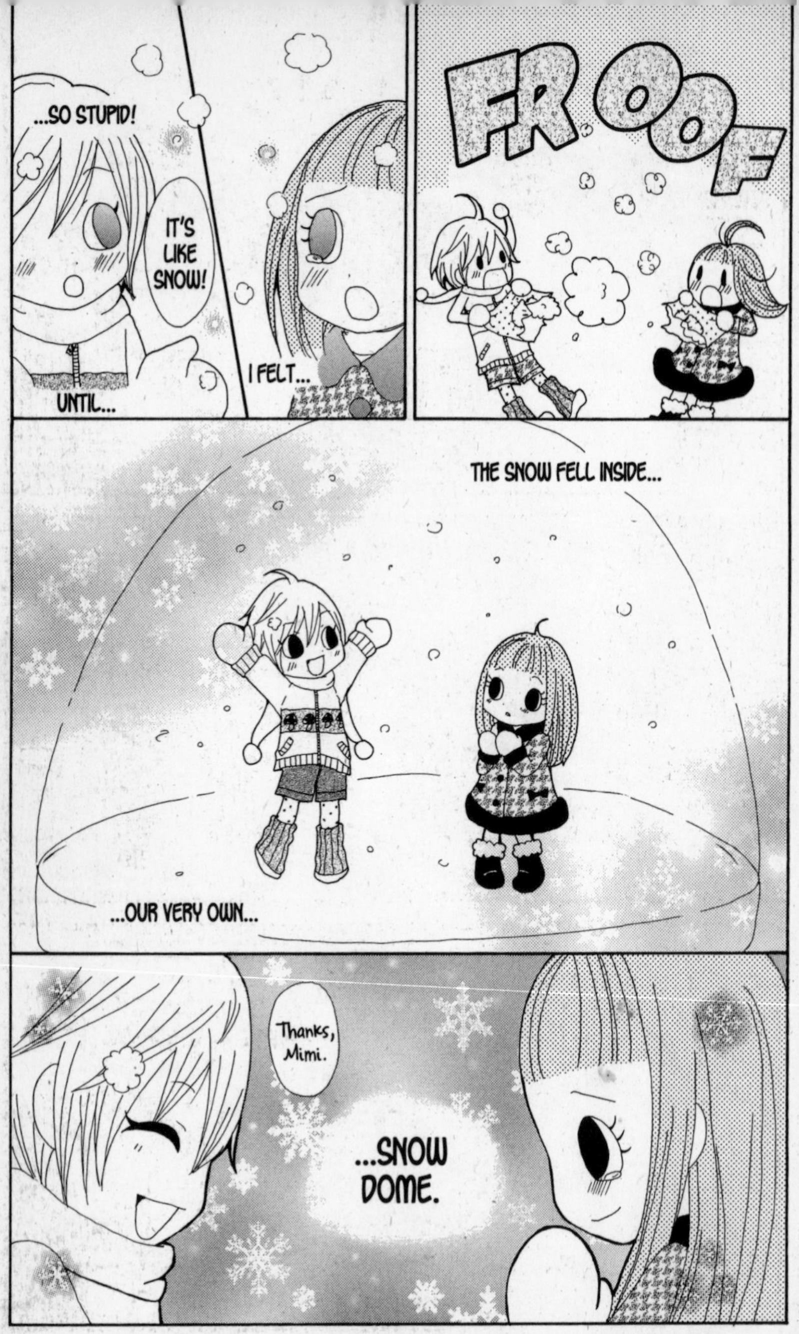
FROOF
I FELT...
...SO STUPID!
IT'S LIKE SNOW!
UNTIL...
THE SNOW FELL INSIDE...
...OUR VERY OWN...
Thanks, Mimi.
...SNOW DOME.

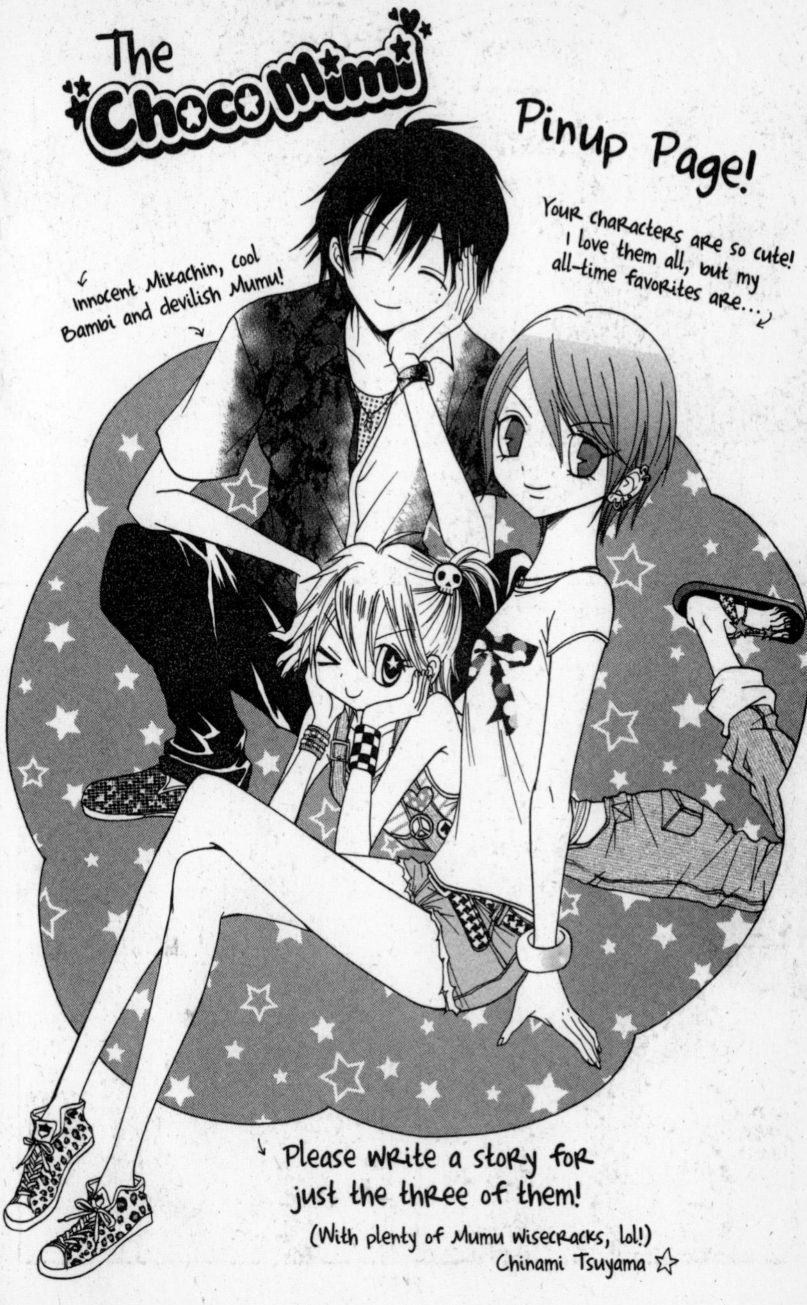
The Choco Mimi Pinup Page!
Your characters are so cute! I love them all, but my all-time favorites are...
Innocent Mikachin, cool Bambi and devilish Mumu!
Please write a story for just the three of them!
(With plenty of Mumu wisecracks, lol!)
Chinami Tsuyama ☆

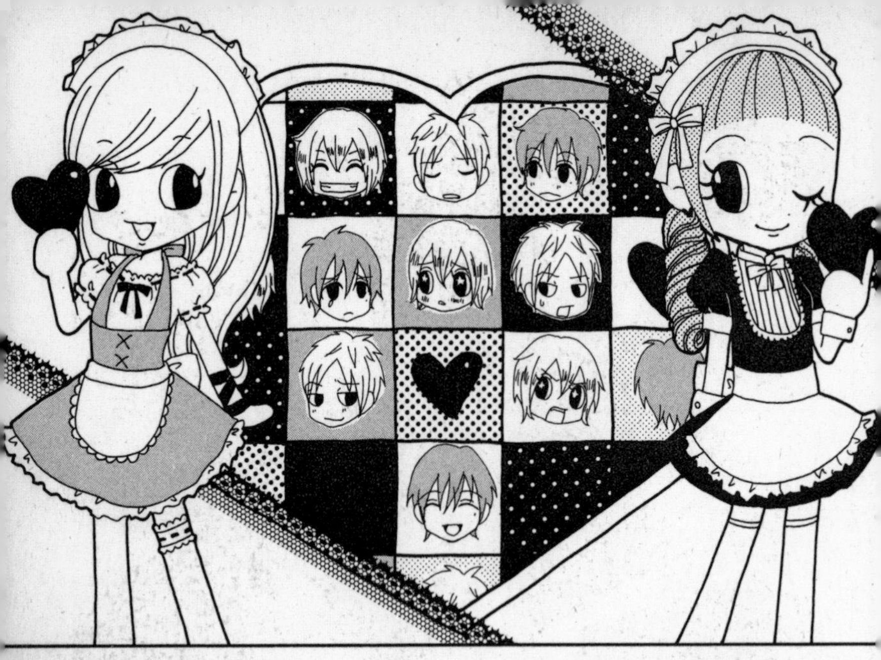

♡ Valentine ♡

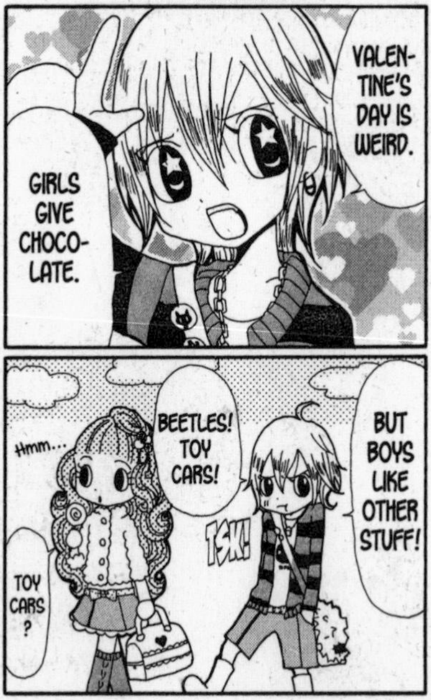
VALEN-TINE'S DAY IS WEIRD.
GIRLS GIVE CHOCO-LATE.
BUT BOYS LIKE OTHER STUFF!
BEETLES! TOY CARS!
TSK!
Hmm...
TOY CARS?

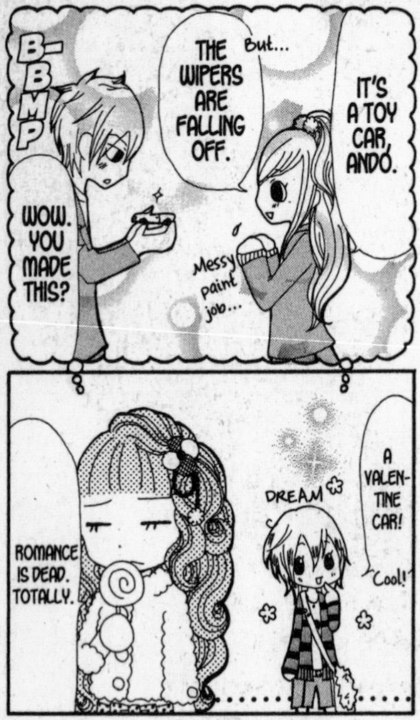
IT'S A TOY CAR, ANDO.
But...
THE WIPERS ARE FALLING OFF.
B-BBMP
WOW. YOU MADE THIS?
Messy paint job...
A VALEN-TINE CAR!
Cool!
DREAM
ROMANCE IS DEAD. TOTALLY.

♡ Chocolate ♡

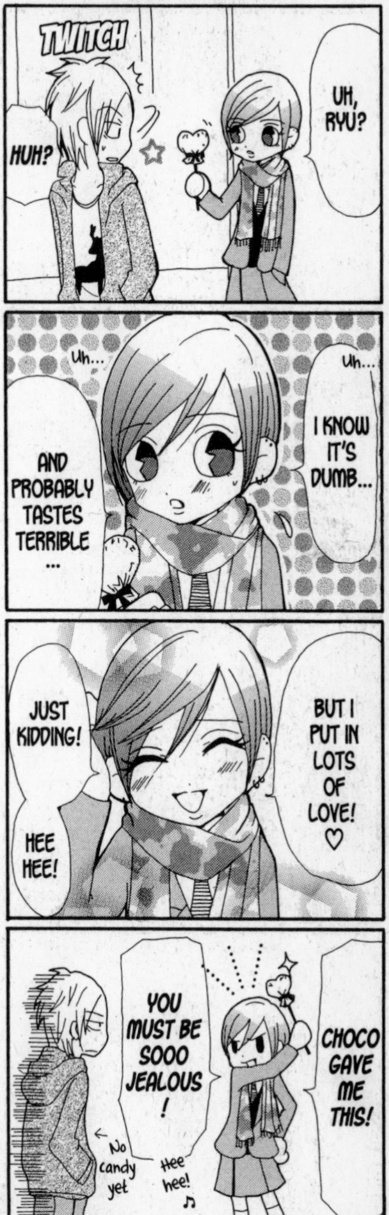

UH, RYU?
TWITCH
HUH?
Uh...
I KNOW IT'S DUMB...
Uh...
AND PROBABLY TASTES TERRIBLE ...
BUT I PUT IN LOTS OF LOVE! ♡
JUST KIDDING!
HEE HEE!
CHOCO GAVE ME THIS!
YOU MUST BE SOOO JEALOUS!
Hee hee! ♪
No candy yet

♡ Courtesy Chocolate ♡

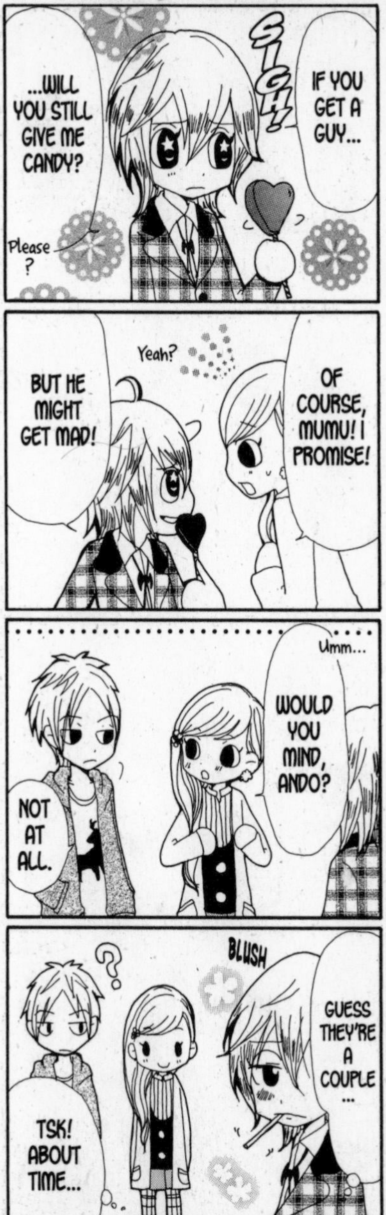

IF YOU GET A GUY...
SIGH!
...WILL YOU STILL GIVE ME CANDY?
Please?
OF COURSE, MUMU! I PROMISE!
Yeah?
BUT HE MIGHT GET MAD!
Umm...
WOULD YOU MIND, ANDO?
NOT AT ALL.
GUESS THEY'RE A COUPLE ...
BLUSH
TSK! ABOUT TIME...

♡ Phone Call ♡

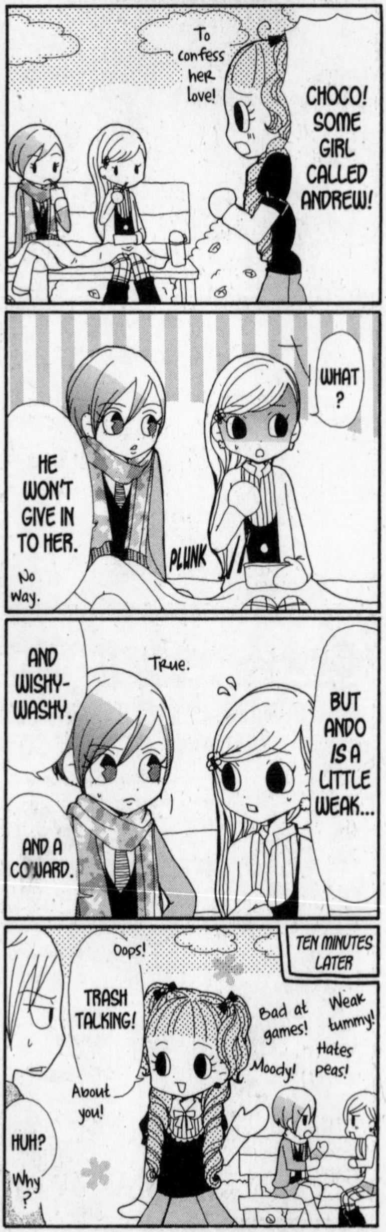
CHOCO! SOME GIRL CALLED ANDREW!
To confess her love!
WHAT?
HE WON'T GIVE IN TO HER.
PLUNK
No way.
BUT ANDO IS A LITTLE WEAK...
True.
AND WISHY-WASHY.
AND A COWARD.
TEN MINUTES LATER
Weak tummy!
Bad at games!
Hates peas!
Moody!
Oops!
TRASH TALKING!
About you!
HUH?
Why?

♡ Special ♡

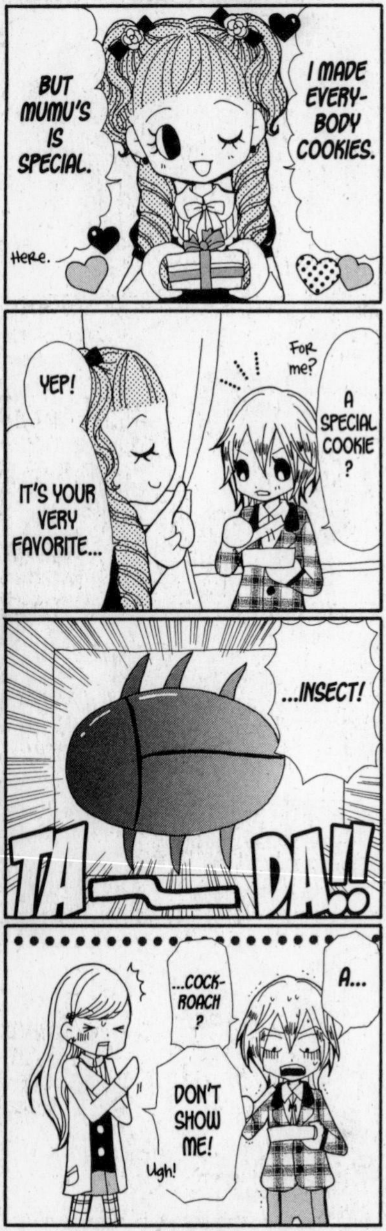
I MADE EVERYBODY COOKIES.
BUT MUMU'S IS SPECIAL.
Here.
For me?
A SPECIAL COOKIE?
YEP!
IT'S YOUR VERY FAVORITE...
...INSECT!
TA—DA!!
A...
...COCKROACH?
DON'T SHOW ME!
Ugh!

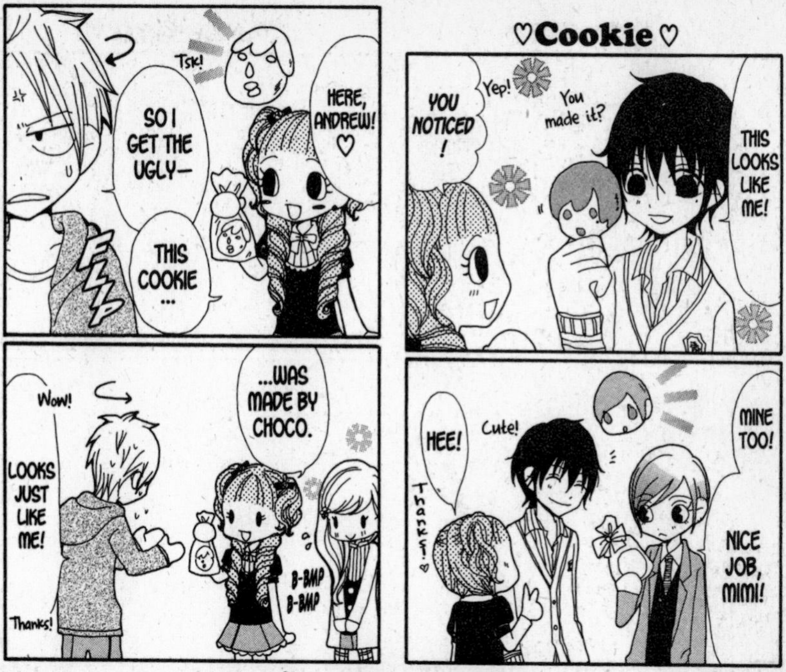
♡Cookie♡
THIS LOOKS LIKE ME!
You made it?
Yep!
YOU NOTICED!
MINE TOO!
NICE JOB, MIMI!
Cute!
HEE!
Thanks!♡
HERE, ANDREW! ♡
Tsk!
SO I GET THE UGLY—
THIS COOKIE...
FLIP
...WAS MADE BY CHOCO.
B-BMP B-BMP
Wow!
LOOKS JUST LIKE ME!
Thanks!

ChocoMimi Fashion Notes

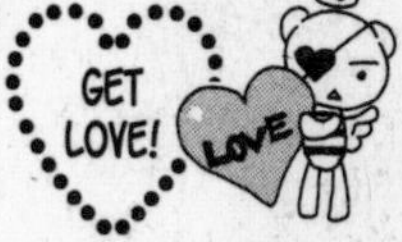
GET LOVE!
LOVE

TRY THESE LOVELY LOOKS FOR VALENTINE'S DAY! MAKE HIS HEART GO B-BMP! ♡

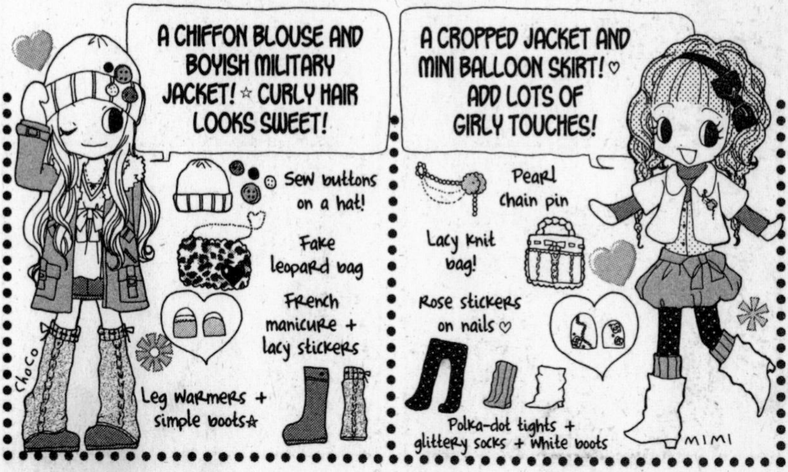
A CROPPED JACKET AND MINI BALLOON SKIRT! ♡ ADD LOTS OF GIRLY TOUCHES!
Pearl chain pin
Lacy knit bag!
Rose stickers on nails ♡
Polka-dot tights + glittery socks + white boots
MIMI
A CHIFFON BLOUSE AND BOYISH MILITARY JACKET! ☆ CURLY HAIR LOOKS SWEET!
Sew buttons on a hat!
Fake leopard bag
French manicure + lacy stickers
Leg warmers + simple boots☆
Choco

♡One Bite♡

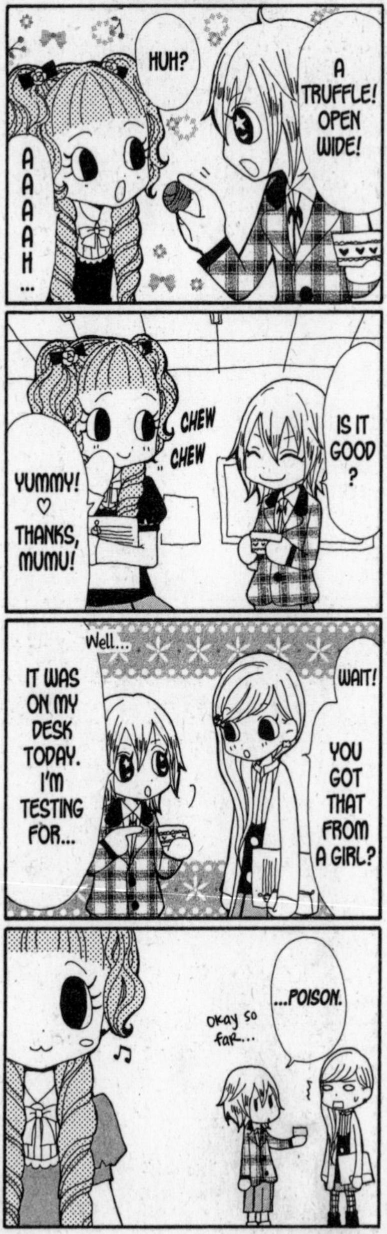
A TRUFFLE! OPEN WIDE!
HUH?
AAAAAH...
IS IT GOOD?
CHEW CHEW
YUMMY! ♡ THANKS, MUMU!
WAIT!
YOU GOT THAT FROM A GIRL?
Well...
IT WAS ON MY DESK TODAY. I'M TESTING FOR...
...POISON.
Okay so far...

♡Big Zit♡

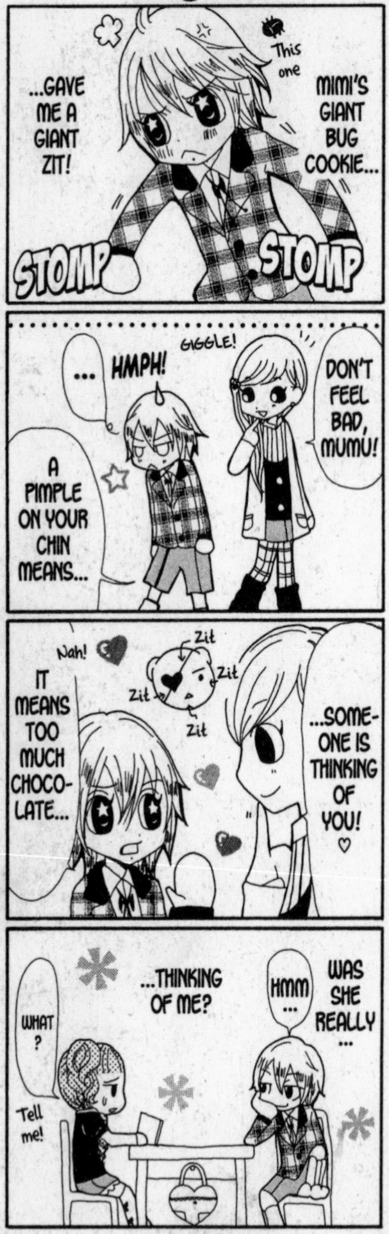
MIMI'S GIANT BUG COOKIE...
This one
...GAVE ME A GIANT ZIT!
STOMP
STOMP
DON'T FEEL BAD, MUMU!
GIGGLE!
... HMPH!
A PIMPLE ON YOUR CHIN MEANS...
...SOME-ONE IS THINKING OF YOU! ♡
Zit
Zit
Zit
Zit
Nah!
IT MEANS TOO MUCH CHOCO-LATE...
WAS SHE REALLY ...
HMM ...
...THINKING OF ME?
WHAT ?
Tell me!

♡ Love Letter ♡

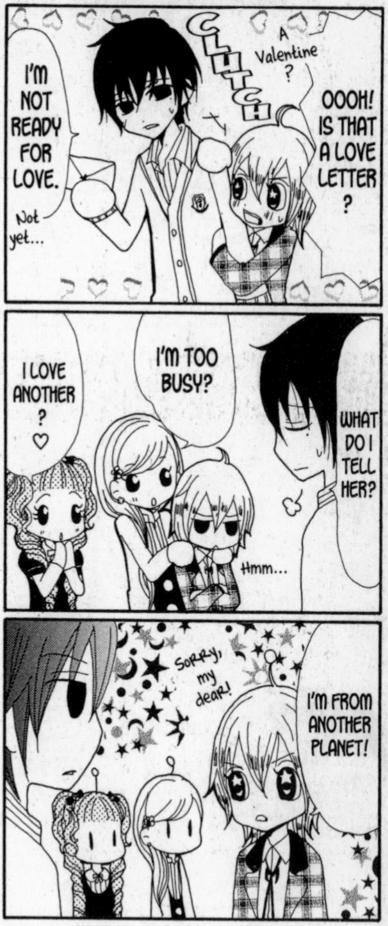

A Valentine?
OOOH! IS THAT A LOVE LETTER?
CLUTCH
I'M NOT READY FOR LOVE.
Not yet...
WHAT DO I TELL HER?
I'M TOO BUSY?
Hmm...
I LOVE ANOTHER? ♡
I'M FROM ANOTHER PLANET!
SORRY, my dear!

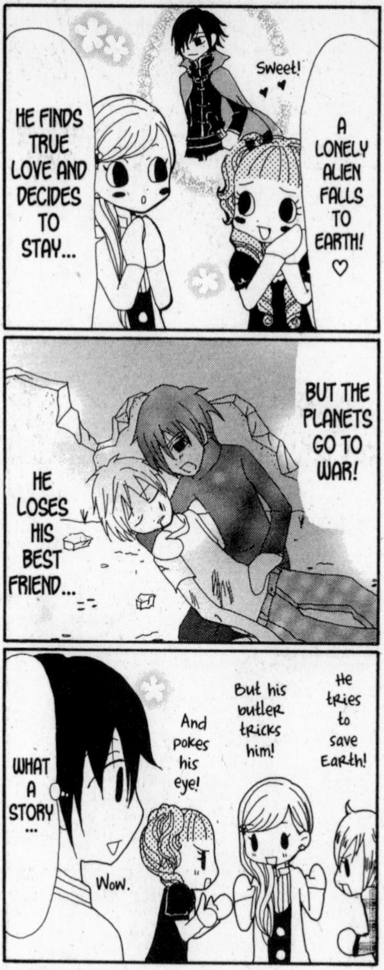

A LONELY ALIEN FALLS TO EARTH! ♡
Sweet! ♥ ♥
HE FINDS TRUE LOVE AND DECIDES TO STAY...
BUT THE PLANETS GO TO WAR!
HE LOSES HIS BEST FRIEND...
He tries to save Earth!
But his butler tricks him!
And pokes his eye!
WHAT A STORY...
Wow.

One hour later...

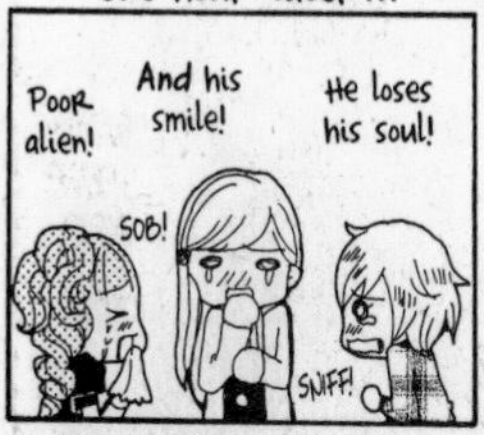

He loses his soul!
And his smile!
Poor alien!
SOB!
SNIFF!

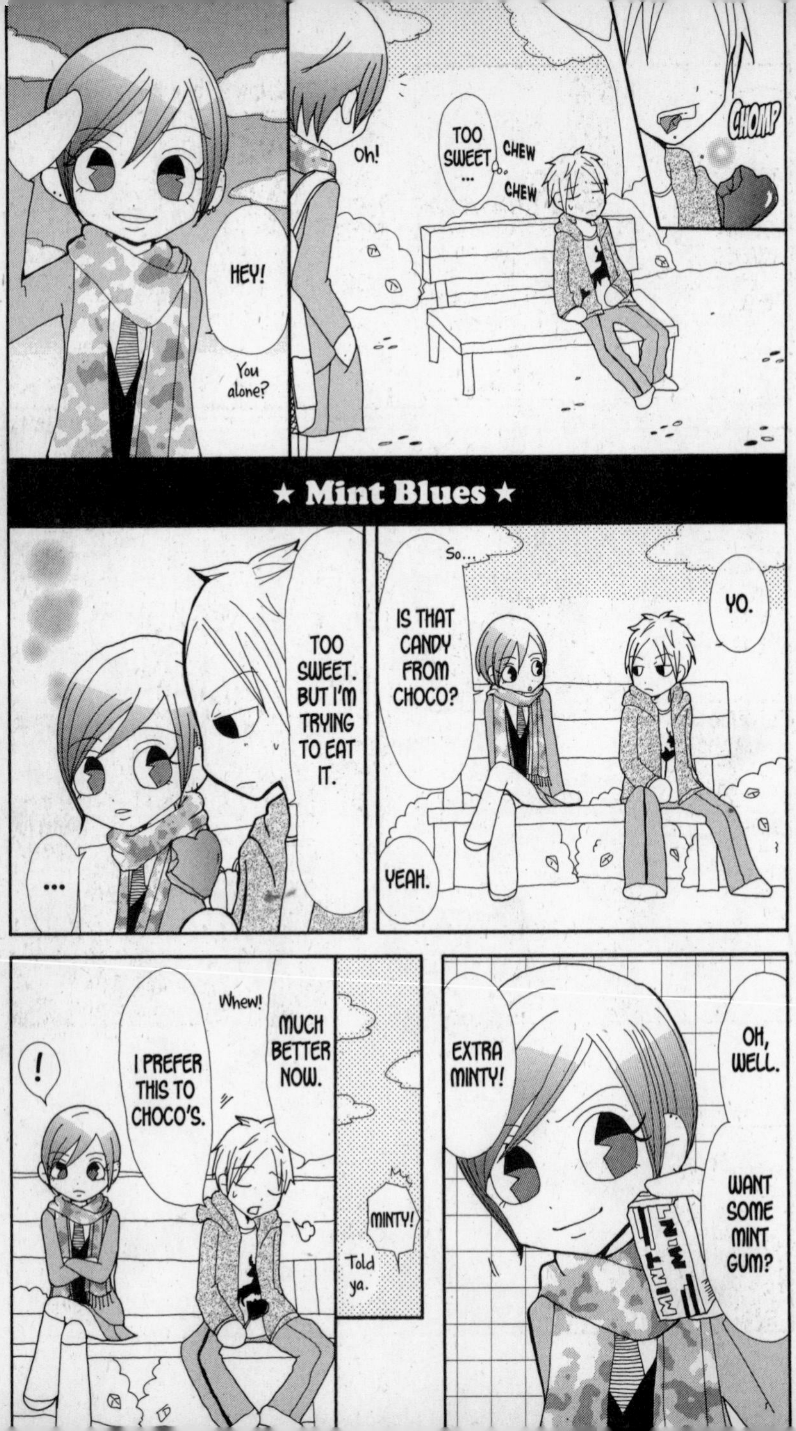
CHOMP
TOO SWEET...
CHEW
CHEW
Oh!
HEY!
You alone?
★ Mint Blues ★
YO.
So...
IS THAT CANDY FROM CHOCO?
YEAH.
TOO SWEET. BUT I'M TRYING TO EAT IT.
...
OH, WELL.
WANT SOME MINT GUM?
EXTRA MINTY!
MINT
MINTY!
Told ya.
MUCH BETTER NOW.
Whew!
I PREFER THIS TO CHOCO'S.
!

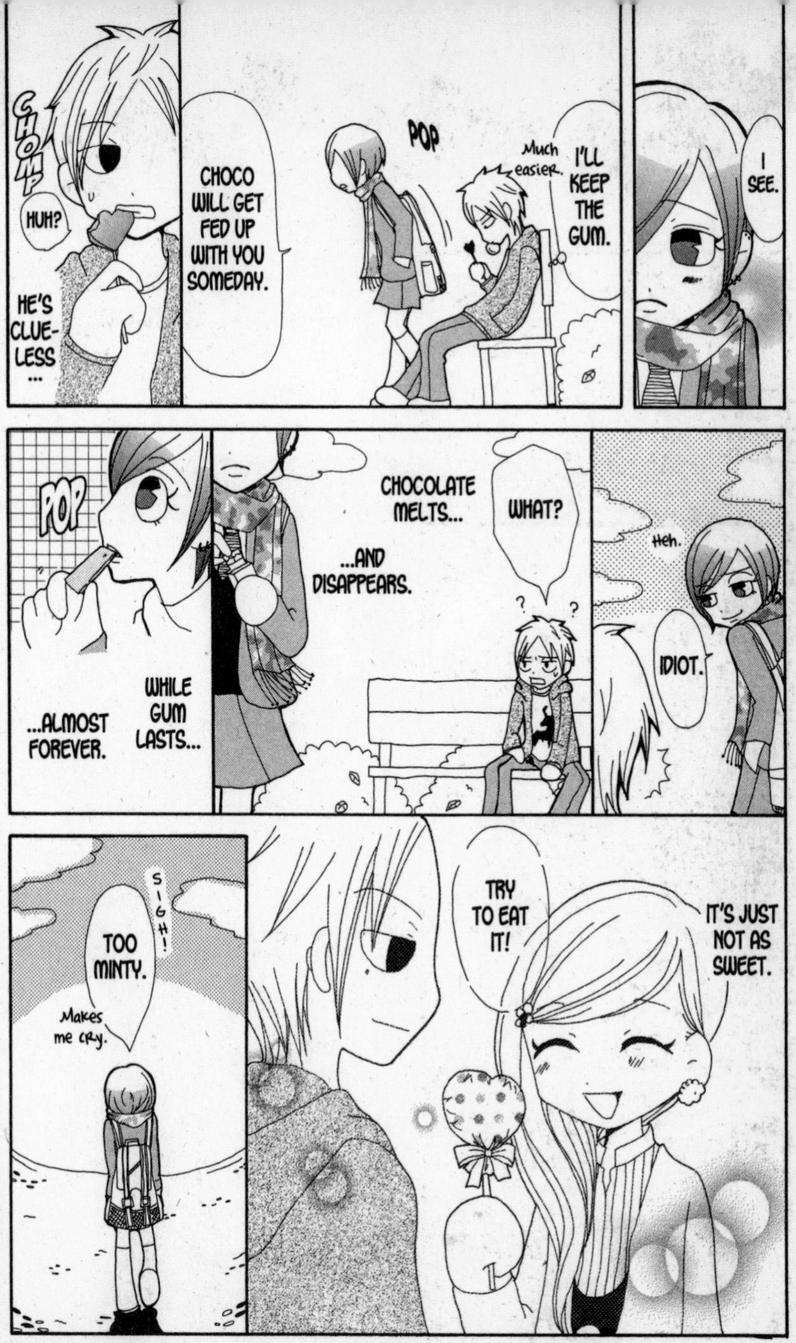
I SEE.
I'LL KEEP THE GUM.
Much easier.
POP
CHOCO WILL GET FED UP WITH YOU SOMEDAY.
CHOMP
HUH?
HE'S CLUELESS...
Heh.
IDIOT.
WHAT?
CHOCOLATE MELTS...
...AND DISAPPEARS.
WHILE GUM LASTS...
...ALMOST FOREVER.
POP
IT'S JUST NOT AS SWEET.
TRY TO EAT IT!
SIGH!
TOO MINTY.
Makes me cry.

Extra 3

2/15
Oops! I forgot!

MIKAMI'S LOVE LETTER...
For...
...Mikami!
From a first-grader...
To Mikami
YO.
A LETTER FOR YOU.
Hmm?
WHAT IS IT?
BLUSH
A... LOVE LETTER.
Here.
GASP!
BUT...
I'M AN ALIEN!
I can't love an Earthling!
WHAT?

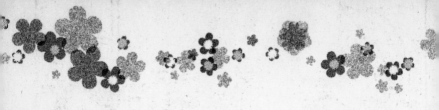

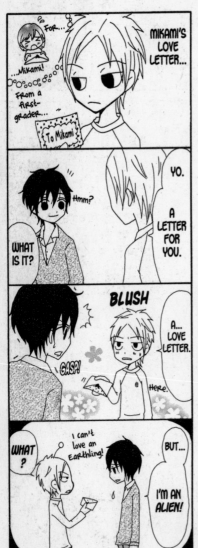

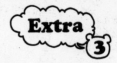

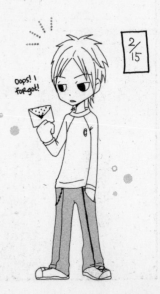

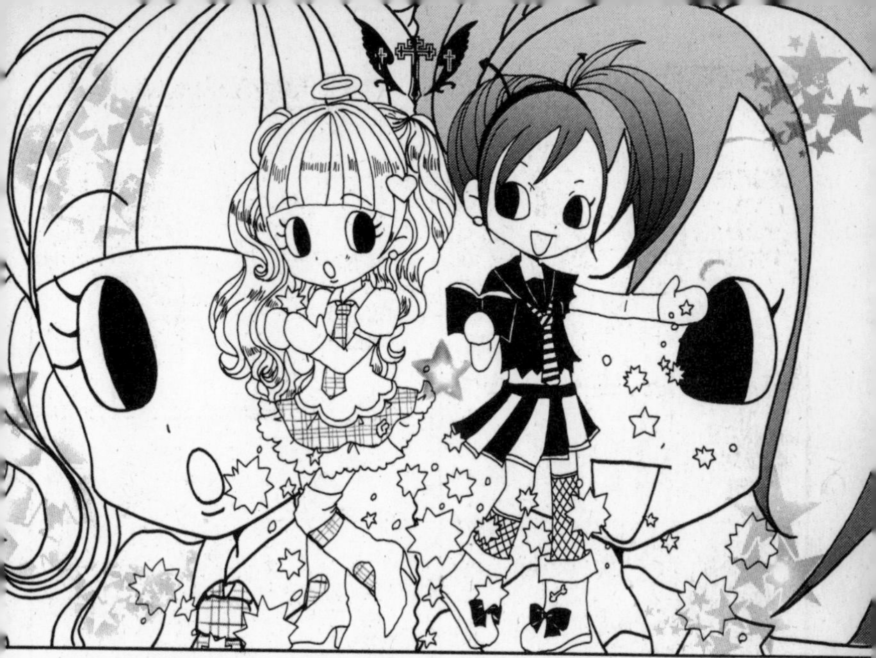

☆ **Party** ☆

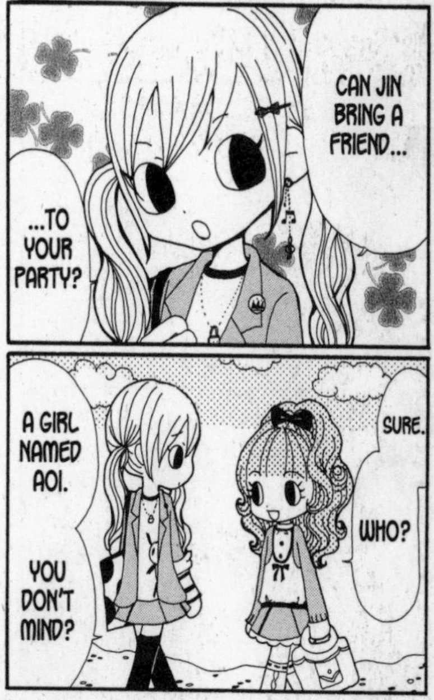

CAN JIN BRING A FRIEND...
...TO YOUR PARTY?
SURE.
WHO?
A GIRL NAMED AOI.
YOU DON'T MIND?

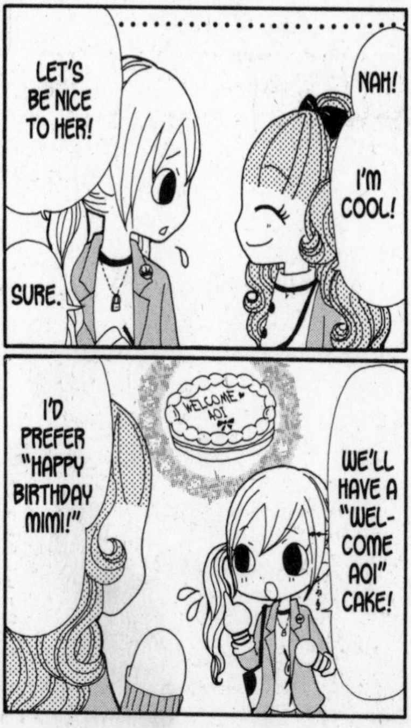

NAH!
LET'S BE NICE TO HER!
I'M COOL!
SURE.
WE'LL HAVE A "WEL-COME AOI" CAKE!
I'D PREFER "HAPPY BIRTHDAY MIMI!"
WELCOME AOI

☆Girlfriend☆

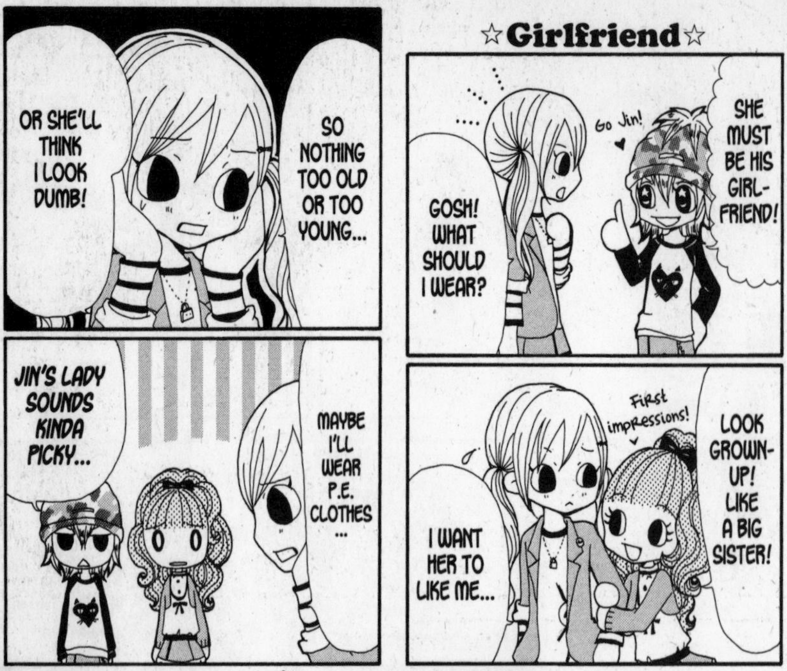
SHE MUST BE HIS GIRL-FRIEND!
Go Jin! ♥
....
GOSH! WHAT SHOULD I WEAR?
LOOK GROWN-UP! LIKE A BIG SISTER!
First impressions!
I WANT HER TO LIKE ME...
SO NOTHING TOO OLD OR TOO YOUNG...
OR SHE'LL THINK I LOOK DUMB!
MAYBE I'LL WEAR P.E. CLOTHES...
JIN'S LADY SOUNDS KINDA PICKY...

Choco Mimi Fashion Notes

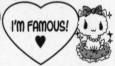

I'M FAMOUS! ♥

BE THE STAR OF YOUR OWN PARTY!
JUST FOLLOW OUR TIPS!☆

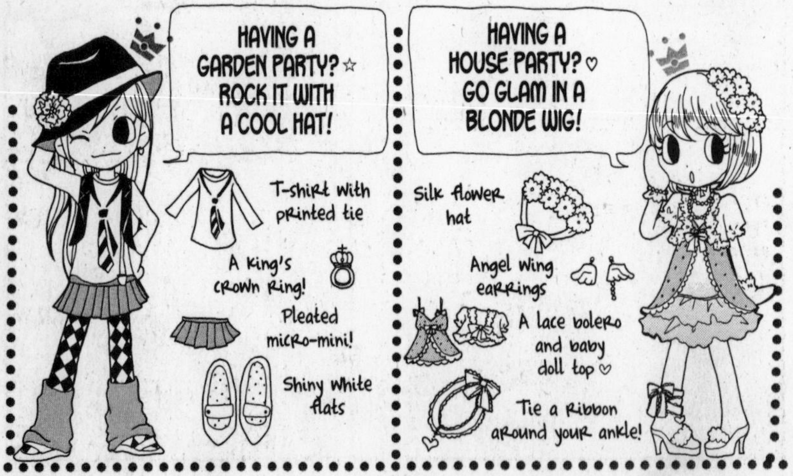
HAVING A GARDEN PARTY? ☆ ROCK IT WITH A COOL HAT!
T-shirt with printed tie
A King's crown Ring!
Pleated micro-mini!
Shiny white flats
HAVING A HOUSE PARTY? ♡ GO GLAM IN A BLONDE WIG!
Silk flower hat
Angel wing earrings
A lace bolero and baby doll top ♡
Tie a ribbon around your ankle!

☆Nice to Meet You☆

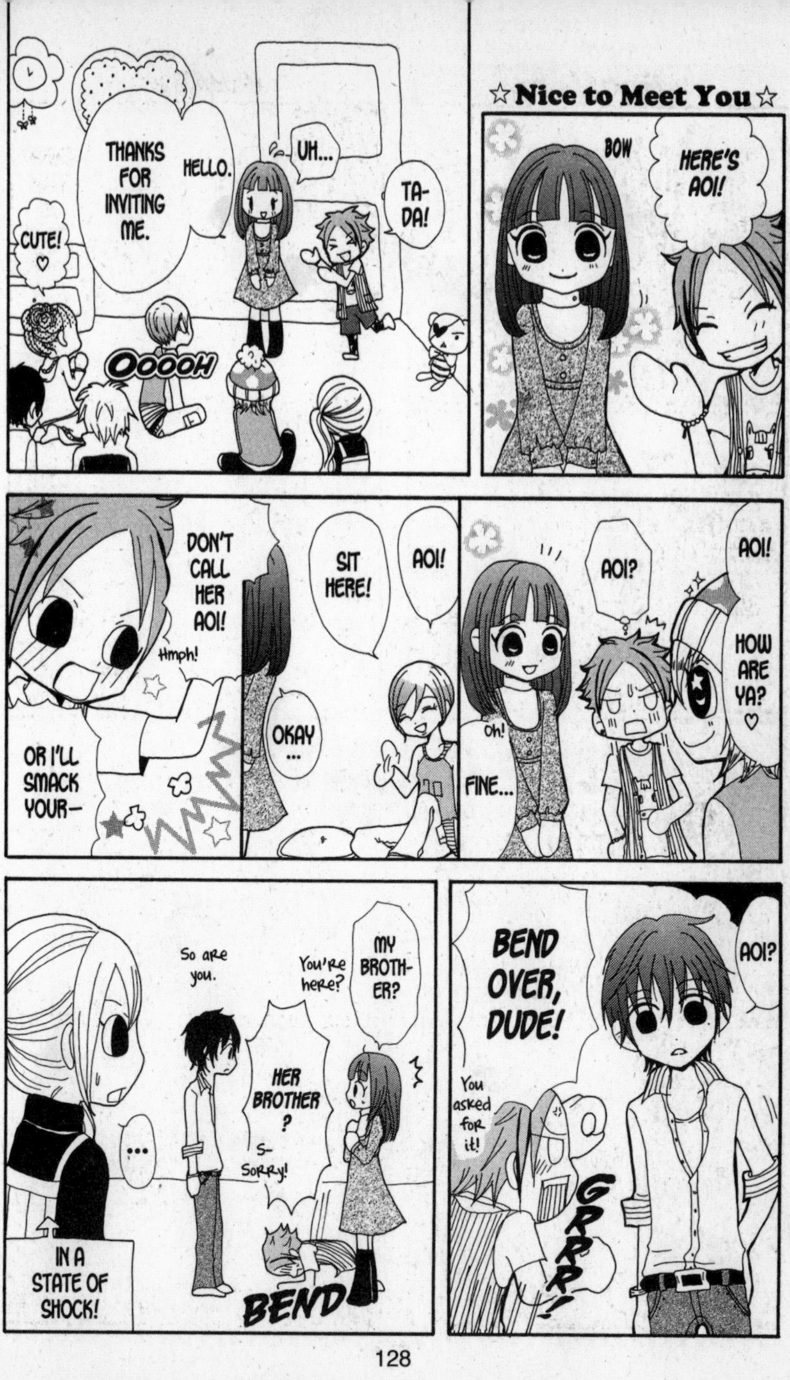
HERE'S AOI!
BOW
TA-DA!
UH...
HELLO.
THANKS FOR INVITING ME.
CUTE! ♡
OOOOH
AOI!
HOW ARE YA? ♡
AOI?
oh!
FINE...
AOI!
SIT HERE!
OKAY ...
DON'T CALL HER AOI!
Hmph!
OR I'LL SMACK YOUR—
AOI?
BEND OVER, DUDE!
You asked for it!
GRRR!
MY BROTHER?
You're here?
So are you.
HER BROTHER?
S-SORRY!
...
BEND
IN A STATE OF SHOCK!

☆ Brother ☆

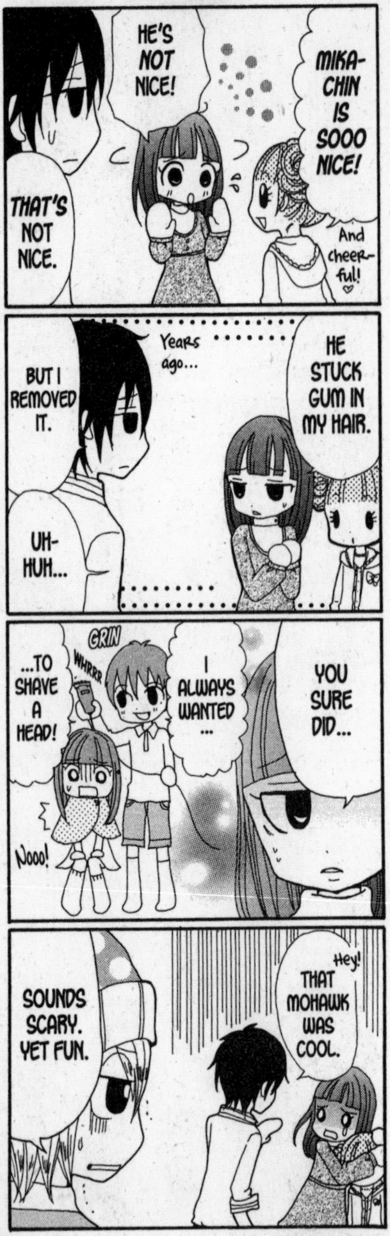
MIKA-CHIN IS SOOO NICE!
And cheer-ful! ♡
HE'S NOT NICE!
THAT'S NOT NICE.
HE STUCK GUM IN MY HAIR.
Years ago...
BUT I REMOVED IT.
UH-HUH...
YOU SURE DID...
I ALWAYS WANTED...
GRIN
WHRRR
...TO SHAVE A HEAD!
Nooo!
Hey!
THAT MOHAWK WAS COOL.
SOUNDS SCARY. YET FUN.

☆ Noodles ☆

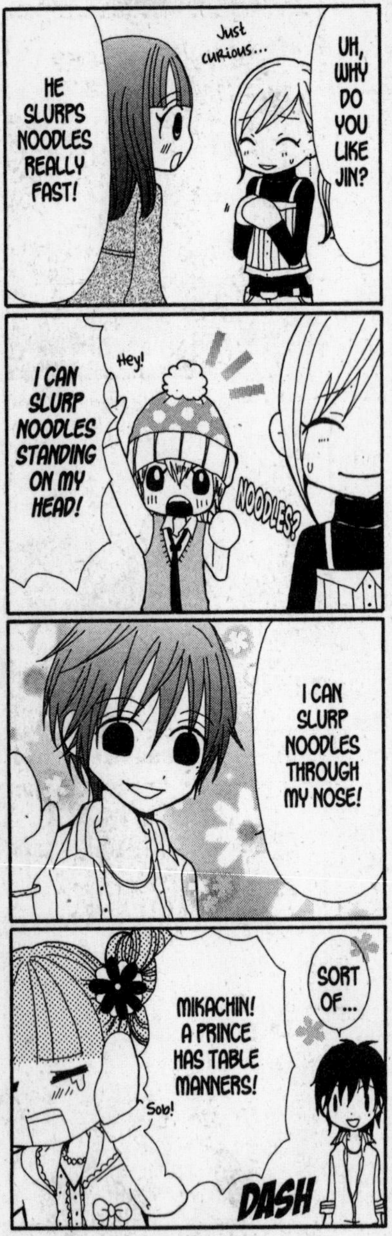
UH, WHY DO YOU LIKE JIN?
Just curious...
HE SLURPS NOODLES REALLY FAST!
NOODLES?
Hey!
I CAN SLURP NOODLES STANDING ON MY HEAD!
I CAN SLURP NOODLES THROUGH MY NOSE!
SORT OF...
MIKACHIN! A PRINCE HAS TABLE MANNERS!
Sob!
DASH

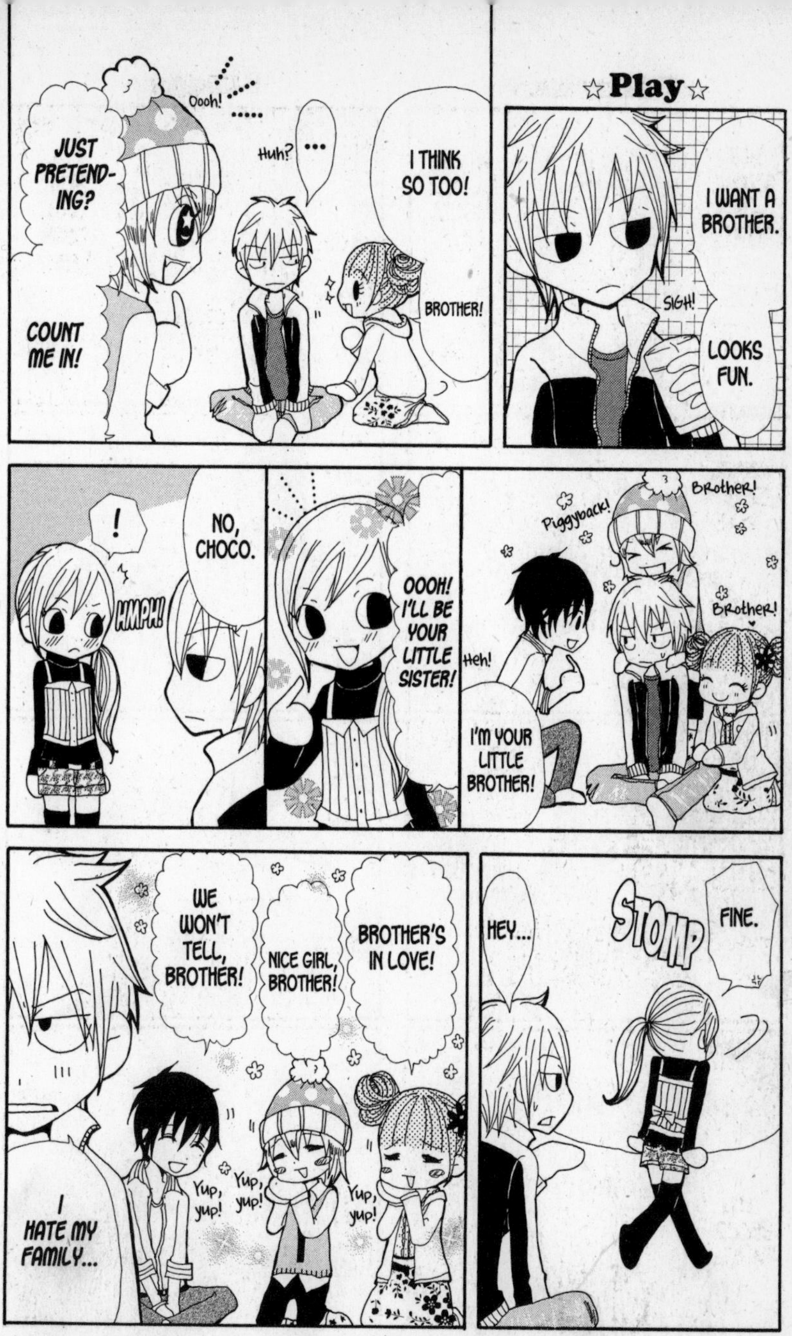
☆Play☆
I WANT A BROTHER.
SIGH!
LOOKS FUN.
I THINK SO TOO!
BROTHER!
...
Huh?
.....
Oooh!
.....
JUST PRETEND-ING?
COUNT ME IN!
Brother!
Piggyback!
Brother!
Heh!
I'M YOUR LITTLE BROTHER!
OOOH! I'LL BE YOUR LITTLE SISTER!
NO, CHOCO.
!
HMPH!
FINE.
STOMP
HEY...
BROTHER'S IN LOVE!
NICE GIRL, BROTHER!
WE WON'T TELL, BROTHER!
Yup, yup!
Yup, yup!
Yup, yup!
I HATE MY FAMILY...

☆ Child ☆

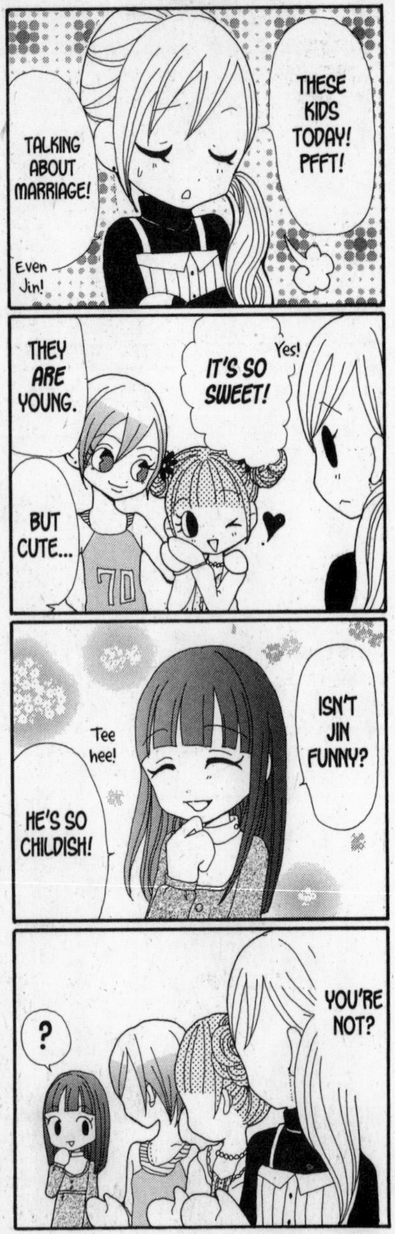
THESE KIDS TODAY! PFFT!
TALKING ABOUT MARRIAGE!
Even Jin!
Yes!
IT'S SO SWEET!
THEY ARE YOUNG.
BUT CUTE...
ISN'T JIN FUNNY?
Tee hee!
HE'S SO CHILDISH!
YOU'RE NOT?
?

☆ Congrats! ☆

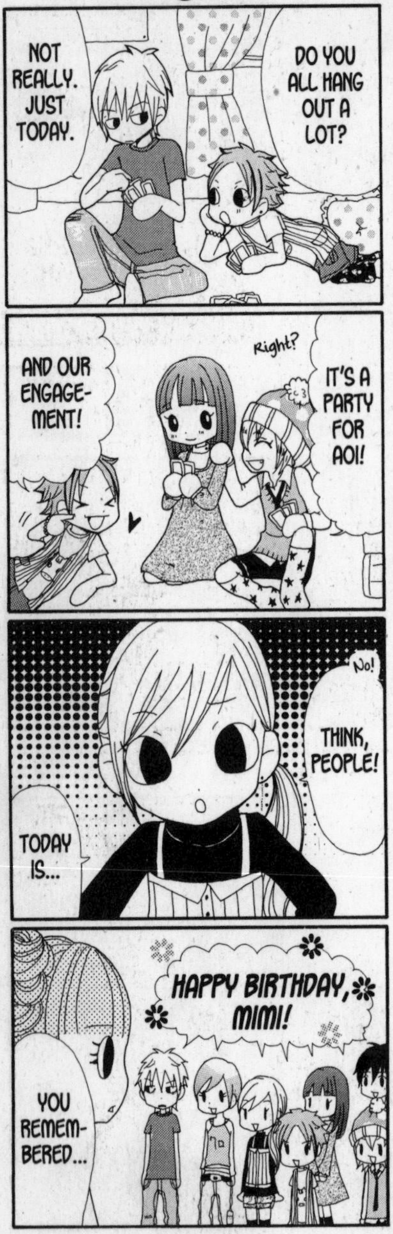
DO YOU ALL HANG OUT A LOT?
NOT REALLY. JUST TODAY.
Right?
IT'S A PARTY FOR AOI!
AND OUR ENGAGE-MENT!
No!
THINK, PEOPLE!
TODAY IS...
HAPPY BIRTHDAY, MIMI!
YOU REMEM-BERED...

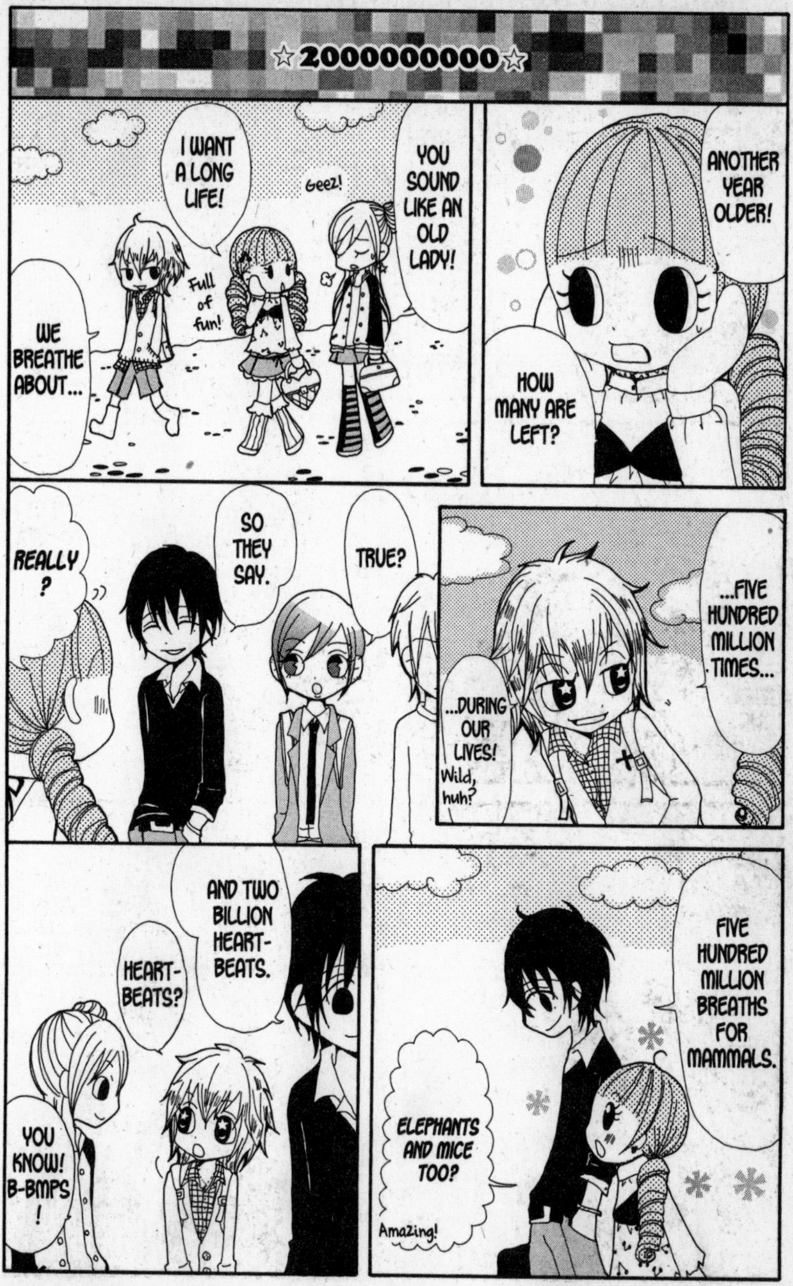
☆2000000000☆
ANOTHER YEAR OLDER!
HOW MANY ARE LEFT?
YOU SOUND LIKE AN OLD LADY!
Geez!
I WANT A LONG LIFE!
Full of fun!
WE BREATHE ABOUT...
...FIVE HUNDRED MILLION TIMES...
...DURING OUR LIVES!
Wild, huh?
TRUE?
SO THEY SAY.
REALLY?
FIVE HUNDRED MILLION BREATHS FOR MAMMALS.
ELEPHANTS AND MICE TOO?
Amazing!
AND TWO BILLION HEART-BEATS.
HEART-BEATS?
YOU KNOW! B-BMPS!

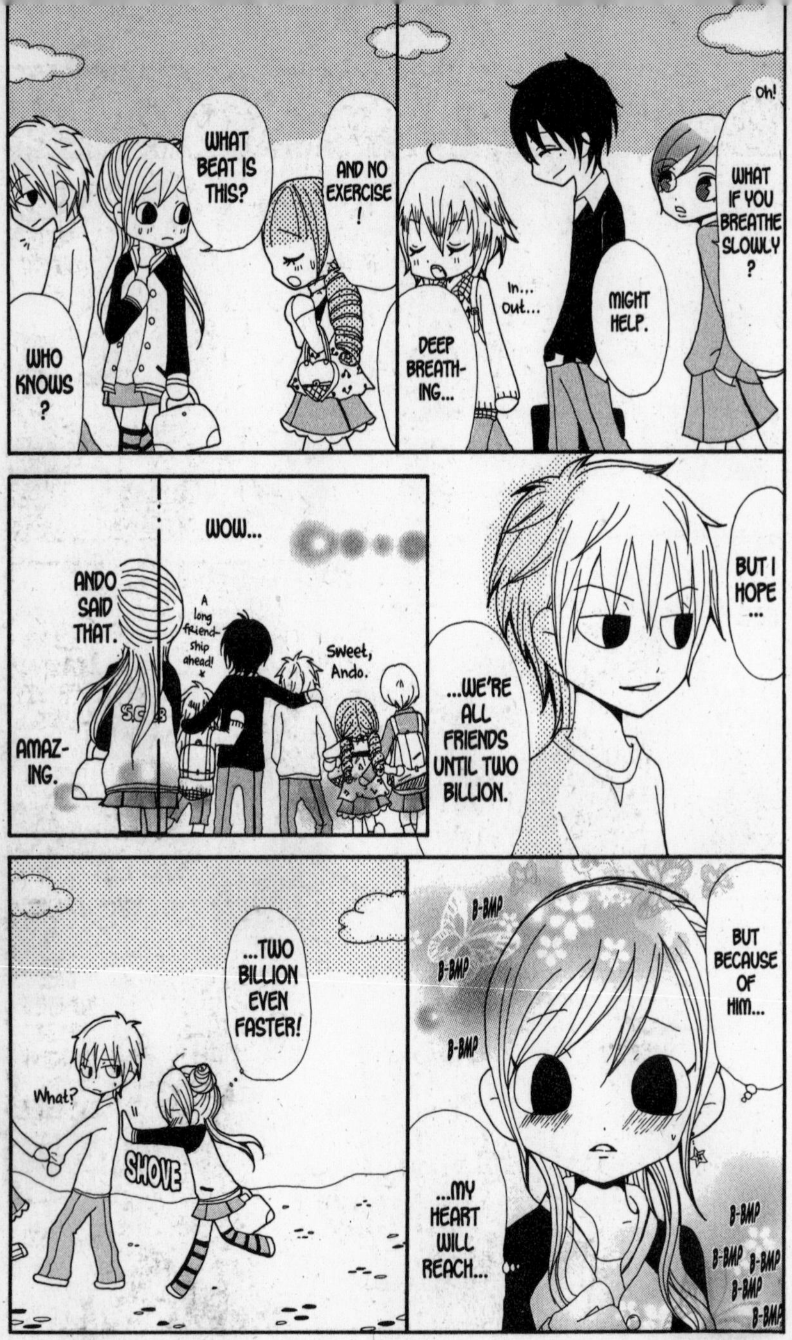
Oh!
WHAT IF YOU BREATHE SLOWLY?
MIGHT HELP.
In... out...
DEEP BREATHING...
AND NO EXERCISE!
WHAT BEAT IS THIS?
WHO KNOWS?
BUT I HOPE...
...WE'RE ALL FRIENDS UNTIL TWO BILLION.
WOW...
Sweet, Ando.
A long friendship ahead! *
ANDO SAID THAT.
AMAZING.
BUT BECAUSE OF HIM...
B-BMP
B-BMP
B-BMP
...MY HEART WILL REACH...
B-BMP
B-BMP B-BMP
B-BMP
B-BMP
...TWO BILLION EVEN FASTER!
What?
SHOVE

All About Aoi

By the Artist

I wanted a girl who was smart, cute, kind—and a little strange. So Aoi was born!

She's the most girly girl in *ChocoMimi* and the most modest. Definitely the quiet type!

Aoi has two older brothers besides Mikachin. They often tell her that girls should be graceful!

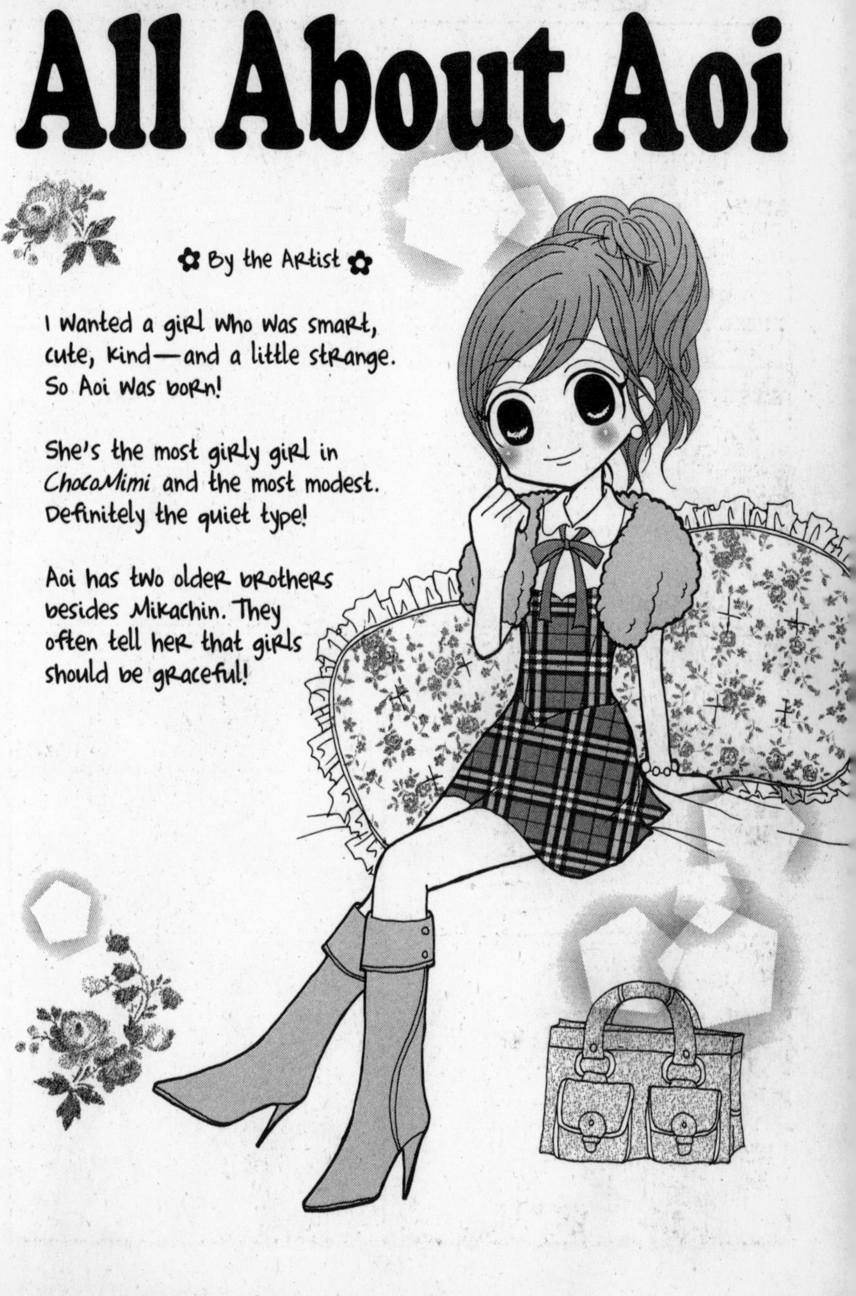

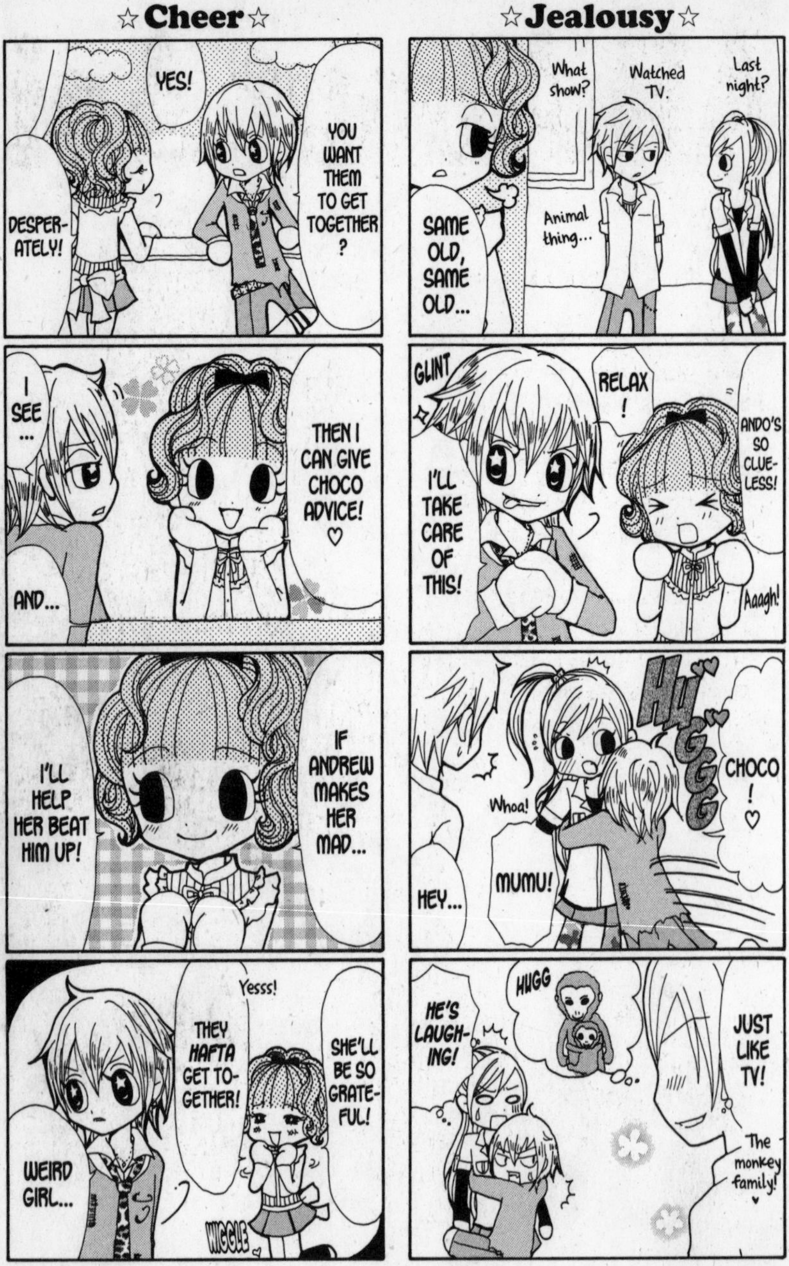
☆Jealousy☆
Last night?
Watched TV.
What show?
Animal thing...
SAME OLD, SAME OLD...
ANDO'S SO CLUELESS!
Aaagh!
RELAX!
GLINT
I'LL TAKE CARE OF THIS!
CHOCO! ♡
HUGGG
MUMU!
Whoa!
HEY...
JUST LIKE TV!
The monkey family! ♥
HUGG
HE'S LAUGHING!
☆Cheer☆
YOU WANT THEM TO GET TOGETHER?
YES!
DESPERATELY!
THEN I CAN GIVE CHOCO ADVICE! ♡
I SEE...
AND...
IF ANDREW MAKES HER MAD...
I'LL HELP HER BEAT HIM UP!
SHE'LL BE SO GRATEFUL!
Yesss!
THEY HAFTA GET TOGETHER!
WIGGLE
WEIRD GIRL...

☆ Two Choices ☆

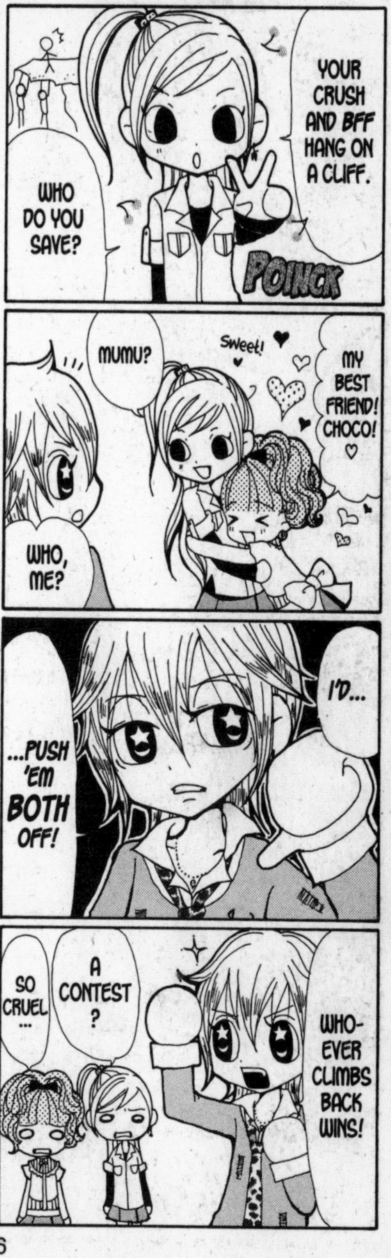
YOUR CRUSH AND BFF HANG ON A CLIFF.
WHO DO YOU SAVE?
POINCK
MY BEST FRIEND! CHOCO! ♡
Sweet!
MUMU?
WHO, ME?
I'D...
...PUSH 'EM BOTH OFF!
WHO-EVER CLIMBS BACK WINS!
A CONTEST?
SO CRUEL...

☆ Book ☆

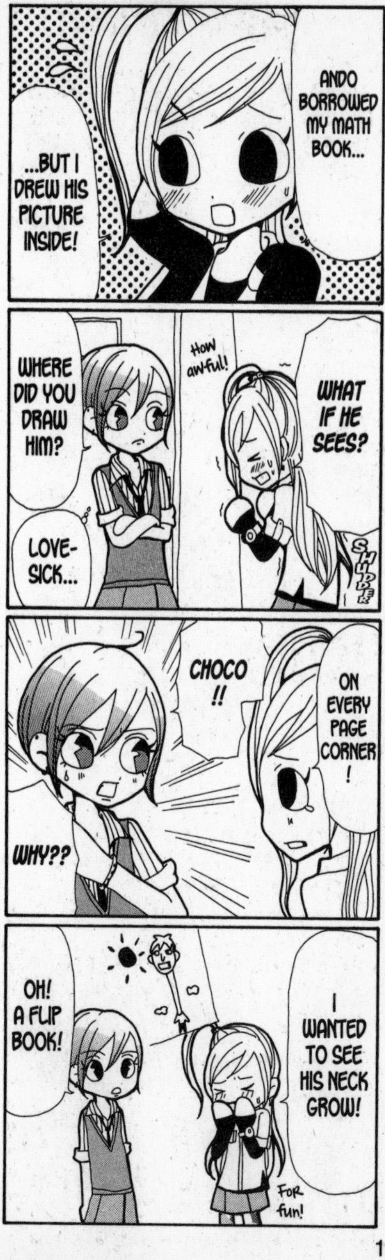
ANDO BORROWED MY MATH BOOK...
...BUT I DREW HIS PICTURE INSIDE!
WHAT IF HE SEES?
How awful!
SHUDDER
WHERE DID YOU DRAW HIM?
LOVE-SICK...
ON EVERY PAGE CORNER!
CHOCO!!
WHY??
I WANTED TO SEE HIS NECK GROW!
For fun!
OH! A FLIP BOOK!

☆Boyfriend☆

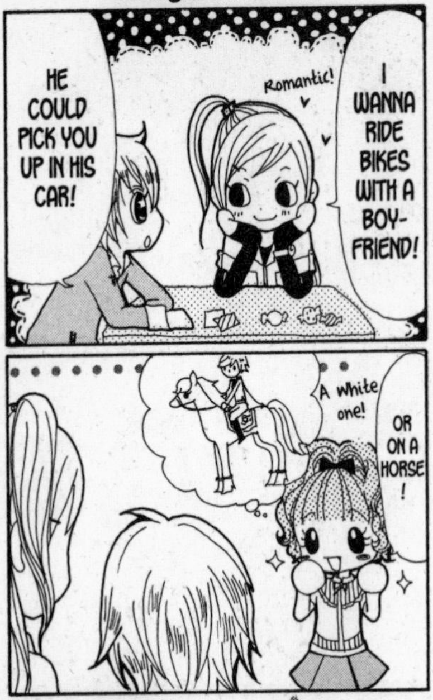
I WANNA RIDE BIKES WITH A BOYFRIEND!
Romantic!
HE COULD PICK YOU UP IN HIS CAR!
OR ON A HORSE!
A white one!

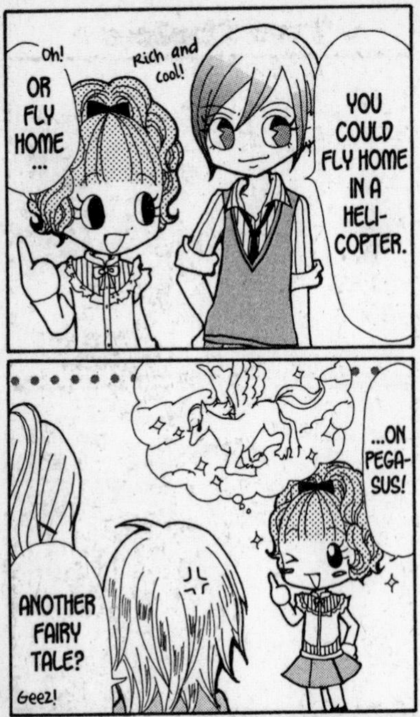
YOU COULD FLY HOME IN A HELICOPTER.
Rich and cool!
Oh!
OR FLY HOME...
...ON PEGASUS!
ANOTHER FAIRY TALE?
Geez!

Choco Mimi Fashion Notes

IT'S A BRAND-NEW TERM!
LET'S GIRLY-UP THAT UNIFORM! ★

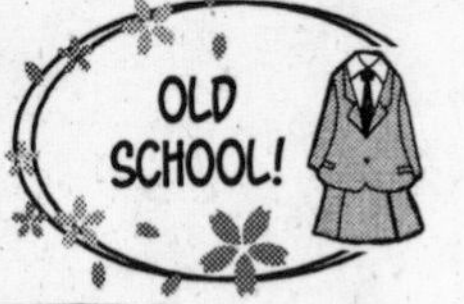
OLD SCHOOL!

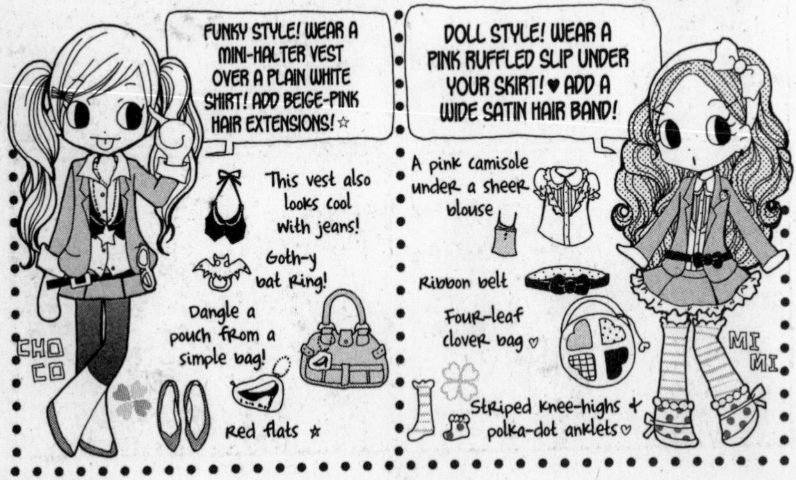
FUNKY STYLE! WEAR A MINI-HALTER VEST OVER A PLAIN WHITE SHIRT! ADD BEIGE-PINK HAIR EXTENSIONS! ☆
This vest also looks cool with jeans!
Goth-y bat ring!
Dangle a pouch from a simple bag!
Red flats ☆
CHOCO
DOLL STYLE! WEAR A PINK RUFFLED SLIP UNDER YOUR SKIRT! ♥ ADD A WIDE SATIN HAIR BAND!
A pink camisole under a sheer blouse
Ribbon belt
Four-leaf clover bag ♡
Striped knee-highs + polka-dot anklets ♡
MIMI

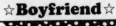

☆ Survey ☆

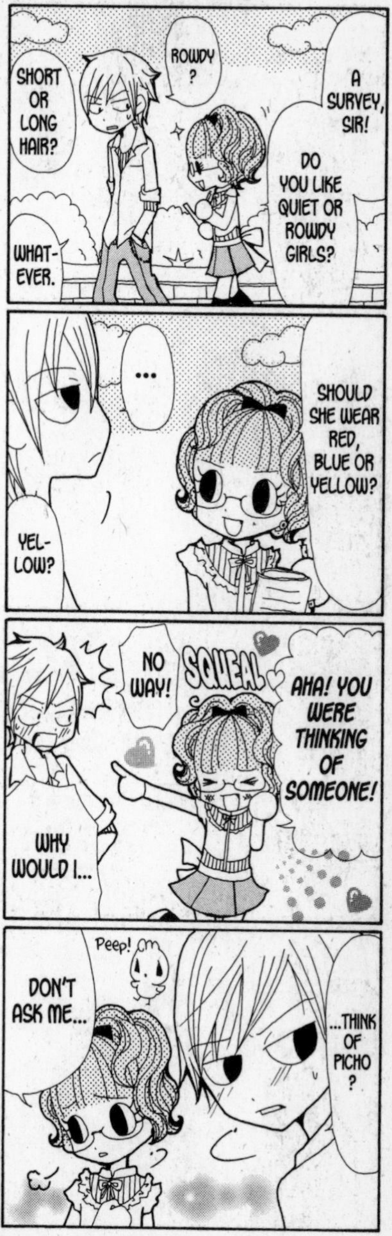
A SURVEY, SIR!
DO YOU LIKE QUIET OR ROWDY GIRLS?
ROWDY?
SHORT OR LONG HAIR?
WHAT-EVER.
SHOULD SHE WEAR RED, BLUE OR YELLOW?
...
YEL-LOW?
AHA! YOU WERE THINKING OF SOMEONE!
SQUEAL
NO WAY!
WHY WOULD I...
...THINK OF PICHO?
Peep!
DON'T ASK ME...

☆ Cooking ☆

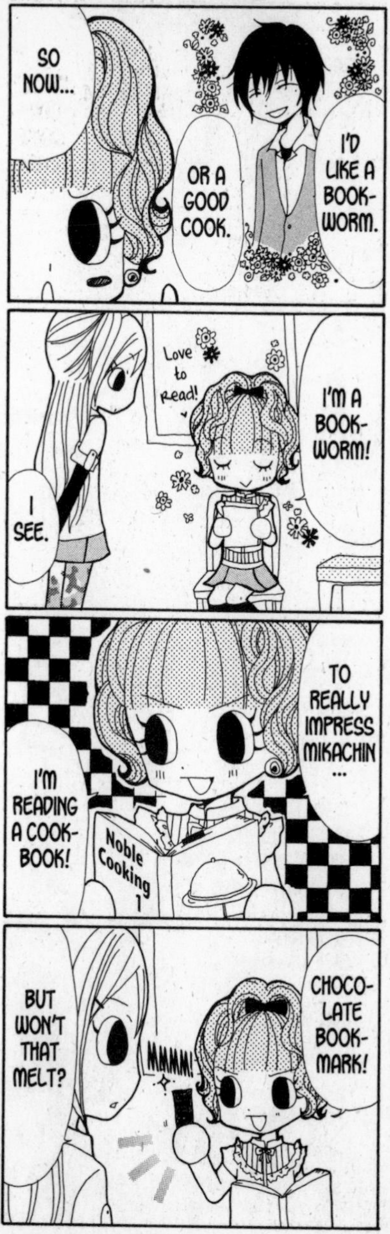
I'D LIKE A BOOK-WORM.
OR A GOOD COOK.
SO NOW...
I'M A BOOK-WORM!
Love to read!
I SEE.
TO REALLY IMPRESS MIKACHIN...
I'M READING A COOK-BOOK!
Noble Cooking 1
CHOCO-LATE BOOK-MARK!
MMMM!
BUT WON'T THAT MELT?

☆ **Close** ☆

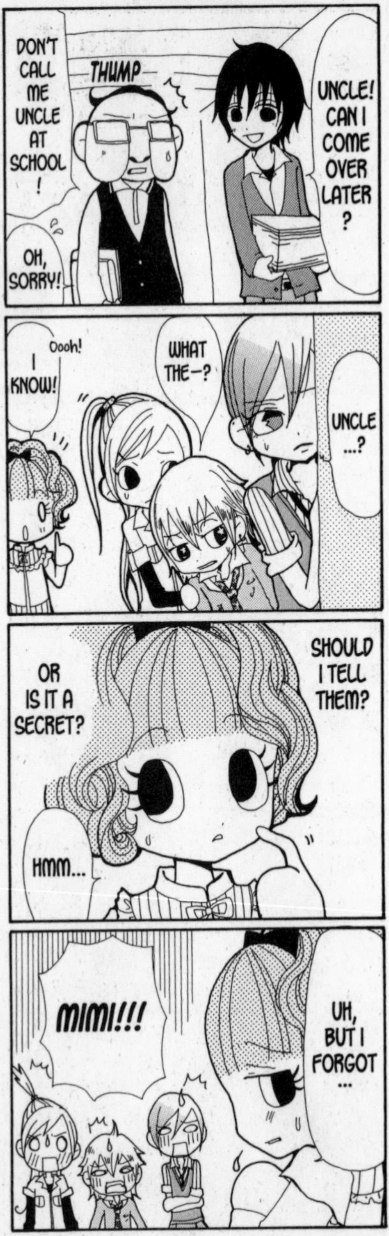
UNCLE! CAN I COME OVER LATER?
THUMP
DON'T CALL ME UNCLE AT SCHOOL!
OH, SORRY!
UNCLE ...?
WHAT THE—?
Oooh!
I KNOW!
SHOULD I TELL THEM?
OR IS IT A SECRET?
HMM...
UH, BUT I FORGOT ...
MIMI!!!

☆ **Relatives** ☆

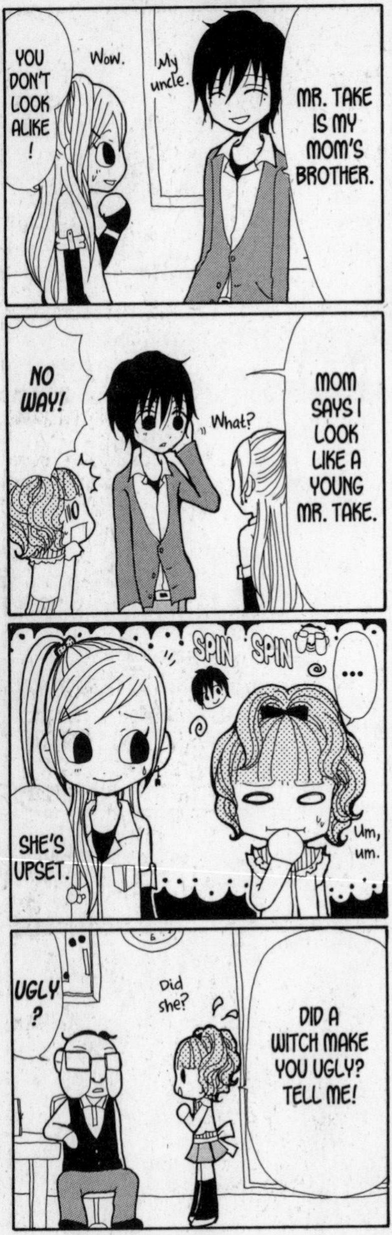
MR. TAKE IS MY MOM'S BROTHER.
My uncle.
Wow.
YOU DON'T LOOK ALIKE!
MOM SAYS I LOOK LIKE A YOUNG MR. TAKE.
What?
NO WAY!
...
SPIN SPIN
Um, um.
SHE'S UPSET.
DID A WITCH MAKE YOU UGLY? TELL ME!
Did she?
UGLY?

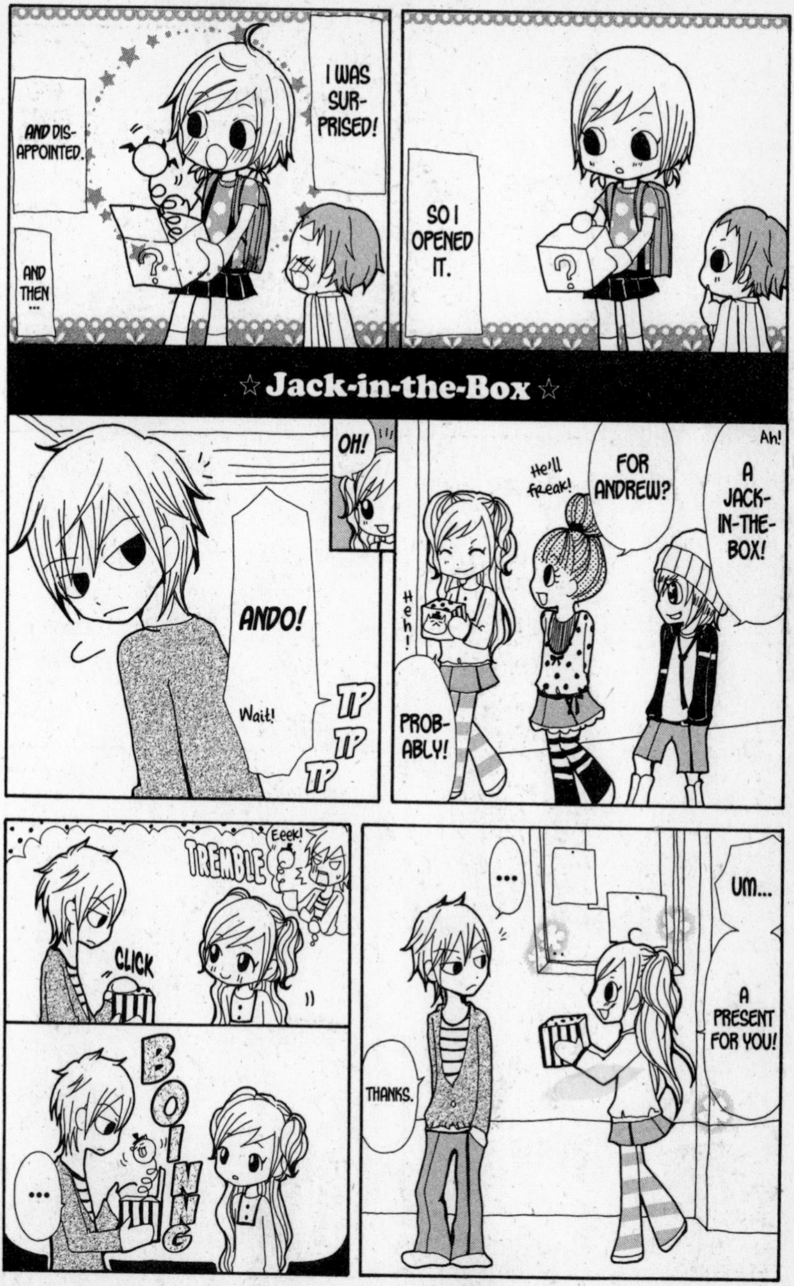
SO I OPENED IT.
I WAS SURPRISED!
AND DIS-APPOINTED.
AND THEN ...
☆ Jack-in-the-Box ☆
Ah!
A JACK-IN-THE-BOX!
FOR ANDREW?
He'll freak!
Heh!
PROBABLY!
OH!
ANDO!
Wait!
TIP TIP TIP
UM...
A PRESENT FOR YOU!
...
THANKS.
TREMBLE
Eeek!
CLICK
BOING
...

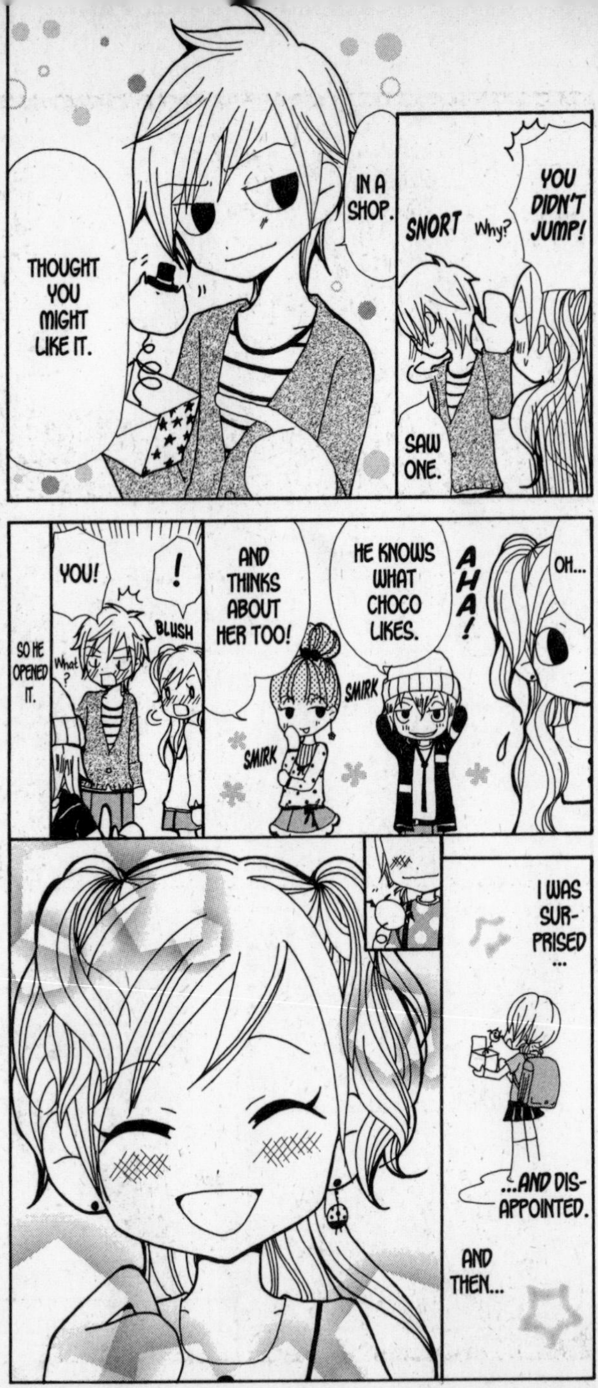
YOU DIDN'T JUMP!
Why?
SNORT
SAW ONE.
IN A SHOP.
THOUGHT YOU MIGHT LIKE IT.
OH...
AHA!
HE KNOWS WHAT CHOCO LIKES.
SMIRK
AND THINKS ABOUT HER TOO!
SMIRK
!
YOU!
BLUSH
What?
SO HE OPENED IT.
I WAS SURPRISED...
...AND DISAPPOINTED.
AND THEN...

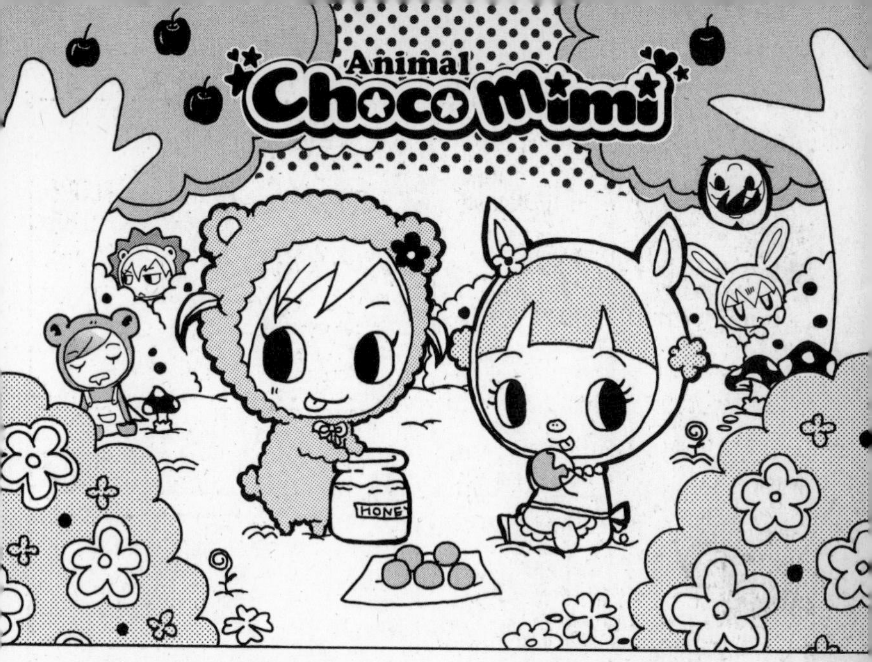
Animal
Choco Mimi
HONEY

Friends

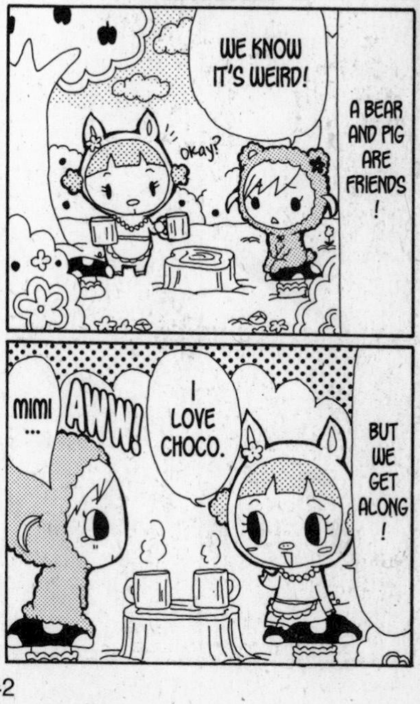
A BEAR AND PIG ARE FRIENDS!
WE KNOW IT'S WEIRD!
Okay?
BUT WE GET ALONG!
I LOVE CHOCO.
AWW!
MIMI ...

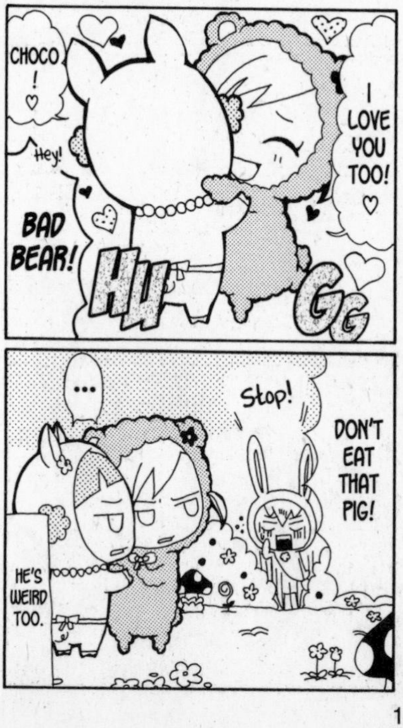
I LOVE YOU TOO! ♡
CHOCO! ♡
Hey!
BAD BEAR!
HUGG
DON'T EAT THAT PIG!
Stop!
...
HE'S WEIRD TOO.

Alone

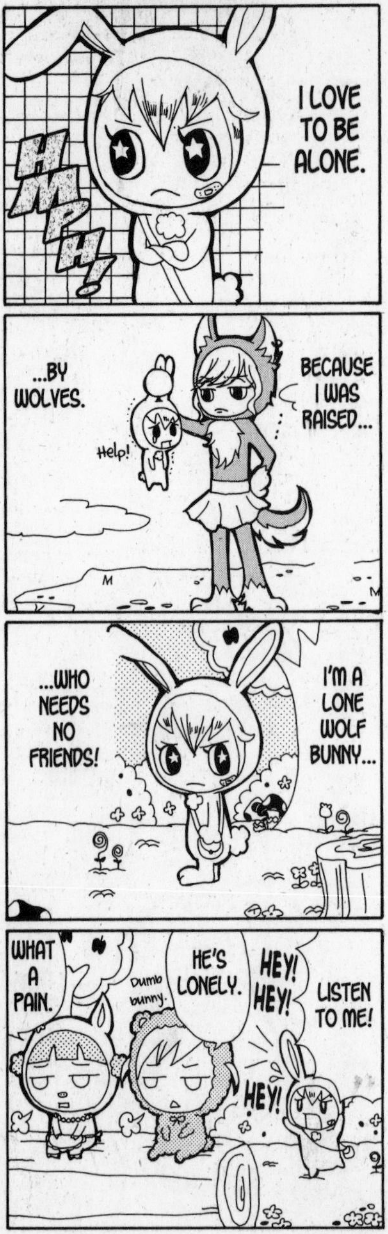
I LOVE TO BE ALONE.
HMPH!
BECAUSE I WAS RAISED...
...BY WOLVES.
Help!
I'M A LONE WOLF BUNNY...
...WHO NEEDS NO FRIENDS!
LISTEN TO ME!
HEY! HEY!
HE'S LONELY.
Dumb bunny.
WHAT A PAIN.
HEY!

Boy

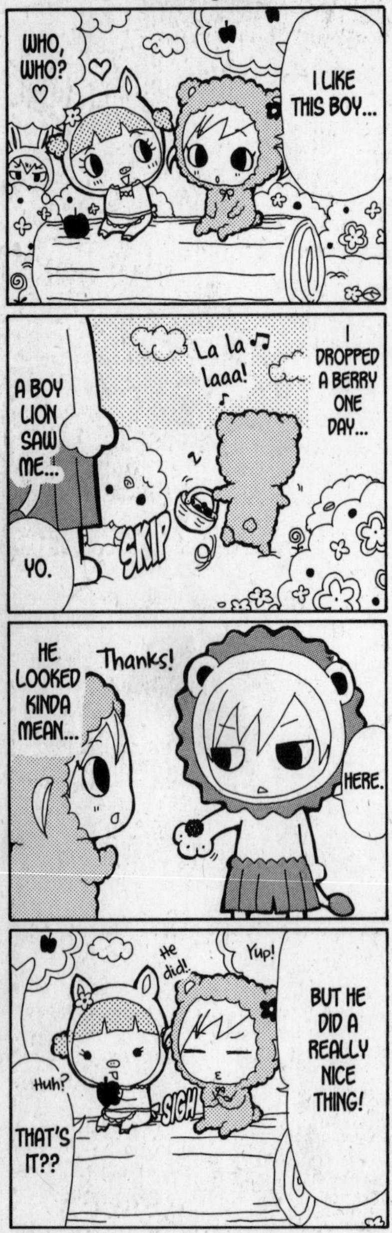
I LIKE THIS BOY...
WHO, WHO? ♡
I DROPPED A BERRY ONE DAY...
La la laaa! ♫
A BOY LION SAW ME...
SKIP
YO.
HERE.
Thanks!
HE LOOKED KINDA MEAN...
BUT HE DID A REALLY NICE THING!
Yup!
He did!
SIGH
Huh?
THAT'S IT??

Flower

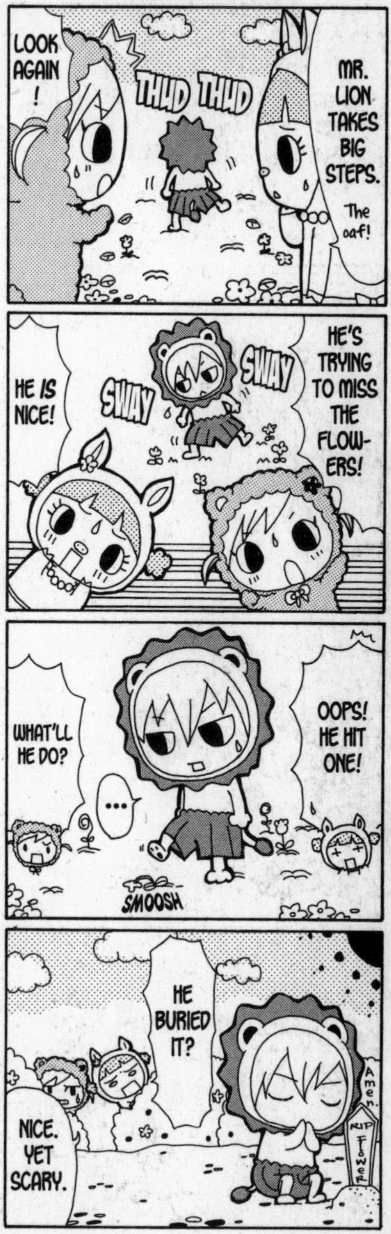
MR. LION TAKES BIG STEPS.
The oaf!
THUD THUD
LOOK AGAIN!
HE'S TRYING TO MISS THE FLOWERS!
SWAY
SWAY
HE IS NICE!
OOPS! HE HIT ONE!
WHAT'LL HE DO?
...
SMOOSH
Amen.
RIP Flower
HE BURIED IT?
NICE. YET SCARY.

Name

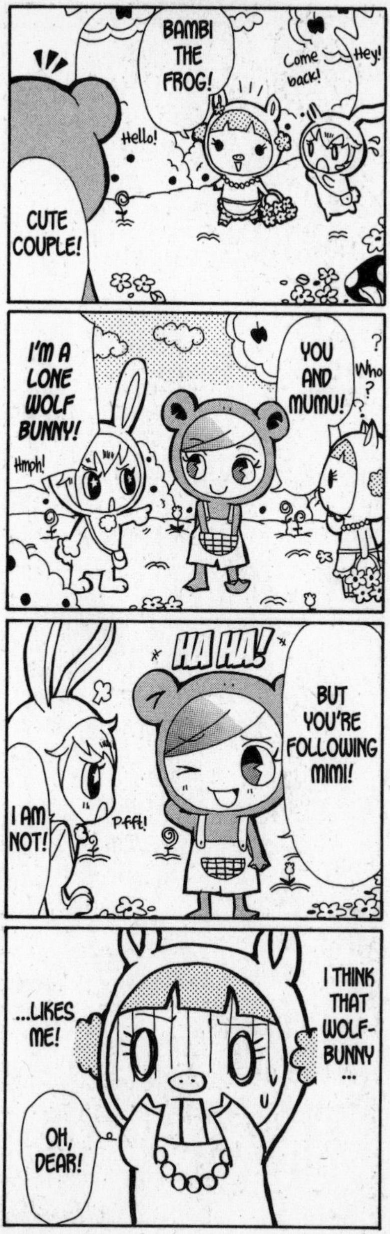
Hey!
Come back!
BAMBI THE FROG!
Hello!
CUTE COUPLE!
Who?
?
YOU AND MUMU!
I'M A LONE WOLF BUNNY!
Hmph!
BUT YOU'RE FOLLOWING MIMI!
HA HA!
Pfft!
I AM NOT!
I THINK THAT WOLF-BUNNY...
...LIKES ME!
OH, DEAR!

Cool

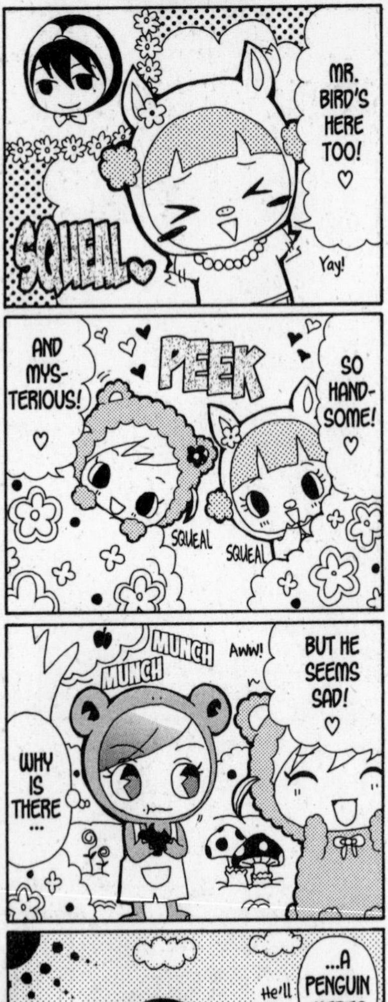
MR. BIRD'S HERE TOO! ♡
Yay!
SQUEAL ♡
SO HAND-SOME! ♡
PEEK
AND MYS-TERIOUS! ♡
SQUEAL
SQUEAL
BUT HE SEEMS SAD! ♡
AWW!
MUNCH
MUNCH
WHY IS THERE ...
...A PENGUIN HERE?
He'll die!
PUF
PUF
SO HOT...

House

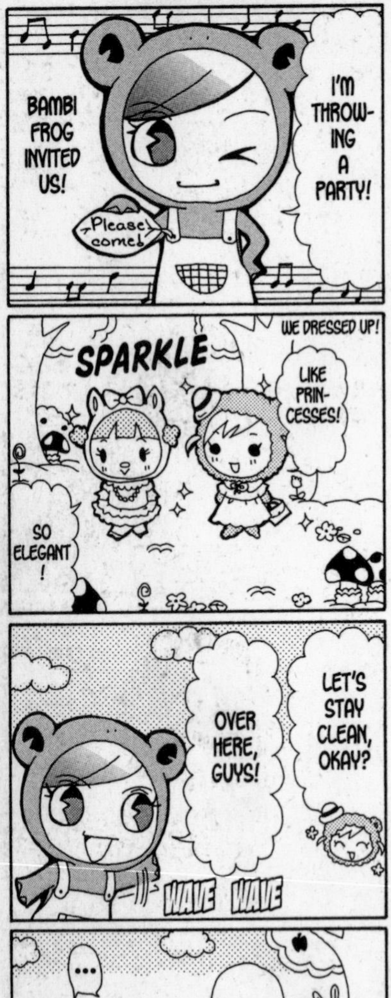
I'M THROW-ING A PARTY!
BAMBI FROG INVITED US!
Please come!
WE DRESSED UP!
LIKE PRIN-CESSES!
SPARKLE
SO ELEGANT!
LET'S STAY CLEAN, OKAY?
OVER HERE, GUYS!
WAVE WAVE
DIVE IN!
...
Bambi
SPLASH

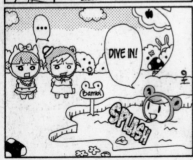

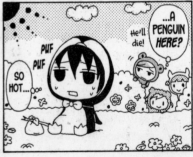

CHOCOMIMI PINUP PAGE!

I'm Yuka Fujiwara, a super ChocoMimi fan. I decided to draw my three favorite characters: Mikachin, Choco and Ando. But I love the pets too! I love everybody, in fact! Thank you for printing my drawings.

Sincerely, Yuka Fujiwara

(Who loves her ChocoMimi-filled room!)

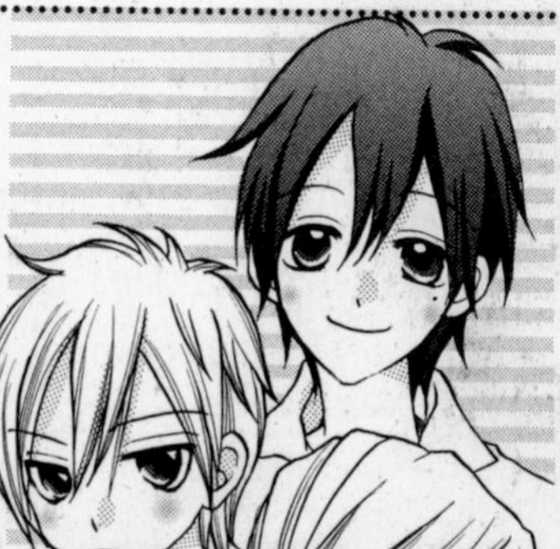

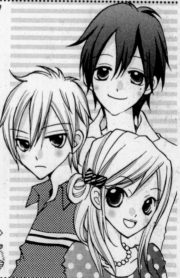

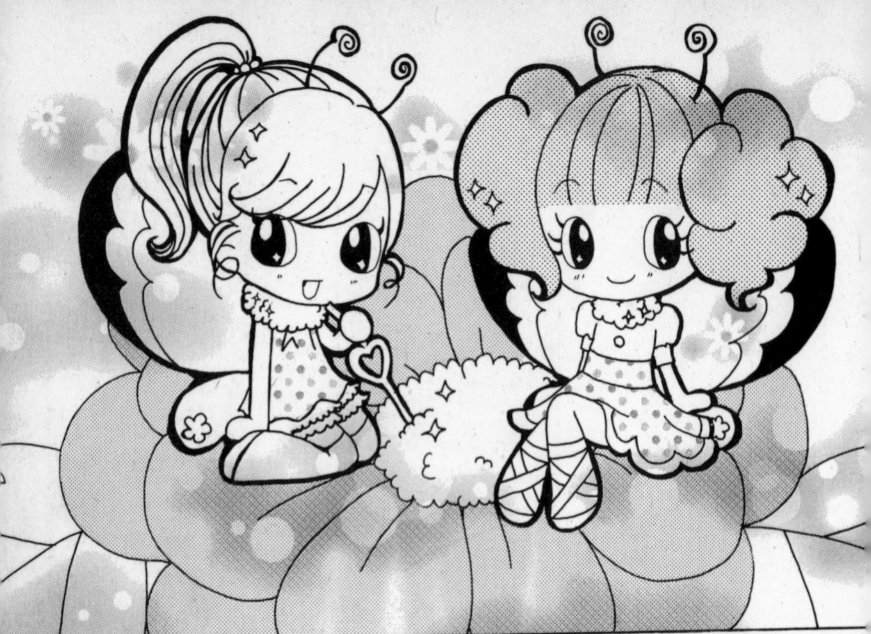

☆Camping Trip☆

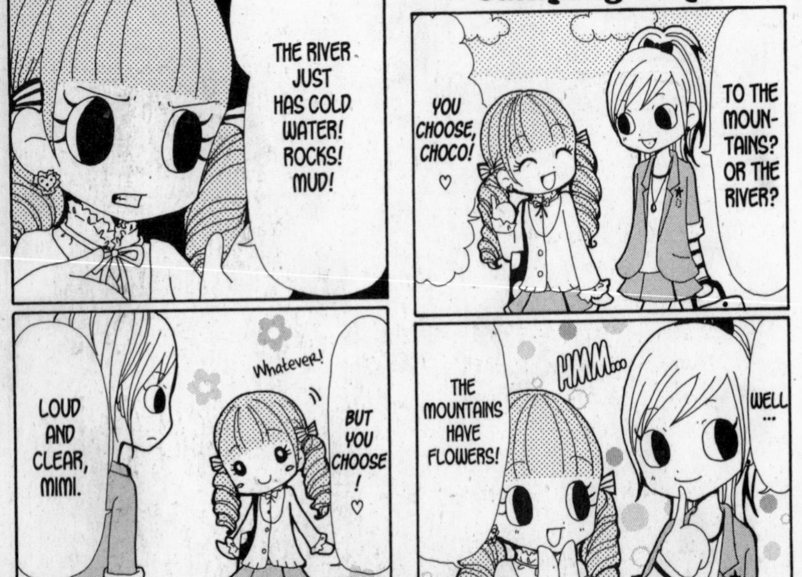
TO THE MOUNTAINS? OR THE RIVER?
YOU CHOOSE, CHOCO! ♡
WELL...
HMM...
THE MOUNTAINS HAVE FLOWERS!
THE RIVER JUST HAS COLD WATER! ROCKS! MUD!
BUT YOU CHOOSE! ♡
Whatever!
LOUD AND CLEAR, MIMI.

☆ Day Camp ☆

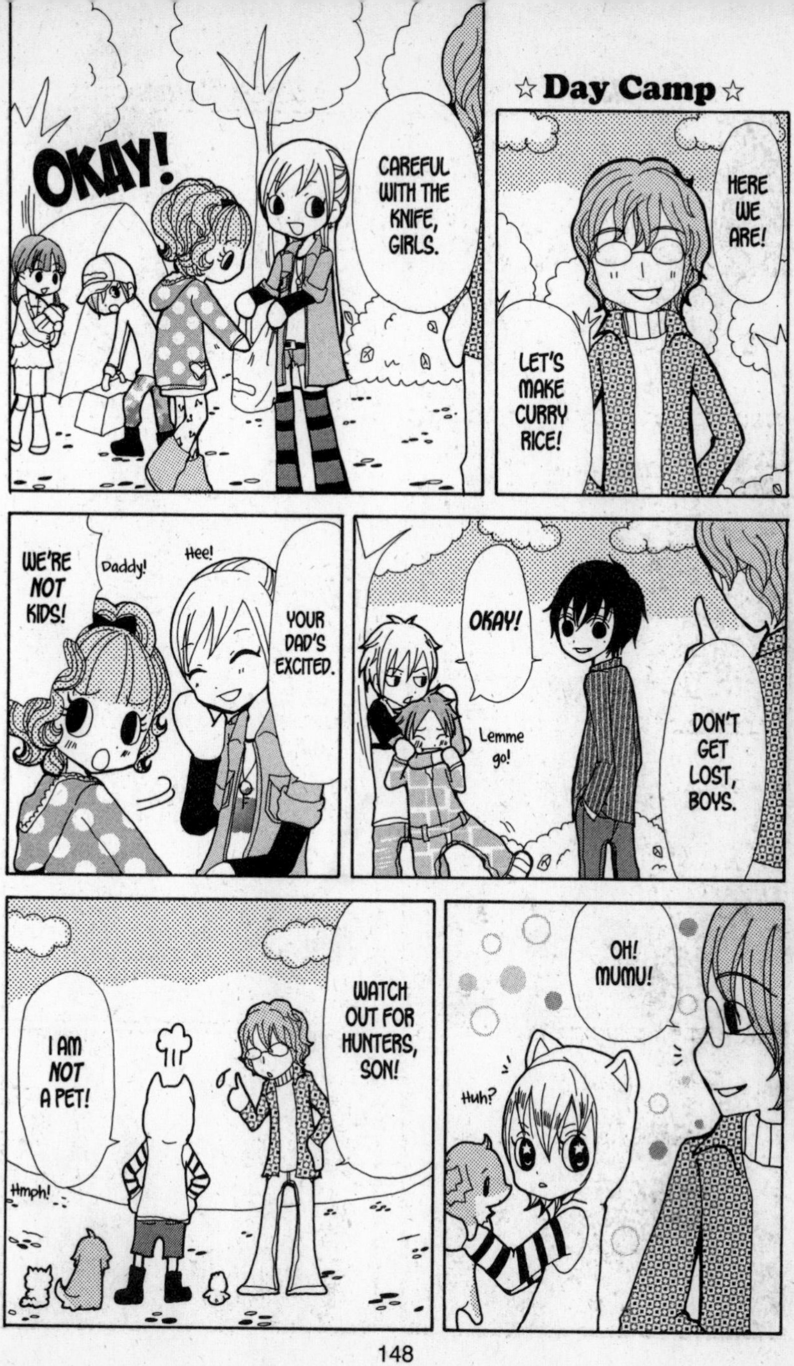
HERE WE ARE!
LET'S MAKE CURRY RICE!
CAREFUL WITH THE KNIFE, GIRLS.
OKAY!
DON'T GET LOST, BOYS.
OKAY!
Lemme go!
YOUR DAD'S EXCITED.
Hee!
Daddy!
WE'RE NOT KIDS!
OH! MUMU!
Huh?
WATCH OUT FOR HUNTERS, SON!
I AM NOT A PET!
Hmph!

☆Rice Cooker☆

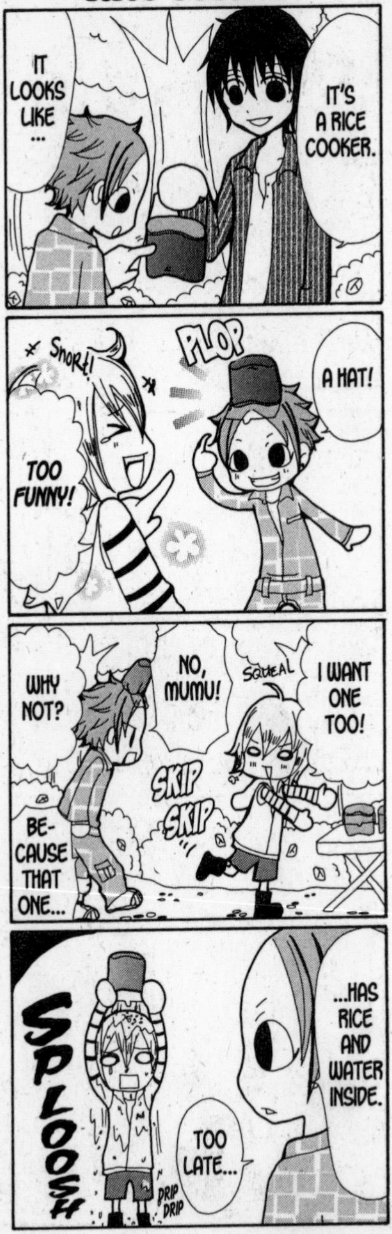
IT'S A RICE COOKER.
IT LOOKS LIKE ...
A HAT!
PLOP
Snort!
TOO FUNNY!
I WANT ONE TOO!
SQUEAL
NO, MUMU!
WHY NOT?
SKIP
SKIP
BE-CAUSE THAT ONE...
...HAS RICE AND WATER INSIDE.
TOO LATE...
SPLOOSH
DRIP DRIP

☆Rice☆

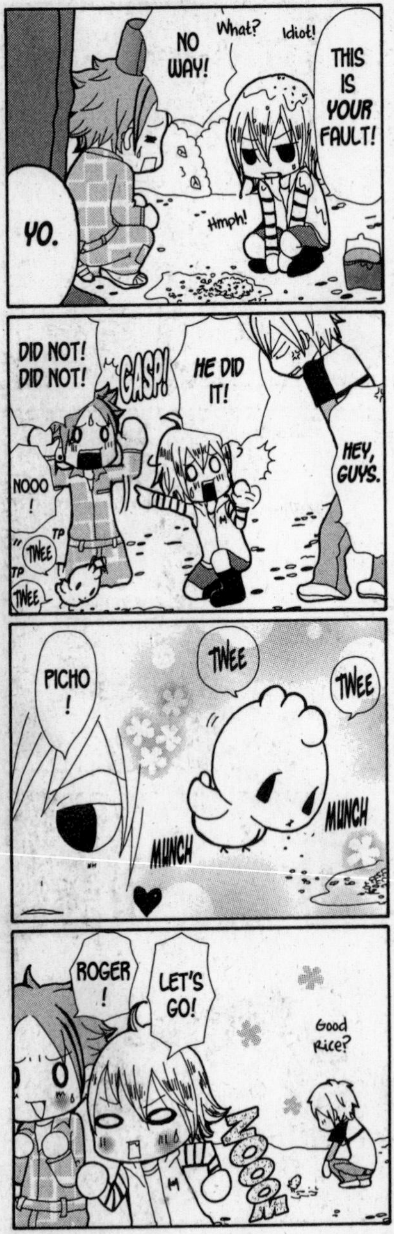
THIS IS YOUR FAULT!
Idiot!
What?
NO WAY!
Hmph!
YO.
HEY, GUYS.
HE DID IT!
GASP!
DID NOT! DID NOT!
NOOO!
TP
TWEE
TP
TWEE
TWEE
TWEE
PICHO!
MUNCH
MUNCH
Good rice?
LET'S GO!
ROGER!
ZOOOOM

☆Fire☆

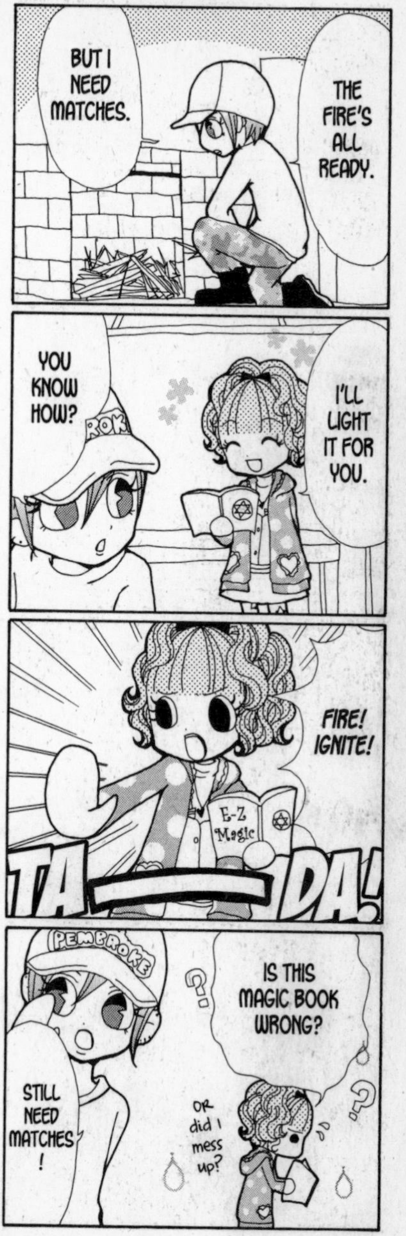
THE FIRE'S ALL READY.
BUT I NEED MATCHES.
I'LL LIGHT IT FOR YOU.
YOU KNOW HOW?
FIRE! IGNITE!
E-Z Magic
TA—DA!
IS THIS MAGIC BOOK WRONG?
OR did I mess up?
PEMBROKE
STILL NEED MATCHES!

☆Firewood☆

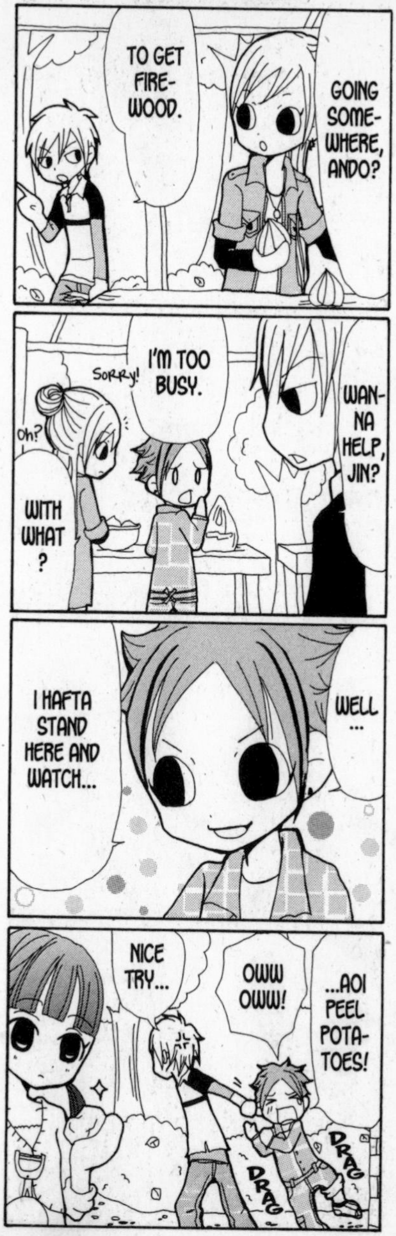
GOING SOMEWHERE, ANDO?
TO GET FIREWOOD.
WANNA HELP, JIN?
I'M TOO BUSY.
SORRY!
Oh?
WITH WHAT?
WELL...
I HAFTA STAND HERE AND WATCH...
...AOI PEEL POTATOES!
DRAG
DRAG
OWW OWW!
NICE TRY...

☆ Riddle ☆

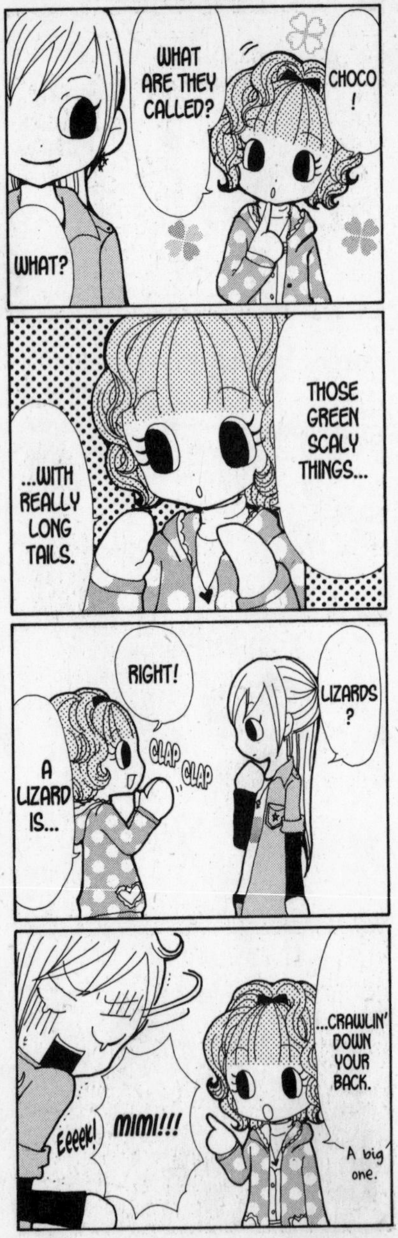

CHOCO!
WHAT ARE THEY CALLED?
WHAT?
THOSE GREEN SCALY THINGS...
...WITH REALLY LONG TAILS.
LIZARDS?
RIGHT!
CLAP CLAP
A LIZARD IS...
...CRAWLIN' DOWN YOUR BACK.
A big one.
MIMI!!!
Eeeek!

☆ Carrot ☆

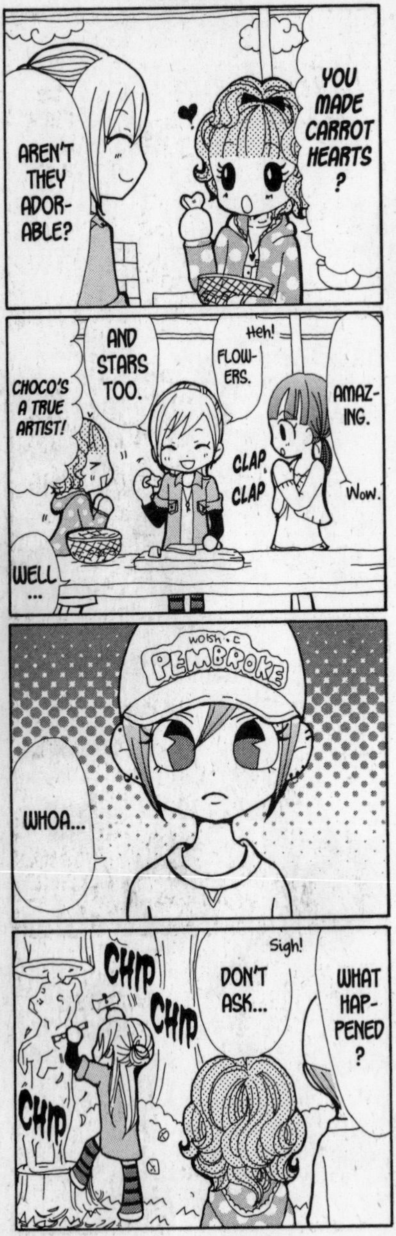

YOU MADE CARROT HEARTS?
AREN'T THEY ADORABLE?
AMAZ-ING.
Wow.
Heh!
FLOW-ERS.
AND STARS TOO.
CLAP, CLAP
CHOCO'S A TRUE ARTIST!
WELL...
PEMBROKE
WHOA...
WHAT HAP-PENED?
Sigh!
DON'T ASK...
CHIP
CHIP
CHIP

☆Finger☆

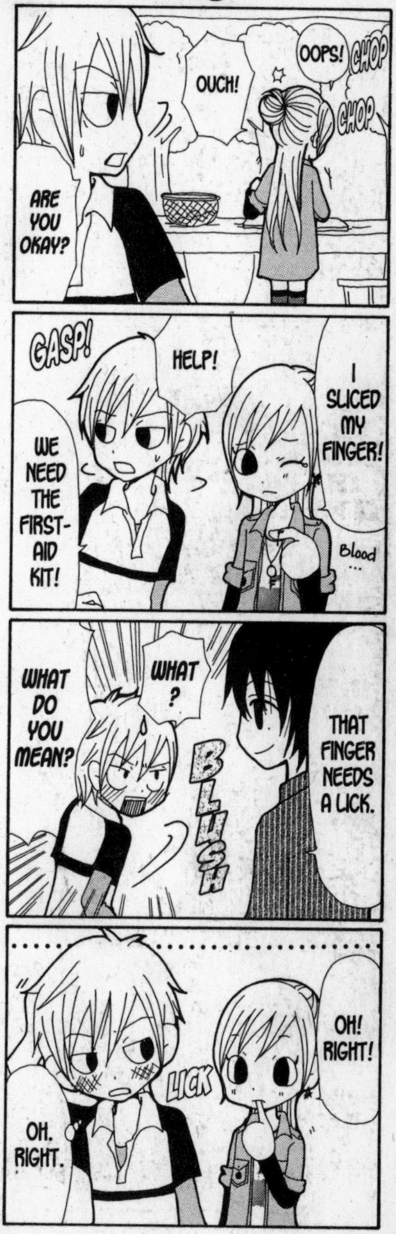
OOPS!
CHOP
CHOP
OUCH!
ARE YOU OKAY?
I SLICED MY FINGER!
Blood...
HELP!
GASP!
WE NEED THE FIRST-AID KIT!
THAT FINGER NEEDS A LICK.
BLUSH
WHAT?
WHAT DO YOU MEAN?
OH! RIGHT!
LICK
OH. RIGHT.

☆Potato☆

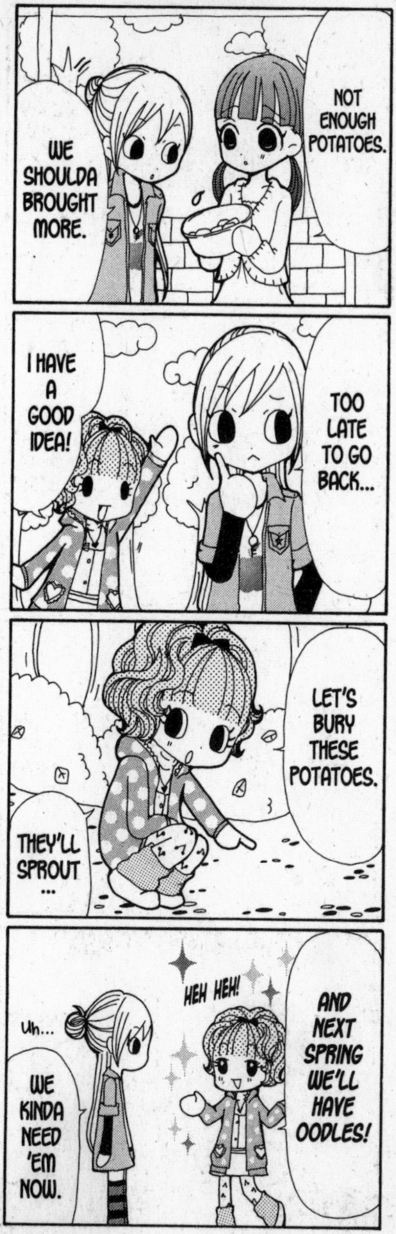
NOT ENOUGH POTATOES.
WE SHOULDA BROUGHT MORE.
TOO LATE TO GO BACK...
I HAVE A GOOD IDEA!
LET'S BURY THESE POTATOES.
THEY'LL SPROUT...
AND NEXT SPRING WE'LL HAVE OODLES!
HEH HEH!
Uh...
WE KINDA NEED 'EM NOW.

☆Panic☆ ☆Memo☆

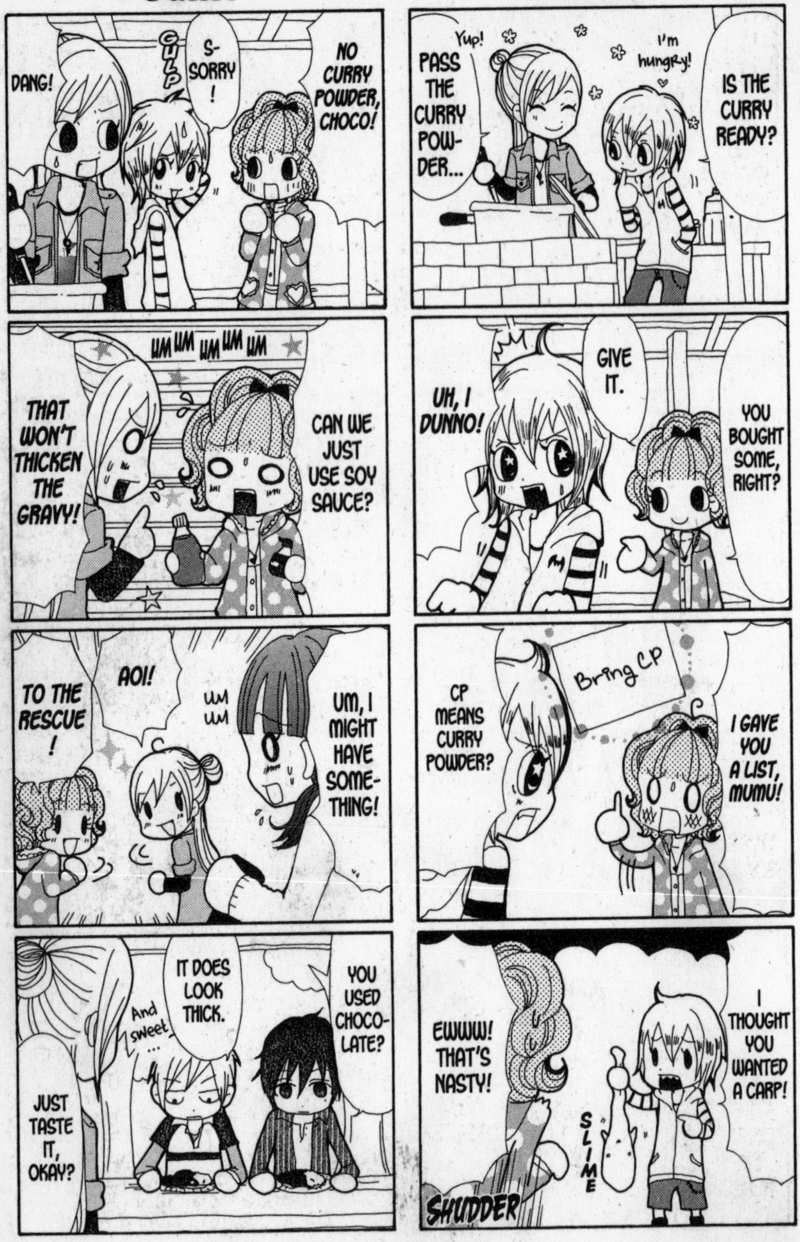
IS THE CURRY READY?
I'm hungry!
Yup!
PASS THE CURRY POWDER...
YOU BOUGHT SOME, RIGHT?
GIVE IT.
UH, I DUNNO!
I GAVE YOU A LIST, MUMU!
Bring CP
CP MEANS CURRY POWDER?
I THOUGHT YOU WANTED A CARP!
SLIME
EWWW! THAT'S NASTY!
SHUDDER
NO CURRY POWDER, CHOCO!
S-SORRY!
GULP
DANG!
CAN WE JUST USE SOY SAUCE?
UM UM UM UM UM
THAT WON'T THICKEN THE GRAVY!
UM, I MIGHT HAVE SOMETHING!
UM UM
AOI!
TO THE RESCUE!
YOU USED CHOCOLATE?
IT DOES LOOK THICK.
And sweet...
JUST TASTE IT, OKAY?

☆ Going Home ☆

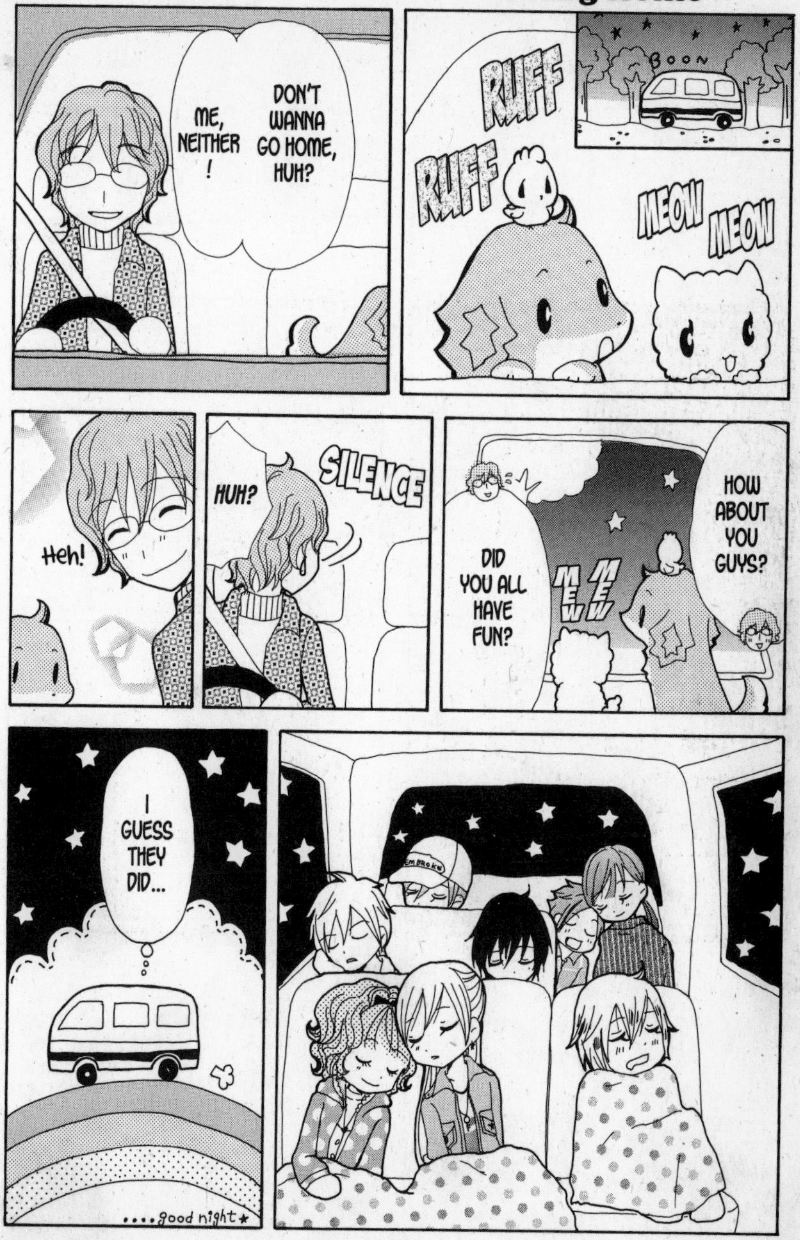
BOON
MEOW MEOW
RUFF RUFF
DON'T WANNA GO HOME, HUH?
ME, NEITHER!
HOW ABOUT YOU GUYS?
DID YOU ALL HAVE FUN?
MEW MEW
SILENCE
HUH?
Heh!
I GUESS THEY DID...
....good night★

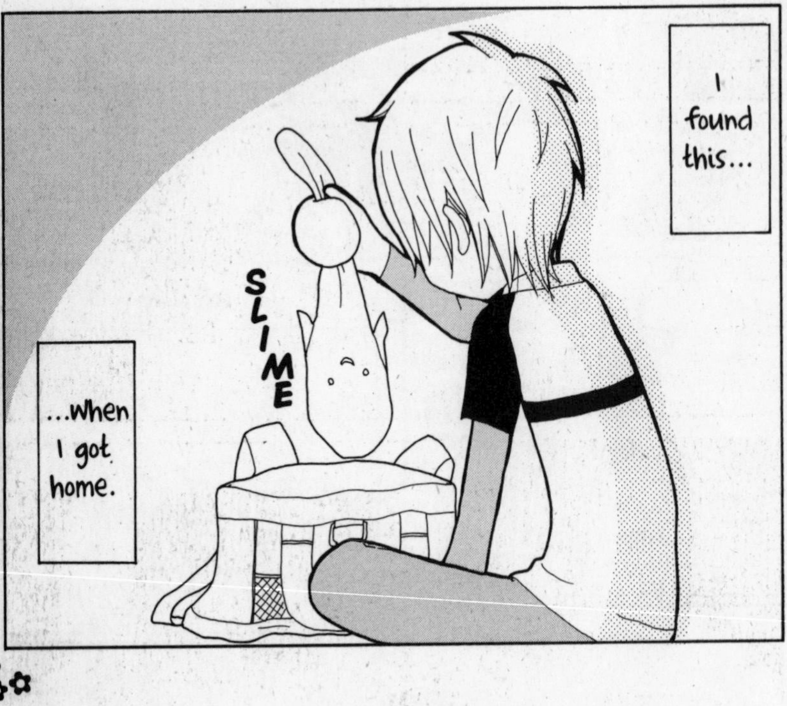
I found this...
SLIME
...when I got home.

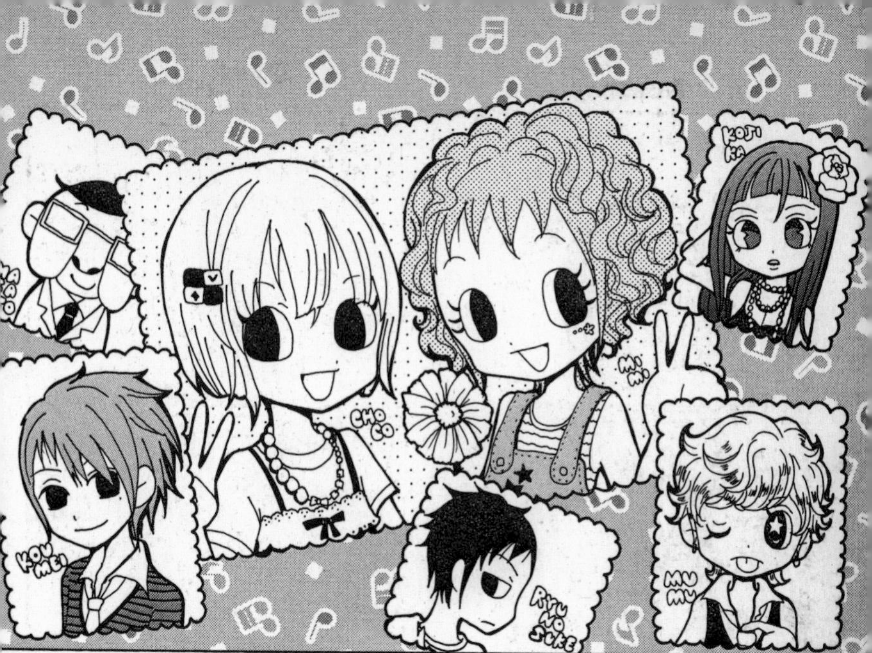
KOJI KA
MI MI
CHO CO
MU MU
RYU NO SUKE
KOU MEI

☆ **Short** ☆

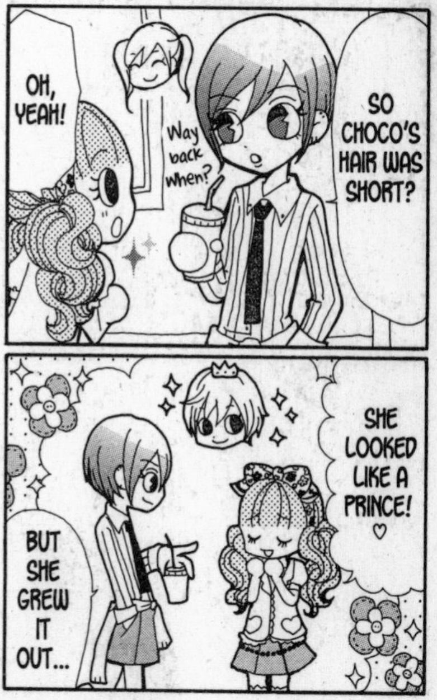
SO CHOCO'S HAIR WAS SHORT?
Way back when?
OH, YEAH!
SHE LOOKED LIKE A PRINCE!
BUT SHE GREW IT OUT...

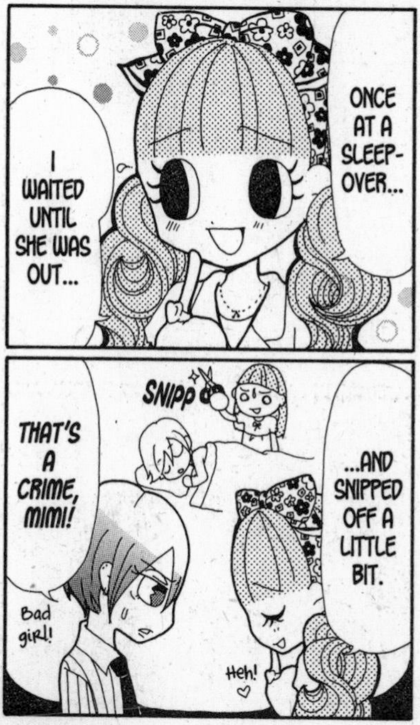
ONCE AT A SLEEP-OVER...
I WAITED UNTIL SHE WAS OUT...
...AND SNIPPED OFF A LITTLE BIT.
SNIPP
Heh!
THAT'S A CRIME, MIMI!
Bad girl!

☆Scarf☆

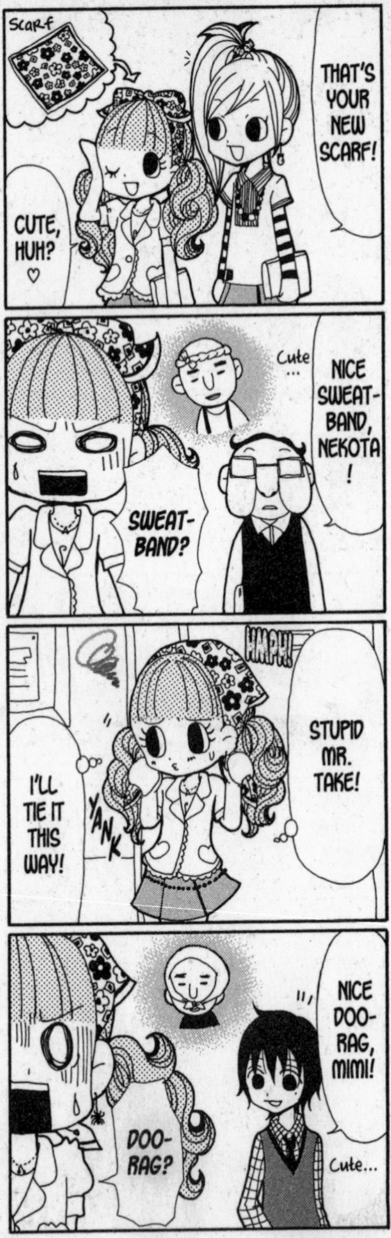
THAT'S YOUR NEW SCARF!
Scarf
CUTE, HUH? ♡
NICE SWEAT-BAND, NEKOTA!
Cute ...
SWEAT-BAND?
HMPH!
STUPID MR. TAKE!
YANK
I'LL TIE IT THIS WAY!
NICE DOO-RAG, MIMI!
Cute...
DOO-RAG?

☆Arrange☆

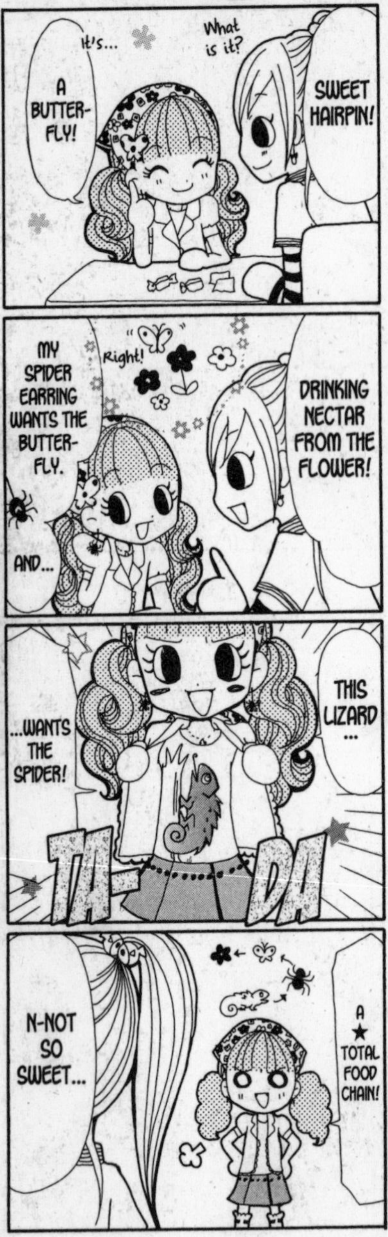
SWEET HAIRPIN!
What is it?
It's...
A BUTTER-FLY!
DRINKING NECTAR FROM THE FLOWER!
Right!
MY SPIDER EARRING WANTS THE BUTTER-FLY.
AND...
THIS LIZARD ...
...WANTS THE SPIDER!
TA-DA
A ★ TOTAL FOOD CHAIN!
N-NOT SO SWEET...

☆Change☆

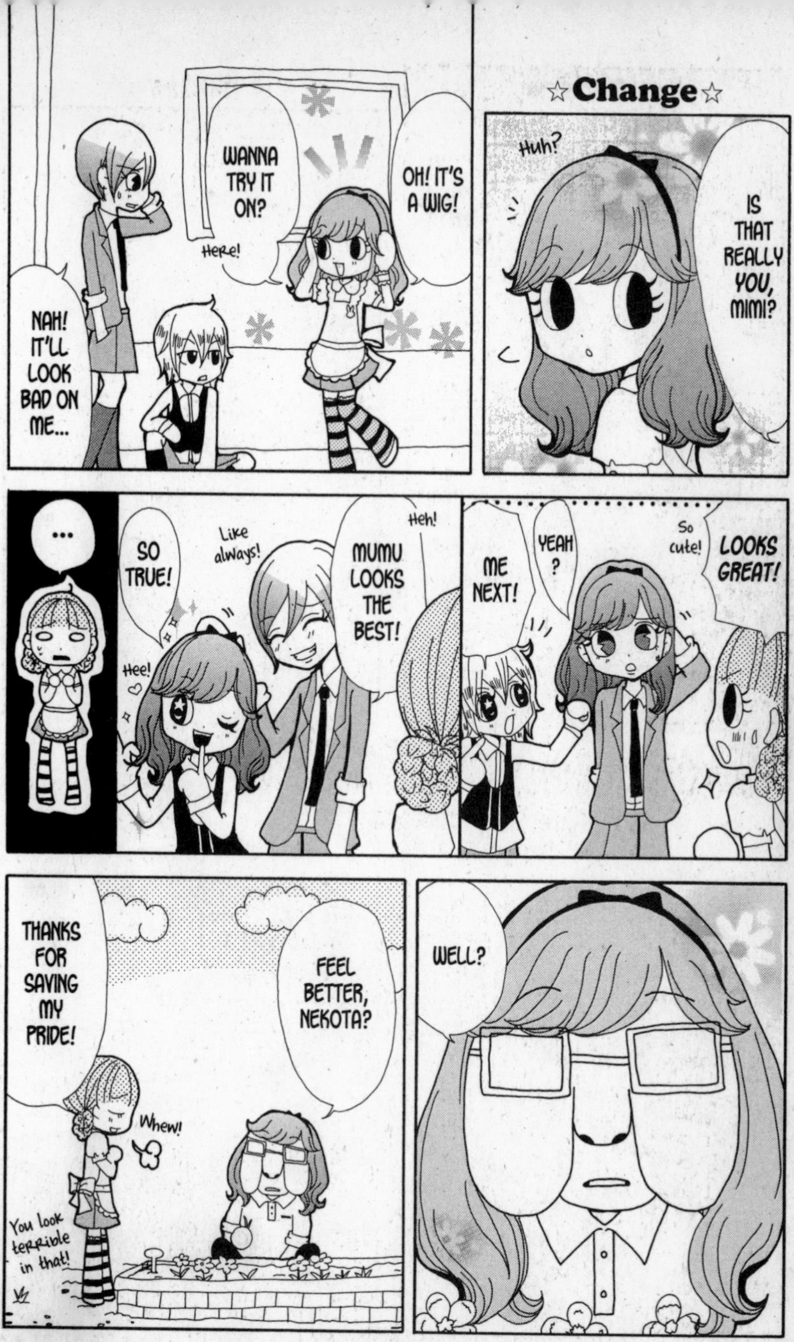
Huh?
IS THAT REALLY YOU, MIMI?
OH! IT'S A WIG!
WANNA TRY IT ON?
Here!
NAH! IT'LL LOOK BAD ON ME...
LOOKS GREAT!
So cute!
YEAH?
ME NEXT!
Heh!
MUMU LOOKS THE BEST!
Like always!
SO TRUE!
Hee!
...
WELL?
FEEL BETTER, NEKOTA?
THANKS FOR SAVING MY PRIDE!
Whew!
You look terrible in that!

☆ Skirt ☆

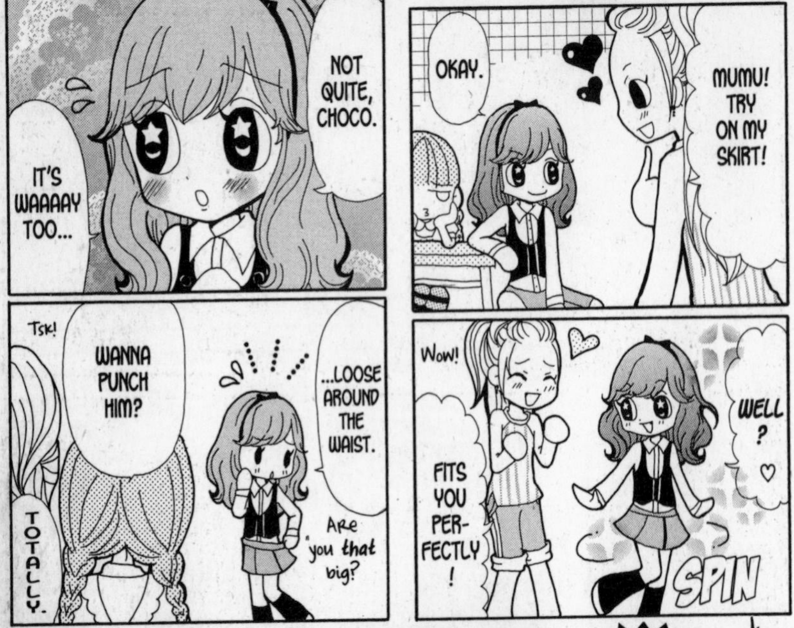
MUMU! TRY ON MY SKIRT!
OKAY.
WELL? ♡
SPIN
Wow!
FITS YOU PER-FECTLY!
NOT QUITE, CHOCO.
IT'S WAAAAY TOO...
...LOOSE AROUND THE WAIST.
Are you that big?
WANNA PUNCH HIM?
Tsk!
TOTALLY.

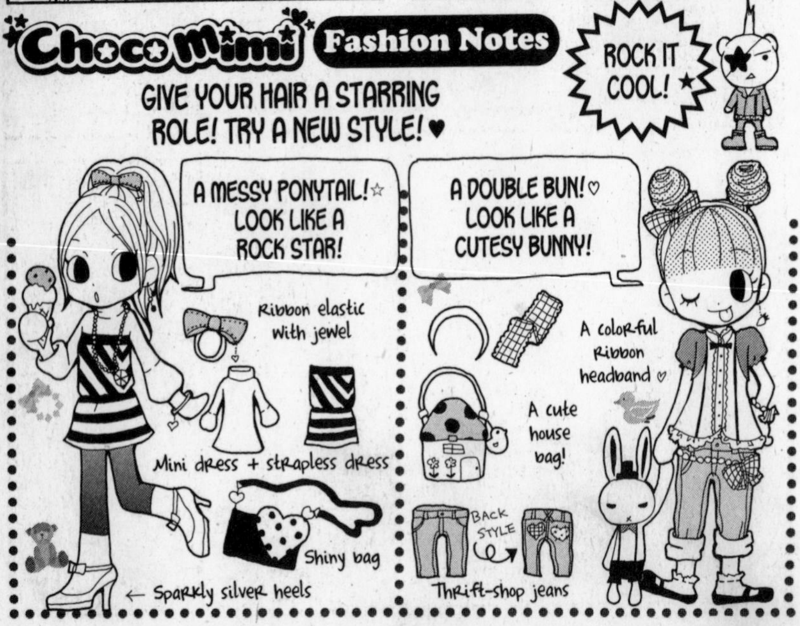
ChocoMimi Fashion Notes
ROCK IT COOL! ★
GIVE YOUR HAIR A STARRING ROLE! TRY A NEW STYLE! ♥
A DOUBLE BUN! ♡ LOOK LIKE A CUTESY BUNNY!
A colorful Ribbon headband ♡
A cute house bag!
BACK STYLE
Thrift-shop jeans
A MESSY PONYTAIL! ☆ LOOK LIKE A ROCK STAR!
Ribbon elastic with jewel
Mini dress + strapless dress
Shiny bag
← Sparkly silver heels

☆ My Style ☆

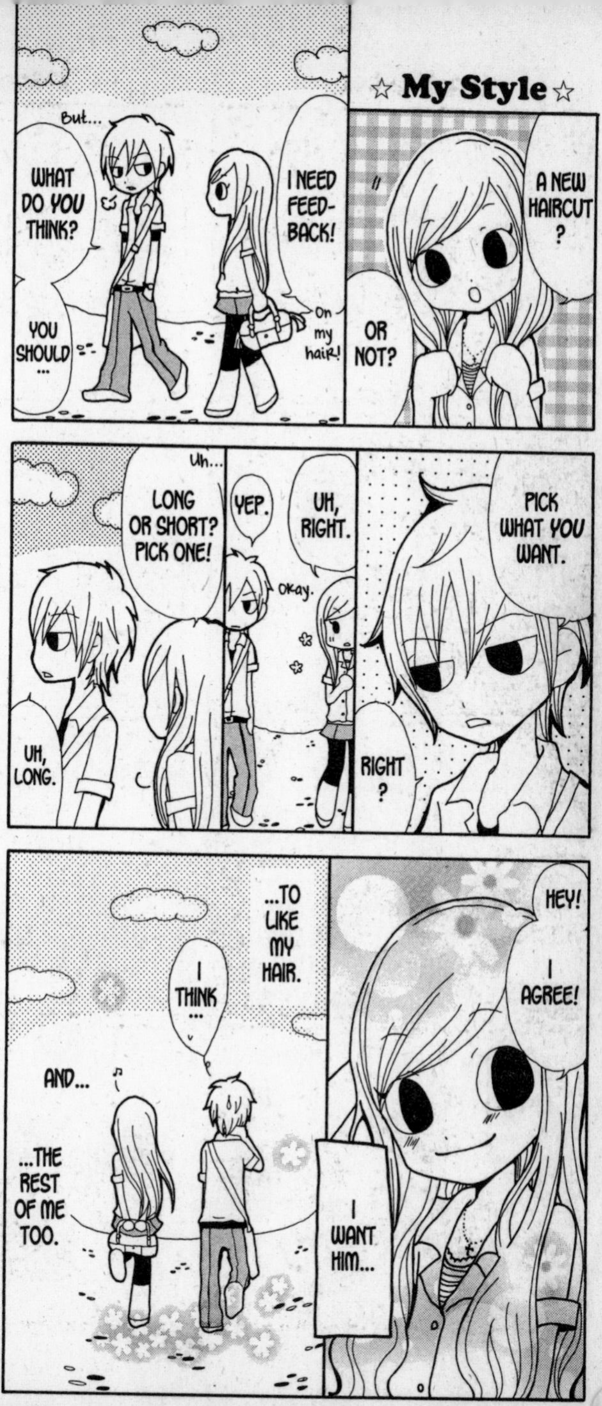
A NEW HAIRCUT?
OR NOT?
I NEED FEED-BACK!
On my hair!
But...
WHAT DO YOU THINK?
YOU SHOULD...
PICK WHAT YOU WANT.
RIGHT?
UH, RIGHT.
YEP.
Okay.
Uh...
LONG OR SHORT? PICK ONE!
UH, LONG.
HEY!
I AGREE!
I WANT HIM...
...TO LIKE MY HAIR.
I THINK...
AND...
...THE REST OF ME TOO.

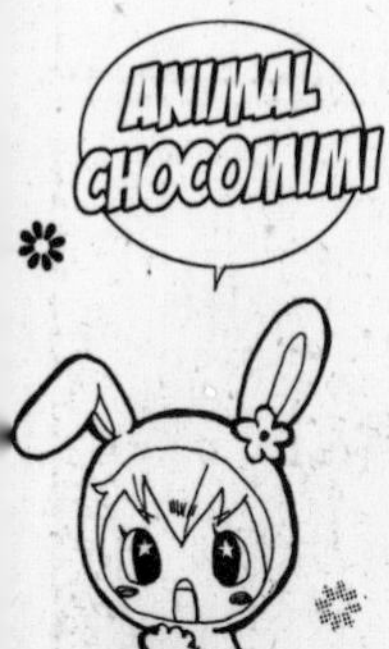
ANIMAL CHOCOMIMI

Cake

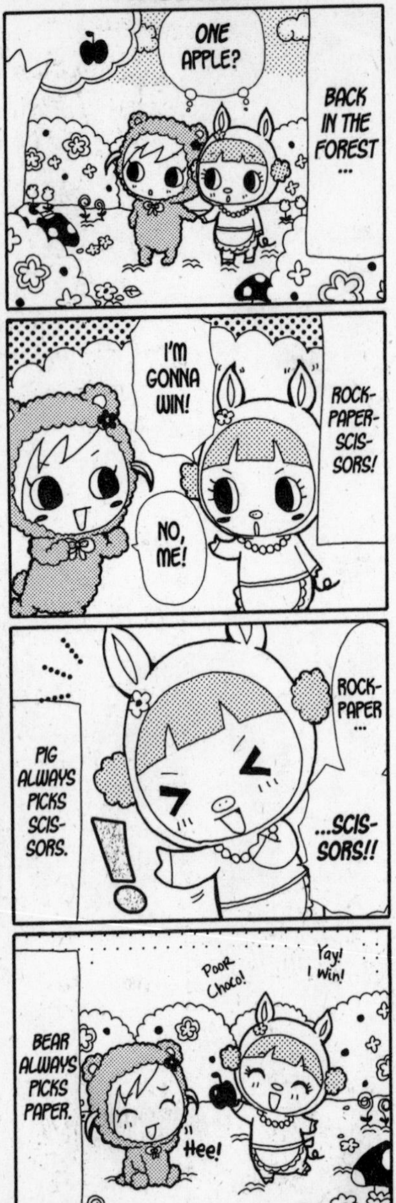
BACK IN THE FOREST ...
ONE APPLE?
ROCK-PAPER-SCIS-SORS!
I'M GONNA WIN!
NO, ME!
ROCK-PAPER ...
...SCIS-SORS!!
PIG ALWAYS PICKS SCIS-SORS.
Yay! I win!
Poor Choco!
BEAR ALWAYS PICKS PAPER.
Hee!

Red

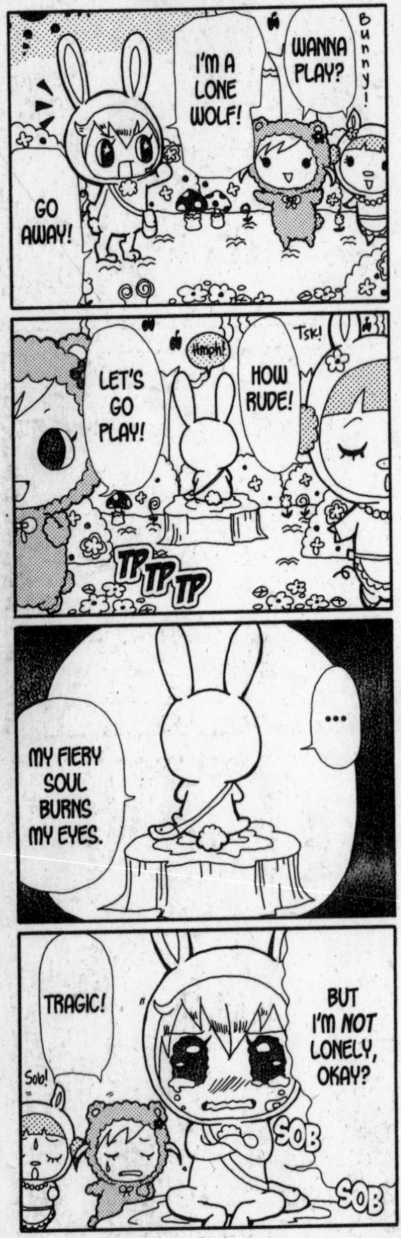
Bunny!
WANNA PLAY?
I'M A LONE WOLF!
GO AWAY!
Tsk!
HOW RUDE!
Hmph!
LET'S GO PLAY!
TP TP TP
...
MY FIERY SOUL BURNS MY EYES.
BUT I'M NOT LONELY, OKAY?
TRAGIC!
SOB
SOB
Sob!

Like

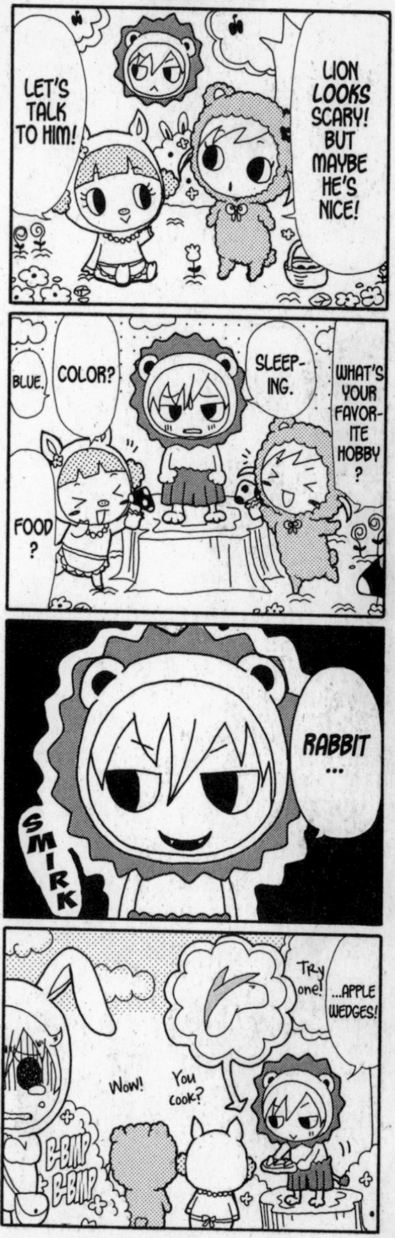
LION LOOKS SCARY! BUT MAYBE HE'S NICE!
LET'S TALK TO HIM!
WHAT'S YOUR FAVOR-ITE HOBBY?
SLEEP-ING.
COLOR?
BLUE.
FOOD?
RABBIT...
SMIRK
...APPLE WEDGES!
Try one!
You cook?
Wow!
B-BMP B-BMP

Spring

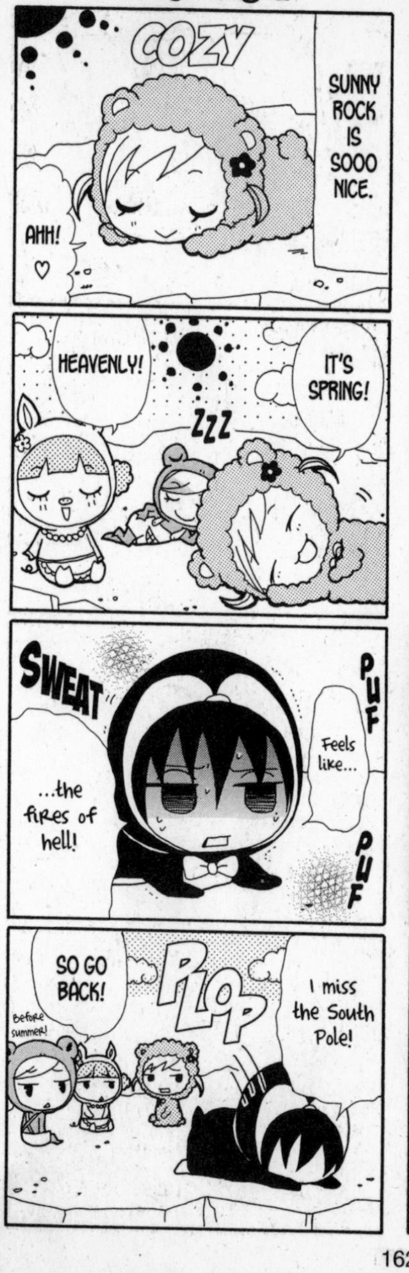
SUNNY ROCK IS SOOO NICE.
COZY
AHH! ♡
IT'S SPRING!
HEAVENLY!
ZZZ
PUF
Feels like...
PUF
SWEAT
...the fires of hell!
I miss the South Pole!
PLOP
SO GO BACK!
Before summer!

Three

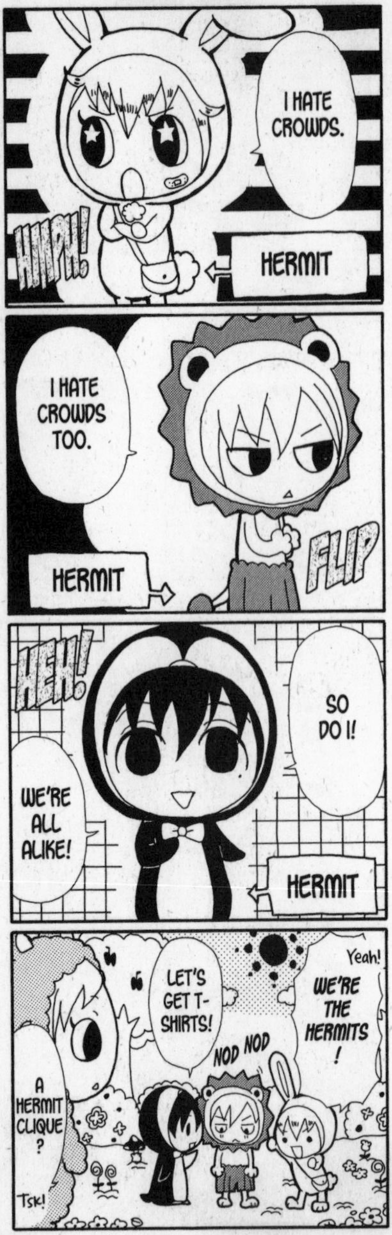
I HATE CROWDS.
HMPH!
HERMIT
I HATE CROWDS TOO.
FLIP
HERMIT
SO DO I!
HEH!
WE'RE ALL ALIKE!
HERMIT
Yeah!
WE'RE THE HERMITS!
NOD NOD
LET'S GET T-SHIRTS!
A HERMIT CLIQUE?
Tsk!

Help

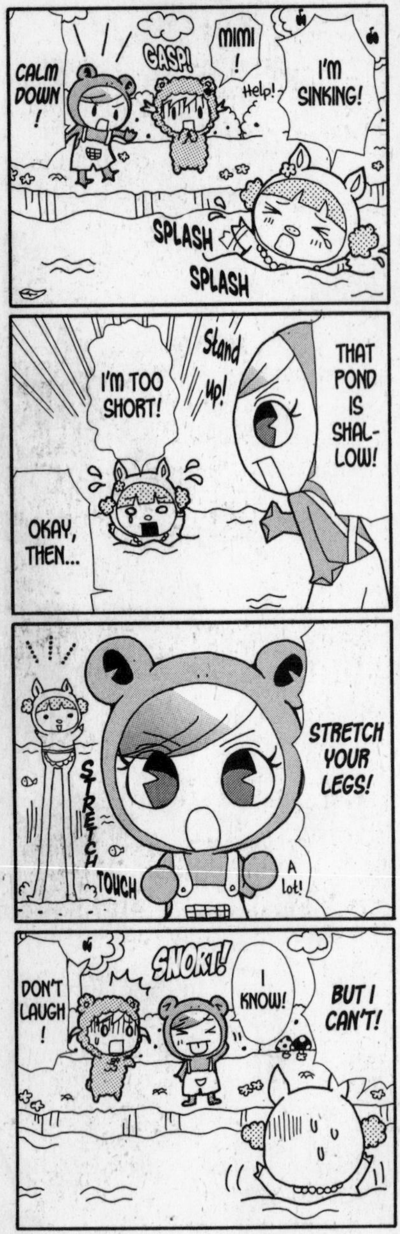
I'M SINKING!
MIMI!
Help!
GASP!
CALM DOWN!
SPLASH
SPLASH
THAT POND IS SHALLOW!
Stand up!
I'M TOO SHORT!
OKAY, THEN...
STRETCH YOUR LEGS!
A lot!
STRETCH
TOUCH
BUT I CAN'T!
I KNOW!
SNORT!
DON'T LAUGH!

Clover

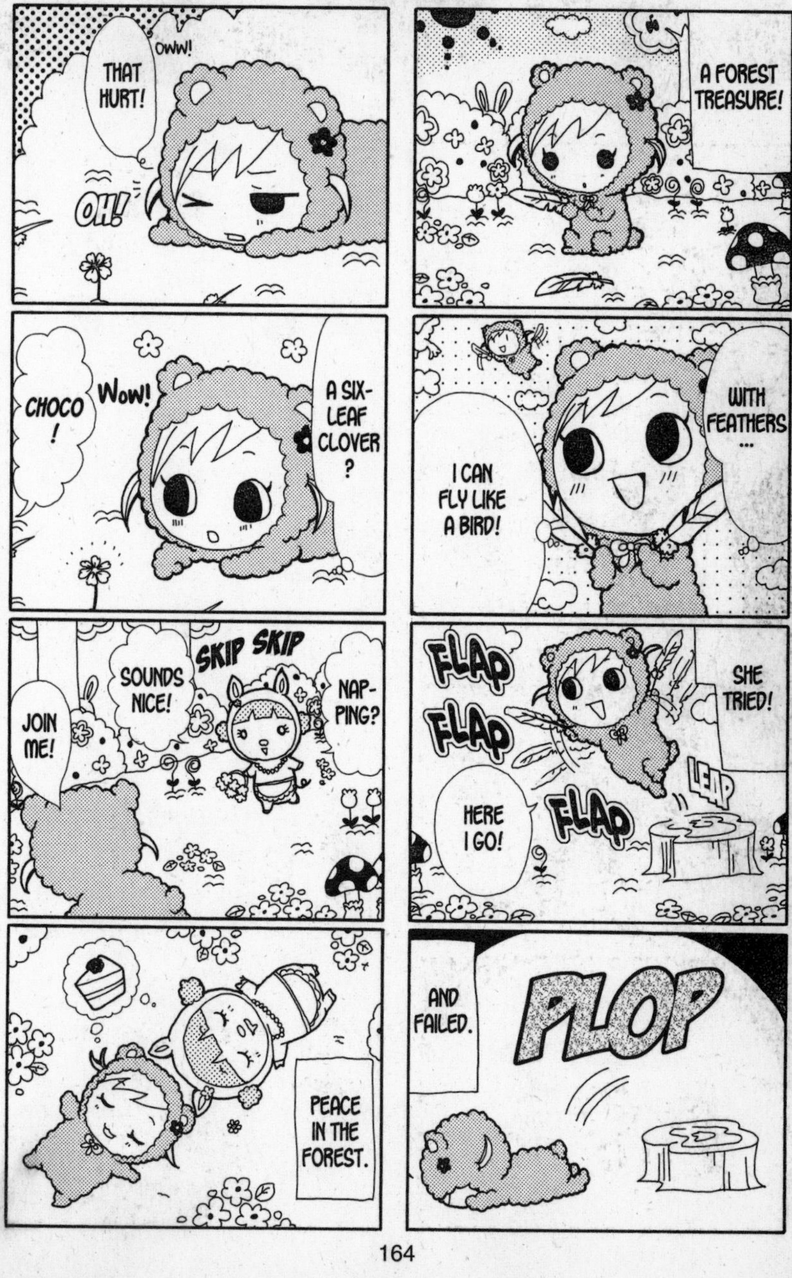
A FOREST TREASURE!
WITH FEATHERS...
I CAN FLY LIKE A BIRD!
SHE TRIED!
FLAP
FLAP
LEAP
HERE I GO!
FLAP
AND FAILED.
PLOP
OWW!
THAT HURT!
OH!
A SIX-LEAF CLOVER?
WOW!
CHOCO!
NAP-PING?
SKIP SKIP
SOUNDS NICE!
JOIN ME!
PEACE IN THE FOREST.

Extra 4

Check out...
...our new shirts!
HERMITS

WE LOOK LIKE A TEAM!
NOD NOD
Yep.
WE DO.
HERMITS
FRIENDS ARE OKAY...
RIGHT?
ACKK!
HERMITS
TOO HOT!
PUF PUF
CAN'T WEAR IT!
TWACK
I quit!
HERMITS

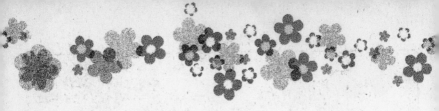

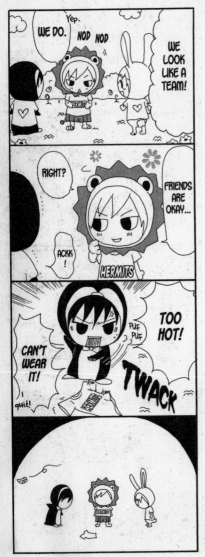

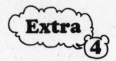

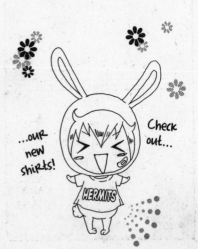

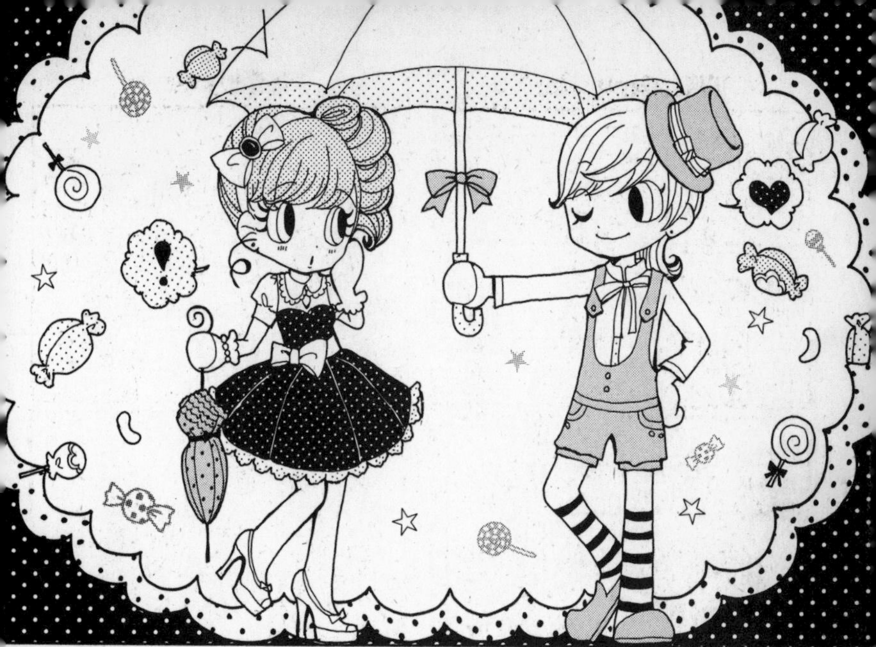

☆Umbrella☆

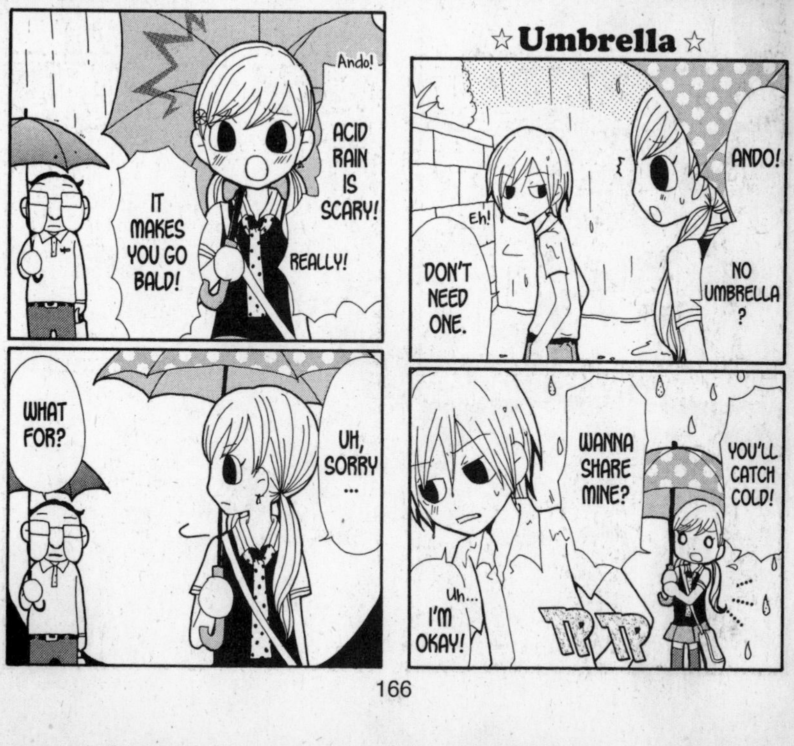
ANDO!
NO UMBRELLA?
Eh!
DON'T NEED ONE.
YOU'LL CATCH COLD!
WANNA SHARE MINE?
Uh... I'M OKAY!
TP TP
Ando!
ACID RAIN IS SCARY!
REALLY!
IT MAKES YOU GO BALD!
UH, SORRY...
WHAT FOR?

☆ Dryer ☆

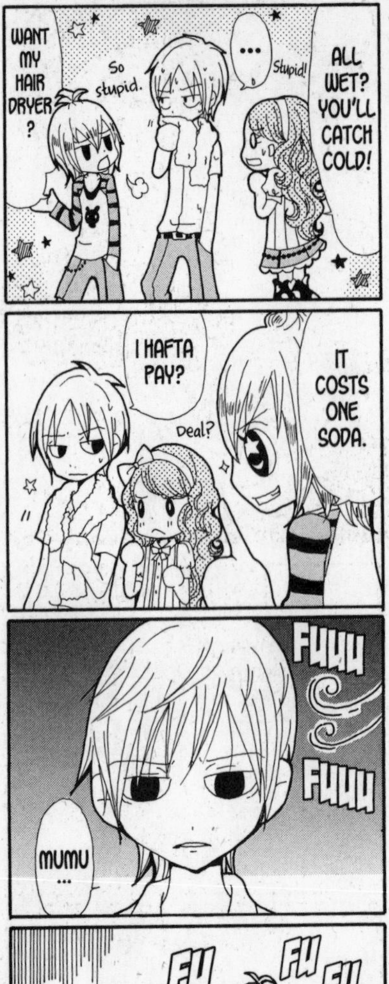
ALL WET? YOU'LL CATCH COLD!
Stupid!
...
So stupid.
WANT MY HAIR DRYER?
IT COSTS ONE SODA.
Deal?
I HAFTA PAY?
FUUU
FUUU
MUMU...
FU
FU
FU
FU
FU
ENOUGH.
Go away.

☆ Window Art ☆

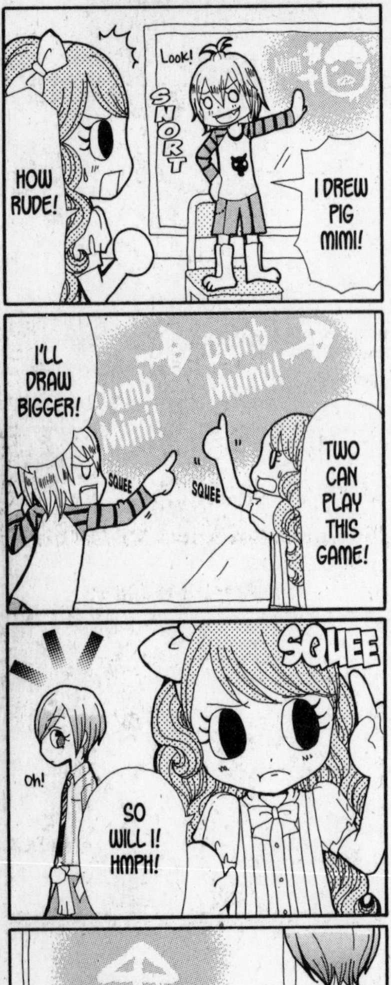
I DREW PIG MIMI!
Look!
SNORT
HOW RUDE!
TWO CAN PLAY THIS GAME!
Dumb Mumu!
Dumb Mimi!
I'LL DRAW BIGGER!
SQUEE
SQUEE
SQUEE
SO WILL I! HMPH!
Oh!
AN UM-BRELLA?

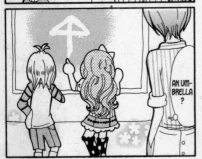

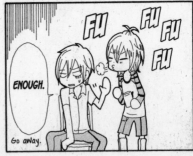

☆Love☆

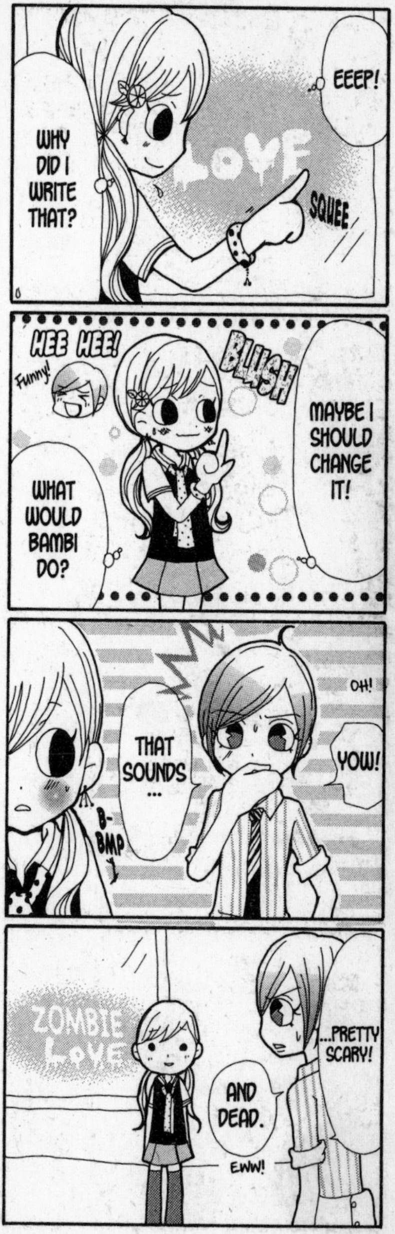
EEEP!
LOVE
SQUEE
WHY DID I WRITE THAT?
MAYBE I SHOULD CHANGE IT!
BLUSH
HEE HEE!
Funny!
WHAT WOULD BAMBI DO?
OH!
YOW!
THAT SOUNDS...
B-BMP
...PRETTY SCARY!
AND DEAD.
EWW!
ZOMBIE LOVE

☆Rain☆

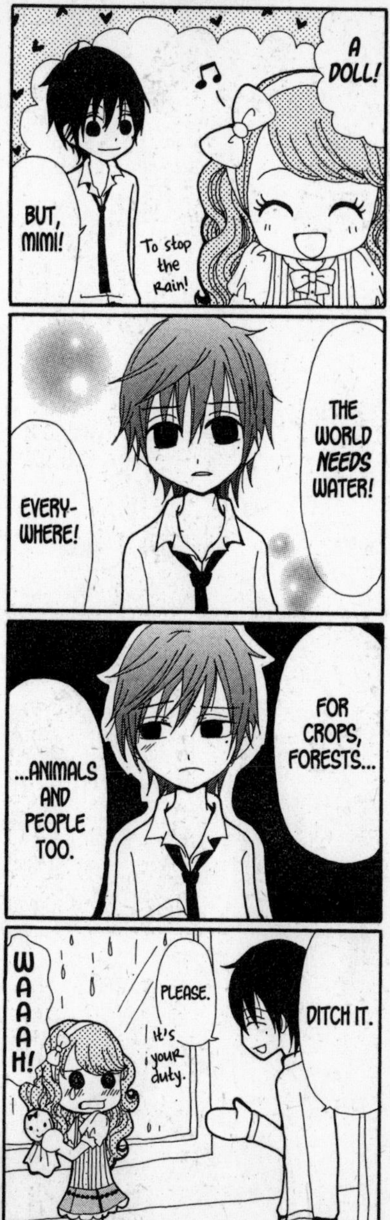
A DOLL!
To stop the rain!
BUT, MIMI!
THE WORLD NEEDS WATER!
EVERY-WHERE!
FOR CROPS, FORESTS...
...ANIMALS AND PEOPLE TOO.
DITCH IT.
PLEASE.
It's your duty.
WAAAAH!

☆Raincoat☆

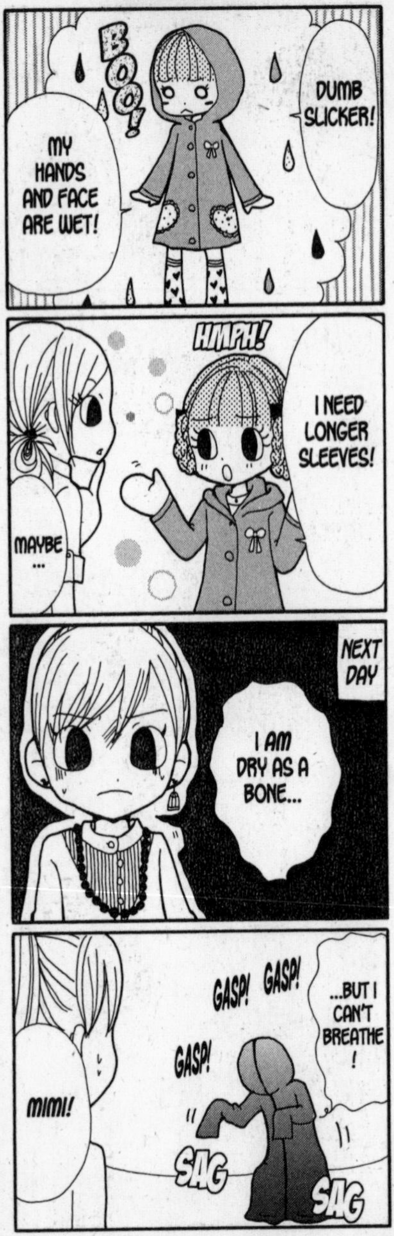

DUMB SLICKER!
BOO!
MY HANDS AND FACE ARE WET!
I NEED LONGER SLEEVES!
HMPH!
MAYBE...
NEXT DAY
I AM DRY AS A BONE...
...BUT I CAN'T BREATHE!
GASP!
GASP!
GASP!
SAG
SAG
MIMI!

☆Rain Boots☆

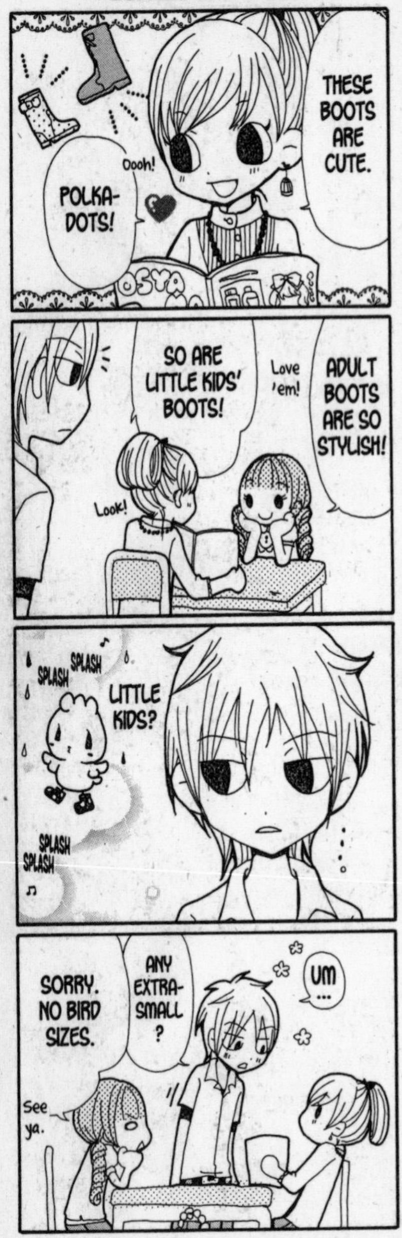

THESE BOOTS ARE CUTE.
Oooh!
POLKA-DOTS!
ADULT BOOTS ARE SO STYLISH!
Love 'em!
SO ARE LITTLE KIDS' BOOTS!
Look!
LITTLE KIDS?
SPLASH
SPLASH
SPLASH
SPLASH
UM...
ANY EXTRA-SMALL?
SORRY. NO BIRD SIZES.
See ya.

☆Love Umbrella☆

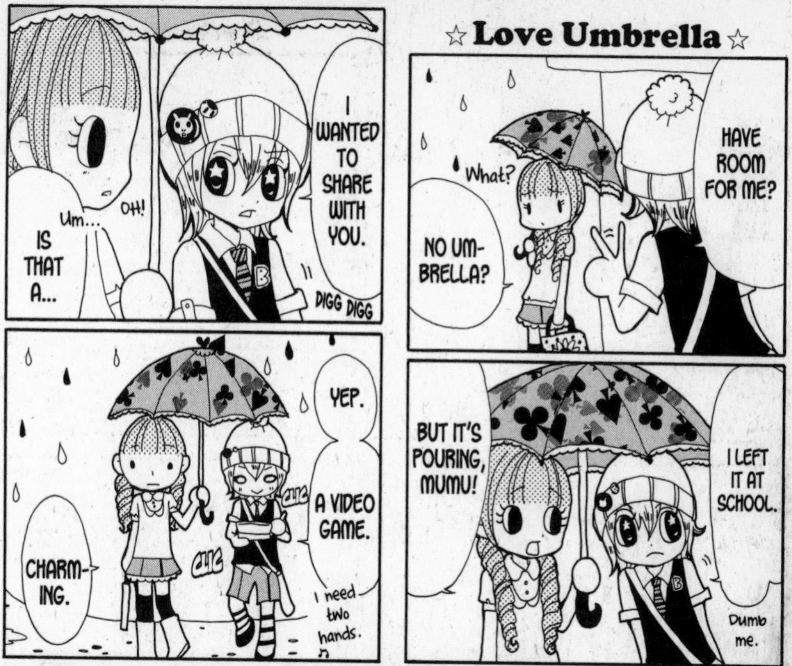
HAVE ROOM FOR ME?
What?
NO UM-BRELLA?
I LEFT IT AT SCHOOL.
BUT IT'S POURING, MUMU!
Dumb me.
I WANTED TO SHARE WITH YOU.
OH!
Um...
IS THAT A...
DIGG DIGG
YEP.
A VIDEO GAME.
CHARM-ING.
I need two hands. ♪

Choco Mimi Fashion Notes

WHERE'S THE SUN?♪

A RAINY DAY FASHION PLAN! ♥

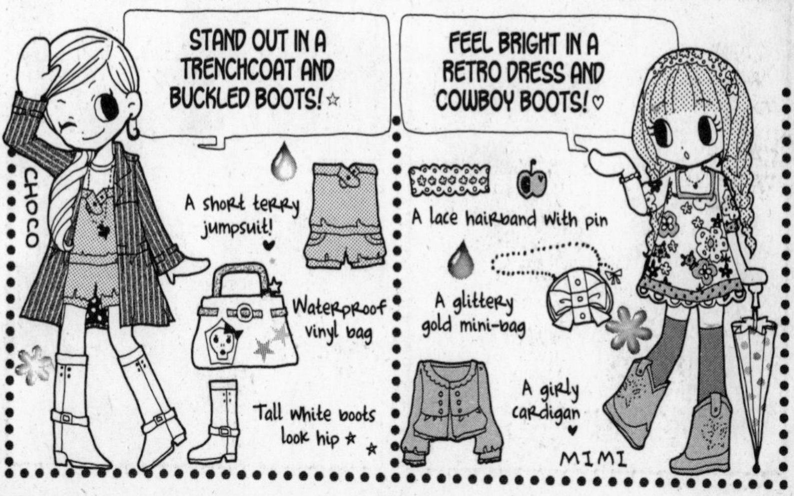
FEEL BRIGHT IN A RETRO DRESS AND COWBOY BOOTS! ♡
A lace hairband with pin
A glittery gold mini-bag
A girly cardigan ♥
MIMI
STAND OUT IN A TRENCHCOAT AND BUCKLED BOOTS! ☆
CHOCO
A short terry jumpsuit! ♥
Waterproof vinyl bag
Tall white boots look hip ☆

☆Hydrangea☆

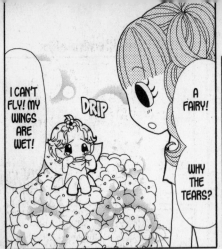

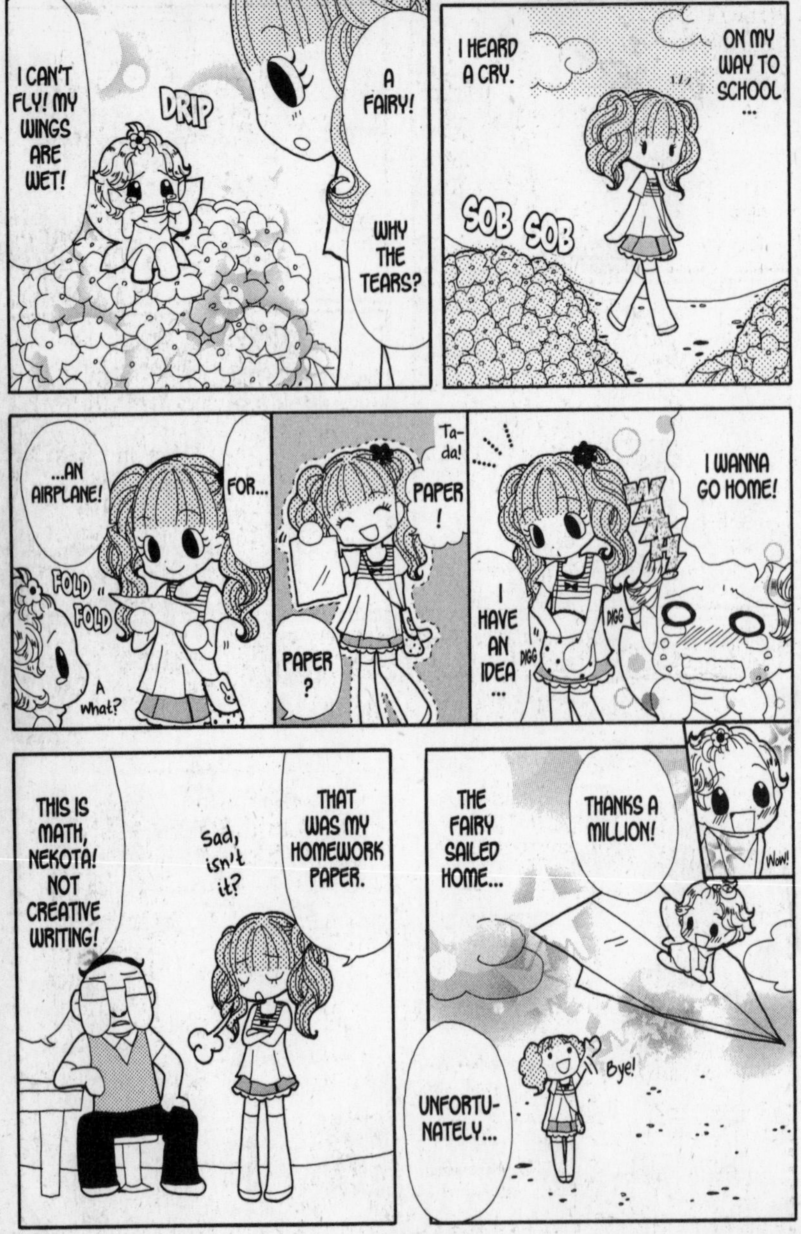
ON MY WAY TO SCHOOL ...
I HEARD A CRY.
SOB SOB
A FAIRY!
WHY THE TEARS?
I CAN'T FLY! MY WINGS ARE WET!
DRIP
I WANNA GO HOME!
I HAVE AN IDEA ...
DIGG DIGG
...!!
Ta-da!
PAPER!
PAPER?
FOR...
...AN AIRPLANE!
FOLD FOLD
A what?
THE FAIRY SAILED HOME...
THANKS A MILLION!
Wow!
Bye!
UNFORTUNATELY...
THAT WAS MY HOMEWORK PAPER.
Sad, isn't it?
THIS IS MATH, NEKOTA! NOT CREATIVE WRITING!

☆Library☆

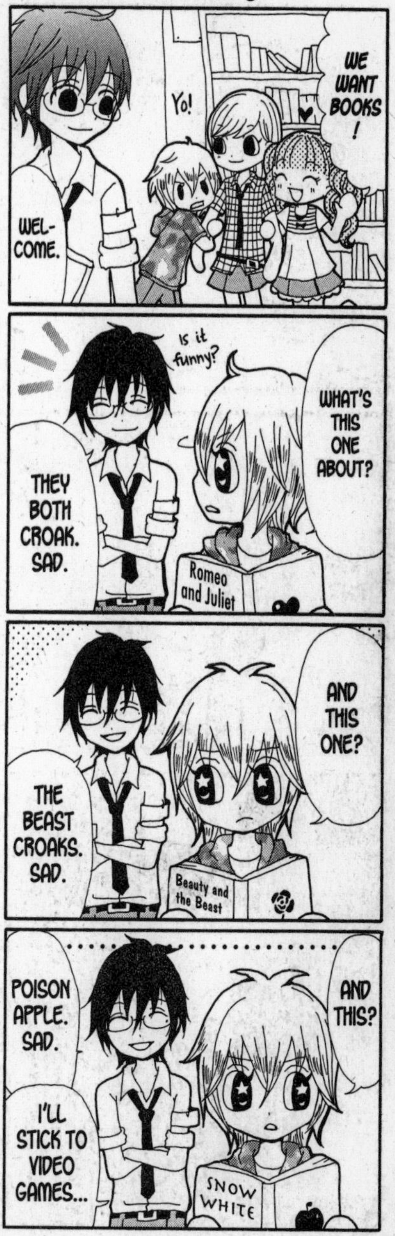
WE WANT BOOKS!
Yo!
WEL-COME.
WHAT'S THIS ONE ABOUT?
Is it funny?
THEY BOTH CROAK. SAD.
Romeo and Juliet
AND THIS ONE?
THE BEAST CROAKS. SAD.
Beauty and the Beast
AND THIS?
POISON APPLE. SAD.
SNOW WHITE
I'LL STICK TO VIDEO GAMES...

☆Crossword☆

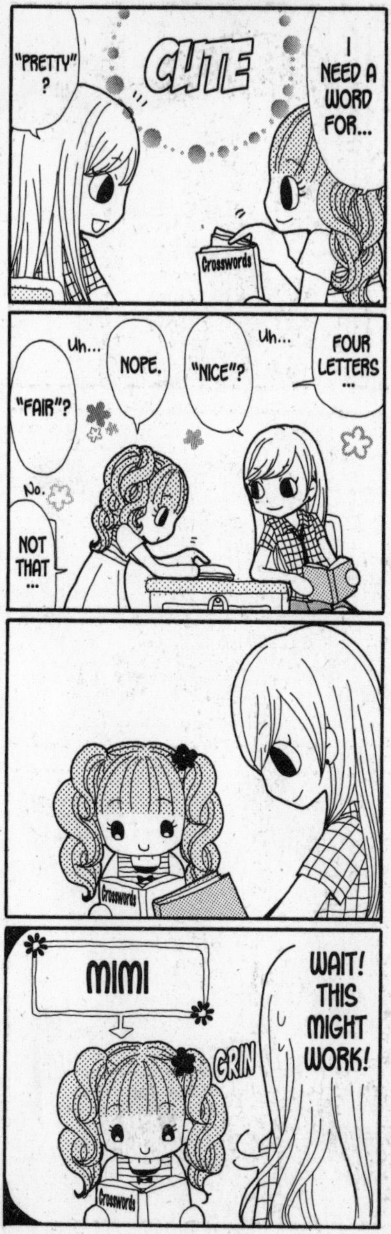
I NEED A WORD FOR...
CUTE
"PRETTY"?
Crosswords
FOUR LETTERS...
Uh...
"NICE"?
NOPE.
Uh...
"FAIR"?
No.
NOT THAT...
Crosswords
WAIT! THIS MIGHT WORK!
GRIN
MIMI
Crosswords

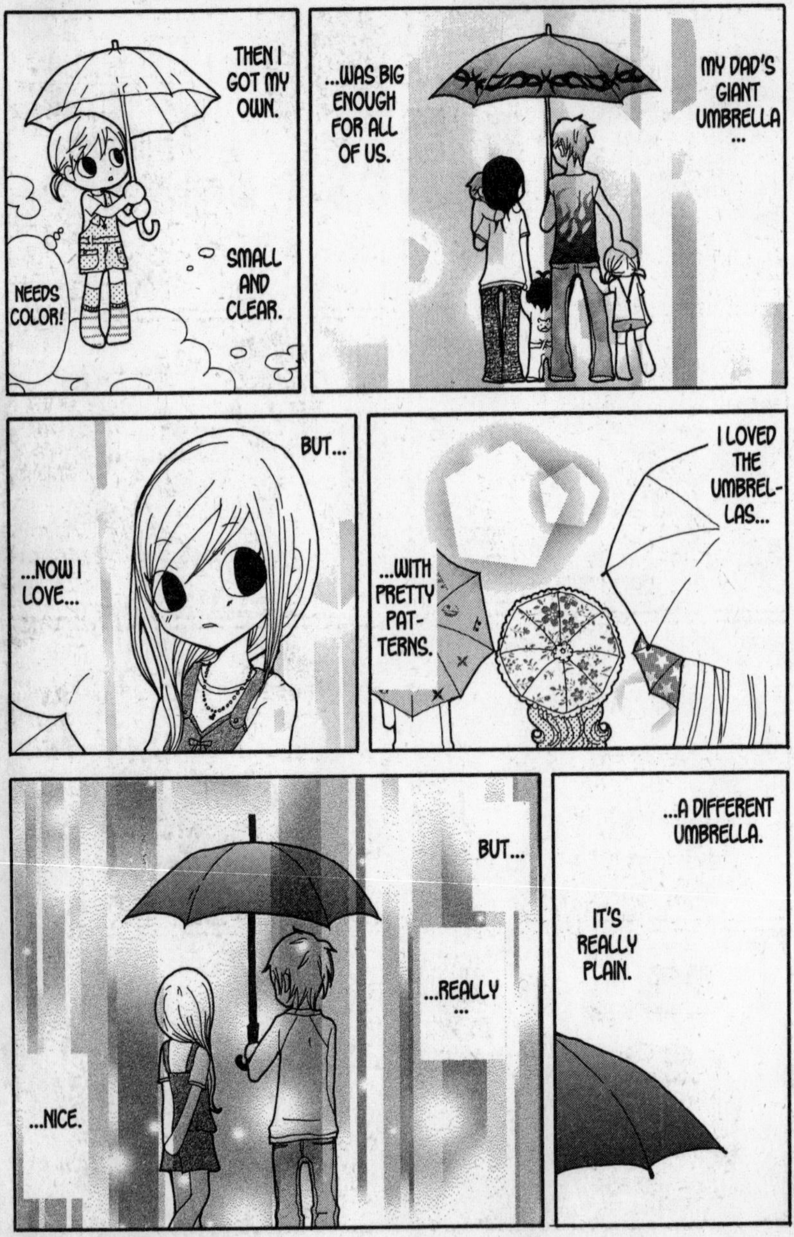
MY DAD'S GIANT UMBRELLA ...
...WAS BIG ENOUGH FOR ALL OF US.
THEN I GOT MY OWN.
SMALL AND CLEAR.
NEEDS COLOR!
I LOVED THE UMBREL-LAS...
...WITH PRETTY PAT-TERNS.
BUT...
...NOW I LOVE...
...A DIFFERENT UMBRELLA.
IT'S REALLY PLAIN.
BUT...
...REALLY ...
...NICE.

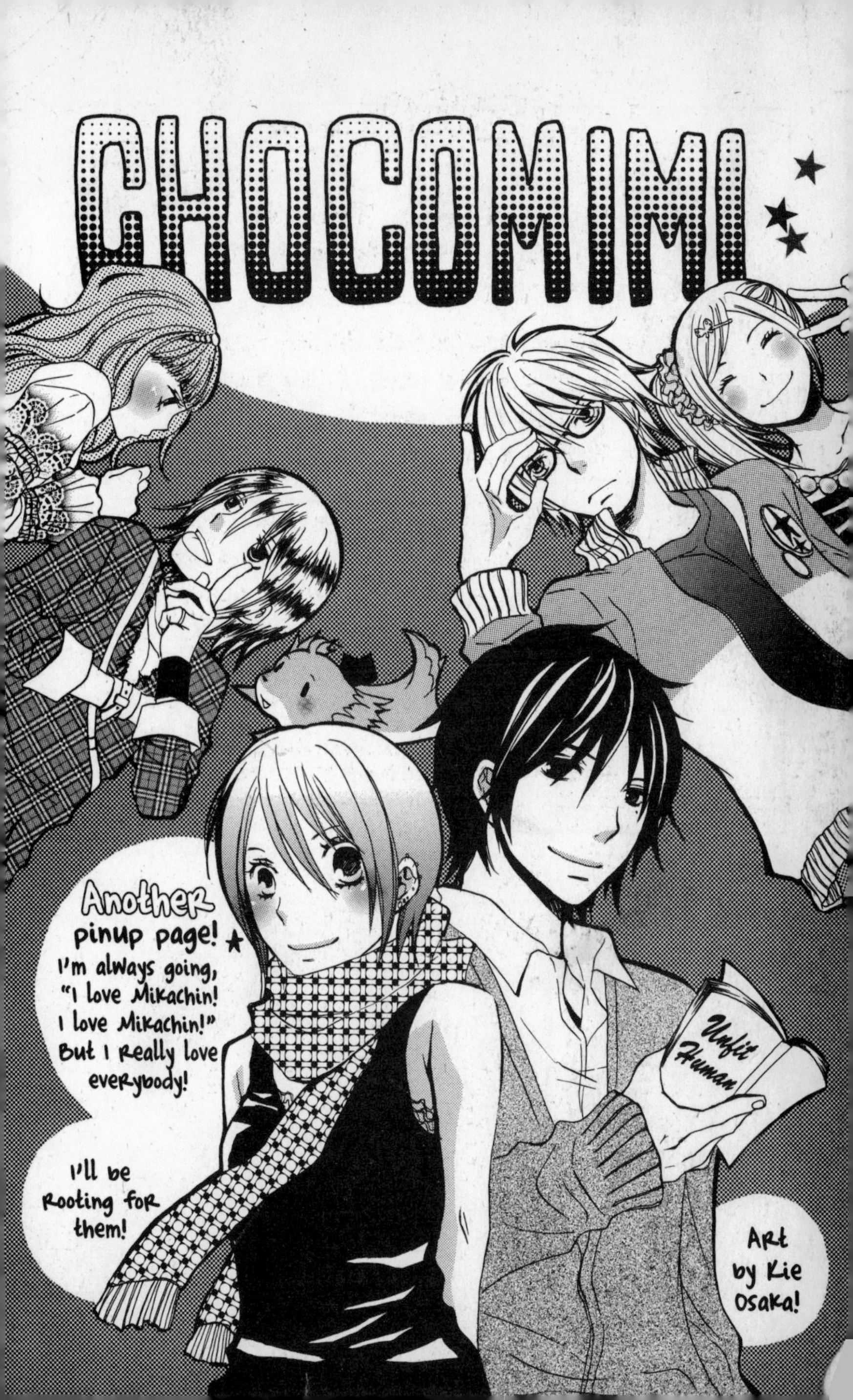
CHOCOMIMI
Another pinup page! I'm always going, "I love Mikachin! I love Mikachin!" But I really love everybody!
I'll be rooting for them!
Unfit Human
Art by Kie Osaka!

AFTERWORD...ish thing

- I'm Konami Sonoda. Thanks for reading my book. You must be so tired!

- My favorite artists drew pinup pages for this issue. A big thank you goes to Chinami Tsuyama, Yuka Fujiwara and Kie Osaka. I love you! ♥

- ChocoMimi is going to be a TV show!* I'm so happy that the ChocoMimi world is growing. Thanks to my cheering section, and especially my manager.

- Hope to see you in volume 4!

*The ChocoMimi live-action TV show aired in Japan on TV Tokyo. Each episode was followed by a short fashion show by Choco and Mimi.

Konami S

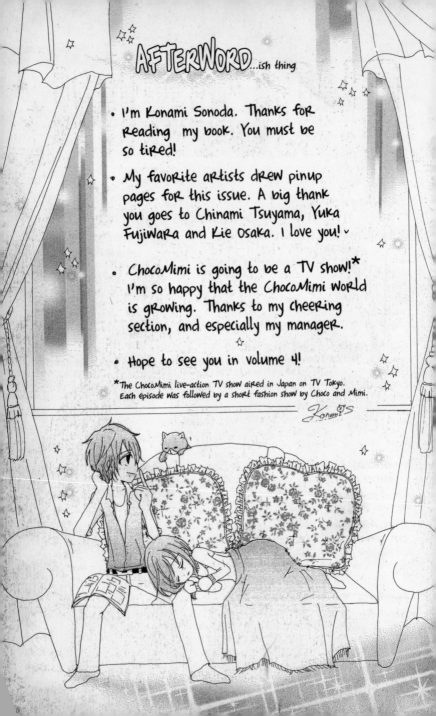

CULTURAL NOTES

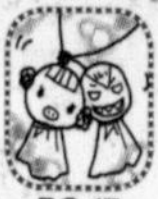
PG.17

★ Sunny day dolls (page 17)

Traditional *teru teru bozu* dolls are hung outside of windows to prevent a rainy day. (If you read volume 1 of *ChocoMimi*, you already know this!)

★ Yukata (pages 46 and 102)

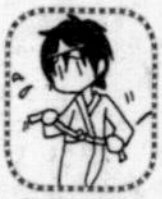
PG.102

Yukata are robelike garments, typically made of unlined cotton. In the previous volumes of *ChocoMimi*, the girls have worn yukata to summer festivals.

★ Yen (pages 69–70, 79)

Instead of dollars, Japanese kids spend yen! One hundred yen is equal to about one dollar.

★ New Year's cards and wishes (pages 97–102)

New Year's Day is the most important holiday in Japan, and people often send greeting cards to their friends and relatives. It is traditional to visit a shrine or temple on New Year's Day and make wishes for health and good fortune. (You can also read about these things in the other *ChocoMimi* books, volumes 1 and 2.)

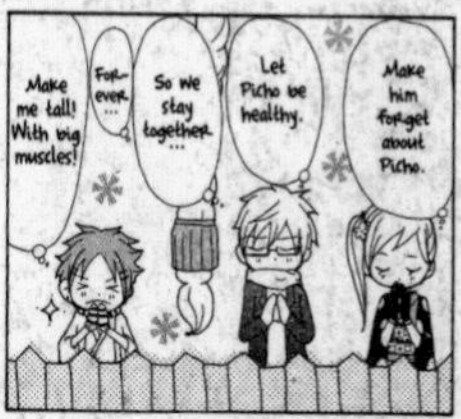
Make him forget about Picho.
Let Picho be healthy.
So we stay together...
Forever...
Make me tall! With big muscles!
PG.102

★ Calligraphy (pages 103–104)

The kids are practicing writing kanji, the characters in Japanese writing that are adapted from Chinese writing. Each symbol conveys an idea. When Mimi put the bottom half of the kanji meaning "red" and the kanji for "heart" together, it looks like the kanji expressing "love."

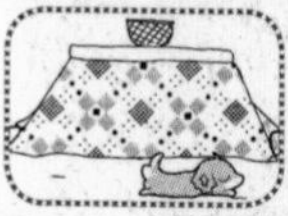
PG.107

★ Kotatsu (pages 106–108)

The low table with the blanket over it is called a kotatsu. These tables have a heat source underneath them—it's helping keep Choco, Mimi, Berry and Chiffon warm on a winter day.

★ Valentine's Day and White Day (pages 117–124)

In Japan, girls give chocolate to boys on Valentine's Day (February 14, same as here!). Then a month later, on March 14—White Day—boys are expected to give gifts to the girls who gave them chocolates.

★ Pimple (page 121)

A type of love forecast is based on where a pimple pops up! It's said that if you get a pimple on your forehead, you are thinking about someone. If it's on your chin, somebody is thinking about you; on your right cheek, you may have a hard time; and if it's on your left cheek, you may dump your current love interest.

★ First names (page 128)

In Japan only close friends and family members are on a first-name basis. Jin is angry that his friends are using Aoi's first name because he doesn't realize they know her.

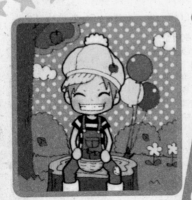

What a long wait for volume 3! And this is the third year of this series, which means that I've aged three years too. Ha ha! But I'd like to keep the soul of an eighth grader for eternity! My adolescence lives on! ★ (In my mind anyway...)

—Konami Sonoda

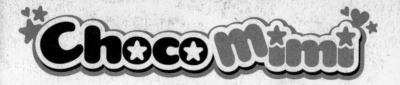

Choco★mimi

VOLUME 3
VIZ Kids Edition
STORY AND ART BY Konami Sonoda

Translation	HC Language Solutions, Inc.
English Adaptation	Janet Gilbert
Touch-up Art & Lettering	Steve Dutro
Design	Fawn Lau
Editor	Carrie Shepherd

VP, Production	Alvin Lu
VP, Publishing Licensing	Rika Inouye
VP, Sales & Product Marketing	Gonzalo Ferreyra
VP, Creative	Linda Espinosa
Publisher	Hyoe Narita

Published by VIZ Media, LLC
P.O. Box 77010
San Francisco, CA 94107

10 9 8 7 6 5 4 3 2 1
First printing, January 2010

www.viz.com   www.vizkids.com

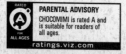

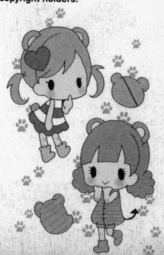

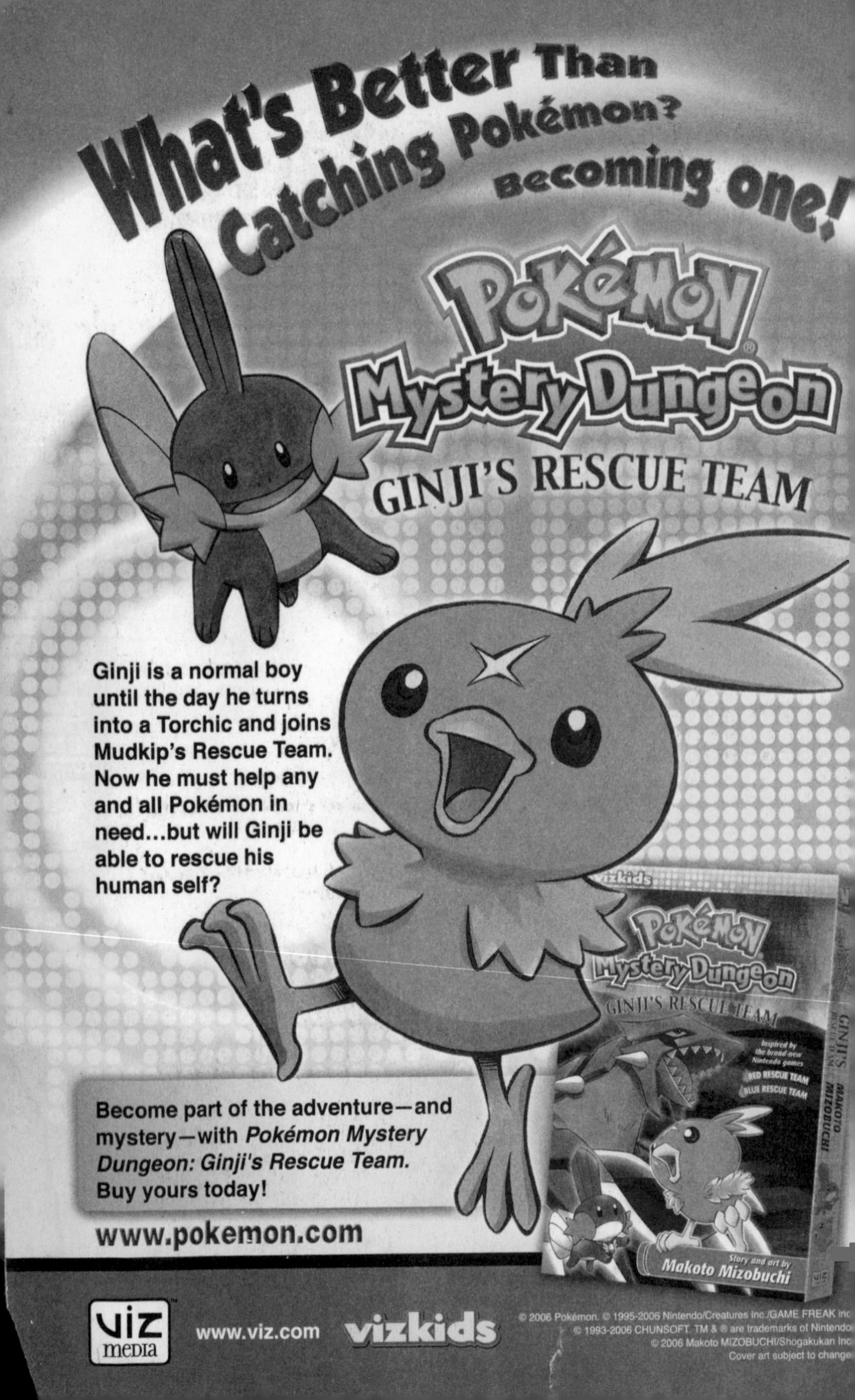

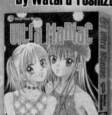
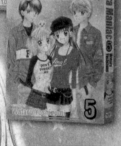

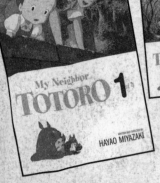
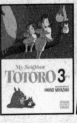
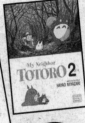
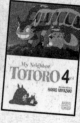
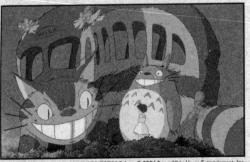

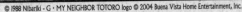

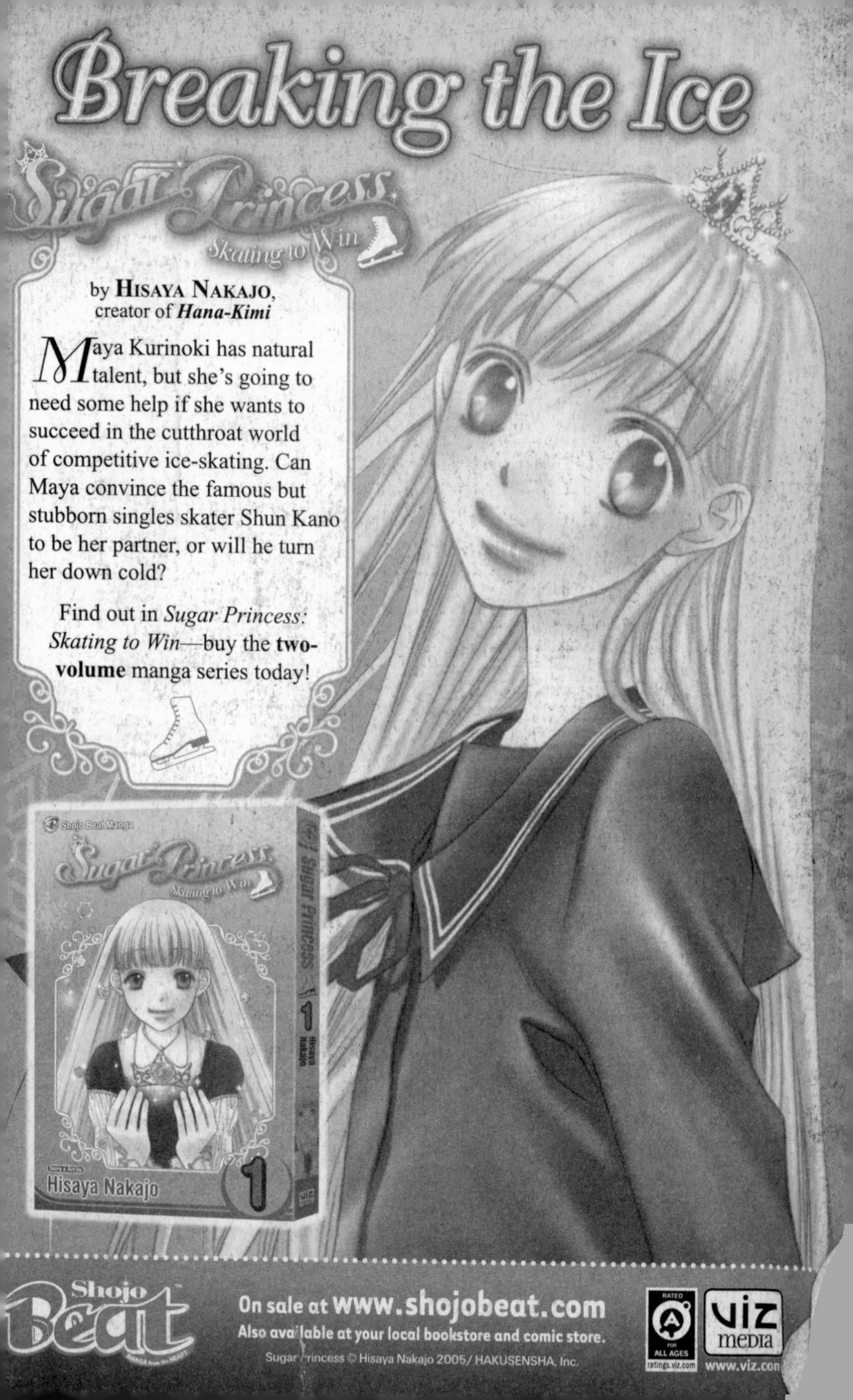
Breaking the Ice
Sugar Princess
Skating to Win
by Hisaya Nakajo,
creator of Hana-Kimi
Maya Kurinoki has natural talent, but she's going to need some help if she wants to succeed in the cutthroat world of competitive ice-skating. Can Maya convince the famous but stubborn singles skater Shun Kano to be her partner, or will he turn her down cold?
Find out in Sugar Princess: Skating to Win—buy the two-volume manga series today!
Shojo Beat Manga
Sugar Princess
Skating to Win
Hisaya Nakajo
1
Shojo Beat
On sale at www.shojobeat.com
Also available at your local bookstore and comic store.
Sugar Princess © Hisaya Nakajo 2005/ HAKUSENSHA, Inc.
RATED
FOR ALL AGES
ratings.viz.com
VIZ media
www.viz.com

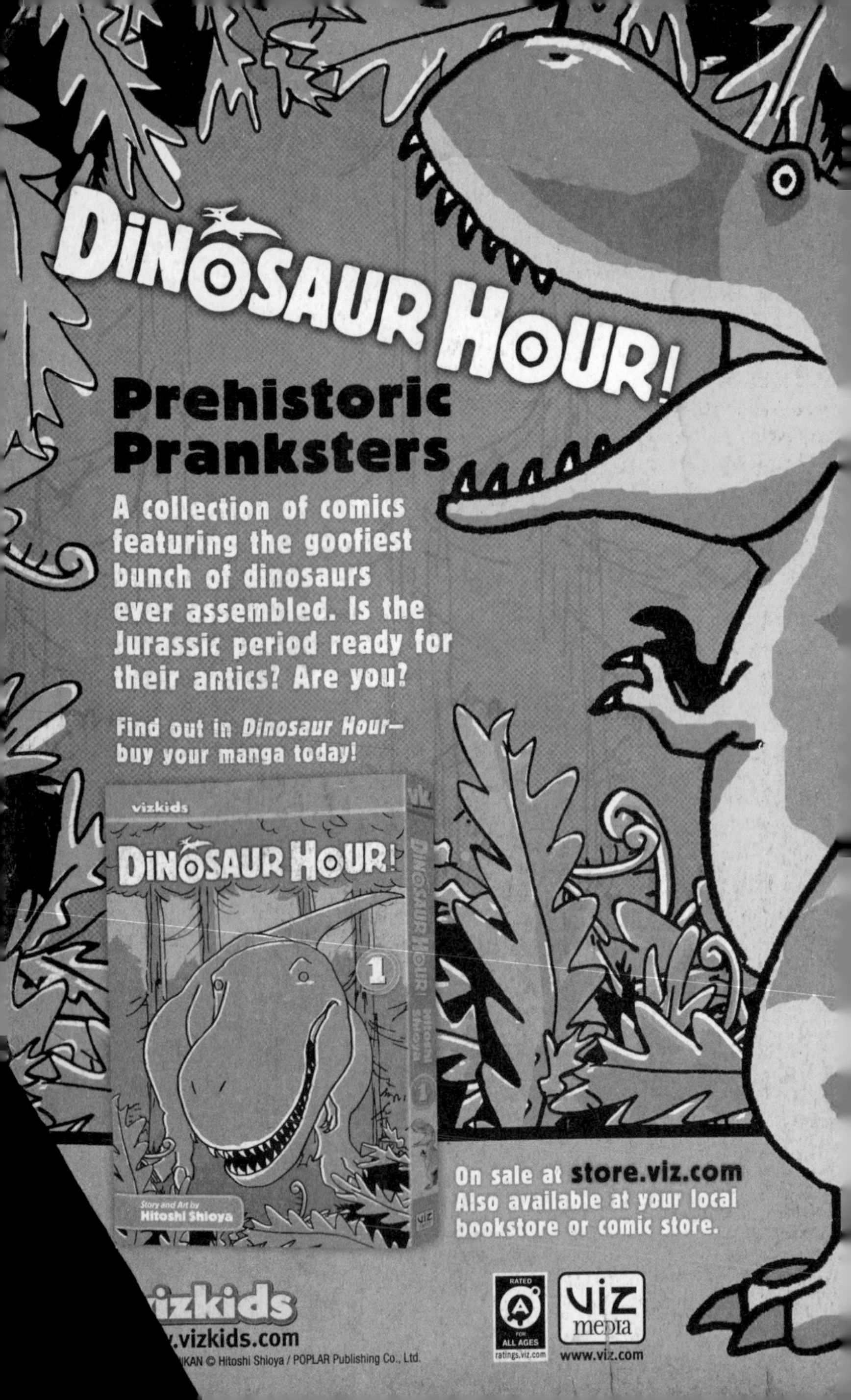
DINOSAUR HOUR!
Prehistoric Pranksters
A collection of comics featuring the goofiest bunch of dinosaurs ever assembled. Is the Jurassic period ready for their antics? Are you?
Find out in Dinosaur Hour—buy your manga today!
vizkids
DINOSAUR HOUR!
1
Story and Art by Hitoshi Shioya
On sale at store.viz.com
Also available at your local bookstore or comic store.
vizkids
.vizkids.com
IKAN © Hitoshi Shioya / POPLAR Publishing Co., Ltd.
RATED A FOR ALL AGES
ratings.viz.com
VIZ media
www.viz.com

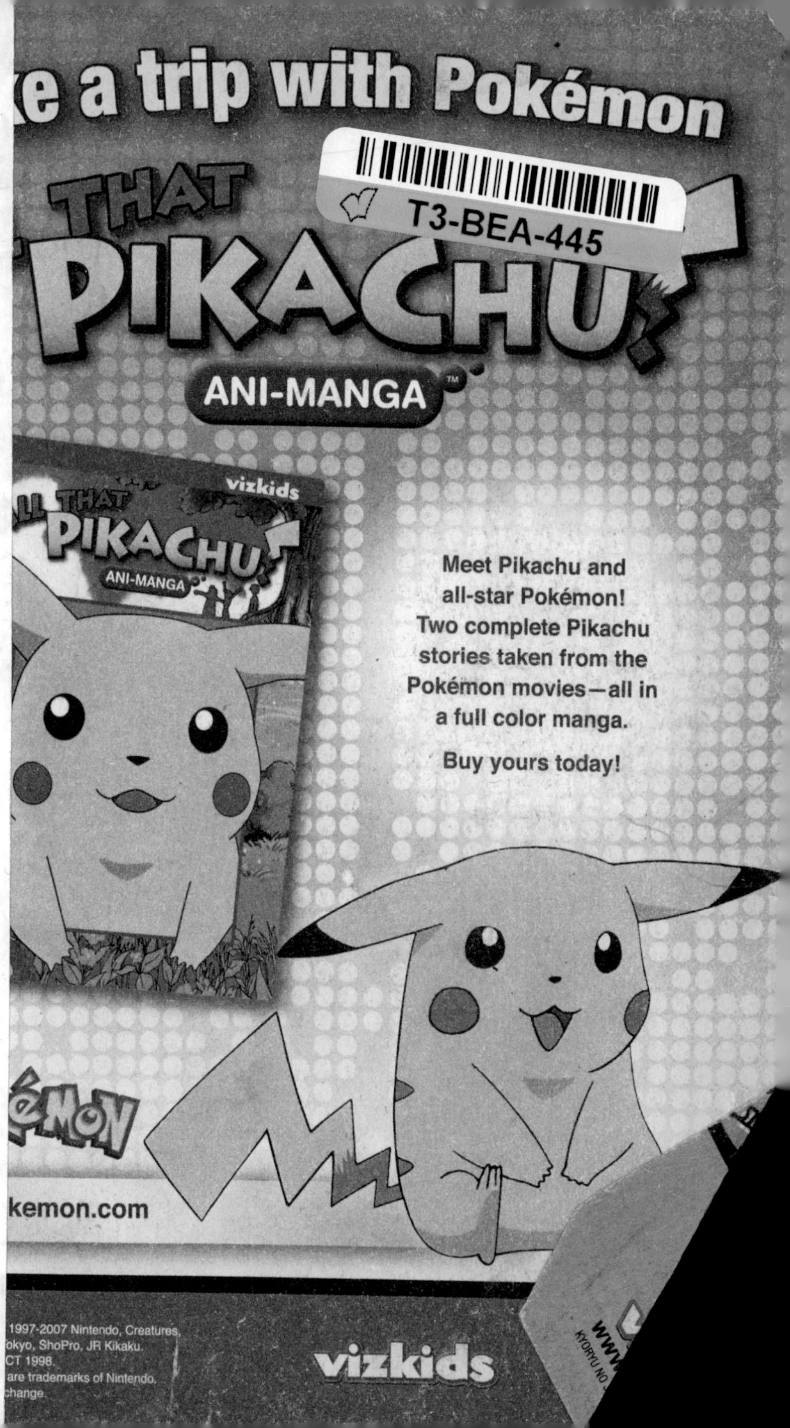

ke a trip with Pokémon
T3-BEA-445
THAT
PIKACHU!
ANI-MANGA™
vizkids
LL THAT
PIKACHU!
ANI-MANGA
Meet Pikachu and
all-star Pokémon!
Two complete Pikachu
stories taken from the
Pokémon movies—all in
a full color manga.
Buy yours today!
kémon
kemon.com
1997-2007 Nintendo, Creatures,
okyo, ShoPro, JR Kikaku.
CT 1998.
are trademarks of Nintendo.
change.
vizkids